A86-2861

The Tattooed
Soldier

The Tattoo

DELPHINIUM BOOKS

HÉCTOR TOBAR

oped
dier

Harrison, New York
Encino, California

Library of Congress Cataloging-in-Publication Data
Tobar, Héctor, 1963-
The tattooed soldier / Héctor Tobar. —1st ed.
p.   cm
ISBN 1-883285-15-1 (acid-free paper)
1. Guatemalan Americans—California—Los Angeles—Fiction.
I. Title.
PS3570.022T38   1998
813'.54—dc21   97-40965
CIP

First Edition
2 4 6 8 10 9 7 5 3 1

Distributed by HarperCollins*Publishers*
Printed in the United States of America on acid-free paper
DESIGNED BY KRYSTYNA SKALSKI

To my mother and father,

two travelers among thousands

in the Guatemalan diaspora

Antonio and the Sergeant

Antonio and Elena

Antonio and Guillermo

Part 1

Antonio and the Sergeant

On Crown Hill

Neither man could claim English as his mother tongue, but it was the only language they shared. The tenant, Antonio Bernal, was from Guatemala. Through the narrow opening of a door pushed slightly ajar, he was speaking to the building manager who was about to evict him from his apartment, a Korean immigrant named Hwang. Both men squinted, each confused by the other's diction, trying to decipher mispronounced words. After several minutes of mumbled exchanges, they began to toss night-school phrases back and forth like life preservers: "Repeat, please." "Speak slower." "I don't understand."

Los Angeles was the problem. In Los Angeles, Antonio could spend days and weeks speaking only his native tongue, breathing, cooking, laughing, and embarrassing himself with all sorts of people in Spanish. He could avoid twisting and bending his lips and mouth to make those exotic English sounds, the hard edge of the consonants, the flat schwa. English belonged to another part of the city, not here, not downtown, where there were broad avenues lined with Chinese pictographs and Arabic calligraphy and Cyrillic, long boulevards of Spanish *eñes* where Antonio could let his Central American *ches* and *erres* roll off his tongue to his heart's delight.

"What?" Antonio said.

"I ask what you say?" replied Mr. Hwang, a squat man in khaki pants and a freshly starched shirt.

"I said, How much time? More time. Time, Hwang?"

"What time? Say again."

"Say what again? Time?"

"No."

"I don't understand."

Antonio was tired, and his accent felt a little thicker than usual.

Mr. Hwang crossed his arms impatiently, as if he suspected that this confusion of tongues was only a stalling tactic, a ruse to postpone the inevitable eviction. Or maybe he was just callous, maybe he didn't care that Antonio had stayed up most of the night worrying about what he would do this morning. Antonio loosened the chain on the door and opened it wide to show Mr. Hwang that the floor of the apartment was littered with clothes and old paperbacks, proof of what he had been unable to communicate with words: he and his roommate were not ready to leave, because they had just begun to pack.

"We are trying, Mr. Hwang," Antonio said slowly. "We are trying."

"If you don't leave by two," the manager blurted out, "I have to call police."

Antonio took a deep breath and tried to compose himself, pushing his glasses up the bridge of his nose, a habit of his at moments when he felt close to violence. They were circle glasses, and when he caught a glimpse of himself in the mirror he would sometimes remember the day he first put them on, a decade ago, when he was a student at the university in Guatemala. "These are my intellectual glasses," he told a friend once. "I can't decide if they make me look like a chemist or a Maoist. What do you think?" He had kept his circle glasses through all his travels, all the way to Los Angeles, and had worn them at his last job, as a bus boy at a now defunct diner on the Westside. One of the cooks made fun of him and called him "professor." Somehow, the ideas and learning that made him strong in Guatemala had slipped away once he crossed the border, lost in the translation.

Granted, he did not speak English well, but who did? That in itself was not an explanation for what was happening to him today. Spanish was as good a language as any other. *In Spanish, I sound like the intelligent person I really am. In English, I am a bus boy.* But even that was dignified work. To have lifted dirty dishes, poured coffee, and worn a servant's brown uniform was nothing to be ashamed of. The little brown cap did not demean him, nor did the name tag that had begun to fade after so many months until it read ANT NI.

Voy a ser uno de los "homeless." It did not seem right to him that a man who loved to read, a man with *Crimen y Castigo* and *El Idiota* and countless other works of real literature scattered on the floor of his apartment, would be called this ugly word. And at the same time it made perfect sense, the logical conclusion to years of living in this cold, alien country. No Spanish equivalent captured the shame and sooty desperation of the condition, and so this compound, borrowed word would have to do: home-less.

"You are making me homeless," Antonio told the manager.

"If you don't leave," Mr. Hwang said in suddenly perfect English, "I will call the marshals."

Antonio pushed his glasses up again. He really would like to hit this *coreano*. There would be some satisfaction in that. But no, he could only blame himself for this fiasco, for having failed at the mathematics of his finances. He had decided to be polite to the building manager, apologetic, because he thought he detected a note of regret in Mr. Hwang's voice when he first knocked on the door to say, "You must leave." But now Mr. Hwang was threatening to call the marshals, the police of evictions. *To have the police come here and treat me like a criminal. I was a bus boy, but that doesn't make me a criminal.* He imagined himself being led away in handcuffs, his arms pulled behind his back, the public indignity of being marched past the neighbors.

"Call the police!" Antonio boomed six inches from the man's face. "Call the police!"

"Thirty minutes!" the manager yelled after taking a step back. "You have thirty minutes!"

"*¡Come mierda!*" Antonio shouted. "*Hijo de la gran puta.*"

"*Sip sae ki!*" the manager hissed in Korean.

The neighbors began to appear almost immediately. Down the length of the first floor, doors snapped open and heads popped out— a dozen nameless acquaintances, people Antonio knew from hallway chitchat, glances and nods on the stairs, their startled, anxious, amused faces illuminated by the severe light of two naked bulbs that hung at either end of the corridor. The man who lived in the adjacent apartment, a lonely-looking and hirsute Mexicano, was standing bare-chested in his doorway, one foot in the hallway, the other in his room, grinning as if he expected to be entertained soon by a fistfight or shoving match. Antonio stared back at him and the other neighbors with his best impersonation of a madman, eyes ablaze, nostrils flaring.

"*¡Me está sacando a la calle!*" he shouted. And then, in English, so that everyone would understand: "He's throwing me on the street!"

More doors opened, and the hallway audience grew. A dozen people were standing in the buttermilk yellow corridor now, along with three children who had been playing with toy cars on the grime-stained carpet of the lobby, next to the rows of mailboxes without any names on them, just numbers. A crowd of brown eyes was trained on Antonio and the building manager, who was known to the residents, depending on their mother tongue, as "*el chino,*" "the manager guy," "*el* manager," or "Mr. Chang." Antonio, who had lived in this building for a year, was one of the few people who knew Mr. Hwang's real name.

"Chang is getting really pissed," said a voice in the corridor. "I never seen him like that."

Mr. Hwang drew back as if to spit, then seemed to think better of it and walked away, leaving Antonio to the fire drill of trying to fit everything he owned and wanted to save into a black plastic Hefty trash bag. His roommate, José Juan, was dumping a large collection of plastic spoons and forks out of a dresser drawer, unperturbed by the shouting. Exhausted and depressed, he and Antonio had fallen asleep just before dawn, only to be startled awake by the pounding of Mr. Hwang's fist on the door and the bright sunshine of midmorning. Then they had argued about what to do with the four-burner hotplate José Juan insisted on keeping even though it was clear now that they wouldn't have anyplace to plug it in.

"Never mind that *chingadera,*" Antonio said, using one of the vulgar Mexican expressions he had picked up during his years in Los Angeles. "Leave it behind."

"But it cost me forty dollars."

After half an hour, Mr. Hwang returned and stood in the open doorway with his hands on his hips, watching Antonio sift through a pile of papers scattered on the dark brown rug. Behind the manager, a crowd of tenants had gathered again.

Antonio glared at him, then picked up a stack of unopened letters from his mother in Guatemala. In between two of the envelopes he discovered a forgotten photograph of his wife and son, taken years ago in Quetzaltenango against a painted backdrop of fanciful lakes and volcanos. *Of all things.* He raised the photograph to his lips and tried to fight off the rush of memories that began to gather and rumble like thunder behind his eyes. *This picture is the sadness of me, the tragedy of me.*

"Hurry," said the voice above him. "Hurry, please."

It struck Antonio as an outrageous invasion of his privacy, to have the manager standing over him as he packed away this photograph.

"I'm doing the best I can," he said.

"You supposed to be out at eleven o'clock."

"We don't have anyplace to go," Antonio shot back. "What are we supposed to do?"

"I don't care," Mr. Hwang said curtly. "Go sleep under the freeway."

Sleep under the freeway. Antonio had heard this phrase more than once in the weeks leading up to this humiliation, as the money in his wallet slowly disappeared and the prospect of eviction became a certainty. Sleep under the freeway. It was almost a refrain in the neighborhood. José Juan had said it once, just five days ago, when Mr. Hwang slipped the final, final eviction notice under their doorway. *"Podemos dormir debajo del freeway."* It didn't sound any better in Spanish.

Elvira Gonzales, the elderly Mexican-American widow who lived down the hall, and who was now toward the back of the crowd staring at Antonio with a sad and disapproving motherly frown, had repeated it too. "Well, *muchachos*, if they throw you out, I guess you'll have to sleep under the freeway. That's what everybody else does. I guess it's warmer there."

Why did people persist in repeating this horrible little phrase? No matter which way Antonio turned the situation and looked at it, he knew he would still be out there in the open, with only a shrub or a piece of cardboard to protect him against the wind, the cold, and the junkies. And now this *chino* was saying it to him. Go sleep under the freeway. It was too much. Antonio wanted to grab Mr. Hwang's plaid shirt and shove him against the very walls within which he and José Juan were no longer welcome. At least that would be poetic justice.

Antonio lunged for Mr. Hwang, his fingers gripping the manager's collar. Seams ripped in his hands.

"You go sleep under the freeway! You! *¡A ver como te gusta!*"

"Mister Manager!" yelled a voice in the hall. "Do you want me to call the police?"

At this, Antonio surrendered to the arms that were pulling at him, separating him from Mr. Hwang.

The crowd completely filled the hallway now. People had come from the other floors to watch the spectacle. They probably expected the police to arrive at any moment. Car crashes and altercations always drew an audience. Antonio had seen this sort of thing before, had been part of the crowd himself on more than one occasion. The promise of real-life violence or chaos was just about the only thing that could entice the apartment dwellers to break the burglar-proof seals on their doors and venture into public space. Fires, gang shootings, marital slugfests that spilled out onto the street: friendships were made and love affairs ignited in these magical moments when people gathered in the hallway, on the sidewalk or the front steps, tugging at the yellow police tape, whispering under the pulsating blue and red lights of an ambulance or patrol car.

But there would be no police cars, no flashing lights today. A few minutes after Antonio ripped the manager's shirt, he and José Juan were ready to go. They left a collection of newspapers, letters, books, immigration forms, and check stubs on the floor. On a wall they left a life-sized poster of Hugo Sánchez, the mop-haired Mexican soccer star. José Juan and Antonio both loved soccer; it was how they became friends in the first place, talking about *fútbol* in the diner where Antonio had been a bus boy and José Juan a dishwasher. When they had steady work, they saved to see games at the Los Angeles Memorial Coliseum, El Salvador versus Guadalajara, Mexico versus Guatemala.

Now they would leave their room to Hugo Sánchez. He seemed to be having a good time, anyway, with his foot on a soccer ball, a beer in one hand, and the other around the waist of a pretty brunette.

Goodbye, room. *Adiós, Hugo.*

At 3:00 p.m. they picked up the black Hefty bag and walked down the corridor, which was now empty and quiet. The neighbors had returned to their apartments, but Antonio could hear the murmur of their voices passing through the closed doors, wooden rectangles that breathed words in a jumble of English and Spanish.

José Juan closed the black iron door of the lobby behind them, and the voices of the Bixel Garden Apartments grew silent. They stood on the bubble-gum- and oil-stained front steps, pondering their options. Go sleep under the freeway: it seemed as good a choice as any. They began walking the nine blocks from their apartment building to the overpasses of the Harbor Freeway.

Antonio and José Juan carried the Hefty bag downhill along Third Street, straining to keep it from scraping the ground. The bag was heavy because it contained everything they owned: clothes, shoe boxes filled with letters from Mexico and Guatemala, two blankets, a framed picture of José Juan's wife, and the four-burner hotplate.

"We should get rid of this stupid hotplate," Antonio said.

"We're not going to be out here forever," José Juan answered defensively. "When we get another apartment you'll be thankful. I'll be eating hot food and you'll be begging me to let you use it. *Ya vas a ver.*"

They walked through a neighborhood of tumbledown wood-frame houses with damp clothes draped over the porch railings, then a street of squat brick apartment buildings. Someone tossed a bucket of water from a third-story window behind them, bringing the merchants out of the first-floor storefronts to complain and hurl insults skyward. A mother pushing a stroller hurried past the scene. The sidewalks were thick with people, but no one seemed to pay any attention to Antonio and José Juan with their plastic bag. They passed a crowded bus stop, mostly women watching the traffic go by with weary, end-of-the-working-day stares. No one bothered to cast them a glance.

Antonio was living on the streets, carrying everything he owned in a plastic bag, and no one would look him in the eye. He was used to being unseen. There was the invisibility of being a bus boy, of walking between the tables unnoticed, a shadow rolling the cart, clearing the dishes. But this was another kind of invisibility. People now made a point of turning away from him, just as Antonio had turned away from the hopeless men he saw in this same condition. Those men pushed their belongings around in shopping carts. Now he could see how practical it was to have a shopping cart.

"I'm tired of this," Antonio said suddenly, dropping his end of the Hefty bag. He felt disoriented, as if someone had spun him around in circles. He wanted to scream at José Juan, at the people on the sidewalk who would not look at him. There was a word the Americanos used when they were angry, a word Antonio liked because it sounded so harsh and mean and ugly.

"Fucking bag," he said in English. "Fuck it."

José Juan let out a sigh and looked up at the sky. The sun was low, but his face was covered in sweat. The freeway was within sight now, an overpass just down the hill, only two blocks away. Without a word, Antonio picked up his end of the bag, and they began walking again.

They reached the freeway and stood underneath it, dwarfed by the immensity of the structure. This overpass was higher than most, an underbelly of concrete covered with a fine network of leafless ivy branches that spread out like capillaries across the gray surface. Water oozed like blood from the cement, and the damp air around them smelled of feces and urine. Antonio could hear trucks passing overhead with hurried rattling sounds, hydrocarbon winds rushing by in their wake.

"Now what do we do?" José Juan asked.

Antonio decided that they should walk a little farther, to the spot where a series of overlapping concrete spans vaulted and curved in the air, the interchange of the Harbor, Hollywood, and Pasadena freeways: inside the shadows cast by all these overpasses and underpasses, on-ramps and off-ramps, there had to be, surely, a place to sleep.

They threw the bag over a cyclone fence and then jumped over themselves, following a trash-strewn path that cut through a slope of ivy landscaping. They walked a few hundred feet to a two-lane transition road where cars passed under a bridge and into a tunnel, the sound of their engines echoing into a fluttering roar. Across this narrow road, hidden in the concrete hollows at the center of the interchange, Antonio could see the makeshift shelters of human beings.

"*Ya llegamos,*" he said. "We're here."

To reach the shelters they would have to cross the transition road, which was filled with rush-hour traffic, two lanes of cars snaking past them at about twenty miles an hour. Inside the cars, everyone seemed to be wearing sunglasses. Antonio stood and waited for a break in the stream of sedans, RVs, trucks, buses. Fifteen minutes later he shouted "Now!" and they ran across the tarmac, dragging the Hefty bag and its hotplate cargo behind them, a blue sports car speeding by on their heels.

Antonio bent over with his hands on his knees to catch his breath, and began laughing as he hadn't laughed for days and days. José Juan smiled broadly. The absurdity of their situation was sinking in. Antonio felt silly, scampering across the freeway with this impossibly heavy plastic bag, like some Mexican comedy act, Cantinflas or Tin Tan.

They examined their surroundings. Now that they had stepped into the shadows, Antonio could see the shelters more clearly. He made out a sofa, a director's chair with the back missing, several mattresses tossed about. Maybe twenty or thirty people lived here. At the moment, however, the lone resident was a black man with a long beard who was sitting on a blanket on the dusty ground. He stood up and walked toward them.

"You must be visiting, right?" He examined the plastic bag at Antonio's feet and shook his head. "Because I know one thing. You sure as hell ain't staying. This spot right here is taken, it's our spot. There ain't no more room here. And we don't need any neighbors. *Comprende?*"

Antonio looked at José Juan. Silently they picked up the Hefty bag and turned around. They were outsiders here, and there was no use arguing with the man. A fresh wave of defeat now, a sense of pointlessness as they ran back across the lanes of traffic and followed the path through the ivy back to the street. Sleeping under the freeway wasn't so easy after all.

The shadows were lengthening as the short March day came to an end. They had been walking for at least an hour, maybe two. Antonio glanced at José Juan and saw that his friend was biting his lower lip, tears welling in his eyes. He is broken, this is too much for him, Antonio thought, the humiliation is too deep. Mexicanos. When they are little boys their fathers won't let them cry, ever, and so they fight it off as long as they can.

They walked back up Third Street, away from the freeway. *Away from that horrible freeway.* Antonio had not felt so lost and alone for many, many years. He wanted to weep too, but he held it in. He felt like a child out here on his own, a boy wandering about in his pajamas, separated from parents and home, pining for his pillow and his bed. They entered a stretch of downtown without pedestrians, passing a large white monolith with a blue sign announcing "Pacific Stock Exchange." Here there were only cars and low, windowless office buildings sealed off with layers of stucco and iron. Electronic eyes scanned garage entrances, unused doorways. Everything was painted tan and gray, as if in imitation of the sky and earth.

A few blocks on, they reached a flat, empty space where even the squat buildings had disappeared. The scent of burning wood wafted through the air. In the growing darkness Antonio saw at least two fires going, the outlines of people. There were several shelters and tents, one resembling an igloo, wool blankets and a blue tarpaulin attached to a round skeleton of wire and wood planks. The shelters were spread across several vacant lots. There seemed to be plenty of room, and it might not be so bad to camp out in the open.

"I guess we can sleep here," Antonio said. "This looks like a good place. I think we can rest here."

The people standing around the tents and shelters seemed to ignore Antonio and José Juan as they set down their Hefty bag by an old palm tree. José Juan found some pieces of cardboard nearby and laid them on the ground. This was where they would sleep. They were on a small hill that rose over downtown, the muddy lot beneath them green with weeds grown thick from the recent rains. The leaves of the palm trees waved in the cool breeze. This place was some sort of geographic anomaly, a lush knoll of wild plants and grasses in the middle of the city.

Hours later Antonio was lying on a mattress of crushed boxes, adrift in a timeless night. José Juan was snoring, tossing and turning, resting finally. Above Antonio the Los Angeles sky stretched in a vast blackness empty of stars, constellations erased by the glowing lights of too much city around him. To his left he could see the skyscrapers on Olive and Grand, so close he could almost make out the faces of the janitors inside. He imagined Mexicanos emptying trash cans on the thirty-second floor, mopping, dusting, daydreaming, sitting in the executive's chair, talking on the phone, doing things they weren't supposed to do.

Sleepless hours passed as Antonio listened to the sounds hidden in the darkness around him, wondering if they would bring new calamities. Voices came from the igloo-shaped tent now, people speaking in Spanish and English, men with Central American accents, lilting voices that felt familiar and comforting. *There must be a hundred people living here, chapines and guanacos too, living here as if it were the most normal thing in the world, as if they'd been here for years and years.* He heard a woman, a gringa, her voice scratchy and insolent. The men called out her name. "Come here, Vicki. *Ven acá*, Vicki." She responded with streetwise laughter. "*Conmigo*, Vicki. Next to me, Vicki."

"You guys are so sick," she said playfully. "That's why I like you so much. Because you're so fucking sick."

It was strangely reassuring to hear their voices, to know that the people who camped here went about their lives like anybody else. He could easily have heard the same squalid dialogue in the building he had just been evicted from. Vicki and the men in the tent laughed together, a rich, human laughter. They sounded happy. But no. What a silly thing to say. How could they be *happy*? That was a word for birthdays and weddings. *The bride and groom looked happy when they left the church.*

Antonio had spent a lifetime turning away from all that was ugly and unpredictable, and yet here he was right in the middle of it. He was sleeping on dirt, exposed to everything, protected by nothing. He was already beginning to feel nostalgic for the yellowing walls and rusty locks of the apartment he had left just a few hours ago. When he rolled over, trying to sleep, his lips touched the soil, grains of earth sticking to his tongue until he spat them out. The taste was not unpleasant. It reminded him of eating dirt, something he must have done when he was less than two, a memory older than words.

* * *

Morning came and the sky was a canopy of whiteness, soft and pale, the diffuse light of dreams. What time was it? Five, six o'clock? Antonio had not slept one minute. His mouth was dry and his eyes ached and stung. José Juan was already up, exploring the lot; Antonio could hear him scratching about in the patches of dirt and weeds. Suddenly he was standing over Antonio, his thick eyebrows arched high in an expression of childlike wonder. José Juan had the almond-shaped eyes and curly black hair of an Arab, which was why Antonio sometimes called him *moro*.

"Are you awake?" José Juan asked.

"What do you think, *moro*? Of course I am. Who could sleep here?"

"Good. I want to show you something. I found something really neat. *No me lo vas a creer.*"

Antonio rose to his feet reluctantly, his back heavy and sore from the night spent on the ground. A car droned by on Beaudry Avenue, and a phlegmy cough sounded from one of the tents. Otherwise the lots were quiet; everyone, it appeared, was still asleep. José Juan walked across the lot where they had slept and stood in a flat patch of red dirt.

"Look," he said, spreading his arms wide to celebrate his discovery. "There's a floor here. Tile. It used to be a kitchen. This was somebody's house."

For a moment Antonio thought that José Juan was trying to make some sort of joke, but then he saw a narrow path of bricks leading to a set of concrete steps. A little farther on were the ruins of a driveway.

"See?" José Juan said. "A family, a rich family used to live here." He walked around the empty property tracing squares and rectangles, the geometry of a home that had been demolished many years ago.

"Right here, this was their garden. That was their garage." José Juan jumped a few steps to his left. "Over here was the bedroom. And see this? These bricks? This had to be the fireplace. See? A fireplace to sit by when it's cold, like it is now. A nice hot fire to keep warm. Can you see it? Can you?"

Antonio looked at the land around him. There was the green hill, with perhaps a dozen tents and shacks perched on its muddy earth. Underneath these ephemeral structures were the ruins of a lost community, a forgotten neighborhood built with brick and cement. On the hill, and on the flat plain that extended from its base, he could see a grid of city streets, blocks of land cut in rectangles and bordered with sidewalks, asphalt avenues with iron manhole covers for the sewers. Dozens and dozens of concrete stairs led from the streets to what used to be front lawns. In all, Antonio counted more than forty demolished lots, a whole section of the city leveled to an expanse of wild grasses.

Only the palm trees had survived the disaster that swept through this place: tall, majestic trees that looked very old, each with a heavy crown of dry leaves near the top, like a lion's mane. To the east, looming over the open plain, were the skyscrapers, an ocean wave of steel and glass. To the west, the empty fields came to an end and the city started again, now closer to the ground: not skyscrapers but stubby apartment buildings, liquor stores, fading stucco houses.

Antonio closed his eyes and tried to imagine what once stood on this barren land. *Elena always said I had an overactive imagination.* He could feel the souls of the children who once lived in this place, their after-school games and innocent wanderings. What sins did their parents commit, he wondered, to bring such destruction upon themselves?

José Juan lay down on the tile floor and stretched out with a lazy yawn. "We have a home, our own little *rancho*," he said. "It's ours. We own it. A nice piece of property next to downtown."

Several hundred yards away, two men huddled around a fire that blazed in an oil barrel, the smoke drifting upward and settling into a thick haze. In Guatemala, Antonio had seen cornfields set ablaze, swirling rains of ash and ember, veils of smoke that lingered for days like fog in the mountain valleys. He remembered bridges that fell into rivers, asphalt and steel swallowed by white tongues of water. He looked at the wild urban grasses before him and remembered the hills near Huehuetenango, where he once encountered a single-file column of soldiers, a camouflage serpent on the march, disappearing suddenly into the dense foliage.

The vacant property, the plastic shelters, the ruined homes. The more he thought about it, the more Antonio began to feel a kinship with the flattened earth around him.

* * *

Sitting on the damp ground of the lot, Antonio opened the Hefty bag to see his possessions swimming around inside, socks and underwear mixed up with spoons and soup bowls. It reminded him of the haste and disorder of his retreat from the apartment building. He worried about leaving things unfinished in the apartment. He rummaged in the bag for his collection of photographs, but could not find them, and this left him feeling unsettled. A moment of déjà vu, until he pinpointed a memory, another day like this one.

On that day many years ago it was not a plastic bag he carried but a cardboard box tied shut with dirt-colored twine. As today, it held all of his possessions, although he could not now remember exactly what he possessed at the time. He was standing in the central square of San Cristóbal Acatapán, the box at his feet, because he was fleeing that horrible little village, taking the first step in the journey that would lead, eventually, to Los Angeles. He was leaving behind a house with floors that were covered with reddish black blood. He had wandered through that house like a sleepwalker, his shoes sticking to the tiles.

There had been a crowd around the doorway when he got there. A man he didn't know, a *campesino*, was kneeling over the bodies, poking a stick into Elena's ribs, trying to see something underneath her corpse. No one had known he was the husband and father until he pushed his way to the front and gasped and fell to his knees. Elena's arms raised above her head, as if she were reaching for something behind her. Wearing a blue apron he had never seen before. Next to her, their baby, his arms and face covered in watery pink splotches, eyes open and fixed.

That's the way the doctors gave him to me when he was born, just out of Elena's belly. Covered in an earth brown film of blood and tissue, mother and son joined by life's fluid. This is something a father can never forget, the son's first cries, the voice of new lungs, the mother's exhausted glow of relief and joy. Antonio would forever relive these two moments as one, the birth and death of his son fused into a single image, the living cry of the newborn and the scream of the father. *And then the moment when my baby opened his eyes for the first time and I realized that they were my own, my legacy, Spanish eyes of Zacapa passed down by our fathers and mothers for generations and generations.*

Someone had dragged the corpses through the house before he got there, painting the floors with their blood, placing Elena and Carlos on the front steps for the crowd to see.

People he didn't know whispered to him that he should leave San Cristóbal immediately. They said the soldiers who killed Elena and Carlos would soon return to finish their work. The family servant, Marisol, ran through the house in a panic, filling the cardboard box with the things he could not remember. "You have to leave," she repeated between sobs. "You have to leave or they'll kill you." Hypnotized by the smudges of blood on the floor and the walls, by the bullet holes he found in a closet door, Antonio would have stayed in that house all day if Marisol hadn't dragged him out. Carrying the box, she led him by the arm to the town square and left him there, by the kiosk, to wait for the bus that would take him away to safety.

The box was still at his feet when the bus pulled in and parked, its engine idling in a loud sputter. He was about to board when he was spotted by Mrs. Gómez, his neighbor, the woman from across the street. He didn't want anyone to look at him, he longed to be invisible, but that was impossible when you lived in a small town and stood in its central square. Antonio did not really know the woman, but he knew she had spoken to his wife quite often. Elena was gone, but Antonio still possessed this absurd fact: she did not like this Mrs. Gómez very much.

Embracing him, Mrs. Gómez offered her *pésame*. She was an older woman with white hair tied in a braid. Tears were streaming from her milky eyes as she lamented the passing of "our Elena." Everything was a jumble, and he did not hear what she was saying. She talked and cried. It occurred to Antonio that the bus passengers around him might think she was his mother come to wish an embarrassed son a tearful goodbye. She should go away: it seemed to him that he should be allowed to suffer alone. And then the stream of her condolences came to an abrupt stop. She fell silent, her eyes fixed on something behind him. Without warning she grabbed him by the arm, squeezing his biceps.

"Oh my God, that's him, right there!" she said, looking over Antonio's shoulder. "He's one of *them.*"

"What?"

"He's one of them. I saw him at your house."

Confused, Antonio turned to see what Mrs. Gómez was looking at.

"Don't!" she said in a fierce whisper, pulling at his arm. "He'll see you. He'll kill you."

"Who?"

"It's them. It's him. One of the men at your house. He killed Elena. He killed the baby. He's one of them."

Antonio felt himself suddenly alert again, the haze around his eyes dissolving, the moment coming into sharper focus.

"*Matones sinvergüenzas.* They're not even ashamed to show themselves," Mrs. Gómez said. "*Asesinos.* They kill someone and buy an ice cream like it's nothing. Nothing!" She pushed him toward the bus.

Look at him. Why are you afraid? The twine that held the box together cut into Antonio's fingers. *Drop the box. Drop it and confront the man.* The box seemed to have a will of its own, pulling Antonio forward, onto the bus. Turning, he caught the outline of a man with a chocolate ice cream to his mouth, diminutive but stout, like a tree stump.

Antonio shuffled along with the other passengers, keeping the vague form of the killer in his field of vision. Moving through the aisle now, he took a seat by the window. He squeezed his hand into a fist for courage and looked out.

The killer was sitting on a cast-iron bench, not thirty feet away, wearing black denim pants and a green sweatshirt, hair stubble-short. He raised the ice cream to his mouth with a chunky, muscular arm. He was dressed like a civilian but looked like a soldier. The shaved head was the giveaway. Antonio memorized his face: the dark features, the long nose, the protruding ears, something childlike in the eyes.

The killer caught Antonio's glance and pulled the ice cream from his mouth, slightly perplexed, as if to say, "Who are you and why are you staring at me?" Antonio did not look away. The killer lost interest and returned to his ice cream.

Antonio saw one more thing before the bus jerked into gear and began to roll forward. On the killer's left arm, the one not holding the ice cream, halfway between the wrist and the elbow, there was a mark on the skin, yellow and black. A tattoo of a yellow animal with its jaws open.

For the next several hours Antonio rode the bus with his feet on the box underneath him. The box with the forgotten, worthless possessions. He vomited out the window, wept into his hands, pounded a fist into his thigh. *I am a coward. I am a coward.* He had failed to summon the courage to jump from the bus in the square in San Cristóbal and confront the man who had killed his wife and son.

El Pulgarcito Express

Guillermo Longoria, retired sergeant in the Jaguar Battalion of the Guatemalan army, lived six blocks from MacArthur Park in a brick building called the Westlake Arms. He kept his one-room apartment meticulously clean, making his bed first thing in the morning and dusting his only furniture, a dresser and an old wooden chair, three times a week. Every Sunday he took a wet rag and wiped down the scratched lime green skin of the linoleum floor on his hands and knees. He worked his muscled arms hard against the scuff marks and the faint outline of dirty footprints, reaching under the bed to annihilate dust balls and loose hairs. No matter how hard he cleaned, no matter that his palms were wrinkled and white from scrubbing, the floor always seemed to be dirty again an hour later. Alone in his room, Sergeant Longoria was waging a war of attrition against the gray film of soot that infiltrated whenever he left the window open, fine particles of automobile exhaust and God knows what else that came creeping in from the streets four stories below.

This self-imposed discipline and Spartan lifestyle set him apart, he felt, from the rabble that lived around him, the Salvadorans, Mexicans, and Guatemalans who filled the Westlake Arms. He saw them in the hallways and stairways, these janitors, garment workers, and housekeepers, scrambling off to work every morning. They were on a sad minimum-wage quest, with no sense of life's greater purpose. He hated them, they were so pathetic.

Longoria considered himself a man of accomplishment. The certificates and diplomas from his military training in the Panama Canal Zone and at Fort Bragg, North Carolina, the newspaper clippings detailing his unit's exploits in Guatemala, were all carefully preserved in an album he kept in the bottom drawer of his dresser. The intellect, strategic vision, and wisdom of great military leaders had been passed down to him. A soldier did not lose those things when he quit the army; he carried them with him wherever he went, even to a city filled with criminals and drug addicts. His neighbors lived in apartments dense with people, two or even three families sharing one room. That was good enough for them, but Longoria demanded better for himself. He made enough money from his job at El Pulgarcito Express to afford living alone.

Longoria's photo album was filled mostly with snapshots of his buddies in the army, pictures of men posing with their weapons and with the company mascot, a brownish mutt named Che. One shot was a close-up of Longoria's forearm when the tattoo of the jaguar was fresh, two weeks new—yellow pelt, black spots, moist red mouth. A certificate from the School of the Americas in the Canal Zone took up an entire album page. There were several newspaper clippings, two of them from *La Prensa Libre*: an interview with Lieutenant Colonel Miguel Villagrán, commanding officer of the Jaguar Battalion, and a report of Villagrán's death in an ambush by "terrorist delinquents." Longoria loved Villagrán even more than his own father, a love that had grown stronger in the years since Villagrán was killed. The album also held a stack of battlefield photographs that Longoria rarely looked at, the last of what had once been a trunkful of war trophies, most of them given away when he left Guatemala.

In the drawer with the album, Longoria also kept his book collection, which consisted of several paperbacks, among them *Vladimir Rashnikov's Guide to Intelligent Chess* and *Fifty Chess Openings from the Grandmasters*. He had three titles by Dr. Wayne García, including *Success and Self-Fulfillment Through Mind Control*.

Dr. García helped Longoria understand his inner urges. He had read all of Dr. García's books, and considered him one of the great thinkers of our time. Dr. García taught Longoria that the mind was like any machine and that he had to control the machine instead of allowing it to control him. If Longoria had read Dr. García's books when he was younger, he might have gone further in the army, might have accomplished more with his life. *Maybe I would have been an officer*. Longoria wanted to meet Dr. García one day.

Besides the dresser, the bed, and the chair, the only other objects in Longoria's apartment were a weightlifting bench and a set of barbells, which he kept stacked like coins in a corner of his room. Although he was a small man, he could bench-press two hundred fifty pounds, almost double his weight. He bathed after each workout, in the morning before he left for work, and in the evening when he came home. Afraid of running out of shampoo, he kept extralarge bottles of silky yellow Suave in the shower. When he rinsed off, he took great pleasure in looking down to watch the dirty water drip off his body, thin black lines swirling down the drain. After just a few hours on the street, the soot was always thick and sticky on his neck and face.

He would not be swallowed by the uncleanness around him. *This place, this Los Angeles, is a cloud of filth, even the sky is muddy brown.* He found condoms and hypodermic needles on the street. There were needles everywhere: in the park, on the lawns, by the bus benches, in the gutters. All it took was one little poke, one little drop of blood to infect you. He'd seen the AIDS cases, right here in front of his building, the old *culeros* so close to death, skeleton men. *If the needle pokes me, my muscles and bones will corrode and I will die here, alone in this room. It will take them weeks to find my body. To die like that is to die without honor.*

Over the years Longoria had learned to spot the AIDS cases and the AIDS-cases-to-be: the hypes, the doomed *tecatos*, the human pincushions. The streets around MacArthur Park were thick with wan-faced heroin addicts. They were stacked in the old hotels and apartment buildings like diseased cords of wood. When they drifted toward him on the street corner, bony hands outstretched for a cigarette or a few coins, he gave them a homicidal stare.

Behind Sergeant Longoria's building was an alley where a group of these heroin addicts lived, adding another layer of scent to the putrid sweetness of the alley's dumpsters. Longoria saw the addicts and breathed in their smell every morning when he took out his trash. This was another of his rituals, something he did every day, even if there was only a single Kleenex in the red plastic waste basket he kept in his bathroom.

The addicts had been living in the alley for about two years. Their cluster of shacks pushed against the unused rear entrance to a medical clinic, under a sign reading *"Clínica Médica Familiar: Un Servicio Para la Comunidad."* Longoria would like to see them flushed out of the alley like shit down the toilet. But there was no one to do it, because no one in Los Angeles seemed to care about trespassing, about people breaking the law.

When they first arrived in the alley the *tecatos* slept in the open air, with a piece of cardboard or a blanket thrown over them. After a few weeks they brought boxes and plastic milk crates to build snug little shelters, then some sheets of plywood to fashion a crude lean-to against the wall. Step by step they added on, and now they had this little settlement with an air of permanence about it, made from things other people had thrown away. The heroin addicts were here in the alley for the long haul.

Longoria made a point of never talking to the *tecatos*. He hardly even looked at them anymore. Only once did he exchange words with them, on a nippy winter morning when he heard a curious noise drifting from their shacks. He was standing in the alley, raising the dumpster's table-sized lid to throw out his trash. Then this unfamiliar sound, a high-pitched tone halfway between a hum and a whistle, and the chatter of voices. When he stepped closer to investigate, the source of the noise became clear: a television set. The heroin addicts were watching television. It couldn't be, but yes, now he could make out the jovial monologue of a weatherman.

". . . the forecast is for heavy snow across the Midwestern states, with icy blasts of arctic air coming down across Lake Michigan. Sorry about that, Chicago! And our hearts go out to the people of Buffalo this morning, Katie, where it's a bone-chilling fifteen below. Ouch!"

Longoria walked slowly past an opening in the wall of blankets and saw a man and a woman sitting on a mattress, bathed in the gray glow of the television screen. Inside, the space was no more than four feet wide, just enough room for two people to sleep side by side. He stepped back and saw a frayed brown wire poking out from under the rotting blankets and cardboard that were the shack's roof. The wire snaked up along the wall of the medical clinic, looped around a water pipe, and disappeared into a window in the Westlake Arms.

Intrigued, Longoria went inside and found the wire dangling from a windowsill in a second-story stairwell, attached by a crude copper braid to another wire that ran along the base of the wall. For a few seconds he stared at the wires in confusion, until he realized that the heroin addicts were using electricity from his building. It incensed him that they would do this. They sure had a lot of nerve, these hypes. This was going too far, *se estaban aprovechando.* Longoria ripped the wires apart, causing a small but fierce explosion of blue sparks that sent a quick jolt of electric current through his arms. He fell butt-first onto the floor. The television noise in the alley sputtered and died.

"Aw shit," a male voice shouted below. "We're gonna miss the rest of *The Today Show.*"

"Go reconnect it, baby," a female voice said. "Hurry. I wanna watch that interview with Whitney Houston."

Longoria got to his feet and stuck his head out the window. "*Ladrones,* you were stealing our electricity! We paid for that. It's not yours, it's not free. It costs money!"

After a short silence, the male voice in the alley called back slowly, "Fuck you, buddy. Fuck you."

*   *   *

They came to the offices of El Pulgarcito Express clutching envelopes overflowing with Mother's Day cards, love letters, and Kodak pictures of the grandson's baptism. They carried cardboard boxes stuffed with vitamins and cold creams you couldn't find in San Salvador or Guatemala City. They took neatly folded bills from wallets and purses and bought money orders made out to relatives in Quetzaltenango, Tegucigalpa, Jutiapa, and Zacatecoluca.

They didn't trust the mail system in their native countries, painfully slow when it functioned at all, so they came to El Pulgarcito or one of its competitors: Lopez Express, Cuzcatlán Express, Quetzal Express, and a half-dozen other outfits with equally quaint Central American names, in storefronts decorated with the sky blue and white flags of El Salvador, Guatemala, Honduras. You paid fifteen dollars and El Pulgarcito promised to deliver your letter within one week, *más o menos*, unless the destination was in one of the "zones of conflict," the euphemism of choice for guerilla-controlled territory, in which case the delivery might take a lot longer.

At the El Pulgarcito office on Pico Boulevard, branch number two, Sergeant Longoria's job was to handle complaints, to listen to the customers whine about the rates, about packages that never arrived at their destinations, about lost checks and money orders.

"My sister said she opened the letter and there was no money order, it disappeared," a corpulent Honduran woman said, waving a receipt before Longoria's face. "Two hundred dollars, gone, just like that! You know what I think? You're just a bunch of thieves, that's what."

Longoria wondered which of the five or so people who worked in this office had taken the woman's money order. Maybe it was Carlos Avilés, the manager, who opened every letter to check for political messages, or maybe it was the owner himself, who wasn't above a little pilfering now and then. Longoria had no doubt this customer was telling the truth, but then again, she was a fool for trusting El Pulgarcito in the first place. She got what she deserved.

"We only guarantee the money order if you buy it here, with us," Longoria said for the third time. "If you put one in and don't tell us, we're not responsible. The company isn't responsible for any of that. This is what our *jefe* says. The *jefe* says those are the rules."

"Oh, so that's how it is?" the woman shot back. "I see. So that's the little racket you've got going here."

Longoria stared straight into her angry eyes. This was his practiced soldier's gaze, his *cara de matón*, the look that said he was one of the serious ones, the type to grin after he hit you over the head with his rifle butt. Anyone from Central America recognized this look. Longoria had the face of the soldier the customers remembered from back home, a Galil at his side, pants tucked into high laced boots, standing with menacing grace on a street corner in Guatemala, El Salvador. Dead dictators and demagogues lived on in these cold brown eyes. It was Longoria's great gift, his strongest personal asset. His stare always chased the complainers away, which was precisely why he had been stationed at the front counter. The Honduran woman put the receipt in her purse, turned around, and walked away.

There was a certain discipline involved in his work, and Longoria liked that. You had to be patient and resist the urge to reach over and slap the woman. Self-control. That was what he was learning from Dr. Wayne García's book, to rein in the initial impulse to strike out and solve the problem with his fists. Sometimes it took more nerve not to hit someone than to hit them.

Longoria liked working at El Pulgarcito because it was an office job. He told people he worked in "the service sector," admiring the orderly sound of this phrase. When he first came to Los Angeles, Longoria had worked in a series of factories, including eight months in a sweatshop on Washington Boulevard where his job was to tend to large vats of acid that turned regular blue jeans into "stone-washed" jeans. This was smelly work, and he felt he deserved something better than noxious fumes. Above all, he wanted a job where he could stay clean and not worry about chemicals eating into his skin.

Longoria the factory worker had begun his search for new employment on a Sunday afternoon, walking into the storefronts along Pico Boulevard to ask the owners if they needed any help. He was turned away at a *discoteca* and a shop that sold religious articles, saints and votive candles of all shapes and sizes. He stepped into a store called La Primerísima, which sold First Communion, wedding, and *quinceañera* dresses. Waves of lacy white fabric gushed from every corner of the cramped space, from the display windows, from hooks on the walls, from the rows and rows of racks on the floor. The young women who worked there laughed at him, asking if he wanted a job modeling the dresses.

His next stop was El Pulgarcito Express. Behind the counter stood a thirtyish pug-nosed man in a square-cut guayabera shirt, the uniform of the well-dressed Latin American businessman. The man turned quiet, his eyes narrowing, when Longoria asked if the company was hiring.

"You're a soldier, aren't you?" he said, staring at Longoria as if he were some sort of zoological curiosity. "I can tell. You're a veteran."

"Yes, *jefe. Así es.*"

"What unit were you with?"

Talking about one's military past was always risky, but Longoria already had an inkling of this man's sympathies.

"*Ejército de Guatemala,*" he answered efficiently, as if he were addressing an officer. "*Batallón Jaguar. Sargento Guillermo Longoria, para servirle.*"

The man in the guayabera broke out in a perfect white smile—a wealthy man's smile, Longoria observed—and embraced him.

"Welcome, sergeant, welcome to El Pulgarcito Express. Of course we have a job for you. You'll work the counter, you'll help with the shipments. How's six fifty an hour sound?"

This was two dollars more an hour than Longoria had ever earned before.

"Consider this your home, soldier. You're part of our family now."

The man was William Duarte, owner of El Pulgarcito. Duarte was a fervent Salvadoran nationalist and self-described "militant" in the right-wing ARENA party; his claim to fame, back in El Salvador, was that his sister was married to a rather influential government minister. He decorated his offices with ARENA campaign posters and the mustachioed portrait of the party's balding presidential candidate, Alfredo Cristiani. In between all the political posters calling for "ORDER, PEACE, WORK" were tourist posters of Salvadoran landmarks: snapshots of palm-lined beaches and tidy cities. Judging from the cars and the clothes styles, Longoria guessed that the posters dated from the 1960s. El Salvador before the war.

After hiring Longoria, Duarte disappeared for several weeks. When Longoria inquired about him, his co-workers said *el ingeniero* Duarte was busy. *El ingeniero* Duarte was tending to his many investments and properties scattered across Los Angeles. They always referred to the owner by this formal title, *ingeniero*, because he claimed to have a degree in civil engineering, though few of his employees really believed this. *El ingeniero* Duarte drove a white BMW and often called the office on his car phone, yelling at his employees to talk faster because the calls cost a dollar a minute and he worked too hard to waste his money on slow-witted people.

When Duarte returned to branch number two, he pulled his newest employee away from the front counter to say he desperately needed a word in private. He grabbed Longoria's arm and began talking with frantic energy, as if he'd been waiting to have a chat with him for a very long time. They sat in a small office in the back, a bare room with only two chairs and a telephone on the floor. Duarte sipped at a milk shake in a Styrofoam cup.

"I can't tell you how much respect I have for our fighting men. In my country, and in yours too, the army is the glue that holds everything together. If it wasn't for the army, we'd still be in the Dark Ages, we'd be living in complete chaos. Am I right, or am I right? Of course I'm right. That's just the way it is. Right?" He lifted his arms, as if to ask how anyone could object.

Longoria nodded in assent and Duarte continued. "We need the army to bring order. Without the army we'd just be a country of poor peasants, illiterates. That's how it is, and you know it too. I can see it in your face. That's why you came here to work with me at El Pulgarcito, because you could see we thought alike. You could sense it as soon as you stepped in the place. We're alike, me and you. We see things the same way. What sign are you, by the way? I'm a Gemini. You're a Gemini too, aren't you? I knew it! I can spot one every time."

Duarte was wearing a pale yellow guayabera with crusty bean stains on the bottom. He had soft hands that had been spared the indignities of physical labor, and a round gut that showed despite his loose-fitting shirt. His moussed hair was combed back neatly and he smelled of cologne, a vanity Longoria found especially irritating. Although Duarte was talking to him like an old friend, Longoria felt uncomfortable in his presence. He had not yet said a word, but Duarte just kept talking.

"Personally, I never joined the army because I had another role to play, with my business and organizing for the party here in Los

Angeles. This is important work. Maybe it's not as dangerous as what you did in the army, but it's important. There are many insidious influences here among the people in Los Angeles, among the Centroamericanos. We have to fight them. We monitor their activities. Once in a great while we organize a little action to let them know we're here. A little letter, a little phone call, sometimes something more serious. The newspapers get all excited and call us a 'death squad,' but it's nothing like that. Just little things. *Acciones.* One day maybe you can help us. We could use someone with your training.

"So, tell me about your training. Did you get to work with the Americans, with the Green Berets? You know, we have a battalion like yours in El Salvador. They're called the Atlatacl Battalion. Yes, yes, of course, you've heard of them. I forget, I'm talking to an expert here! The American training is simply the best, isn't it? These gringos know what they're doing. Just look at their soldiers, real warriors. For starters, they give them a lot to eat. For years and years our soldiers were always so skinny and small, and then we learned from the Americans that we shouldn't skimp on the food for the fighting men. Little things like that it took us a long time to learn. You have that same look now, that healthy look. What's the word? Robust. That's it. You're small but robust. You're in fighting shape."

Duarte insisted on hearing about his military career, so Longoria told him about Fort Bragg and the Panama Canal Zone, about the John F. Kennedy Center for Special Warfare and the School of the Americas and how he had diplomas from both. Longoria said he had been impressed by North Carolina, by the antiseptic army base, the nicely stocked PX, everything so orderly and well thought out. He expected the rest of the United States to be like Fort Bragg, but then he came to Los Angeles and was badly disillusioned. What he remembered most about Panama was the unrelenting heat and the American officers who seemed to be two or three feet taller than all the Guatemalans and Salvadorans around them. There was the training in jungle warfare and no time to see the canal itself, which was something of a disappointment. When he wasn't training, all he did was sleep.

Longoria spoke quietly, looking down at the carpet as he talked. He thought he should remain humble before his boss. When he looked up he saw that Duarte's eyes were wide open, the face of a child listening to a fantastic bedtime story.

* * *

"This room is so sad, Guillermo. You should decorate it. Put something on the walls, a poster at least. It's like a cave in here. It makes me sad to visit you. My bathroom has more personality than this."

Reginalda Peralta was the only woman Longoria had ever granted the privilege of staying overnight in his room. A twenty-three-year-old native of the port city of La Unión in El Salvador, she had long, curly black hair and full lips the color of red wine. She was frank and outspoken, a common trait among Salvadoran woman, Longoria believed, especially the ones from the big cities. They had a date every Saturday afternoon.

On this particular Saturday, Reginalda was sitting next to him on the edge of his bed in a tight polyester black skirt and a frilly yellow rayon blouse. It was the awkward, obligatory intermission between the time they entered his apartment and the moment they started having sex. As usual, Longoria didn't say much, though Reginalda felt compelled to fill these minutes with something resembling conversation. As she talked, her small feet tapped against the green linoleum.

"Do you like my new shoes?" she asked, raising her black pumps into the air. "I bought them on Broadway. Just fifteen dollars. The shine never goes away, it's permanent. Nice, huh?"

When Longoria first met her, she had been wearing tennis shoes and a silly Taco Bell uniform covered with bean and avocado smudges. It was last summer, on a day when the hot, dry air had left Longoria feeling especially weary and spent. He was eating alone, as he always did, his face buried in the bland but inexpensive Mexican food before him. He looked up and saw a woman wearing an aquamarine shirt and a small rectangular name tag. Her curly hair was tucked under a purple baseball-style cap that had a yellow bell on the front, and she was wiping the tables in the outdoor dining area, stacking discarded cups and paper wrappers on a bright orange tray. It was late afternoon, a few hours past lunchtime, and Longoria was the only customer left.

It was not his habit to talk to women he didn't know, to begin a conversation out of thin air, but Reginalda intrigued him. She frowned as she scrubbed a rust-colored salsa stain from a plastic tabletop. Longoria looked at her lonely eyes, the hurried, resentful way she wiped the tables clean, and decided that she was as angry and disillusioned as he was. Life has not been fair to me, she seemed to be saying. I deserve better than this, I wasn't meant to wash salsa off tables. He felt he instantly understood everything there was to know about her. His natural inhibitions were overwhelmed by the desire to talk to her, to reach out to her with words, and he said the first thing that came to his mind.

"People should learn to throw away their own trash, don't you think? It's a bad habit people have, to leave their trash for someone else. *Son unos maleducados.* If people were more polite, if they were more considerate, you wouldn't have to pick up after them."

Reginalda's forlorn mouth broke into a wide smile. She dumped the trash in a plastic receptacle and looked briefly into his eyes.

"You're right," she said. "People *are* inconsiderate."

Longoria had the feeling that he had stumbled upon a great, unspoken truth. They talked for a few minutes, mostly about the sad state of a world filled with so many ill-mannered people, until Reginalda's supervisor emerged from the kitchen and told her to stop goofing off and get back to work.

Now, six months later, Longoria's meetings with Reginalda followed a strict schedule, just like everything else in his life. He saw her once a week, sometimes twice, rarely more than that. But he never missed a date either. He didn't think he should see the same woman for too long, but he was becoming attached to her anyway. He liked her because she talked endlessly, even when he wasn't listening. She didn't care if he was quiet, and she seemed to know the texture of his past, even though he had never spoken of the things he had seen and done.

Their date today had been like many others over the past six months. He met her at her apartment in Pico-Union, near Olympic Boulevard. They rode the bus downtown to Broadway to see a matinee at the Million-Dollar Theater—Pedro Infante, the Mexican cowboy crooner, in *Soy de Mi Pueblo*. Then another bus ride back to MacArthur Park, where they took a quick walk around the lake without exchanging more than a half-dozen words. He bought her some *churros con chocolate* from a street vendor and they made a beeline for his apartment.

Next to him on the bed, Reginalda tapped her new black shoes on the green linoleum and rambled on about her cousin's upcoming wedding.

"They're going to have the reception on the patio behind the house. She lives down on Century Boulevard, near Watts."

Longoria reached down and took off her shoes while she was still talking, tossing them on the floor. It was the signal to begin. She looked at the fallen shoes for a few seconds, laughed quietly, and began tugging at the buttons of his shirt. She took a wet bite at his bare chest and soon they were undressed, reaching for each other in a desperate meeting of skin and tongues, the tangle of their bodies on the narrow bed. His desire for her, for her thin arms and wide face, was growing stronger with each passing week. It confused him deeply, his weakness before the pull of this small woman, but he surrendered to it anyway. Ten minutes of groping, and then she put a square packet into his hand, a condom. She was underneath him now, curves of coffee-colored skin, their naked bodies pressed together in an extended caress, a flowing language of kisses and thrusts and scratches.

When their lovemaking was over, the silence between them returned, broken only by the sounds of the building, children and their mothers speaking through the walls, toys falling to the unseen floor above them. Longoria wondered if his neighbors could hear him making love to Reginalda. It bothered him to think that his intimate sounds, his moaning and Reginalda's muffled shouts, might serve as entertainment for people in the surrounding apartments. Maybe they didn't hear him. He tried to be quiet, putting his hand over

Reginalda's mouth and keeping it there even when she bit it. He mulled this over. Of course they could hear him: after all, he heard everybody else.

At night, from about ten until one or two in the morning, an orgiastic chorus of Spanish lovemaking radiated from the ceiling, the floor, the walls and windows around him: "*¡Ay amor!*" "*¡Así! ¡Así!*" "*¡Qué rico!*" It was enough to drive a single man who was alone in his room to touch himself, a moral weakness Longoria occasionally succumbed to, even though he always remembered the admonition of Lieutenant Colonel Villagrán, who once told him it was a "faggot's habit."

"Don't play with yourselves, soldiers. It weakens the spirit. Think like warriors, not like faggots. That's why we take you to the brothels, to attend to these needs. Do it the right way, the natural way. The army will see to everything. There will be no 'self-service' in the barracks."

Longoria left Reginalda on the bed and went into the bathroom, where he pulled a three-foot stretch of toilet paper from the dispenser and wrapped it around the condom. He carefully placed the neat bundle at the bottom of his waste basket. Then he turned on the shower and waited for the hot water to wash the sex and perspiration from his body. In a few minutes he was completely clean.

* * *

Guillermo Longoria had not joined the army by choice. He might have avoided being a soldier altogether if he hadn't gone to the movies on a Sunday afternoon to see *E.T. The Extra-Terrestrial* at the Lux Theater in Huehuetenango. He was seventeen years old and still filled with youthful innocence, the son of a peasant woman who grew corn on two acres of hillside. His life revolved around the soil, the cycles of rain and harvest. He did not yet know the world.

He was supposed to be in town to buy soap. "Get the soap and come right back," his mother had said. She was a stern and very short woman, with deep creases in her dark orange-brown skin and a slight Indian lilt in her Spanish voice. "I know what you're like, Guillermo. Don't wander around the market and don't get into any trouble."

Two hours' walk and a long bus ride later, the soap had been purchased, white powder with specks of blue that made his nose itch when he sniffed at it. The soap was in a plastic bag placed carefully between his two feet as he sat in this forbidden place, the movie theater. Guillermo was just two rows from the front, so close to the screen that he felt his seat was moving when the camera panned across a scene. They showed two kinds of movies at the Lux, Mexican and American. Guillermo preferred the latter. He looked up at *E.T.* and marveled at the movie's wide, clean streets and the impossibly large houses. For two weeks he had been saving for this ticket, and now he was finally in the packed theater, elbow to elbow with dozens of *campesinos,* men and women with sun-baked necks and faces watching the bright Technicolor images in muted awe. The suburb on the movie screen seemed to Guillermo more like a playground than a neighborhood. He watched a boy pedal his bicycle across the perfect pavement of a cul-de-sac, across open streets where there was not a single car or bus in sight.

He had seen other American movies before, mostly action pictures with exploding cars and gunfights. But he had never seen a movie with a house like this, room after room filled with televisions and toys, closets packed with more clothes than anyone could wear in a lifetime, a cornucopia of gadgets and appliances. It made sense that the Extra-Terrestrial would go to the United States. He would never come to Guatemala to be cooped up inside a little adobe house with a cement floor like the one where Guillermo lived. In the United States, E.T. had a whole refrigerator of food to indulge his appetites. What would he eat if he were to visit Guillermo's house? A tortilla with some beans and a pinch of salt?

On the screen, the cuddly little alien stood before a television set, fumbling with a remote control.

If I were in that house I would feel like E.T., like some small creature in a far-off world, making sounds no one understood.

E.T. drank beer from the refrigerator. He was alone in Elliot's house, getting drunk. He stumbled into the little sister's closet and put on her clothes and a silly hat.

Suddenly the house lights came on and the screen turned a blinding white. The theater filled with a confusion of voices, whistles of protest. The people in front of Guillermo turned to look back at the projectionist in annoyance. "Put the movie back on!"

The exit doors to the right and left of the screen burst open with a loud crack. Fatigue-clad soldiers appeared in each doorway with machine guns in their hands.

"*¡El ejército!*" a woman cried out. "Run, *muchachos*, run. It's the soldiers. Run before they get you!"

The theatergoers exchanged glances of incipient panic. *This is not happening. We're supposed to be at the movies.* Peasant men stood up and held their straw hats at their chests, women placed protective arms around their small children. Next to Guillermo, a boy began to crawl under his seat, squirming on the sticky syrup of the theater floor. A young man with a scar on his cheek sprinted up the aisle toward the lobby.

"Nobody move!" a muscular voice shouted from the back of the theater. "Everyone stay where you are!"

Guillermo turned around and saw soldiers spilling through the doors that led to the lobby. The soldiers looked too young, boys with high Indian cheekbones, dwarfed by their black rifles. The man with the muscular voice stood at the head of the aisle and surveyed the scene with self-satisfied authority. He wore tall boots and camouflage fatigues.

"Okay, you sons of bitches," he muttered as he lumbered down the aisle. "Now you'll see I mean business. *Ya van a ver, hijos de la gran puta.*"

He climbed up on the small stage just below the blank screen. All eyes turned to him; he was clearly the officer in charge. For a moment Guillermo was excited by the drama of the scene, so much like part of a movie, though not the movie he had just been watching. This soldier up on the stage was something of a cross between a Mexican comedian and one of those American action-adventure heroes who carried big guns and set off so many explosions.

"The women and girls can leave. The men and the boys will stay," the officer shouted. "Every boy over fourteen stays right here. And get your documents out. We're checking documents today. Anybody without proof of military service goes straight to the *cuartel.*"

Women in embroidered peasant blouses began stepping out of the rows, crying as they separated from husbands and sons, holding the hands of small boys and girls in shoes too big for their feet. Two soldiers pulled a man from his seat and dragged him to the front of the theater. One of them reached into the man's pocket and handed the officer some wrinkled documents. The officer shook his head and jerked his thumb over his shoulder.

"You're twenty-three years old and you haven't done your military service?" he said. "Sergeant, take this lazy yellow piece of shit and put him in the truck. *Al cuartel con este maricón.*"

The soldiers grabbed more men and boys from their seats and formed them into a line along the aisle. The officer checked documents; those with a blue stamp on their identity papers, proof of military service, were allowed to leave by the door on the left, while the others—all but a handful—were pushed, dragged, and kicked toward the door on the right.

A tall, skinny *campesino* with a wispy mustache stood before the officer, his head bowed. The officer glanced at the pathetic man before him and took in the surroundings, a second-rate theater with holes in the seats. He seemed suddenly disgusted by the cheapness of the drama he had concocted. After inspecting the man's papers, he pointed with a limp finger to the door on the right.

Finally it was Guillermo's turn to stand before the corpulent officer. He produced his papers, uncertain of the consequences.

"No seal on this one either," the officer said listlessly. "Another one for the barracks."

"But I'm not eighteen yet, *jefe*," Guillermo protested weakly.

"Don't tell me what the regulations are, you bastard. You think I don't know the regulations? You'll be eighteen soon enough."

Guillermo felt strong arms pulling at his collar. He tripped and nearly fell into the front row of seats. Another soldier pulled him up and shoved him through the exit door into the hot whiteness of the day. Before his eyes could adjust to the sunlight, he felt sharp pains on his legs and shins. He was running a gauntlet of soldiers who were kicking him, trying to trip him. After a few strides he fell to the ground, scraping his forearm on the asphalt; then the sensation of being lifted into the air like a sack of beans and landing on the wooden bed of an army truck.

A boy next to him was crying, his face buried in cupped hands. The man with the wispy mustache was bleeding from a cut to the forehead. They were all heaped up against each other. The truck began to move over a potholed road, tossing the men around like tourists on a carnival ride.

At the barracks, soldiers shaved the stringy hair from Guillermo's head and issued him a uniform. That night he slept in a stiff cot, weeping quietly. He knew his mother would be angry with him because he didn't listen to her and just buy the soap and come back home. If he were a good son, he wouldn't have gone into the theater and he wouldn't be in the army now.

3
Instant Shelter

At this point, anything would do. A glass of milk, a chicken sandwich, a *torta* like the Mexicans made with that round bread shaped like a pregnant woman's belly. Antonio had not eaten since yesterday, before the eviction.

He was sitting on a piece of cardboard, legs crossed, a blanket over his shoulders. The camp was in shadow, the sun still hiding behind the silhouette of the Financial District skyscrapers to the east. From time to time he heard rats scurrying up and down from their nest in the crown of a palm tree. Antonio and José Juan had moved their cardboard mattresses next to the whitewashed concrete wall of a basement, all that remained of a building that had otherwise dissolved into dust and pebbles. José Juan, ever resourceful, had found some plastic sheets nearby that he was going to use to build a lean-to. He was a bundle of Mexican energy, making the best of the situation, always finding something to do.

Antonio's hunger was an acid stream that flowed upward from his belly to his throat. Smoke signals from his stomach, a request from the intestines to the feet and legs: *Stand up and find some food.* He knew that they gave away groceries at the Unitarian food bank, thick blocks of orange cheese that you could eat with bread to fill you up. He should go soon, to get a good spot in line behind the bleary-eyed women who were always there two hours before the place opened. If he didn't move quickly the women would take all the good tomatoes and bread, leaving behind the stale loaves that only the homeless would eat.

But Antonio did not feel like moving from his patch of pebbles and dirt. A trip to the food bank would stave off the hunger for a few hours, and then he would have to start searching for food all over again. The effort seemed pointless, like building a wall of sand to stop the sea. And he would have nothing to show for it but the degrading memory of having waited in line, in the beatific glow of the church volunteers who smiled stupidly at the resentful winos, the impoverished mothers, the homeless immigrants.

"*Tengo hambre,*" José Juan said, appearing suddenly with another sheet of plastic. "Let's get something to eat."

Antonio ignored José Juan and the protests of his own stomach. He had forgotten something, and this had triggered another one of his famous depressions. He could feel it covering him, a somber rain, those leaden moments when even the breeze had too much weight, when it seemed his skin would collapse under the burden of so many thoughts, so much sadness. He could not remember when his wife and son had died. He could remember their birthdays—September 23 and May 15—but he could not place the date of their deaths.

What kind of father would forget? If she were alive, Elena would smile at him and say, "Of course you don't remember, Antonio. You always forgot everything. Anniversaries, phone numbers, appointments. You always forgot."

Elena is gone too many years. She has left me alone in this city of food lines and plastic cheese. Elena did not live to see this Los Angeles that I know, the empty sky, the only stars the lights of the skyscrapers that come on at dusk and watch over me like a thousand glass eyes. One moment he might be a normal man, someone with hopes and desires like anyone else, and the next he wanted to curl into a ball. To lie down and let his body seep into the ground. A moment of rest.

Vaguely aware that José Juan was still standing there, Antonio allowed his eyes to drift across the landscape. Saturday morning in downtown Los Angeles. On Third Street a car zoomed past the vacant lot every minute or so, streaks of waxed metal screaming out a Doppler hello and goodbye as they headed for the bridge that somersaulted gracefully over the Harbor Freeway into the Oz of the Financial District. Antonio sat just a few blocks away, in a checkerboard of rubble-covered lots where weeds poked through crumbling layers of concrete, brick, and asphalt.

"*¿Qué te pasa?*" José Juan asked, squatting down to look his friend in the eye like a mechanic checking under the chassis.

Antonio turned away.

"You look like you're dead," José Juan said. "All sad and everything. Say something, talk to me." He grabbed Antonio by the shoulders and shook him like a doll.

"Hey, listen to me. Snap out of it. *No te agüites.* I hate it when you get like this."

He hates me when I get like this. Who can blame him? Poor man, to have put up with Antonio for so long. What have I done to deserve such a patient friend? José Juan did not seem to like the Antonio who wanted only to sleep, the friend who seemed to be on the verge of suicide every few weeks.

"Go ahead and suffer then," José Juan said, standing up and shaking his head. He drifted off toward Third Street.

Antonio was left alone to watch the camp coming to life around him as the sun crested the skyscrapers, filtering through the blue patches in a half-cloudy sky. Here and there he saw white men in nylon jackets and olive drab parkas, and one gangly old man with a long white beard who looked like a caricature of Father Time. The Latino men in the tent next to Antonio and José Juan stepped out into the daylight and rubbed their bloodshot eyes. The Vicki from the night before stood among them, a heroin-pale woman of indeterminate age and angular features.

"Aw shit, look where I am," Vicki said, squinting. When her eyes had adjusted to the light, she saw that Antonio was staring at her and gave him the finger.

Embarrassed, he turned his attention to another encampment, where two black men were hanging clothes on a rope stretched between palm trees. A third man, a long-haired white, started a fire in a circle of rocks, balancing an old barbecue grill over the flames. Soon the scent of pinto beans began to drift toward Antonio, and his stomach growled again. As far as he could tell, the three men lived together in the shelter of milk crates, blankets, and corrugated tin that teetered behind them. The white man sat down on a crate by the fire and ran his fingers through his oily hair, an old instinct toward neatness reasserting itself. He rubbed his palm over the stubble on his face, then stood up and took off his shirt to expose a concave chest, bony and pale. He knelt and poked his head into the shelter, pulled out another shirt, and put it on. He was still stooping as he paced around the fire, as if his body carried the memory of living in that cramped space.

All the people here seemed to have the same vacant expression and hunched posture. They looked like walking question marks.

Refugees. That was the term for people who lived like this, in makeshift tents, on barren ground. This was something new. He did not know that gringos could be refugees.

These gringos don't deserve this.

Years ago, when Antonio lived in Guatemala, he had an electric idea of Los Angeles. It was a place of vibrant promises, with suntanned women in bikinis and men carrying ice chests brimming with beer. It was a city of handsome, fit young people, all with a bounce in their step. Long before he set foot in this country, Antonio felt that he knew California because he'd seen it come to life over and over again on his television set. In Antonio's homeland, the words "Los Angeles" sparkled, like sunlight glimmering off a mountain lake.

And now this. Skinny question-mark men with dirty bodies and unshaven faces, hanging clothes on a line strung between palm trees, in a lot in the center of the city.

Antonio began to imagine that he was somehow responsible for their plight. If his own mind were not clouded with so much pain, they would not exist. *They are what I feel.* Somehow he had tainted the prosperous Americanos with his condition. The pathos of these men was his own creation, an extension of his tortured past, the curse of a man with a dead wife and son. He wanted to apologize to these gringos, to say, "I'm sorry. It's all in my head. My head is full of all this trash, you see." He hadn't meant to put them in this horrible predicament. It was all his fault, and they could go home now, back to the lives they had before, to their beaches and ice chests. As soon as Antonio went away, they would slip back into their fit American bodies.

He closed his eyes for several minutes, meditating in a dizzy darkness, wondering if he could make them disappear. They were still there when he opened his eyes, men with teeth and skin yellow like ivory. They were as real as his hunger. He shook his head vigorously, like a dog shaking water out of its fur. He had been out here in the open air too long and was suffering some sort of psychological reaction. If he had a medical dictionary he would look up the symptoms. Hallucinations, delusions. If he stayed here he might lose his mind completely.

It was important not to lose control.

The men in the next lot went about their morning chores with a serious and practiced efficiency, making coffee, dishing out the beans with a small plastic spoon. Even here in a barren lot, it seemed, people could settle into a domestic routine. With two plastic buckets that looked like beach toys, one of the black men brought water from an unseen source at the bottom of the hill.

A few minutes later José Juan returned, carrying several pieces of scrap wood.

"Let's go get food," he insisted. "We need to eat."

Antonio stood up. Together they hid the Hefty bag with all their possessions in one of the bushes that ringed the empty lots. Turning onto Third Street, past the last of the camps, they stepped over a cyclone fence that had been cut apart. A sign was still attached: Coming Soon: Crown Hill Hotel and Finance Park

* * *

They could see the man from half a block away, reaching into the brambles to pull out the Hefty bag.

"Hey, you!" Antonio called out in English, dropping a sack of groceries from the food bank and breaking into a run. Startled, the man began to walk away with José Juan's hotplate tucked under his arm, taking long, gangly strides. Antonio sprinted to catch up with him and tackled him from behind. The two men fell to the ground with a thud, Antonio landing on the thief's back, pounding him into the weed-covered soil.

Antonio rolled him over and formed his hand into a fist over the man's face. "Bastard!" he shouted.

The thief raised his arms meekly and cried out, "Please don't hit me!" He was the older man Antonio had seen before, pasty-faced, his long beard stained yellow just below his mouth.

We have almost nothing, and this man wants to take it from us. Antonio drove his fist into the man's face, the nose cartilage snapping under his knuckles. Another punch, this one like hammering nails into the ground, a clenched fist to the temple. A weak scream from the thief, and then one more punch, to the mouth.

"Don't fuck with me!" Antonio yelled. "*Hijo de la gran puta, no te metes conmigo.*"

It felt good to hit this man, to feel his own arms doped with adrenaline, to feel his wrists cut through the air as he pummeled the man's face. Antonio stopped when his knuckles began to throb. For a moment he felt strong and free; fury was a much better drug than self-pity.

He walked away and left the man moaning in the dry grass, the milky skin of his face already swelling purple and black. The thief smelled of urine and stale wine; Antonio wondered if the odor would linger on his hands. He wiped them against his trousers, then picked up some dirt and rubbed it quickly between his palms.

José Juan gave him a disgusted, incredulous stare.

"What?" Antonio asked. "What did I do?"

José Juan did not answer.

"He was taking our things," Antonio said. He shrugged his shoulders and went to collect the scattered groceries. The old man was still lying on his back by the bushes, moaning loudly. A pathetic, theatrical moan. Antonio unwrapped a block of cheese and bit off a piece. The plastic taste was not satisfying.

"Why did you hit him like that?" José Juan said finally. "He's just an old man. You didn't have to hit him."

Another moan from the wounded man in the bushes, who turned over onto his stomach.

There was revulsion on José Juan's face. *He's looking at me as if I were an animal.* Antonio took an angry bite of cheese and saw the red patches on his knuckles, the dirt embedded in his fingernails. This was what José Juan saw, the stains of the old man on his hands. *He thinks I beat the old man up for sport.*

Antonio began to feel like the ugly person in José Juan's gaze. To beat up a *viejo* who was too anemic and emaciated to defend himself was not an honorable act. *It was my temper coming out again. My famous, uncontrollable temper.* The men in Antonio's family had a genetic propensity to bouts of rage. They liked to scream, to shout, to bare their teeth to their wives, sons, and business partners. *Elena said she was afraid of my "reacciones violentas."* In family lore these outbursts were blamed on Antonio's peasant ancestors in Zacapa, a dry region on Guatemala's eastern frontier, where men still settled accounts with rifles and machetes. Antonio's grandfather was from Zacapa. A Zacapaneco took it seriously when you doubted his manhood. A Zacapaneco would shoot a man who stared at his wife. When Antonio or his father or one of his uncles raised his voice at a family gathering, people said, "That's the Zacapa coming out."

Antonio had never hit a man before. True, he had grabbed the building manager by the collar and pushed him against the wall, but he hadn't drawn blood. He had been known to raise his voice, to open his jaws, pantherlike, and scream in rage, but he did not think of himself as a violent person.

He blamed his actions on the surroundings. The exposed lots and the dirt and the hunger seemed to demand violence of him. Living out here on the street, you had to prove you were a man. To beat someone up had a purpose here.

I must become a Zacapaneco. Only the blood of Zacapa that runs through my veins will protect me now.

* * *

"I'd rather be up here than down there on the row, that's for sure. You're on the mountain, it's kind of nice, you know, up here with the trees and the breeze."

Frank liked to talk. He was a stout man, perhaps a former athlete, healthier than most of the men in the camp, and his freckled face was the light brown of *chocolate con leche*. He wore gloves that didn't match, one brown leather, the other gray wool. Antonio had awakened on his second morning in the camp with a great thirst, and had wandered around for an hour in a futile search for water. Finally he fought off his growing suspicion of the homeless people around him and approached this black man, who lived in a tent a few lots over from Antonio and José Juan.

At first Frank wore his own mask of distrust, eyes inspecting the stranger, sizing up any potential threat. "Yeah, I can tell you where the water is," he said. "That's an easy question." He pointed down the hill that he called "the mountain" to a liquor store on Glendale Avenue, two blocks away. There was a spigot behind the store, and the owner didn't mind you filling up a little bucket now and then. Slowly the sense of mutual distrust began to disappear. Several other nuggets of advice and observations followed.

Frank said he used to live on Skid Row but now preferred these weed-covered lots.

"Up on this mountain nobody bothers you. Except for the crack-heads and the prostitutes, I guess, but even they're kinda mellow here. It's hard to explain, but it's true. Down on the row you can get stabbed in your fucking sleep. People'll knife you for your wallet. The row is a fucking snake pit." He paused, cleaning his teeth with the corner of a matchbook. "Yeah, the row is a fucking snake pit. That's what it is."

Frank's shelter was on a choice piece of real estate where the little plateau of Crown Hill dropped off sharply, providing a panoramic view of the Harbor Freeway, the Financial District, and City Hall, a stubby white stone building dwarfed by towers of glass and steel. Frank and his companions had set up an old couch on the edge of the cliff to take in the view. Frank was sitting there now, leaning back and stretching his legs, like a suburbanite entertaining a guest in his living room.

"You met the Mayor yet?" Frank asked, and laughed at Antonio's startled expression.

The Mayor, it turned out, was Frank's friend and tentmate, Larry

Greene, who had won his nickname because he went to the Board of Supervisors meetings every Tuesday to tell the county to raise the General Relief payments.

"He makes nice speeches," Frank said. "Heard him talk at the board once. A real orator, the Mayor is. He's got his name on a couple of lawsuits too. *Greene versus the County of Los Angeles.* Has a nice sound to it, like a boxing match. In this corner, Larry Greene, homeless man. In that corner, L.A. County. The county's a real heavyweight. The Mayor's got a good left hook, but the county's got the fancy lawyers, the best money can buy. The Mayor's lawyer is a do-good volunteer in a wrinkled suit."

The Mayor emerged from the tent, a black man with a sad, gentle face. He wore blue jeans and a navy blue watch cap pulled down low, almost covering his eyebrows.

"Are you talking shit about me again, Frank?" he said with a playful smile. "Taking my name in vain?"

"Indeed I am. Talking about the G.R."

"Two hundred and ninety-seven dollars!" the Mayor snapped. "That's how much G.R. is." He paused and shook his head solemnly. "Don't know why they call it relief when it don't relieve nothing."

"Tell it, Mayor," Frank said. "Tell it."

"What can two hundred ninety-seven dollars a month do but keep you broke?" His gentle features turned harsh as he spoke, as if he were suffering the indignity anew. "You go to the check-cashing place, they take out their chunk. That's a whole little Mafia right there. Go to a regular bank, and they laugh at you. You get angry, you raise your voice, and they call the security guard to throw you out because you're stinking up the place and making all the legitimate customers nervous. That's how it is. A runaround for poor people. That's how I see it."

Frank and Antonio sat on the couch, contemplating what the Mayor had said. The silence stretched out for a minute or so, the space between the three men filled with the unspoken sense that they were powerless against such overwhelming injustice.

"What did you say your name was?" the Mayor asked finally.

"Antonio."

"Good to meet you. You're new here, right?" He shook Antonio's hand. "Seems to me I saw you come in a couple of days ago. You and another Latin. There's all sorts of Latins here now, more every day. I wonder why that is? You know why that is?"

Antonio shook his head. It was a good question.

"They're good people, the Latins. We all get along here, you know what I'm saying? There's no trouble here because this ain't like the row. In the row you're just a number, just a body on the sidewalk. Here we all got our little piece of earth. I guess you can say we've got a small investment in the community." He laughed at the irony. "And the Man, he leaves us alone because he's afraid to come in here. The place looks scary to him, all this rubble and shelters and shit. He doesn't understand it. He's afraid because this is our territory. It's like a liberated zone. Know what I mean?"

Antonio wasn't exactly sure what he meant, but he nodded politely. The Mayor excused himself, shook Antonio's hand again, and disappeared into the tent.

"See," Frank said. "Told you he made good speeches." Then, lowering his voice to a whisper, he added, "The Mayor's okay as long as he takes his meds. Once he gets off his meds, it's another story."

Frank leaned forward on his couch and pointed across a few hundred yards of undulating green hills to the freeway and the sky-scrapers beyond. "I've spent so much time here I started me a new hobby," he said. "Watching accidents." He told Antonio that he had seen fourteen so far, fender-benders, sideswipes, flip-overs: he collected them, keeping notes in a green loose-leaf binder with Sylvester the Cat on the cover.

"That down there is the Harbor Freeway," he explained. "The most dangerous stretch of freeway in California. I read that in the *Times*. And it's true. People switching lanes so much they can't help but run into each other. Trying to get over to the Santa Ana, the Pasadena, the Hollywood. Sideswiping each other and shit. It's the funniest thing I ever seen."

Antonio sat and watched the traffic. From this vantage point, a good half-mile away, the freeway ran quiet, like the sound of wind. The cars sped along, then slowed down, bumpers almost kissing, as if engaged in an automobile courtship ritual. Frank took the matchbook to his teeth again, cleaning patiently without taking his eyes off the freeway. Soon Antonio began to feel sleepy, hypnotized by the repetitive rush-rush of so many trucks and vans, Volkswagens and convertibles. All those cars and destinations. He dozed off for a second, awakened by the snap of his head falling forward.

"Kind of relaxing, isn't it," Frank observed.

Antonio wiped the sleep from his eyes and stood up.

"Thank you for telling me about the water," he said.

"Nice to meet you, *amigo*," Frank said. "Where'd you say you were from again?"

"Guatemala."

"Oh yeah. That's by Mexico, right?"

An hour later Antonio was sitting on his cardboard mattress, leafing through the Mexican soccer scores in *La Opinión*, when he heard excited shouts from Frank's camp.

"Whoa! A double flip!"

Antonio looked up and saw Frank slapping palms with the Mayor, in the style of American athletes.

"Did you see that, Mayor? Did you? Right over the center divider! Ka-pow! Oh man, that's fifteen! One-five."

* * *

José Juan scratched his head, his fingers deep in his curly hair, now a repository for bits of dirt and blown grass. He had been working diligently on the new shelter for several hours, but now he was looking at the assembled wood scraps and plastic sheets on the muddy ground as if he had just become aware of what he was actually doing.

"I'm finished, done for," he said. "I'm living on the streets. Everything is over for me. *Se acabó.* This is it."

He must be thinking about his family again, Antonio surmised. When you live with someone long enough, when you suffer with them, you begin to recognize the patterns of their moods. José Juan always scratched his head when he thought about his family. It had been more than three months since he sent money to his wife and children in Morelos, and weeks since he had enough for a long-distance phone call home. That was why he came to Los Angeles in the first place, to be a better provider for his family, so his children could have the pretty things they deserved.

"My wife and kids, they must be wondering what happened to me," José Juan said, digging at his scalp. "My mother will think I'm dead. But my wife will think I've gone off with another woman, a *gabacha*, a blondie. She told me that when I left home. She cried and said, 'I know I'm losing you forever. *Te voy a perder.* You'll find a *gabacha* and you'll fall in love.' I told her that would never happen. But now that's what she'll think, that I've gone off with a gringa." He buried his face in his hands.

Antonio reached over and put an arm around his friend's shoulder. "It's okay, *hombre*. It's okay."

As the sky began to turn a more ominous shade of gray, Antonio realized it was his turn to take charge.

"Let's get going with this," he said. "We'll drown if it starts to rain."

With six rotting two-by-fours José Juan had rescued from an alley on Alvarado, they began to erect a roof. They drove the planks six inches or so into the ground, braced them upright with bricks and chunks of concrete, then lifted several plastic sheets and old blankets over the frame.

José Juan looked at the makeshift shelter and frowned. "We're only going to be here on this mountain for a little bit, but we might as well make the best of it," he said. His spirits seemed to lift. "All it takes is one good job to get us back in a real apartment. Three weeks of work and we'd have enough for a down payment. Maybe I should go bother that Armenian guy again. If that guy paid me my money then we wouldn't have to stay here."

"Why do you keep bringing that up, *moro*?" was Antonio's testy reply. "*El Armenio* is never going to pay you. Just get that through your head."

"He might. The court says he has to."

Antonio had been listening to his friend talk about *el Armenio* for months. A building contractor of dubious repute, he had hired José Juan and a few other immigrant workers at a street corner on Santa Monica Boulevard in Hollywood. Three weeks into the job—the construction of an apartment building in the Los Feliz district—he had asked the crew to work late. Overtime was promised. The men stumbled around in the darkness, plastering walls on the exterior of the three-story building, until one of them, a Salvadoran, slipped off a scaffold and broke his ankle. When the crew refused to work in such dangerous conditions any longer, *el Armenio* fired them on the spot, cheating them out of their last six days' pay.

The other workers figured they had no recourse because they were *ilegales*. But José Juan, with his usual perseverance, had taken the case to small claims court, winning when the contractor didn't show up. The judge tacked a $200 penalty onto the $360 in wages the contractor already owed. José Juan had been counting on this $560 for two months, carrying around a stack of forms from the court as if he expected them to be transformed into cash at any moment. The contractor, however, was nowhere to be found. The dog-eared judgment of the small claims court was now tucked inside the Hefty bag.

"Just forget about it," Antonio said. He dragged their cardboard mattresses into the new shelter. "Thinking about it will only make you angry."

José Juan looked up at the sky, now completely overcast. Suddenly the day had become blustery. Their new roof fluttered in the wind. "One day. One day soon *el Armenio* will pay."

Antonio shook his head and sighed. He knew what it meant to be taken advantage of. That was what happened when you worked as a bus boy, cut lawns and planted flowers for strangers, when your best hope for a job was to stand with the crowds at the infamous street corners. There were certain employers who looked at men like Antonio and José Juan, saw the Mayan and Aztec in their eyes or heard the Spanish handicap in their speech, and took them for defenseless bumpkins. And it wasn't just the employers. The same type of person would sell you a radio that didn't work or a car without brakes, or rent you an apartment without heat or water.

Antonio had learned to appreciate simple common decency. For example, at the Culver City diner where he and José Juan became friends, they always paid him on time, and the waitresses gave him his fair share of the tips. Mr. Finkel, the owner, had declared bankruptcy but had managed to give each of his workers a week's severance pay before closing the place down.

No sooner had Antonio and José Juan put the last touches on the shelter than it began to rain, first a light sprinkle, then a downpour. They crawled inside and listened to the drops pattering on the plastic roof, which sagged just a few inches above their heads.

An hour passed and the rain did not stop. Pools of water began to form in the plastic canopy. Antonio examined the bruises on his knuckles, a reminder of all that had happened in the last three days: the eviction, the nights under the sky. Even the beating of the old man seemed like it was ages ago. The beating and the bruises on his knuckles seemed perfectly normal.

I can't get any lower than this. This is the lowest. Where did I go wrong?

When he first came to Los Angeles, Antonio thought of it as the place where he would redeem himself, undertake a new beginning. He remembered the feeling of tempered hope when he arrived at the airport and everything was so new and orderly compared to home. He looked at the clean-shaven police officers, for instance, and knew immediately that they wouldn't accept a bribe. In those first few months in California he had aspired to study literature at UCLA, to continue the education that had been cut short in Guatemala.

Antonio had not advanced beyond night-school English classes. Eventually he had learned what every other immigrant in the city seemed to know already. It was a fact of life that when you came to the United States you moved down in social station and professional responsibilities. Women with medical degrees became laboratory assistants, accountants became ditch diggers. Los Angeles made you less than you were back home. People accepted this because they still made six times more money than they could in El Salvador or Mexico, even though everything was twice as expensive.

Everyone took a step down, but Antonio had dropped further than most because he carried the unbearable burden of what he had seen at his house in San Cristóbal so many years ago. His Guatemalan memories were a bloodstained cloth that hung over him just as the rain-soaked roof hung over him now, threatening to collapse and inundate him: the inescapable sense of having failed Elena, his first and only love, of having failed Carlos, his son, of having allowed them to die alone. The feeling of being responsible for their deaths had only grown stronger over the years, with each new Los Angeles failure. He had allowed the many threads of his life here to come undone. Among other things, he had neglected his application for political asylum, ignoring the pleas of the caseworker at the Central American Refugee Center who told him he needed to show more backbone. "You won't get *asilo político* unless you try harder, Antonio. Don't be lazy." Dispirited by the never-ending immigration paper chase, he had allowed his tourist visa to expire, slipping into the caste of "illegals," the *indocumentados*.

Antonio soon found himself settling for jobs that were clearly beneath him. He stood under the baking sun at the on-ramp to the Santa Monica Freeway, selling oranges for two dollars a bag: a dollar fifty for the guy from the produce market, fifty cents for him. He worked in a garment factory and at MacArthur Park, selling roach powder that came in little yellow boxes with Chinese writing on the back. He pushed heavy square carts filled with ice cream and *paletas* up and down the streets of South-Central, block after block, ringing the little bell that brought the black children running out of their stuffy apartments.

Elena was ambitious, she aspired to something more. She thought a man with an education should put it to good use. But he liked the street jobs because he was on his own. Restaurants he did not like because he found it difficult to be polite and obliging. He could not hide his indignation when people spat out orders for coffee and called him Pepe or José or Pedro just because he was wearing the bus boy's uniform. He pushed his glasses up on his nose and gave the rude customers his meanest I-spit-in-your-face stare.

I have too much pride. A bus boy with too much pride is a contradiction in terms. An illegal immigrant with too much pride is doomed to unemployment. Only Mr. Finkel, the Culver City restaurateur, tolerated Antonio's sour disposition. Mr. Finkel was a Polish Jew and seemed to recognize something in Antonio, the face of concealed trauma, perhaps, the disoriented, resentful eyes of the exile.

Antonio was used to being tall. In Guatemala he towered above family and friends. But Los Angeles made him short. It made him stoop and it cast him out with its untouchables, the lifters of dirty dishes, the silent sweepers of bathroom floors, the men and women who placed their hands in the city's toilets and urinals, scrubbing everything antiseptic-clean.

After an hour of steady rain, the plastic roof began to leak. It was too flimsy. Water soon soaked Antonio's hair and dripped down his neck, covering his back and chest with lines of icy wetness. First he shivered, then he began to sneeze.

Elena would be horrified to see what I've become.

* * *

The search for building materials took them through the open fields of rubble and weeds on a scavenger hunt for plastic, planks, pipes, anything they could use to shore up their shelter. Antonio came upon the rusting frame of an automobile left by thieves who had stripped it for parts. Windblown plastic bags bounced across the landscape like tumbleweed. There were white steel appliances, bed frames, a dollhouse with the roof missing. At the base of "the mountain" José Juan spotted a twisting stairway, a hundred steps climbing up the hillside. The only signs of human habitation were the scattered tents of the homeless men, the American refugees. Occasionally they came upon a car parked on one of the abandoned streets, its windows covered with newspaper and towels, suggesting that people lived inside.

They found a rain-soaked mattress and decided to drag it back to their shelter. The mattress was heavy, so they stopped to rest.

"Hey, look," José Juan said. "Words."

Stamped into the concrete was the name of a street: SAPPHIRE AVENUE. Forgetting the mattress for a moment, Antonio and José Juan walked along the sidewalk with their heads bowed to the ground, like penitent monks. On the next block they found another name, DIAMOND STREET, and then one more, EMERALD STREET. And finally: A.J. SIMMONS, CONTRACTORS, 1919. INSPECTED, CITY OF LOS ANGELES.

"There were people living here in 1919," Antonio said.

"Maybe there was an earthquake," José Juan said. "Or a fire."

Antonio wondered if he could take this information, piece it together, and come up with a theory to explain why all the buildings had collapsed, why there were vacant lots in the center of Los Angeles.

When they were dating, Antonio remembered, Elena had taken him to the only Mayan ruins in Guatemala City, a place called Kaminaljuyú. It was a minor outpost in what had been a vast empire, centuries dead. The abandoned Mayan city was little more than a series of earthen mounds covered with wild grasses, fenced off from the modern residential neighborhood around it. Walking through the ruins was like walking through a park. People played soccer games around the old temples, flew kites. The grass mounds of Kaminaljuyú looked much like the land on which Antonio now found himself, ten years and thousands of miles later.

Elena talked at length that day about the Mayans and the science of archaeology. She had studied anthropology with the vague idea of becoming an archaeologist. For some reason Antonio could remember only one of the things she told him, a principle of the science: "A vacant building collapses faster than an occupied one." This theory helped explain why the old buildings and temples had crumbled in just a few hundred years.

"In archaeology, a hundred years is almost nothing."

Antonio was staring at the remnants of some concrete stairs, lost in his thoughts, when José Juan tapped him on the shoulder.

"Let's go," he said. "It's going to get dark soon."

They returned to the mattress, dragging it back to their shelter. Along the way José Juan found two sheets of plywood, which he used to reinforce the roof. When the rains began again, the water did not seep through.

* * *

It was early evening, and the rain had finally stopped. The sky was beginning to clear over the vacant lots, the storm front passing to the east, patches of blue opening in the west. Antonio watched the migrating clouds and tried once more to remember the date his wife and son died.

There are still things that I remember. Carlos was a happy baby who took his first steps on a Sunday, in a restaurant called Los Arcos, walking away from his father across the tile floor.

It was seven years ago, of that he was more or less certain. But the exact date eluded him. It was the last of the numbers that made up the almanac of his short family life, along with Carlos's birth weight, the number of hours Elena spent in labor, their wedding anniversary, their son's last shoe size. To know the date was a measure of his loyalty and devotion.

We named him Carlos Martín Bernal, in honor of my grandfather and of San Martín de Porres, the black saint from Peru, the little statue Elena prayed to in the church altar when she was pregnant.

The date marked the beginning of his descent, the long fall that ended in this vacant lot filled with homeless people and puddles of rainwater.

I was Elena's husband for three years and she loved me for all my flaws. She said that when we met the first thing she noticed about me was my sad student wardrobe, my wrinkled, worn-out pants and shirts. When we were dating she bought me new clothes.

Elena was killed three weeks after she wrote a letter. Antonio could still remember that it was exactly three weeks. Elena wrote the letter because she could never remain silent in the face of an injustice. Elena was reckless. She marched in demonstrations without covering her face, she made love without taking precautions. Elena's letter caused her death and the death of their son, but Antonio would always love her for her recklessness, for the whirlwind of her voice. If words were colors, Elena's letter would have been painted in vibrant hues of crimson and orange, a landscape like the winter sunsets in Los Angeles, vast and full of hope.

High clouds were fanned across the horizon in long furrows, like a freshly plowed magenta field. Dying sunlight reflected off the crystal skyscrapers to the east, a constellation of office lights beginning to glow.

In Antonio's country, where there were many natural beauties, the sunsets were ordinary and predictable. Dusk arrived and passed in a single flat shade of orange. Here in Los Angeles, nightfall was often a sweeping and multihued event, with a majesty that suggested the coming of the millennium, the end of a planetary journey.

Someone once told Antonio it was the pollution in the air that made the evening sky this way. Like everything else in Los Angeles, even the beautiful sunsets were man-made.

January 26, 1985. Or was it the twenty-seventh?

The Source of the Infection

The old man sat chewing on his cigar, scratching his nubby fingers against the concrete table while he waited for Longoria to move. The chess pieces stood cryptic and immobile, a puzzle Longoria could not solve, little black and white soldiers on a green and white field imbedded in the table. Five minutes, and Longoria had not moved. He was already a knight and a bishop down, and he didn't want to make any more mistakes. The clock ticked and ticked, crying out for Longoria to move-move, move-move, move-move. The old man, a Cuban named García, kept scratching at the table, his fingers working in a rhythm that matched the ticking of the clock.

"Will you please stop that?" Longoria said irritably.

"What? What am I doing?"

"You're scratching the table. It's making me nervous."

"Stop trying to intimidate the sergeant," a Mexicano named Lopez yelled from another table. "Can't you see the man is trying to concentrate? Maybe if you let him concentrate he'd beat you for once."

The chess tables were in the northwest corner of MacArthur Park. Longoria had first come to this park on weekend mornings to jog. One day, about two years ago, he had drifted over to watch the chess players, drawn by their intense faces as they leaned over the tables. He liked the idea of men coming to the park to sit and think. The players were Latino and white, black and Cuban, Jewish and Filipino. Even the occasional *chino*. People talked English here, mostly, and Longoria liked to practice his English.

In Spanish you say "*caballo*." In English it's "knight." "Checkmate" is English for "*mate*."

Since taking up this new hobby, Longoria had built a small

library on chess strategy. It wasn't enough to play; the thing was to win, and Longoria rarely won.

Someone once told him that no two games of chess are alike. If only they were, if only he could spot the patterns, it would be easier. The secret, he had read in his books, was to anticipate what your opponent was going to do. But with García it was never the same move twice. The old man was tricky and always seemed to be thinking two or three moves ahead. In Longoria's chess books they called this "developing your board vision," something Longoria had yet to master. Chess wasn't like war, where you could use your strength and courage to impose your will, to overcome your mental mistakes. García was sickly and flabby, an old walrus of a man with tobacco-colored stains on his skin, but he played chess like a real stud.

Longoria had played twenty or so matches with García and had never beaten him. It didn't look like he was going to beat him this time, either. Exasperated, confused, Longoria finally moved a piece to stop the ticking of the clock. Somebody standing behind him immediately muttered his disapproval.

García responded quickly, bringing his fat hands over the board to move a rook and call out, "Check!"

Ten minutes and a few moves later, it was checkmate.

"You lost again, sergeant."

"One day I'll beat you."

Together they looked at the board, the arrangement of the pieces at checkmate, the landscape of Longoria's defeat.

"You started off good with the Sicilian defense, but then you seemed to lose your nerve," García said.

"Black is supposed to play defense."

"Yes, *hombre*, but we're not playing for the world championship here. This is the park. Black doesn't always play defense. Eventually you have to come after me. *No tengas miedo*. I always tell you the same thing, but you're stubborn and you don't listen. Don't be afraid, just attack."

After watching some of the other games and quietly debating strategy with García, Longoria left the chess tables and walked home to the Westlake Arms. Six blocks to go over in his mind what he had done wrong, where his strategy had failed him. The first thing he did when he stepped into his room was to reach for the chess books in the dresser's bottom drawer. Lying on the bed with Rashnikov's book, he turned to "Opening Strategies for Black."

"As black, defend carefully," Longoria read, "but be prepared to take the initiative from white and strike at the appropriate time."

Longoria studied his books for hours, the damp air of his austere room filled only by the Sunday afternoon sounds of the Westlake Arms. At night the sounds of lovemaking were sharpest, but during the day the noise of children dominated the apartment building's acoustic universe: eager, treble-toned voices of boys and girls, balls bouncing down the narrow corridors, tricycles squeaking across the floor in the apartment above him, boys opening windows and calling to their playmates across the inner courtyard. They were American-born children, and their talk was like no language Longoria had heard before, a crazy mixture of schoolyard English, the Central American Spanish of their parents, and the strange, Mexican-influenced argot of the neighborhood.

"*Fíjate, vos, que ese vato* from *La Mara* got in a fight with that dude from *la* Eighteenth Street who lives down the block. Yeah, right there in the class. Real *chingazos. El de La Salvatrucha estaba* bleeding *y todo.*"

The children argued with their siblings and pleaded with their mothers. The mothers did not allow their sons and daughters to play outside, in the free-fire zone of the street, or on the front steps, where a platoon of gang members held sway, so every shout and whisper the children made was trapped inside these arsenic green walls, drifting into Longoria's room as he lay on his bed and tried to read about chess and Dr. Wayne García's prescriptions for inner peace through mind control.

"To control the mind is to enter into another universe, a world we did not know existed. It is a world independent of our urges, where we free ourselves from the demands imposed upon us by thousands of years of instinct and cultural training. Hunger, lust, loneliness, and fear have no place in this new universe. To enter it is to . . ."

It was impossible to concentrate with all the noise the children were making. There was great disorder in the voices, too much shouting. *Do I live in a playground or an apartment building?* From outside his door came the muffled sounds of a bike crashing to the thinly carpeted floor of the hallway. A brief pause. Then the shrieking scream of a girl, perhaps five years old, crying out to her mother in fear and pain. He wanted all these voices to go away, he wanted to be left alone. Their voices were like metal in his mouth. Time stopped when the voices and the crashing of toys and bicycles filled his room. "Mami, Pepe won't give it to me. Give it to me!" Insolent children. Out of control. Why couldn't their parents keep them quiet? Their parents should tell them to respect their neighbors.

Longoria did not behave like this when he was a child. Longoria the child knew a life only of work, hunched by his mother's side, baby fingers squirming like worms in the black earth.

* * *

Guillermo was still a child when the army pulled him out of the Lux Theater. Slowly the army made him a man. But in those first days in the barracks there had been only disorder. You expect the army to be organized, but when you're a draftee and they send you to one of the cannon-fodder infantry units, you learn the truth. They were roused from their sleep before dawn, made to run in circles around a muddy field. Calisthenics and truncheon blows seemed to be integral elements of the training. Two officers stood on the field and yelled orders, contradicting one another and then getting into heated arguments, right there in front of the men. If you slipped in the mud or fell behind in the line of joggers, the soldiers struck you on the shoulders or the back with their batons, or they kicked you with their boots. They were skilled at kicking and striking you without actually fracturing bones. Sometimes, for variety, they elbowed you in the stomach. One day when Longoria was jogging, the man in front of him slipped and he tripped over his body, hitting the wet ground with a slapstick splash. Longoria tried to scramble to his feet, but he wasn't fast enough to escape a kick to the rib cage. He was sore for three days and had trouble sleeping.

They gave him a uniform that didn't fit, about two sizes too small. Longoria was five feet four inches tall, and this uniform was made for someone even shorter and much skinnier—a child, perhaps. In the line of jogging recruits there was a young man who looked more like a little boy, barely fourteen. The uniform Longoria was wearing would fit him. Longoria's shirt was so tight he found it hard to keep it tucked in. He ran a few yards and his stomach started to show. He was afraid that the pants would rip and they would punish him with more baton blows.

After four days of training, four days of being rousted out of bed before dawn, Longoria's fifth day in the army began with an unusual silence. No reveille, nothing. He watched the sunrise through the barracks window for the first time, the sky turning crimson over the muddy training field. Two hours went by. Longoria and the rest of the men sat on their cots, afraid to move without orders, expecting an officer to walk through the door at any moment. But the entire day passed, they were given nothing to eat, no officer showed up, no soldier came through the door telling them to stand at attention. They just stayed by their cots, watching through the windows as afternoon became evening. The camp outside seemed to be deserted.

Longoria and his fellow conscripts were sitting in darkness now, in this barracks of rough-cut wood, the night breeze blowing through cracks in the walls. He had not eaten since yesterday, and he was very hungry. In the cot next to him, the man with the wispy mustache began to speak. His name was Alvaro.

"*Se olvidaron de nosotros*," said Alvaro. "They just left us here and forgot about us. Maybe we can try to sneak out."

"No, this is some kind of test," Longoria said. "A test to see if we're loyal. They want to see if we'll stick around. And if we don't, they'll shoot us down."

Alvaro stroked his mustache. "You're right. I wouldn't put it past them. They'd shoot us in the back."

Without warning, the barracks door sprang open. A bulky officer strode into the room, trailing the smell of stale liquor. The conscripts jumped to their feet and stood next to their cots, arms at their sides, as they had recently been taught to do. Several soldiers followed behind, one of them carrying a portable radio.

The officer began to speak, his words slightly slurred. He was the officer from the movie theater, a Captain Elías.

"You've all been working so hard. All that running and shit. Running and running. You've been such good draftees, we've decided to come and . . ." He seemed to have lost his train of thought. "What was it we were going to do, sergeant?"

"You said we would entertain the men, sir."

"Yes, that's it. Entertain." He snapped his fingers at one of the soldiers. "Music!"

The soldier turned on the radio, fumbling with the dials until marimba music came on. The deep resonance of the wooden instrument reminded Longoria of dancing at so many weddings and village fiestas.

"Louder," Captain Elías called out, and the soldier turned up the volume. The music blared, rattling the tiny speaker.

Longoria and Alvaro exchanged looks. The song was a nostalgic waltz that only increased Longoria's sense of foreboding.

"Well, what are you waiting for, you *maricas*?" the captain said with a sneer. "Dance. Take a partner and dance."

No one moved.

"Are you refusing an order, you faggots?" The captain grabbed the man nearest him by the shoulders. "Dance, you faggot, dance." When the conscript only stood in place, trembling, Captain Elías picked him up off the ground and threw him against the flimsy barracks wall.

Elías moved to the center of the room. "When I give an order you will *obey*."

The soldiers proceeded through the barracks, forcing the conscripts into pairs. A few cots from Longoria's, one of the soldiers slapped a reluctant conscript across the face, dropping the man to his knees. Longoria was paired with Alvaro. They began a halfhearted shuffle across the cement floor, barely touching each other.

"No, not like that," yelled the captain. "Put your arms around each other. Do it with feeling."

The soldiers were all laughing, showing gold and silver teeth, shaking their heads because Elías was crazy and drunk and funny.

Longoria wrapped his arm around Alvaro's waist, feeling deeply humiliated, because he was acting against nature by holding a man the way you were supposed to hold a woman. Alvaro's palms were sweaty and he smelled of onions. A soldier pushed Longoria from behind, and his face brushed against the stubble on Alvaro's cheek.

They danced for thirty seconds or so, until the radio announcer's voice came on abruptly, followed by a commercial for deodorant soap. The men released each other and stepped apart.

"Why are you stopping?" Captain Elías said. Yawning, he sat down on a cot and closed his eyes. "Keep dancing," he said faintly. "Dance."

Longoria and the other conscripts shuffled across the floor to the sound of the radio commercial.

A few minutes later Elías fell asleep and began snoring, the moist vibrations audible over the din of the radio. The music played on, and the conscripts kept moving in a joyless waltz, steps everyone knew from childhood, steps Longoria first practiced with his mother in the cramped space of their little cinderblock house.

* * *

He was called Guillermo when he was a child. In the army he became "Longoria." Longoria knew things Guillermo never dreamed of. The army was a cruel place, it was not for weakhearted people. But the army made you a man. The army made you do terrible, violent things, but they were things that had to be done. You had to love the army, because if you didn't love it you were finished. They might as well bury you, because if you didn't believe in what you were doing you'd go crazy, you'd spin out of control. Longoria had seen this happen to men, to good soldiers, the blood and life disappearing from them like water going down a drain. It was because they didn't believe.

This thing they were fighting was a cancer, and sometimes the children were contaminated with it too. You killed the cousins and the uncles to make sure the virus was dead. That's what the officers said, and you had to believe it. The parents passed the virus along to their children. It made you want to kill the parents again and again, even after they were dead, because if it wasn't for the fucking parents you wouldn't have to kill the children. Guatemala was like a human body, that was how Lieutenant Colonel Villagrán explained it, and if you didn't kill these organisms the body could die.

The noisy children who lived in the Westlake Arms could not be contaminated with the virus because they were not in Guatemala, because they could not grow to take up arms against the government. These children were rowdy and insolent, but they did not carry red flags, they did not threaten Guatemala's sovereignty. They only rode bicycles and bounced balls.

This was the worst thing to remember, the sounds children make when they are dying. The flutter in the throat. Crying because they're bleeding all over the floor and it doesn't make any sense. They cry because when you stand there in your uniform and shoot them they feel like their fathers are punishing them for doing something wrong. And you, in your camouflage skin, are in the room with them, watching this happen. You are the one who put the bullets in their bodies. The little boys feel their hearts winding down. *Why did you shoot me?* they ask with their eyes. *These are the last thumps of the tiny drum in my chest.* Their eyes turn dreamy and faraway when they feel the blackness coming. The little boys see the darkness and call for their mothers. "*Mamá.*" They don't want to be alone in the dark. "*Mamá, Mamá, Mamá.*" Only bullets can stop that sound, only more bullets can stop them moaning for their mothers.

There were days when Longoria thought the same kind of infection was spreading here in Los Angeles, although the symptoms might be different from the ones in Guatemala. Los Angeles could use a thorough cleansing. If he were still in that line of work, he would start with the *tecatos* in the alley. Then he would deal with the gang members who sat on the front steps of his apartment building, the boys who shaved their heads and covered themselves with tattoos to look like men. The cholos had guns hidden in the folds of their loose-fitting clothing. They could use some disinfection. But no, this work would have to be left to someone else. Longoria wasn't up to combat anymore. He had to accept this. Someone else would have to worry about cleaning up Los Angeles. Longoria had done his part in Guatemala, he'd made his contribution, made the sacrifices.

Small bodies in secret cemeteries, piled on top of each other in pits. By a bend in the river. Under the ruins of a church turned to ash. In the muddy soil of an abandoned cornfield. Could their bones be lighter than soil? If the bones of the children floated to the top, people might know what Longoria did. Who could know? Who were the witnesses? The children knew, but they were only sand now, sand children. The other Jaguars knew, but they were in it with you. They would never tell. Longoria would never tell, not even Reginalda, especially Reginalda.

To live forever with the voices of boys and girls, their last words, the calling out to their mothers. That was the biggest sacrifice. All of them cried before you silenced them for good, and a lot of them shit and pissed. Even now, the smell reminded him of death.

It took a lot out of a soldier to see this and hear this and live with it. You were never the same again.

* * *

They were walking by the lake in MacArthur Park, Reginalda clinging to his arm. She had attached herself to him again, enveloping him in the cocoon of her perfume, making a public display. Longoria wanted to pull away, but if he did she would get upset with him and pout. He didn't want her to pout because he liked it when she talked. So he let her cling to his arm, this out-in-the-open touching that so many women seemed to need but that Longoria would probably deny to anybody but Reginalda.

If the guys at the chess tables saw him, they would tease him later on and his face would turn red. He wouldn't have brought her to the park if he'd known she was going to hang on to him like this. They would make vulgar macho jokes about his sex, about the things they imagined he did to her. He would feel like a little boy caught with his fly open.

"I don't care what you think, I didn't like that movie," Reginalda was saying, her black pumps snapping on the asphalt path. She was enjoying every step of their walk through the park, arm in arm, just like a normal couple. "Even if the blood is fake, it's disgusting to me."

"If it's not real it can't be disgusting."

Another Saturday afternoon date, better than most. After the movie, an American thriller with subtitles, Longoria had splurged for a change, taking her to the Mi Guatemala restaurant on Alvarado for a big *comida*. *Carne asada*, black beans, fried plantains. Just like the menu promised, a meal to remind you of home. They listened to the marimba, four men tapping at the hand-carved wooden instrument, playing the classics that made everyone nostalgic, made them wonder why they were living in Los Angeles. At *"Luna de Xelajú,"* a song about a romantic moonlit night in Quetzaltenango, people started dancing in the narrow space between the tables and the band, older couples shifting back and forth in an easy waltz. After she pleaded with him, Longoria even danced two songs with Reginalda, cheek to cheek. In the six months he had known her they had never danced before.

Now, an hour later, they were strolling through the park. They stopped in front of a stout woman selling mangoes from a flimsy metal cart in the narrow shaft of shade created by a palm tree.

"I'm usually not down here in the park," the vendor offered without being asked. "I'm usually up on the sidewalk. But the police are chasing people away. They won't let us sell up there. If you come back later I'll be on the sidewalk. Up there."

The vendor took a mango in her left hand. With a few quick strokes of her knife she cut it open in the shape of a fleshy yellow flower and stuck it on a stick. The juice dripped down Reginalda's chin as she bit into it.

Longoria was wiping her face with his sleeve when he first noticed a scratchy sound coming from the band shell on the western edge of the park. He stopped to listen. It was a woman's voice on a loudspeaker, some kind of rally. The patter of clapping hands followed, then an echoing shout. The meeting seemed to have a religious overtone. More applause now, rising in volume, wafting across the park, making even the mango vendor raise her head in attention.

"What's going on over there, Longoria?" Reginalda asked. "What are they celebrating? Is it a holiday?"

Without answering her, Longoria began walking toward the rally.

"Hey, wait for me!"

Slightly more than a block away, Longoria saw people formed in concentric semicircles, T-shirts glimmering white in the bright sun. They were holding signs and blanket-sized banners busy with letters, though he was still too far off to read what they said. The crowd rose above and away from the band shell and its concrete stage, hundreds of people filling an amphitheater of wooden benches. Hundreds more spilled onto the gentle slope of the park's grass embankment and stood under the eucalyptus trees holding sky blue and white Salvadoran and Guatemalan flags. Longoria was getting closer, and the voice on the stage began to sharpen into clear, angry words. He could make out the messages on the banners now.

SOLIDARIDAD CON LA REVOLUCION SALVADOREÑA
ALTO A LA REPRESION EN EL SALVADOR Y GUATEMALA
APOYO TOTAL A LA LUCHA ARMADA

Longoria stopped on the asphalt walkway, his mouth agape.

"What is it?" Reginalda asked behind him.

Again he did not answer. What he was looking at was too incredible for words. He could not believe that these people were being allowed to gather in a park in Los Angeles and mouth their hateful ideas freely and openly.

A swarthy man in jeans and leather sandals walked by and smiled at Longoria. "*Buenas tardes, compañero.*" On his shoulders was a boy waving a little red flag with a white star and the letters FMLN.

Longoria could feel his face and ears turning crimson. *Compañero.* This was a Communist word. Someone had called him *compañero.*

"How much are they paying you to be here?" Longoria snapped at the man. "Who's paying you?"

The man smiled again and looked at Longoria with amused bewilderment, as if he were speaking in tongues. The little boy wrinkled his forehead and waved the tiny Communist flag. They stepped past him, heading for the mango vendor.

Longoria charged down the asphalt path toward the band shell, holding back a scream with each step. He had come three thousand miles from his country to find these people again, these Communists, up to their old tricks. *This is a real kick in the pants.* Reaching the grass embankment, he plunged into a mass of demonstrators with their backs to him, bumping their shoulders and arms as he worked his way forward. No one seemed to care. They were all gazing up at the stage, eyes fixed on the small, fair-skinned woman at the podium. He looked at the speaker for a moment and saw her raise her fist in the air, the Marxist hand signal of radical students and guerrilla fighters. *¡Idiotas!* he wanted to shout. *You are like sheep. You're being tricked by her pretty words.* Suddenly everyone around him sang out in chorus, "*¡Presente!*" To his left, an old woman in a ragged dress threw her fist into the air, and Longoria stifled a bitter laugh. *In Guatemala we knew how to handle these people. In Los Angeles they are allowed to operate freely. In Los Angeles we cannot stop them.* Longoria kept pushing forward, the bodies packed tighter as he got closer to the stage. Speaker and audience were caught up in a chant, the speaker calling out names, the audience shouting back "*¡Presente!*"

Finally he reached the front, where youngish men and women were pressed against the concrete stage, looking almost straight up at the speaker's thick eyebrows and flat peasant face. She was barely as tall as the podium. From his vantage point just to her left, Longoria could see her feet, white thongs standing on tiptoe so she could reach the microphone.

"*¡ . . . Mientras haya pueblo, habrá revolución!*"

A shout rose from the crowd behind him, the voices ascending and echoing against the bare arc of the band shell. It seemed strange to Longoria, incongruous, to see this small woman leading the mob, directing their energies like an evil conductor. It didn't seem right to him that there was no one to stop her from spitting forth her blasphemies. It would be so simple to silence her, to reach up and stuff his fist in her throat and muffle the words.

Turning away from the stage, Longoria looked at the audience, their eyes focused with intense hope on this small woman. Her amplified voice reached a climax, and a thousand brown-skinned fists rose simultaneously in the air, surrounding him like a forest of bare, knobby tree trunks.

Probability

They were on their way back to Crown Hill after picking up a frozen chicken at the Unitarian food bank when José Juan spotted him, a dark, stubby man walking down Third Street with a bowlegged gait. A peasant without his straw hat, Antonio would think later. The sight of this man caused José Juan a moment of frantic distress. Like a fugitive who's just seen a police officer, he searched quickly for avenues of escape but found none.

"José Juan Grijalva!"

Seeing his friend's alarm, Antonio asked in a whisper, "What's wrong?"

Before José Juan could answer, the bowlegged man had run up to greet him with an exaggerated smile. "I don't believe it. It can't be you."

José Juan feigned pleasant surprise to see someone from his hometown, a place called Anenecuilco. The man's name was Ramiro, and he was the cousin of José Juan's *compadre*. He reached up and gave José Juan a heartfelt embrace.

"How have you been?" Ramiro asked in a vaguely accusatory tone. "*¿Qué te has hecho?* The whole town is wondering what happened to you. Not a word for months and months. Your wife is so worried."

José Juan had always been quick on his feet, but even so, Antonio had to marvel at the story he began spinning.

"I've been working in a machine shop," he said with false humility. "I'm making so much money, 'mano, it's embarrassing. I shouldn't tell you, but I know you'll get it out of me eventually. Fifteen dollars an hour! Can you believe it? I still can't. I'm in the union, though, so they take out a little chunk for that. Plus, the payments on the Chevy and the rent for my *condominio* aren't cheap either. You know how it is. You come to this country and you make lots of money, but somehow you end up spending it all."

"So true," Ramiro interjected.

"*Así es.* Here you work and work. There's no stopping. It's not like back home, is it? There's no rest here, no time to sit down for a *copita* every night with your friends. How does that one song go? '*Una jaula de oro.*' Yeah, that's what it's like, a cage of gold."

José Juan went on to explain that he had come downtown to help his friend Antonio move into a new apartment. If he hadn't written or called home, it was because he'd been waiting to surprise his wife with a call on their wedding anniversary.

To Antonio's amazement, Ramiro seemed to accept all this as true, his *campesino* eyes widening as the tale went on. "I had no idea things were going so well for you," he said stupidly.

José Juan gave him a nonexistent phone number, and the two countrymen embraced, promising to meet again soon.

As Ramiro disappeared down Third Street, José Juan let out a low sigh. The effort of his lie had left him pale and shaken, like a man who's just stumbled away from a car accident. It was his worst fear, running into someone from his hometown. He didn't want anyone in his *pueblo* to know he was living on the streets, no better than the poorest man in Mexico. This was why José Juan never called his family. He was sure they would know the truth the moment they heard his voice. They would hear his shame on the telephone line and remember that he left home bragging about all the success that would come his way.

"Of all the people to meet on the street, it has to be that *pendejo*," José Juan said with a nervous laugh. "What bad luck I have."

It seemed like incredibly bad luck, to encounter a familiar face from your tiny village in a city of nine million people. José Juan had been betrayed by the laws of probability, but Antonio was not surprised. A few months earlier, while riding in the back of a gardener's pickup truck on the Hollywood Freeway, he had noticed a car in the fast lane, a rusting Datsun with four people packed into the back seat.

The driver looked exactly like María Paredes, a schoolteacher who lived down the block from Antonio and Elena in San Cristóbal Acatapán. Antonio looked hard at this woman as she bounced along at fifty-five miles an hour, her long black hair tied in a thick braid. He told himself that he must be imagining things. Then, as the Datsun pulled away, Antonio saw the bumper sticker: "I ♥ San Cristóbal Acatapán."

There were so many Latinos in Los Angeles now, thousands upon thousands of Mexicanos, Guatemaltecos, and Salvadoreños, more than he ever imagined. He had come to the States expecting to be surrounded by blond, blue-eyed gringos, not a Spanish-talking sea of brown faces. Even the Mayan Indians of his country, people who had lived in the same little *aldeas* in Guatemala since before the Spaniards came—even they were here. He remembered coming across a group of Indian women one day, not far from the vacant lots where he and José Juan now lived. They were wearing their traditional dress, embroidered *huipiles* and long rainbow-striped skirts. He watched them, these ancient people of the corn, as they walked through a canyon of brick tenements, their leather sandals scraping along the oil-stained sidewalk on Bixel Street. What were they doing here, in this place where not a single stalk of corn could grow? It saddened him to find so many of his countrymen transported, as if by some dark magic, to this freeway-covered plain, wandering about Los Angeles in an amnesiac daze, far from even the memory of the soil.

"You know what this means, don't you?" José Juan said, interrupting Antonio's thoughts. "Now Ramiro is going to tell everybody in my *pueblo* he saw me. Dressed in rags. He's a big *chismoso*, like everyone else in that town. He'll tell everybody."

Dressed in rags. Antonio hadn't thought much lately about what they looked like. He had begun to forget the threads that dangled from the bottom of his pants, the little holes that had appeared in his shirt, the layer of sweat and grime that perpetually covered his skin. He caught a glimpse of himself in a store window, a cluttered *botánica* overflowing with votive candles. Moving closer to the glass, he could see that his hair was so matted it looked like he was wearing a small helmet. His khaki pants had turned stiff and gray with a smooth sheen of dirt. Lines of soot and dried sweat covered his face, the image of a caveman. Antonio was gradually leaving the company of men, slipping backward on the evolutionary tree.

What would Elena say if she saw him like this? Elena liked him to dress well. Elena was a little vain, she abhorred foul odors, she liked to shower after they made love and sometimes before. She would not make love to the grime-caked man Antonio had become. *If she saw me like this she would turn away in disgust.*

Even here in Los Angeles, after Elena died, he had always showered every morning, wrapping his body in clean shirts and pants, a new, sanitized shell for each day. Now the scent from each day had seeped into fabric and skin: the long walks to the food bank, the tossing and turning at night, his body in bitter communion with the wind and soil. His fingernails were black, and the itching in his crotch was becoming unbearable. His scalp itched too. More than itched; it burned. "Stop scratching yourself, *cabrón*," José Juan finally told him. "You look like a monkey."

"We need to take a bath," Antonio said. "More than a week already. *Ya es mucho.*"

From Frank and the Mayor, Antonio had learned that most of the camp dwellers took showers at one of the missions on Spring Street, although they considered it a last resort because the experience was especially degrading. One of the mission volunteers, a deputized homeless person, made you take off your clothes in a locker room and then hustled you and a dozen other naked men into the shower, where you stood shoulder to shoulder with whatever sample of Skid Row humanity happened to wander in that day.

The Mexicanos, on the other hand, always looked clean but never set foot in the missions. How did they do it?

"Where do you guys shower?" Antonio asked a man everyone called Chino because of his Eurasian eyes. "*¿Dónde se bañan?*"

"*En el río,*" Chino answered.

"The river? What river?"

"You know, the big one, the one that's past Los Angeles Street where all the factories are."

Antonio couldn't hide an expression of disgust. The Los Angeles River was a giant concrete channel that cut a path through the center of the city. At the bottom of this huge chasm ran a brackish stream; except for a few weeds that poked their way through the cement, it contained no signs of natural life. During heavy rainstorms, the pathetic trickle became a raging torrent of fallen trees and trash bobbing in white water: tires, furniture, bottles, cans, newspapers, and bicycle frames from the suburbs upstream.

"That?" Antonio said. "That's not a river, that's a sewer."

"No, it's not that bad," Chino answered. "There's sewer pipes that come in with green water that has lots of chemicals and oil in it. We stay away from those. But if you go to the middle the water's cleaner. We don't go all the way in, we just splash ourselves. You can even wash your clothes and let them dry on the cement in the sun. *Te deja la ropa bien limpia.*"

Antonio didn't want to shower in the mission, and he was afraid of being poisoned if he went to the river. In Guatemala rivers were known to be carriers of disease. It seemed he would be condemned to more days of filth and grit, until José Juan came up with a solution: they could go back to their old apartment building and use the showers. On each floor there was a communal bathroom. Once Antonio and José Juan got past the front door, it would simply be a matter of climbing the stairs and sneaking into one of the bathrooms. They would have to trespass, but they would be clean.

An hour later they stepped out the back door of their erstwhile home into the sunlit, fetid air of the alley, feeling like new men.

Now I am closer to the man Elena knew. If she saw me, maybe she would kiss me.

* * *

When the sun rose the next morning, Antonio had no idea whether it was Monday or Wednesday or Saturday. Not knowing the day depressed him. It was another sign of his withdrawal from the world of normal people, from clocks and calendars, healthy meals and locked doors. So strange to live in a world where the days had no names. Maybe it was Saturday, Antonio guessed. He rose and crawled out of the shelter to see half a dozen girls in their best dresses—pink, blue, yellow chiffon—playfully skipping down Third Street. Their mothers, roundish women with black vinyl purses, shepherded the children briskly past Antonio and the other wretched people who lived in shacks and tents.

"*Andale, apúrale,*" the women called out. Hurry up! The rustling of the girls' shiny dresses and the click-clack of their mothers' high-heel shoes could mean only one thing: church day.

Antonio turned to José Juan, who was busy cleaning his toenails with a toothpick. "Hey, *moro,* it's Sunday," he announced.

"So what," José Juan said, eyes on his feet.

"Well, let's go do something."

"Like what? What could we do? Go to church? Pray for money? No thank you."

It seemed to Antonio that if it was Sunday he should be out somewhere doing what people did on Sunday. They got the family together and found a patch of lawn or beach to sit down and gossip and take in the sun.

"Let's go to the park and walk around the lake like everyone else does." The cheerful vision of the girls in the chiffon dresses had lifted Antonio's spirits.

After some gentle persuasion, José Juan agreed. They dusted themselves off and headed for MacArthur Park, where all the other Guatemaltecos and Salvadoreños and Mexicanos went, a little Parque Central almost like the ones back home.

A block away, people were already trying to sell them things. They were on Seventh Street, where commerce oozed from the concrete pores of the sidewalk: pirated cassette tapes, ersatz leather wallets, plastic toy battle tanks arranged in neat rows. Heavyset women in checkered aprons perched above the merchandise on folding chairs. They did not like to barter: "You're not in Mexico or El Salvador now. The price is set. I have children to feed. *No andas con esas babosadas.*" Farther on, across the street from the park, Antonio heard the restless voices of the black market, anxious packs of slick young men who paced the street corners in imitation Italian shoes.

They looked everyone straight in the eye, the better to tell who was a policeman and who wasn't, who had money and who didn't, and offered one-word descriptions of their wares: *micas*, immigration documents; *seguros*, social security cards; *llamadas*, long-distance phone calls.

The first thing Antonio noticed about the park itself was the green lake that never moved or breathed, a resting place for discarded bottles and condoms, a liquid trash can. A lawn rose around the water's edge in a steep incline, people arranged on the crabgrass like spectators in an amphitheater. The grass itself was marked with long scars, the tread marks of police patrol cars in hot pursuit of a suspect.

Antonio took one step into the park and tried to remember what he was thinking when he decided to come here. This was where people came to relax, and he needed to relax too, to forget and unwind. But everything about the park defied leisure. He had wanted to sit on the grass, but the grass was yellow and dying. The benches were occupied by a variety of anemic souls on the verge of unconsciousness. He watched a blond woman with a pus white complexion rocking on the bench as if she were trying to put herself to sleep.

"Why are we here?" José Juan complained. "It's a waste of time."

Antonio thought about the question. "It's better than being at the camp," he said finally. "I'm tired of the smell of all those drunks."

"But this place is filthy too."

"There are families here. It's the families that I like. The babies and the mothers. See?"

Antonio pointed to a woman who was walking along the narrow asphalt path that wound around the lake with an infant in her arms. Parents, girlfriends, lovers—all the "normal" people were walking around the park at a moderate pace, slowly enough to revel in the illusion of a pleasant stroll by the lakeside, fast enough to avoid being accosted by one of the men lounging on the grass. After a moment Antonio and José Juan joined the pedestrian flow behind two women pushing strollers and a *norteño* father with a baby on his shoulders, in shiny new cowboy boots.

Antonio and José Juan stepped around an amputee who had

planted himself in the center of the path. A little on they encountered a grandfatherly man wearing a baggy charcoal gray suit and carrying a bulky camera. He tried to interest them in a portrait, pointing to a sandwich board covered with sample photographs and the words "*Retratos: Sólo $2.*"

"*Por favor*, let me take your picture," he pleaded.

Antonio had no money but tried to look as if were considering the offer. All the photographs were at least fifteen years old, he guessed from the hairstyles and clothes, which belonged to a time he did not recognize, long before he came to this country. He looked closer and saw that in this distant age the park grass was greener and the palm trees were free of graffiti. Small boats floated on the lake.

"*No, gracias, hermano*," Antonio said to the photographer. The old man turned away, muttering to himself as if he had been cheated.

They drifted toward the small playground in the northern half of the park, a patch of sand with a set of swings, a slide, and a simple merry-go-round bearing two boys who were pumping their brown legs into the heavy sand like tiny acrobats. They spun too fast and fell in a splash of sand and laughter.

Every morning, mothers streamed down to the playground from the old brownstones in the neighborhoods that ringed the park. They came because they were tired of being locked inside their apartments all day, afraid of a neighborhood of criminal horrors where even the sidewalks were thick with graffiti. So they took a deep breath and held their sons and daughters tightly by the hand, eyes focused straight ahead until they reached the park and the children could finally run free. Now they stood guard around the sandbox, twentyish Mexicanas and Centroamericanas in jeans and T-shirts, single women who had just stepped into modernity, whose stance told everyone that they were far from home and wouldn't be pushed around by men any longer.

Antonio had reached a sanctuary, an oasis of everyday life. Leaning on the waist-high fence that circled the playground, taking in the sounds of the children, he could imagine himself a father again, watching his two-year-old son spin on the merry-go-round, jump off the swings. For a moment he lived in a fantasy free of loss and regret.

Then one of the mothers gave him a dirty look, as if she thought he might be a child molester simply because he was wearing grungy clothes and smiling at young children.

Turning away from the woman's stare, Antonio saw that José Juan had fallen asleep on the grass behind him, his arm thrown across his eyes, his mouth a pink circle open to the sky. Antonio looked at the adults gathered on the lawns around the playground. Men with Cuban accents stood in a circle throwing dice on a patch of dirt. Next to them were five stone tables with chessboards painted on the surface. A dozen spectators had gathered around the seated chess players, their eyes fixed on the boards, the plastic pieces, the silent confrontations. The faces of so many men locked in concentration seemed to hold the promise of intellectual stimulation, something Antonio had been missing lately. He left José Juan asleep on the grass and walked toward the chess players.

Most of the men were in their fifties and sixties; they wore dark clothes and smoked cigars and coughed too much. It seemed like a club, a group of intimates. Not wanting to intrude, Antonio took in the action from a polite distance, standing ten feet from the nearest table. Four games were going on at once, but most of the attention was focused on one of the older players and a man in his late twenties or early thirties, with full lips, a long, narrow nose, and cropped hair cut nearly to the whiteness of his scalp. Everyone else was in sweaters and coats, but the younger chess player was wearing a navy blue T-shirt that clung to his muscular frame. A soldier, Antonio told himself. They get their heads shaved when they're in the army, and they never change. Antonio had seen men of his ilk here before, the former soldiers who were now drug dealers, criminals, and hustlers of all sorts.

The younger player lifted his left arm and picked up a chess piece. One of the spectators shook his head, disagreeing with the tactics. For several seconds the man's bare arm was suspended above the table while he decided whether to move his rook. He finally put the rook down, then propped his chin in his hand to await the other player's response. The arm was raised just long enough for Antonio to make out the tattoo of a yellow animal.

* * *

Longoria had never come this close to winning. The other players stopped their games to gather around his table. An audience had formed, half a dozen men looking over his shoulder, watching him, stroking their chins, staring at the board as if it might be some sort of mirage. It seemed they were about to witness a historic victory. Longoria had reached the endgame and was ahead by a bishop and a rook. For once García looked worried.

Concentrate. Be careful not to make a mistake, but remember to attack.

Longoria was moving in for the kill. He set down his rook on the penultimate row, two moves away from the final trap.

"Oh no!" someone said, and the men standing around him let out a loud collective sigh. García smiled and quickly took Longoria's rook. A few minutes later Longoria had lost his bishop too. García picked up a half-smoked cigar from the table edge and lit it in triumph.

"Well, sergeant," he said between puffs. "It pleases me to observe that you are losing once again."

Longoria lifted his eyes from the board and looked for help. The two men standing behind García were shaking their heads, clearly losing interest now. On the lawn to the left of the tables, another man was standing on the grass, staring at Longoria in a peculiar way. He looked like someone from Guatemala. An innocent, provincial, friendly kind of face, the face of someone you feel sorry for because you know they're Guatemalan and thus gullible and luckless by definition, the whole host of things Guatemalans are famous for. *Una cara que da lástima.* Longoria turned his attention back to the board.

* * *

The recognition seeped into Antonio's consciousness through layers of disbelief and confusion, finally registering with great clarity, the light-flash of truth. After so many years, the soldier from San Cristóbal, the killer of Elena and Carlos, was sitting right here in front of him playing chess, just a few feet away.

The son of a bitch is in Los Angeles.

It seemed so incredible Antonio wanted to laugh out loud. Then, for an instant, his mind reversed course. The tattoo and the face were so familiar they could only be an illusion. How many times had Elena appeared to him in his dreams, caressing him in his sleep? How many times had he seen Elena's face in the features of a passing stranger, his heart racing with impossible hope, all the pain lifted for an instant, until the mirage dissolved. And yet this tattooed soldier had never appeared in any of his dreams. Antonio had never seen him again until the moment he came to life at the chess tables.

The soldier raised his tattooed arm to rub his temple while he studied the board. He looked perplexed, pained and vulnerable. He glanced up at Antonio and the other men standing around him with a plaintive expression, as if to say, What should I do, what's my next move? The shaved head bent and moved its eyes back to the board, as if the man could force his will upon the complex geometry of the game.

The longer Antonio looked at this man, the sharper the memory became. In San Cristóbal, all those years ago, in another park, not so different from this one, while Antonio waited for a bus by the kiosk. The soldier on the iron bench, eating an ice cream. The blood of Elena and Carlos still sticky on the floor of the house, just a block or two away. Here was the man who cut into their flesh, painting the floor with their wounds. A box at Antonio's feet as he waited for the bus. Antonio falling, spiraling with his box, falling for many years, landing in Los Angeles. The skin had puckered around the soldier's eyes; the younger features Antonio held in memory were now molded into this other face, covered with the faintest sheen of weariness. The killer's face. Antonio spun in the flux between decades and countries, time and space distorted. He was in a park in Guatemala, a park in Los Angeles. The present, the past, somewhere in between.

There could be no doubt this was the same man.

Suddenly Antonio realized that he was not standing still, that he was shifting back and forth on his feet like a boxer, drawing attention to himself. The tattooed soldier was going to look at Antonio again and recognize him.

Instinctively Antonio took a step back. He began to tremble, the ground seeming to rise and fall underneath him. *Get on the bus, hurry. On the bus.* He was too close to this man. Once a killer, always a killer. Even the concrete table where the soldier was sitting began to look menacing, a stone animal that could come to life and swallow him whole. Antonio had to get away. He would slip off unnoticed past the pepper trees. But no, the tattooed man was not running after him; he was still sitting in front of the chessboard, he had not moved. He had only put a pawn down, raising his hand to his chin again, showing Antonio the tattoo again, as if to mock him.

You see, I am the same man. The proof is in the skin. What will you do now, refugee?

Antonio tried to catch his breath. The tattooed man did not know him. *He did not recognize me that day in San Cristóbal, so why would he remember me today?* Antonio felt exhilaration in this discovery, a falling away of his fears. The soldier would never recognize him. A girl with long braids pedaled past Antonio on a tricycle, her father just behind her on a bike much too small for him, his long legs bent awkwardly, like broken wings. They were both laughing. Antonio wasn't in Guatemala anymore. There was no reason to be afraid.

The old man sitting at the table took a satisfied puff on his cigar. "Checkmate," he said.

Part 2

Antonio and Elena

A Zoo for the Generals

Elena Sosa was sitting in the cafeteria at the Universidad de San Carlos when the man who would become her husband entered her life, gift in hand. She was eating alone, reading *Nicaragua Avenged*, an account of the assassination of Anastasio Somoza, thinking that the bastard got what he deserved. Immersed in the gory details of the dictator's demise—he was blown up by bazooka-wielding guerrillas—she did not notice as her future mate walked across the linoleum floor and sat down at her table.

"Elena, I bought this for you, I hope you'll like it," he said.

Startled, she looked up from her reading and saw a nervous young man with round-frame glasses, a hardcover crimson book in his outstretched hand, beads of perspiration on his forehead. He was in one of her anthropology classes. She had talked to him three, maybe four times. It took a moment, but then she remembered his name. Antonio.

"The other day, in the seminar on Quiché rituals, you were talking about how you'd love to learn the language," he explained. "So when I saw this in the bookstore, I thought of you. I thought you might like it. You don't have one already, do you?"

Elena took the book and examined the title: *Bilingual Dictionary of the Quiché and Spanish Languages*, printed in gold leaf on the cover. By Dr. Francisco Trujillo, Universidad de Sevilla. It must have cost him a fortune. She opened it and looked at the columns of words from the ancient Mayan language, the exotic glottal sounds and their Spanish equivalents. *Baatz'*: spider monkey. *Balam*: jaguar. A yellow ribbon, a place marker, dangled from the spine. She flipped to the Cs, and a scent like wet cement drifted upward from the newly printed pages.

What sort of boy would give an expensive gift to a girl he hardly knew? She was touched by his kindness, but also a little embarrassed for him. "It's the most beautiful book I've ever seen," she said.

The nervous young man broke into a wide smile. This Antonio was abnormally tall for a Guatemalan, but not quite settled into his body, a recent inductee into the fraternity of manhood.

"I'm glad you like it," he said.

After an awkward silence Elena flipped the pages of the book to the Spanish side and looked up *"gracias."* She reached over, gave him a demure kiss on the cheek, and took great delight in saying, *"Qamov!"*

That night she carried the dictionary around at home, leafing through it when she did her chores, pronouncing words, resisting the sarcastic remarks of her father, who said he couldn't think of anything more useless than to learn a language "only a few barefoot Indians can speak." Elena wasn't one to care much what her father said. She'd always done things her own way, a trait her father claimed she'd inherited from her mother, who died just hours after Elena was born. Her father had always told her to avoid political movements, so she brought home revolutionary leaflets and left them scattered around the house in the most conspicuous places. Her two sisters always stayed out of the sun, lest their cinnamon complexions darken; Elena became a sun worshiper, lounging in the tiny backyard in a bathing suit, setting up her lawn chair and towel not far from her father's small chicken coop. Her sisters shook their heads and called her a crazy woman, a *chiflada.*

"I want to be brown," she told them with a defiant smirk. "I want to be brown and dark like the earth."

After their next Quiché seminar Antonio sought her out once more, an act that seemed to require great courage on his part. Short of breath from running to catch up with her, he was perspiring again. They spoke as she walked to the campus bus stop past the Faculty of Architecture, its powder blue walls covered with revolutionary graffiti that promised, among other things, "Unconditional Support for the Popular Struggle!" They went past a two-story mural of an ape wearing an army uniform complete with medals and epaulets, the painted banner at the foot of the wall declaring, "A Zoo for the Generals, Power for the People."

"It seems to me that the Quiché language is indispensable to us, that every Guatemalteco should learn it," Antonio was saying. "The language of the Maya is in our blood, after all. We can't deny it. It's who we are, where we come from."

She watched him as he walked, this man she had ignored up to now, and decided he was not bad-looking, even if the hair on his upper lip was trying a little too hard to be a mustache. There was a gentleness to him; he seemed untouched by the harshness and arrogance that had contaminated the rest of the male species on campus. He was bookish but not without charm, and was obviously infatuated with her. Why hadn't she noticed him before?

"I think you're being overly romantic," she said as they reached the bus stop. "I agree, it's important to know about our indigenous roots, but let's not romanticize the past. After all, the Mayans practiced human sacrifice."

He made a point of agreeing with her: "Of course, of course."

They talked for about fifteen minutes, discussing *indigenismo* and the Guatemalan novelist Miguel Angel Asturias—long enough for Elena to conclude that he was not quite the hapless boy he seemed when he approached her with his gift. "Thank you for the dictionary," she said as her bus pulled up to the stop. "I read it every day. It's the most practical thing anyone's ever given me. I really do treasure it."

She boarded the bus and took a seat. To her surprise, Antonio was still standing on the sidewalk, looking up at her with a smile. She waved and mouthed, *"Adiós."*

"Liyik!" he shouted as the bus began to roll away. "Look it up! It means peace!"

*   *   *

Antonio could not have been more different from the men Elena had known before. All of her boyfriends had been revolutionaries, organizers of boisterous protests, makers of eloquent speeches. Ernesto

Sanchez, her first boyfriend ever, was also the one responsible for her political awakening. He was a short, curly-headed man with a thick mustache and one long bushy eyebrow, his chest and even his back covered with a forest of black hair. When Ernesto spoke, Elena could see Guatemala's future in the narrow slits of his brown eyes, a just nation, the country she wanted to live in, a country without open sewers and barefoot children begging on the streets. He assigned words to ideas that she had long understood but never heard spoken. He had shelves of books that explained all the poverty and injustice her family and her country suffered, books with titles like *Open Veins of Latin America* and *Guatemala: Occupied Country.*

It was Ernesto who introduced her to the language of the revolution, who taught her the meaning of terms like "proletariat" and "organic struggle." He pronounced the words *"revolución"* and *"pueblo"* in a smooth, aphrodisiac baritone. They made love in his apartment nearly every afternoon for three months, in a bedroom lined with dusty, allergy-inducing tomes, including a twenty-volume bound set of the collected works of V. I. Lenin. And then he left for Costa Rica, driven into exile when his name appeared on a list of "subversives" targeted for death by the "Lorenzo Amaya Anti-Communist Brigade," two days after he had made a now legendary speech calling the army chief of staff "goat face." From exile he wrote her letters that gradually diminished in both frequency and passion, until they finally stopped coming altogether, just four months after he'd gone away. Rumor had it that Ernesto had found himself a Costa Rican girlfriend.

Her most recent boyfriend, Teodoro Pereira, was the current president of the student association. She had dropped him after discovering that he was dating at least one other woman, maybe two. Every time she heard him open his mouth at a rally or a march, she muttered *"hipócrita"* under her breath. He'd make an angry speech against the suspension of civil liberties, then lie to her a few moments later about where he was last Wednesday afternoon, making up some pitiful excuse, saying he was at such-and-such meeting when she knew full well he was off somewhere with Filomena or María or Teresa.

"Teodoro, I can't tolerate this anymore," she told her lover during their final confrontation. "You make a fool of me and every woman who is blind enough to fall under your influence."

Teodoro looked stunned, and for a moment genuinely hurt. He gave her a theatrical pout. But when Elena wouldn't buy this act, he slipped into a sly grin, the look of a boy caught stealing cookies.

"I treat women the same way I treat everyone else," he said smoothly. "As equals."

That was the problem with her revolutionaries: the same masculine chemical energy that made them so brave in the face of the dictatorship also drove them to distraction whenever there was a pretty woman around.

It seemed the revolution would never be free of machismo, even now that the Marxist-Leninists were gaining sway. The Leninists had begun to impose a strict bourgeois morality on the rank and file, declaring that monogamy was preferable to the dissension caused by so much incestuous cross-dating. Philandering was a serious threat to the movement because the enemy would take advantage of any kind of internal rift, so the Leninists cracked down on the Don Juans, telling them party discipline demanded that the comrades keep their pants on. But the change was only superficial: all the leadership positions, Elena had noticed, were still held by men. "This Leninism, or whatever they call it, is just the same machismo," she told one of her women friends. "Machismo with a more serious face."

The Leninists were gaining influence because the movement had come under violent attack. During the day, soldiers dressed as civilians came to kidnap professors and students; after the sun fell, graffiti artists worked until dawn to cover the university walls with the spray-painted names of the dead: Professor Juan Peralta, Ana Saravia, Julio Gomez Asturias . . . The walls seemed to have an insatiable appetite for the names of dead students. Elena became more discreet. She stopped distributing revolutionary leaflets at the markets, and when she went to a demonstration she always tied a blue bandanna over her face, leaving only her brown eyes to display her anger.

When Antonio entered her life, Elena was ready for a change, ready to meet someone outside the movement. The old Elena might have been irritated by Antonio's quiet, obliging manner; the new Elena found it refreshing. After the storms and choppy seas of her revolutionaries, Antonio would be a calm lake of patience and thoughtfulness. And he was nice to look at, with features that were at once masculine and vaguely feminine, somewhere between the Mayan and the Spaniard. His gentleness she found erotic, hinting at untapped reservoirs of passion. She was flattered that someone this handsome would be so completely infatuated with her: she was willing to forgive herself this small vanity, which in no way could be mistaken for a revolutionary value.

After class, in their brief talks during her walk to the bus stop, she learned that even though he wasn't directly involved in campus politics, he did work on the university's literary journal, *Provocaciones*, which was edited by his friend Gonzalo.

"Of course, it's impossible to publish anything these days without touching on the social issues," he said in a matter-of-fact tone. "At least half the submissions are political. Especially the poetry. That's what people want to write about. The revolution."

"To tell you the truth, I haven't read your journal," she answered. "I don't have time for such things, really. Literature is a luxury for me now. Given our economic situation, it's a luxury for the country too."

"There always has to be room for poetry, for literature," he insisted. "Poetry is like water. We can't live without it."

"How can you say that? I'm surprised at you. What a petit-bourgeois thing to say. It's not like water. Poetry is not like water," she said with rising vehemence. "You can live without poetry. But without clean water, like so many of our people, that *is* impossible."

Hours later, Elena regretted her little speech, deciding that she sounded too mean, too masculine; she blamed it on the lingering influence of Teodoro and the other revolutionaries. But to her surprise, her brief tirade had not angered Antonio; he merely raised his eyebrows, a gesture of enlightenment or amusement, she couldn't tell which. In this conversation and others, he never seemed to take offense when she disagreed with him, didn't try to prove that he was really smarter than she was, didn't seemed to feel threatened or intimidated. Once, after they had stood at the bus stop for twenty minutes talking about Quiché cosmology and the Mayan calendar, she realized that he had not once condescended to her. Here was a man who was more inclined to listen than to argue.

Finally they went out on a formal date—at Elena's suggestion. They had dinner at a Chinese restaurant and talked about Federico García Lorca and Russian literature, his favorite topics. She told him she was surprised that someone as reserved as he was would be drawn to the sensuality of García Lorca. "Really, Antonio, all that suppressed sex. The jealousy, the passionate love. It doesn't seem like you." He blushed and quickly changed the subject, saying how tragic it was that a man as talented as García Lorca died when he was just thirty-eight years old, shot by Franco's Falangists. "He had his best writing ahead of him."

All of his fervor was for books. Antonio said he had learned about politics through literature, by reading Steinbeck and Upton Sinclair and the Mexican novelist José Revueltas, among others. "That's interesting," Elena responded, "because I did things the other way around. I discovered literature and art through politics." Her Marxist boyfriends had given her revolutionary poetry to read, like *Vamos Patria a Caminar*, by Otto René Castillo, the Guatemalan writer turned guerrilla fighter who was one of the movement's first martyrs.

Antonio had signed up for the class on Quiché rituals to better understand the *Popol Vuh*, the Quiché Mayan book of creation, which he called "the very first book in Guatemalan literature."

"Your friends might not think that reading the *Popol Vuh* is a revolutionary act, but I do," he said. "People talk about honoring our Mayan past, but how many really do it, how many take the time to understand our roots. To feel the Indian in us. Hardly anyone. Even among all these revolutionary students, to call someone *indio* is still an insult."

Antonio was smart, but like so many other men, he needed a woman to take care of him. His glasses were usually dirty, covered with dust: she was tempted to reach up, pull the circular disks off his face, and wipe them clean so she could see his copper eyes without having to look through those spotted lenses. His height made him somewhat clumsy, like an adolescent after a growth spurt. It occurred to Elena that she could take this tall man, who was still almost a boy, and mold him into the lover she had always wanted. He would be beautiful, intelligent, respectful, and passionate, and he would never lie to her. She would buy him new clothes to replace his faded slacks, those unbecoming windbreakers. She would train him in politics, teach him everything he needed to know.

"Let's stop by the university," she said one afternoon as they embarked on another date. "There's something I want to show you."

It was a Sunday. No students walked on the green lawns, no one filtered in and out of the powder blue buildings. Only the graffiti-covered walls spoke, announcing the coming proletarian revolution to flocks of birds plucking insects from the grass. She took him to the Faculty of Accounting. Turning the corner of the building, she pointed with an outstretched hand. "This is what I wanted to show you. They just finished it yesterday." A huge mural of Che Guevara rose above them, curls streaming from beneath his red-star beret, his face rippling across the wall. Eyes that conveyed a Christ-like kindness, a father looking down approvingly at his Guatemalan children.

"A friend of mine designed it," she said reverently. "Isn't it beautiful?"

She drew his attention to the string of words that ran underneath Che, painted on a long white ribbon held aloft by a crudely drawn dove: "The revolutionary is guided in all his actions by great feelings of love."

"He wrote that in one of his books," Elena said. "It's one of the guiding principles of my life."

Antonio adjusted his glasses, reading and rereading the line.

"That's the problem with the left," Elena continued. "They don't understand the meaning of love. They think that love is something abstract. They don't know that love means you don't lie. Does a real revolutionary lie to the people, to his friends? Does he lie to the woman who loves him? No."

Antonio seemed slightly perplexed.

"Oh, never mind," she said. "I just wanted you to see it. Let's go eat."

An hour later they were sitting at a table in the now familiar Chinese restaurant, admiring the decor. A large mural of Shanghai covered one wall, framed paintings of Guatemalan quetzal birds another. They had been dating for about six weeks. He adjusted his glasses and leaned over, his broad face opening into a wondrous smile.

"You know, I've been meaning to tell you, and please don't take this the wrong way, that I think you're very, very beautiful. You have such beautiful Mayan features."

Elena felt a twinge through her body, a rush of warmth that gathered and gelled below her waist. *Why doesn't he reach over and kiss me right now, the fool.* She considered reaching across the table and kissing him herself, then decided this would be too rash, even for her: she might scare him off. That was one move he would have to make on his own.

In the afternoon they went to see a movie, *The Elephant Man.* The theater was nearly empty, but a couple toward the back was necking furiously. *Good, maybe Antonio will get an idea or two.* Elena shifted in her seat and leaned against him, the movement causing springs to creak loudly. He stiffened for a moment, then relaxed. He put his arm around her, and she rested her head on his shoulder. The movie was in black and white, but nothing else about it registered. He leaned down and kissed her tentatively, tight-lipped, as if he'd never kissed anyone before, the sort of peck you give your sister. Elena tried hard not to frown. His next kiss was better. The third was better still, a gentle meeting of moist lips, tender and slow. By the fourth kiss, mouths slightly open and tongues greeting each other for the first time, he started to get the hang of it.

She would teach this amateur to kiss even if she rubbed her lips raw in the process.

* * *

In the Parque de la Concordia, underneath the sparse shade of a withered tree, Elena and Antonio held each other, oblivious to the flaking paint on the cast-iron benches, the dusty patches in the lawns, the clutch-grinding roar of trucks and buses on nearby Sexta Avenida. She stroked his straight jet black hair, traced the outline of his wide nose with her finger. Why did she feel so much tenderness for this clumsy, quiet man?

They were lying on the grass now, kissing softly. He reached under the cup of her bra and touched her nipple, exploring, questioning her skin. He was getting bolder. Soon she wouldn't be able to stop him. Arching her back, she placed her hand on his. Over his shoulder she saw a man in a wrinkled charcoal suit, his eyes wide under a mane of white hair. This stranger was focusing quite clearly on the movement of Antonio's hand on her breast. She pulled away.

"Antonio, my love, we need to be alone somewhere. People can see us here. We need to go somewhere with walls and a door. A door with a lock."

"A lock?" he said.

"Yes. Maybe a car would do. Can you borrow someone's car?"

"I'll try. Maybe I can get my father's Volkswagen."

They straightened their clothes and left the park, heading for her bus stop near the National Library, a trek through ten blocks of narrow city streets clogged with cars and trucks. Elena held a tissue to her face against the acrid smell of automobile exhaust. Three blocks from the stop they heard a distant chanting, whistles, the sound of an angry crowd.

"It's some kind of protest," Elena said. "Let's go see what's happening. I want to see."

Antonio hesitated, but before he could speak she took him by the hand and led him in the direction of the crowd: there used to be dozens of demonstrations in downtown Guatemala City, and now there were hardly any. Elena didn't want to miss this one.

From a block away they spotted the protesters, four hundred men in pale green uniforms, a few holding signs, their bodies filling a narrow street near the chambers of the Congreso de la República.

"It's the garbage workers," Antonio said.

The street began to echo with the crash of steel shutters slamming as the merchants closed up their shops; there was sure to be trouble now, the throwing of rocks, the breaking of windows, the setting of fires. The protesters were dark men with furrowed faces, not one of them, it seemed, younger than forty. They were the lowest caste of government workers, Guatemala's untouchables. Some carried the large burlap bags they used to collect the trash. Their mouths opened into decaying smiles as Antonio and Elena walked through their ranks hand in hand, two idealistic students come to show their solidarity with the working class, the youth in support of the older generation. Standing among them, bumping into their bodies on the crowded street, Antonio and Elena could just detect the scent of rotting vegetables, sour milk, moldy bread.

"¡Justicia!" they yelled. "¡Queremos representación!"

Antonio and Elena reached the front of the demonstration and saw a line of police officers in steel blue uniforms, batons at their chests, blocking the protesters' advance.

"Elena, maybe we should leave."

"What courage these people have," she said, ignoring him. "It's against the law for them to strike. They want the right to strike."

"Isn't it too dangerous to be here?"

"You can leave if you want to. I'm staying."

"No. I want to be with you."

With the policemen blocking their way, the garbage collectors began drifting down one of the side streets, stopping traffic, weaving around cars as the drivers inside leaned on their horns to no avail. The honking made the workers laugh. Following the lead of a worker with a bullhorn, they headed for the National Palace.

"¡Vámonos, compañeros! ¡Al palacio!"

One of the garbage men worked the sidewalk, passing out flyers. Elena thought she and Antonio must look silly, the clean-faced couple in a grimy sea, until it dawned on her that she was standing in the middle of an illegal demonstration with her face uncovered. She scanned the crowd for the cameras of the military intelligence agents who would record her presence here. Her stomach turned as a man drew alongside Antonio and placed a blackened hand on his shoulder. "Thank you, *compañero*," he said before quickly disappearing into the crowd.

They reached the broad plaza of the Parque Central, within sight of the National Palace. She looked over at Antonio, who was suddenly beaming.

"This feels like a dream, to be here, surrounded by these men," he said. "It feels good to be here. It feels like something we should do."

Elena stopped and kissed him on the cheek. She was proud of him. Of course he was too naive to realize the danger they might face. Maybe she didn't have the right to lead him into trouble: he was in love with her and would follow her anywhere. Taking his hand again, she led him away from the marching workers to a fountain in the center of the plaza where a group of shoeshine boys was watching events unfold from a safe distance.

A line of soldiers guarded the wrought-iron gate at the front of the National Palace, a limestone green building of round columns and ornate cornices. The soldiers, part of the Presidential Guard, wore camouflage uniforms that looked incongruous in the urban setting, and carried Israeli Galil rifles that seemed too big and too menacing for them. There was always a surplus of boyish faces and big guns in front of the National Palace.

From her vantage point at the fountain, Elena could see the soldiers standing at attention, and the pale green backs of the garbage collectors across the street that separated the plaza from the palace. They seemed content to chant slogans and whistle at the soldiers. Several minutes passed. Without warning, four policemen and two soldiers bolted from behind the guards and sprinted across the street. Plunging into the crowd of protesters, they set off a panic, a flurry of voices and pleas, and then the workers scattered, running toward the fountain, a wave of men falling backward in unison like blades of tall grass in a windblown field.

A rifle shot rang out and echoed across the plaza, sending flocks of birds skyward from the trees. The four policemen were carrying off the man with the bullhorn, one holding each limb; he was barefoot now. Other policemen and soldiers were seizing more men, apparently at random. The shoeshine boys next to Elena grabbed their boxes and began running. Antonio squeezed her hand tighter, as if to say, I am still here, I am not running. More men came rushing from the palace, beefy men in polo shirts, jeans, and tennis shoes, soldiers in disguise. For the first time Elena noticed two white Jeeps without license plates parked to the right of the palace, each with tinted windows, a death-squad signature.

Soon the plaza was empty. Only a few placards lay scattered on the cobblestones. As Elena guided Antonio away, she turned to see a garbage worker being pushed into one of the Jeeps. He was kicking the soldiers, trying to get away. Then a pistol butt to the head, and his body surrendered, dropping to the asphalt. They lifted him into the Jeep. He would probably never be seen again. They would torture him, disappear him, mutilate his body.

"I hate them." Elena walked faster, pulling Antonio by the hand. "Soldiers! *¡Animales!* They're not even embarrassed to be seen. In the middle of the city they take people. In the middle of the afternoon!"

One day there would be prisons for these men. A zoo for the gorilla generals who ordered silence. Iron cages for the ape soldiers who grabbed people from the street in broad daylight. Elena wanted to live to see this day.

7 Teodoro's Hands

As soon as she opened the front door and saw Marvin, Elena knew what had happened. She could see it on his face, the eyes heavy in sorrow, the stunned drowsiness. Marvin Chang, the jaunty companion and best friend of Teodoro, standing now at her front door, his hair uncombed, his clothes wrinkled, as if he had slept in them. She knew what he was about to say, but for a moment she held on to the hope that it might not be true. For a moment longer, she would imagine she lived in a country without such horror. Marvin had never come to her house before, but perhaps there was some other explanation for his presence here.

"Elena, Teodoro is dead," he said in a flat voice. "We found his body this morning."

Before she could say anything, he went on.

"They came for him Wednesday. In the middle of the day. They just walked into his house and grabbed him." He was suddenly talking in a rush, as if he would soon run out of breath. "They had machine guns. They put him in a Jeep. We found his body on the road to Chimaltenango."

Marvin began to sob, and Elena embraced him. He trembled in her arms. Teodoro had treated Marvin like his younger brother. Marvin was quiet and shy, trailing after Teodoro at rallies, poetry readings, parties.

He pulled away abruptly. "They cut off his hands! I saw his body. He didn't have any hands!"

Bile began to rise from her stomach, and she lifted a hand to cover her mouth. She leaned against the doorway to keep from falling and shuddered a dry heave. *Teodoro is twenty-three years old and has so much more to live.*

She told herself she would remember this moment, standing here, for the rest of her life. Marvin in blue jeans, tears running down his cheeks, racing for his neck. The sudden, palpable emptiness, the presence of death, the absurdity, to be discussing the mutilation of her former lover while standing at the front door of her house on a sunny tropical day, a scratchy radio playing in the distance, the children from the next house racing toy cars.

Marvin tried to compose himself, wiping the tears from his face. "His mother spent an hour looking for his hands in the weeds by the side of the road, but she never found them. She said she didn't want to bury him without his hands. She looked like she was in a trance."

Teodoro caressed me, held me in his arms. He wore a silver band on his right ring finger.

She gave Marvin a kiss on the cheek before he left, and worried about him as he walked away. What would he do without Teodoro to shadow?

Alone in the house with her thoughts, Elena paced the living room. Teodoro was bright and beautiful, even with his flaws. His fingers were short and stubby. She sat down on the couch, slumping on the thin green cushions, and began to weep. She felt his presence on this spot and remembered sitting next to him, putting her palm to his, laughing playfully. "My hands are so much bigger than yours, Teodoro! My hands are so ugly, like an Amazona."

There was no avoiding it: she felt responsible for his death. If she hadn't dumped him, she would have been able to protect him. A woman should use her love as a shield against the things a man can't see or refuses to see. Teodoro was brilliant, but he had blind spots. *He didn't think I noticed when he looked at other women.* Teodoro was strong-willed, too stubborn to realize he was in danger. *If I had been with him he would have listened to me. A woman has a sense for these things. I was the only woman he took seriously.*

As the day passed and word of Teodoro's death spread, people came by to offer their condolences, as if she were a widow. They all thought that Teodoro had left her and that she still carried a torch that would burn even brighter now that he was gone. Each visitor added another layer to the story of Teodoro's last hours. They sat in her tiny living room and talked to fill the silence because Elena didn't know what to say.

"After the soldiers took him away, his mother went to the police station to ask if they had her son, and they laughed at her," María Teresa, her friend from the anthropology department, told her. "Those pigs. *Animales*. You know how they are."

Teodoro's torturers put a *capucha* on his head, María Teresa had heard, a bag full of caustic chemicals that singe your lungs. She recounted more details, with a detached, morbid fascination. "His brother said they found cigarette burns and machete cuts."

Next to arrive was Agustín, a former suitor and current treasurer of the student association. "Teodoro was completely surprised when they showed up at the door. He didn't even try to run away." Agustín tried to bite his nails, but there was nothing at the tips of his fingers but pink flesh. "They knocked him to the ground. They grabbed him by the shirt and dragged him down the street."

Agustín was afraid of being arrested, but he was going to stay in Guatemala City anyway, lying low, hiding out somewhere.

"Teodoro went down like a brave man," Agustín said. "That's what everyone is saying. He didn't lose his dignity—if it's possible to maintain your dignity in such a situation. They say his tongue swelled up from the tortures. He could barely talk toward the end."

Elena wondered about the source of all this information, how people could know so much about something that supposedly happened in the darkness of clandestine jails.

Pedro Lara, one of the most radical members of the student association, arrived in tan slacks, penny loafers, and a blue sports coat, as if he were on his way to a dinner engagement, and kissed Elena on the cheek. "I came to say goodbye." He was going to Mexico that very evening, into exile. Given the circumstances, he seemed unusually calm, as if he had been expecting this moment for a long time. "At this point I'll be more useful to the movement outside Guatemala. If I stay here, let's face it, they'll probably kill me. They might show up anytime. I'm even worried about how I'm going to get to the airport."

He lit a cigarette and lowered his voice to a whisper. "People are worried about what Teodoro might have said. No one would even suggest, of course, that he betrayed the movement. But believe me, Elena, it's in the back of everyone's mind." He paused to let this thought sink in and looked her in the eye. She revealed nothing.

"Think of all the names he carried in his head," Pedro continued, "everyone he knew, everyone in the student association. They say you'll give up your own mother if they turn up the electroshocks high enough. We're helpless in the face of these barbarians."

Pedro had talked to someone who was in a cell next to Teodoro, a student who had been taken the same day but for some reason was released. The student heard Teodoro crying for his mother. Every time they hit Teodoro he would say, "I'm sorry, I'm sorry."

Pedro put out his cigarette, embraced Elena one last time, and said that if there was any justice in this world they would see each other again when Guatemala was liberated. Maybe in five years.

"Be careful, Elena. They might have your name. Teodoro might have told them you were one of the leaders even though you weren't."

Before she could argue, before she could say that Teodoro would never betray her, Pedro was gone.

The next day Teodoro's picture appeared in the paper, one column wide, the size of a passport photograph. The headline read: "Student President at National Univ., 3 others, dead; 6 missing." The picture was at least four years old, pimply skin smoothed out by a generous photographer's airbrush. He was wearing a suit and tie and looked like a teenager going to church on Sunday, not like the man she knew.

She cut out the picture and tucked it into the corner of the framed Sacred Heart of Jesus, the forlorn Christ with the pulsating organ in his hand. She prayed a novena, nine Hail Marys in a row, three for Teodoro with the *capucha*, struggling to breathe, three for the Teodoro who apologized to his torturers, three for the Teodoro who left this world without hands. He was in Purgatory, and her prayers would help him pass through to Heaven. Silly beliefs she learned from her aunt, but it seemed like a time for faith. She lit a candle and left a glass of water by the picture so that Teodoro could replenish himself while his soul was stranded in the world of in-between.

* * *

She met Antonio in front of the Chinese restaurant and french-kissed him right there, reaching up on tiptoes to meet his lips. He seemed a little startled; after all, they were on a crowded sidewalk across the street from a sad little park filled with ice cream carts, retirees, and blind vendors of lottery tickets. A shoeshine boy standing nearby smiled at them, teeth like a white beacon in a face blackened by shoe polish.

Elena wrapped her arms around Antonio and buried her face in his neck. Just touching him was a release, a lifting of burdens.

She began to tell him about Teodoro but paused, surprised by his look of pale sleeplessness, a numbness that mirrored her own. She led him into the restaurant, and they sat down in one of the booths.

"What's wrong, *amor?*" she asked. "*¿Qué te pasa?*"

He looked at the table and rubbed his temples, his fingers moving in quick circles.

"Tell me," she insisted.

"Gonzalo," he said finally. "He's disappeared. They took him from the university."

Another blow. Anyone could be picked up, at any time, from any place. *A poison cloud is swallowing the people around me.* Who would be next?

The death squad abducted Gonzalo at the campus bus stop by the Faculty of Architecture—the same bus stop where Elena and Antonio had first talked. A slate-colored Jeep pulled up and disgorged four armed men in civilian clothes. There were six or seven people at the bus stop, but one of the armed men had a picture in his hand. Like Teodoro, Gonzalo was caught completely by surprise. They grabbed him and threw his books to the ground. For two days his parents had been making the rounds of the police stations, army bases, hospitals, even the morgue.

"I helped him edit *Provocaciones* a few times," Antonio said. He narrowed his eyes, as if he were trying to find meaning in a story that had none. "He filled it with revolutionary poetry because that's what people submitted. Everyone at the university wants to write about love and revolution. Sometimes people get carried away and throw in a line about the armed struggle. But they're just words." He rubbed his forehead, squeezed his temples.

"They're probably torturing him right now, this very second. They're going to kill him because they want the names of the poets," Antonio said loudly enough for everyone in the restaurant to hear. "They're going to kill him because he won't tell them. Because he has too much honor."

Elena reached across the table and squeezed his hands; she could feel the pulse in his fingers. *"Calmate, amor."*

"What's happening to our country?"

Antonio wore that childlike look of distress and tragic loss that had become so familiar these past few days. Everyone she knew had come to wear this face. She was a member of a generation perpetually in mourning, a generation whose brazen voice had faded to a somber whisper. Obituaries for teenagers and men-boys, condolences for twenty-year-old widows.

She placed her fingers on his lips. "Antonio, please, no more sadness today. No more news."

Suddenly the restaurant felt like a coffin. Without a word Elena stood up and led Antonio outside into the searing midday light.

"Can you still get your father's car?" She had remembered that this was the afternoon of their planned escape in the Volkswagen.

He nodded.

"Good, let's go somewhere, right now," she said, her voice rising with excitement. "Let's not wait. Let's leave the city for a few hours. I want to imagine we live in another country for an afternoon. I want to be alone with you. I want to be happy today."

She looked into his eyes, red behind the round disks of his glasses.

"I want to feel alive."

✳ ✳ ✳

The Volkswagen struggled up the steep hills on the outskirts of the city. The engine sputtered, and even the overcrowded buses sped past them, baskets of food and produce stacked on the roofs, passengers clinging to the doorways, a thick cloud of diesel fumes billowing from the rear. This was the main road out of the capital, a winding four-lane highway rising from the crowded city to the countryside, a panorama of coffee plantations and patchwork cornfields growing on steep hillsides. Elena watched the city disappearing in the valley below. *Let Teodoro's memory fade with the city. Let it shrink away. I am not his widow. I loved him once but he is part of my past.*

Antonio's plan was to drive to Lake Amatitlán, pull onto one of the side roads at the far end, and find a secluded place to park. They were just a kilometer or so from the lake when traffic began to slow. There was some sort of checkpoint up ahead: the National Police, three officers in sky blue shirts and navy pants, loose belts of rifle cartridges dangling from their waists.

When Antonio reached the checkpoint he handed his identity documents and the car registration to an officer with a thin Hitler mustache of the type still worn by many older men in Guatemala's provinces. The officer leaned against the Volkswagen door and looked down at the open leather wallet on Antonio's lap. "What's that?" he asked. Antonio's student identification card had caught his eye.

"Step out of the car," the officer said in a voice that was neither threatening nor polite.

Antonio opened the door and stood on the asphalt road, avoiding the officer's eyes.

"So, you're a student." The officer waved the identification card as if it were contraband. "That nest of troublemakers."

"I'm a literature student, *jefe*. That's all."

"This car isn't registered in your name." He turned to one of the other officers, a man holding a rifle, the barrel pointing to the sky. "*Sargento*, this guy's one of those troublemaker Marxists from the university."

Elena's heart began to race. They were going to take Antonio away, right here, while she watched. They were going to drag him into that police car, and she would never see him again. And it was all her fault; she had talked him into coming here because she wanted to make love to him.

"It's my father's car," Antonio was saying as he pointed to the document in the officer's hand. "See, it has the same last name."

The police officers wore pins on their uniforms with little quetzal birds. They were letting the other cars pass through. All three of them were gathered around Antonio, staring contemptuously at this university student who had been so bold as to wander into their checkpoint.

"What are you doing here?" the officer with the rifle asked. "This is an area of guerrilla activity. Did you know that? See if this son of a bitch is carrying any weapons in his car."

The officer with the mustache opened the Volkswagen's front hood. He asked Elena to step outside while he checked underneath the seats. Finding nothing of interest, he told her to get back inside.

"This car is not registered in your name," he repeated, and shoved Antonio toward the patrol car. Antonio was a foot taller than the policemen, but he looked small and helpless as they pushed him down into the back seat. Elena could see the back of his head, and then he turned around to look at her and she caught his brown eyes, sad and doomed. His lips moved silently, forming the words "Don't worry." While the officer with the rifle leaned in to talk to him, the third officer opened the patrol car's front door and sat down, pulling his hat over his face. Elena could see Antonio shrugging his shoulders and opening his arms in a gesture of exasperation. The officer stepped away from the patrol car and walked over to the Volkswagen.

"So are you going to take care of this, or what?" he asked Elena. "Your boyfriend says he doesn't have any money."

Elena breathed a sigh a relief: they wanted a bribe. Suddenly the situation was familiar, understandable, part of the natural order of things. The National Police were always looking to make a little extra money on the side. She reached into her purse and produced a twenty-quetzal bill. The officer frowned and went to consult his partners. A moment later he waddled back toward Elena and the Volkswagen.

"Ten quetzales more."

"I only have five."

He took the money, and in no time Antonio was stepping out of the patrol car. The policemen patted him on the back, smiling as if it had all been an unfortunate misunderstanding.

"Be more careful next time, *licenciado*," the officer with the rifle said with a wink.

Antonio started the Volkswagen and drove off without saying a word. They were a good mile or so down the road when he started to laugh, a strange, manic sound.

"I thought they were going to shoot me. I really thought they were going to shoot me!"

"Those crooks," Elena said. "That big show, and all they wanted was a bribe."

Antonio guided the car off the main highway. They were on a hillside overlooking the lake, a tourist spot that had fallen into decay when the government built an oil-burning power plant on the shore. Dilapidated weekend homes rose on tall stilts at the water's edge. The Volkswagen moved onto the rough surface of a dirt road, and they came to a bend covered by the canopy of a thick grove of trees.

"No one will bother us here," Antonio said. "No one uses this road anymore."

He turned off the engine, and the air filled with birdsong and the rustling of leaves. Elena looked through the pitted glass of the front windshield. Brush and sweet-gum trees lined the roadway; palm-shaped leaves hung over the car, enveloping them in a shady cocoon.

They were alone.

Teodoro's severed hands lying in the grass by the roadside.

Gonzalo's books tossed to the street like so much trash.

What was Gonzalo reading, what books did he have when the death squad came for him?

Was Teodoro alive when they cut off his hands?

They would kill Gonzalo to silence his poets.

Teodoro would not betray me, ever.

Elena took a deep breath and reached out to touch Antonio's cheek. He sat still, looking straight ahead. She watched him breathing slowly with his eyes closed. Her own fear and tiredness began to slip away.

"We're still alive," she said.

"That's right. We are."

Antonio lowered the Volkswagen's back seat to create a small, cozy space, oval-shaped. Lying on her back, Elena gazed out the curving arc of the rear window and saw a patch of sky framed by the verdant arms of trees, two enormous clouds drifting across the narrow blue canvas. Antonio put his arm across her waist. She pulled him on top of her. *My beautiful man. My tall lover.* His head was bent against the Volkswagen's shell. He began kissing her neck, her forehead. *We're still alive.* She kissed him on the mouth, and as their lips lingered she felt her sadness dissolve and float away, rising into the sky to join the migrating clouds. *Squeeze me tighter, swallow me, show me the way.* No killers, no fear, only her lover, only his straight black hair, the olive-tinted skin, the buttons of his pale blue shirt, the last obstacle of his khaki pants and the imitation leather belt that resisted her for a few seconds.

Elena laughed. She had undressed him in record time. She was still fully clothed and he was naked, the pants at his ankles in a crazy knot with his shirt, socks, shoes, and diamond-patterned boxers.

"I'm cold," he said.

On his knees, straddling her, testicles dangling above her waist, sex stiff and pointing skyward, he took off her blouse, her bra. With a strong tug he pulled off her jeans, tight as a second skin, and she felt the thrill of being naked under the beautiful blue sky, feeling the cool shady air against her bare breasts and legs.

Gradually he became less tentative, but his movements were still jerky and ungraceful. She let her fingers glide across his bare back and wrapped her legs around him. Finally she reached down and guided him into her. And yes, *yes, there you go, that's it, my love. Like that. Así.* And suddenly she is with Teodoro, in the musty bedroom of his apartment, and he is on top of her, looking at her with his green-gray eyes, the smooth lover.

Why have you come back here, Teodoro? I thought you were dead. Go away. Leave me alone.

This was where she wanted to be, in the Volkswagen with Antonio, this caring man who could release her, save her, shelter her from harm. He was pushing against her, moving faster now, and she leaned up to suck on his nipples, to kiss the handful of hairs on his chest.

She reached for Antonio's hands. Then she put his fingers in her mouth, sucking at the living skin, wishing she could swallow the marrow in the bone. She sucked harder, and it was like pulling a trip wire. His muscles gathered tight and then released and he rolled off her.

The Volkswagen filled with silence. Slowly the sounds of the forest returned, gathering resonance, flowing through the car's open windows, the subtle creak of heavy branches swaying in the breeze, the strange calls of tropical birds, the echoing songs.

Elena took Antonio's hands again. It was the first time she had ever made love without a condom or diaphragm. She was almost certain she would get pregnant. It took only a few quick calendar calculations to realize that she was probably becoming pregnant at this very moment, the microscopic union taking place as she lay on her back in a Volkswagen.

"I've never done this before," Antonio said. "Not with anyone, ever."

I knew that, my love. "Neither have I," she said.

The Window

The old bus puttered along a black ribbon that cut through a forest of cornstalks two feet taller than the tallest man. Elena had not been so deep in the countryside for many years and was surprised by the abundance of the land, the dark richness of the soil, the fleshy sheen of the narrow leaves that sprouted from the stalks like spokes on a wheel. There was a tiny golden crown on each plant. The *campesinos* here worked the land with manic industry, as if they feared God would punish them for leaving any spot unplanted. Corn climbed the round bellies of the hillsides, filling narrow, rocky ravines, clinging tenaciously to the steepest slopes, stalks rising even from the edges of cliffs, like stiff green divers poised to jump into the precipice below.

Inside the bus, bodies jostled back and forth in unison. Elena stared at the corn-happy landscape in a trance. She was married, a fact that still seemed impossible twenty-four hours later. There had been a civil ceremony in which she signed her name with Mrs. Bernal and her friend María Teresa looking on as witnesses. She wore a new white sundress with purple and yellow flowers. The whole thing lasted no more than five minutes, not even a chance to linger with her new husband in the registrar's office before Antonio's mother hustled them off to her house.

"It's not safe, son, to be out in public too long."

Mrs. Bernal had sent them on this road, the Pan-American Highway, a name that sounded much too pretentious for the two-lane potholed strip of asphalt before them. She had convinced them to seek refuge from the terror of the capital in a small town where no one would know who they were. "Any fool can see it's only a matter of time until they come after you. It's too dangerous to be a student in this city. It's a death sentence." A stern and attractive woman with strands of gray in her hair, Antonio's mother was now the provider of cash and shelter and would not be disputed. Without money and with a baby on the way, they had no place else to turn. Antonio had resigned himself to the plan, his face a white flag of surrender.

Elena looked out the bus window at signs announcing towns with Quiché Indian names, Hispanicized centuries ago: Chimaltenango, Tecpán, Chichicastenango. On this road to safety she had already seen three army trucks rumbling along, each one filled with young soldiers whose alert and frightened faces suggested that battles were being fought nearby.

She looked across at Antonio, sitting with one foot in the aisle, his hand fixed to the bar on the seat in front of him. Here was her husband, a stranger, a man with gestures and habits that were still unknown. Married couples were supposed to share a daily, mundane intimacy. It worried her that she hadn't known Antonio long enough to find out what was annoying about him.

The journey began to feel more like an ending than a beginning. *This is internal exile. They are sending me to this nowhere village to serve my sentence.*

With each town they passed Elena felt the person she was before her pregnancy slipping further away. In the capital the revolution continued without her. Some of her friends were organizing clandestine cells now, giving their new creations brave names, the Worker-Student Front and the University Movement for Proletarian Democracy. They were taking the struggle to a more advanced stage. Elena was leaving them behind, betrayed by her well-functioning ovaries, her efficient fallopian tubes.

I am selfish. I would rather be pregnant and safe than face the dangers of the movement and the city. I am spoiled. I lack the convictions of a true revolutionary.

But then she remembered the face of Che Guevara and the slogan on the wall. *A revolutionary is motivated in all her actions by great feelings of love.* There could be nothing wrong in accepting the love of a man and loving the child you conceived together. Beyond the movement there was this other responsibility, to child and husband. Antonio was a year younger than Elena, only twenty, and he would be lost without her. The easy thing would have been to find the secret doctors who helped young women with these problems, but the moment to make that decision had come and gone very quickly, like the kilometer posts that were disappearing behind her, marking the progress of her escape.

It was impossible to shake the feeling that she was running away. Everything in the puzzle of events seemed to point in two directions at once. Maybe it was because she was pregnant, because her body was becoming stranger every day, because everything around her seemed to be moving more slowly, because the light seemed brighter, blinding and white. She looked out the window and saw cornfields and more cornfields. With each kilometer the forest of green stalks seemed to grow thicker. *I will be lost in all this corn.* Three times during the drive to San Cristóbal she broke down. Each time Antonio wrapped his arms around her.

"*Amor*, why are you crying?" Antonio looked distressed, helpless, impotent before the stream of her tears. "What's wrong?"

Each time she stopped crying only because she could see Antonio was about to break into tears himself. He was the picture of distress, a man on the brink of collapse. She imagined him bolting from the bus and disappearing into the corn.

Antonio had not been the same since they found Gonzalo's body. "I've never had a friend murdered before," he said to her, almost apologetically. "I've never known anybody who died." Rumor had it that Gonzalo had withstood the tortures inflicted upon him without naming any of the insolent poets who filled his magazine with calls to insurrection. More than one writer had been saved from certain death, including the author of a brilliant satirical poem about the army chief of staff and his mistresses. After the initial shock, Antonio had slipped into a deep depression, a side of him she did not know, a near total gloom colored with long silences. In between these moods he had begun to show the first flashes of irritability. Three days ago she had caught him looking at her with an odd, resentful stare, as if she were to blame for this mess they were in. As if she were to blame, somehow, for Gonzalo's death.

Each time the bus stopped she got out to go to the bathroom.

When the driver stopped for twenty-five minutes to visit a relative in a town in San Marcos, she went twice. They passed through two military checkpoints and three operated by the local civil defense patrol, peasants armed with sticks and machetes. At each checkpoint all the passengers lined up to have their documents examined. At one stop she handed her passport to a peasant and watched as he held it upside down and pretended to read it.

The highway that had wound so steadily through the hills and cornfields came to an end when the bus reached a river crossing. A series of boulders blocking the road and sticks bearing red flags announced that the bridge was gone. Once more the passengers disembarked and lined up to have their documents inspected. After showing his identity card to a *campesino*, Antonio wandered away from the line to the edge of the demolished roadway, now just two sandwiches of asphalt and concrete jutting into the air. In his round glasses, standing above the riverbank with his hands on his hips, he looked like an engineer. Maybe he should have studied engineering instead of literature, Elena thought.

"The war," Antonio whispered in her ear. "The guerrillas blew up this bridge."

Elena wanted to see for herself. She stepped to the edge of the roadway. Forty feet below her, blocks of asphalt swam in the river, muddy water swirling around them. The bridge supports, pillars of thick steel blackened by dynamite, had taken up a gnarled, snakelike dance. The perpetrators had left their signature cheerfully spray-painted on the concrete base: "One More Victory in the People's Struggle!"

Here was a rumor come to life: the revolutionary war in the countryside. *The guerrillas are real, they exist. Now I know they are not just a romantic fantasy.* Men and women had come to this spot secretly, at night perhaps, to plant dynamite and close down the roadway. No army column or air force jet had been able to stop them. And yet Elena was puzzled. They were in Totonicapán province, not far from San Cristóbal Acatapán, a place supposedly untouched by the war, which was being fought much farther north and west of here, according to the newspapers. She had only to look at the ruins of the bridge

swimming in the water for the authority of the newspapers to dissolve, triumphant "dispatches" from the provinces revealed for what
they really were: army propaganda.

I always knew those hacks were lying to me. I knew it.

Elena was at once excited and frightened. There were truths out
here in the countryside, secrets hidden by curtains of corn. She imagined guerrilla fighters losing themselves in the fleshy leaves, building
impenetrable fortresses in the hills and mountains that rose above the
highway. For the first time she began to embrace the idea that living
in the provinces might not be so bad.

They returned to the bus, which followed a path cut in the riverbank and crossed over on a rickety Bailey bridge under the watchful
eye of the civil defense patrol, machetes and clubs in hand. After all
the stops and checkpoints, it was sunset by the time they arrived in
San Cristóbal.

The town sat high on a bluff. From a distance the white facade of
the church could be seen first, pale orange in the fading sunlight. The
bus climbed up the steep grade with a labored grunt and grind. Elena
wondered if it would gain strength now that it was near its destination, like horses do when they know they're almost home. The last
turn before entering town took them past the municipal cemetery, a
tiny metropolis of crosses and marble funeral vaults overlooking the
valley of cornfields below.

* * *

They moved into a nineteenth-century house with chunky stone walls
that were perpetually cool and clammy. Antonio's mother had rented
it for them. It was spacious and airy and had a little courtyard in the
middle with a fountain. Yellow and red tiles covered the floor and kept
the temperature ten degrees cooler than it was outside. Elena thought
she would catch a cold if she spent too much time in this house. She
kept telling herself to buy some throw rugs but always forgot. The
windows were huge portals with sills deep enough to hold a tray of
food. She liked to open the shutters of splintering wood and sit by the
window to feel the breeze, a book in hand.

Weeks passed and Elena came to know the patterns of the sea-son, the richness of the sky and the clouds. Settling into her new life in exile, she decided that what she liked most about this otherwise desolate little settlement were its cobblestone streets, eight or nine blocks in the center of the town. The rest of the streets were dirt paths that became impassable rivers of mud or clouds of dust depending on the weather. Antonio and Elena lived on one of the paved blocks, on Tercera Avenida. The cobblestones were quaint rectangles with round-ed tops, like hundreds of tiny loaves of gray bread.

After just a month or so it seemed that everyone in town knew them. She sat reading by the window, and they greeted her with "*¿Cómo está usted, Doña Elena?*" or "*Buenas tardes, Doña Elena.*" There was a sincerity to their words, a ring of unhurried cheerfulness you didn't hear in the capital. She marked the passage of time by the people who passed her window each day, mostly a parade of street vendors. There was the man who sharpened knives, the girl who sold tortillas from a basket balanced on her head, the boy who brought the newspaper, the woman who sold charcoal from a wheelbarrow that rattled as she pushed it along the cobblestones, the man who fixed shoes and announced his arrival with a long, wailing chant: "*Zapaaaaaatos. Zapaaaaaatos. Zapatos para cooooomponer.*"

They smiled at her through the window and called her *doña*. She thought that she wasn't old enough to be called *doña*, that she hadn't done enough in life to earn that title of respect. Maybe after the baby was born she would have earned it.

She spent the days at home alone while Antonio worked. Her swelling womb was the factory of great shifts of emotion and disposi-tion. Sleep could overwhelm her at any time of the morning, after-noon, or evening. She talked to few people besides Antonio and was amazed by how much she enjoyed the hours of silence. Just the sounds of the town outside to keep her company, the eyes of the polite but inquisitive neighbors, the occasional question about the baby masking other, unasked questions: "Who are you and why are you liv-ing in this town that nobody visits, not even the gringo tourists?"

They stood out, a cosmopolitan middle-class couple in a village of not more than twenty-five hundred people. In this provincial mes-tizo society of squat men and women, Antonio was tall, Europeancomplected, with an intellectual air he couldn't seem to shake. Elena spoke too loudly for a woman, she was too direct: housewives in this little town were supposed to behave more demurely.

Their most persistent questioner, Mrs. Gómez, lived and worked across the street. A gray-haired woman with distrusting eyes, she smelled of vinegar and always wore the same print dress of faded blue. She ran a little bodega with a long glass-covered counter and cans of Mexican coffee and bottles of expired medicine stacked on shelves that reached to the ceiling. Three or four times a week Mrs. Gómez walked across the cobblestones to engage a reluctant Elena in conversation about the weather and similarly innocuous topics.

"I keep calling that man in Quetzaltenango, but he never brings my Bufferin and my Incaparina. How am I supposed to run a business without *mercadería*? When he gets here I'll give him a piece of my mind, that's for sure."

It took a half-dozen or so such conversations before Mrs. Gómez finally got to the point.

"A nice day, Doña Elena, don't you think?"

"Yes, Señora Gómez. Very nice."

"The clouds. So tall today. Have you ever seen such clouds?"

"No, Señora Gómez. Never."

"Are the days this pretty where you come from?"

"Excuse me?"

"Well, you're not from here, right? Everyone knows that. So I wondered, are the days this pretty where you come from?"

"No. Not at all. The air is never this clear. The sky is never this blue in the capital."

"Ah," Mrs. Gómez said with a victorious raising of her eyebrows. "I see. Yes. They never are this clear in the capital, are they?" After a pause, ostensibly to look up at the beautiful, cloud-laden San Cristóbal sky, Mrs. Gómez asked her next question.

"So, what brings you to our little town, Doña Elena? I mean, since you're a *capitalina* and all."

Elena swallowed and tried to remember the exact wording of her much rehearsed answer.

"My husband works for the Department of Public Works. They

transferred him here from the capital. A shortage of workers in Totonicapán, apparently."

"How unlucky for him. I mean, you're both so far away from your homes. Your families."

Elena thought she detected a sarcastic smirk on Mrs. Gómez's face. "No. Not at all. We wanted to get away from the city. Like you say, the sky is never this clear and bright in the city."

"I see. But to be transferred from the capital to such a small town. How is it possible? A demotion, no?"

"Señora Gómez, I think you have a customer waiting. See?" Elena pointed at a boy standing in the bodega doorway, a bill and coins in his hand.

"What does *he* want?" Mrs. Gómez said with a frown.

"*Buenas tardes*, Señora Gómez."

"*Buenas tardes.*"

* * *

It was Elena's prerogative as a middle-class woman to have someone come and help with the cleaning and the chores. For the first time in her life she had a servant, María de la Soledad, Marisol for short. She was a scrawny woman, only twenty-four years old but already the mother of four daughters.

"No sons yet, *señora*, but we're still trying. My *viejo* will keep getting me pregnant until I give him at least one son." Elena wondered how Marisol could be so thin after having four children, the youngest eight months, but thought it would be impertinent to ask.

Marisol was a walking encyclopedia of folk wisdom about pregnancy.

"Don't cry while you're expecting, or your baby will carry sadness for the rest of his life."

"*Caldo de pollo* makes the baby strong, but if you have too much your baby will cry at night because of the onions in the soup."

With no one else to talk to, Elena came to rely on Marisol's advice and experience. "Marisol, I want to ask you about something," she said one day as the servant scrubbed clothes in the washroom behind the kitchen, slapping wet fabric against a stone basin. "I'm having strange cravings. I'm craving ice. All I want is ice in my mouth. I could eat a bucket of ice. What do you suppose it means? Is it some sort of sign? Does it mean my baby will be hard and cold?"

Marisol thought for a few seconds, then looked up from the wet clothes.

"I think it means you're hot, *señora*. Don't go out in the sun so much."

In the morning Elena and Marisol washed clothes in the stone basin and hung them on lines stretched across the small sunlit square of the inner courtyard. In the afternoon, after cooking lunch and putting dinner on the stove, after Marisol swept out the house, they would move to the cool air of the bedroom to fold the laundry. The routine repeated itself day after day. Cooking, cleaning, washing, folding. Marisol left at four and Antonio arrived home an hour later. A repetition of chores, interrupted by time for reading and letter writing.

On the day her pregnancy entered its sixth month, Elena was in the bedroom with Marisol when she heard a noise filtering in through the shuttered windows, a sandpaper sound. Feet shuffling on the cobblestone street outside. She put down the sheet she was folding and opened the shutters. Sunlight flooded the room, dust dancing in the bright beam. Leaning on the windowsill, Elena looked out and saw a barefoot boy with straight jet black hair and a cowlick. His face was blank and numb, a look of exhausted resignation. He and another boy carried two long poles on their shoulders, attached to a small table that held a pine coffin painted canary yellow and barely two feet long. They were *campesinos*, and their clothes were dusty and threadbare, once-bright colors muted by wear. The procession reached the patch of street in front of the window, and the tiny coffin floated in gentle bounces across Elena's field of vision.

"My God," she whispered.

"What is it, *señora*?" Marisol asked anxiously behind her, looking up from a stack of towels.

"It's a funeral," Elena answered. "For a baby."

Marisol glanced out the window. "That is sad," she said with only a trace of sentiment, picking up another towel. As an afterthought, she added, "Those babies die so easily."

Across the street, Mrs. Gómez stepped onto the narrow sidewalk in front of her store to watch the procession and bless herself, an almost perfunctory gesture, the casual up and down and across of the arm and forefinger, like brushstrokes of holy paint on the face and shoulders.

"Which babies are those?" Elena asked. "The ones that die so easily."

"The ones from that neighborhood, *señora*. Sometimes they bury three or four in one month."

"In one month?"

"Yes."

"Why so many?"

Marisol looked perplexed. No one, it seemed, had thought to ask her that question before. "The air is bad in that neighborhood," she said finally. "It makes the babies sick."

"What neighborhood is that?"

"Colonia La Joya. That's where those people are from. See how dirty they are? It's a *limonada*, a slum they built in the ravine by the old bridge." Seeing Elena's distress and confusion, Marisol added with mild exasperation, as if the explanation were too obvious to bother with, "The babies get diarrhea. It's because they're poor. Even poorer than I am."

Elena turned back to the window and watched the slow procession reach the Parque Central a block away, then disappear down a side street. There were about twenty people in the group—just one adult man, the rest women with flower-print shawls covering their heads, and shoeless children with the soles of their feet calloused lime white. Aquamarine paper streamers attached to the bier fluttered in the breeze.

Elena thought it was both the saddest and most beautiful thing she had seen so far in her new home.

* * *

The newspapers from Guatemala City gathered in a stack by the window. Elena seldom opened them, and when she did, she rushed through the pages as if her haste might shield her from the picture of a corpse or the obituary photograph of a friend or acquaintance. She was seven months pregnant, indisposed, in no condition to hold banners or paint slogans on walls or run from tear gas canisters. For the moment she would simply try to pass the time, watching the street vendors of San Cristóbal through her window and writing long letters to her sister.

Querida Hermana: I am so bored. You would not believe the slowness of this place. The clocks move like turtles in San Cristóbal.

Her mother-in-law had told her not to write home, but she defied orders and wrote regularly to family and friends in Guatemala City. The letters to her sister she sent via a second cousin who surreptitiously hand-delivered them because their father destroyed the letters he found in the mailbox. She got only one response for every half-dozen letters she sent, but she kept writing because she was afraid she would be lost to San Cristóbal forever if she stopped. Already she wondered if her speech was slowing, if there was a new lilt to her Spanish. You could hear the Indian influence in the Spanish here, though no *ladino* would admit such a thing.

The letters were a promise to herself that she would return home.

Boredom and depression are frequent dance partners, I have discovered. The trick, little sister, is to keep busy. If there were a good music teacher here, I would take piano lessons. If there were a place to dance, I would take dance lessons. Instead, I read. Twenty novels in six months. I have read enough Borges and Cortázar to write a doctoral thesis on Argentine literature. Antonio is very excited about this new hobby of mine, and we fill the evenings with long literary conversations. I have taken up cooking also, a feminine art I have too long neglected.

Her husband patiently suffered her experiments with black beans, vegetables, and chicken. Every two weeks or so they took the bus to Quetzaltenango, the nearest city of any consequence, to go shopping and sit in the cafes and remember the life they had before. Antonio and Elena sat sipping coffee and tea on the colonial balcony of the Pensión Bonifaz, looking out across a plaza at a municipal building with a façade of Greek columns.

Whenever Antonio talked about his job, he sounded defeated. The Department of Public Works provided little in the way of excitement or interest. With each passing day he seemed lonelier, further adrift. "All I do is sit around and listen to the secretaries. They're always asking me to get the fan fixed. Today the big event was the arrival of our yearly supply of carbon paper. Can you imagine? Carbon paper! This is what I've been reduced to." Elena found this hysterically funny and couldn't stop laughing, until the laughter finally infected Antonio and he began to lose his sad face. She took his hands and looked into his eyes and told him they both needed to be strong now. They would be partners in seclusion, each strong for the other.

She decided to like being a wife. She would settle into this role. There was time to read, and as soon as the baby was born she would start to explore San Cristóbal.

This was what it meant to be a woman. You faced the difficulties, accepted them, and then adjusted. She would have new dreams, new plans. Perhaps they could move to Mexico. Save enough money to move to Mexico or the United States. A place where they could be safe and their daughter, or son, could be educated. A place where you could speak your mind and there were no soldiers on the street.

I will wait and see what I do next, little sister, after the child is born. One thing is certain: I will not be one of these women who stay at home all day with the baby. I am determined to enter the world.

* * *

Eight months pregnant, she was a slave to the calendar. The event would happen very soon, but not soon enough for Elena. Headaches one day, backaches the next, dizziness in between.

She was sitting in her chair by the open window with the sun at her back. A gentle draft blew through the dark rooms of her house, a cool antidote to the oppressive midday heat. There was nothing to do but wait and follow the signs from her body, the kicking inside her.

With a book in her lap she slipped into sleep. She dreamed that she was reading *El Gráfico*, leafing through it in search of the names of her friends and the poets Antonio knew. But she found only blank pages. Someone had stolen all the photographs and articles from the newspaper. She ran out of the house in her bare feet, stubbing her toes on the cobblestones, looking for Antonio because she was scared and needed to tell someone all the articles were missing.

A woman cried out in the distance. Elena sat up, startled. Was the cry part of her dream? The book that had been in her lap was on the floor, the bookmark still in place. Now, with her eyes open, she heard the cry again. With some difficulty Elena rose from her chair and moved to the window.

There was another funeral procession, this one with just three people. At the front was a man in a straw hat and soiled work pants, a machete tied around his waist. He was carrying a small casket on his shoulder. Behind him came a woman and a little boy. The woman had a tissue to her face and a shawl covering her head. It was her crying that had jolted Elena awake. The man's cheek rubbed against the rough, unpainted surface of the tiny pine box, just big enough to hold a newborn child. The woman and her son held hands, eyes fixed to the cobblestone street, but the father showed the town and its inhabitants a proud Mayan stare. Cold anger holding off grief. Elena caught his glance, dark brown eyes, penetrating and embittered. He looked straight at her as he walked by with the casket on his shoulder.

This man meant to tell her something with his eyes, some truth, some message, words transmitted in silence.

Why is he looking at me with such hatred? He doesn't know me. The pine box floated past.

And then the message of his eyes seemed painfully clear. *My child has died. Yours will live.*

She stepped away from the window and reached for her belly, surprised that this man, the father of the dead child, had seen and sensed her eight-month roundness. She saw herself as she must look to him: a bourgeois housewife, clean and well fed, a woman who would deliver her baby in an antiseptic hospital far from the slum dwellers and their virulent shacks.

"It's not my fault," she whispered to herself.

In less than a minute the small funeral procession disappeared through the plaza to a side street that led to the old whitewashed church and cemetery on the other side of town. Short of breath, Elena sat down on the edge of her bed.

After her baby was born, she would go to this place where the children were dying, Colonia La Joya. She had been in San Cristóbal for eight months and had yet to see this slum on the outskirts of town. She had been locked up in this house too long, afraid of her own shadow. As soon as her baby was born and she was strong enough, she would visit this place, this *limonada*.

She wanted to see its streets and hovels, its killing air, with her own eyes.

9
Microbes

At the point where the cobblestones ended and the dirt streets began, Elena paused. She was headed for the poorest corner of this poor town, a place "decent people" talked about with bated breath, warning her about muggers and rapists and child pickpockets who would free her of her last centavo. People in Guatemala City spoke the same way about the neighborhood where she was born and raised. Elena pressed ahead. She had put off this day for too long. Carlos was six months old now, at home with Marisol while Elena undertook her exploratory expedition to Colonia La Joya, the place where so many babies were dying. La Joya, it was called, absurdly. The Jewel. La Joya would bother her until she finally saw it.

Following the water-carved grooves that coiled through the dirt, Elena walked down an unpaved street that was littered with boulders. Goats and starving dogs ambled by, little more than walking rib cages. Burning trash stacked into small pyramids sent a sticky, sweet smoke into the air. The houses here were made of adobe bricks plastered over and painted white, yellow, and sky blue, the earthen flesh underneath showing where the plaster had cracked and flaked away. A woman sat in the doorway of one of the houses, her head snapping back gently as a young girl ran a brush through her hair in long, luxuriant strokes.

At the bottom of the hill, where the street ended, Elena reached a narrow path that led into a thicket of waist-high brush. Following the directions Marisol had reluctantly given her, she took the path and found herself walking into a ravine above a thin, rocky river, not much more than a stream. At a great distance she saw two girls standing knee-deep in the river, filling plastic basins. They raised the containers to their heads to carry them in the Mayan style, water splashing over the edges and soaking their necks and backs. *I must be close.*

An Indian woman passed in the opposite direction, carrying an empty basket against her side, not bothering to look up. Branches and prickly leaves brushed against Elena's pants. She congratulated herself for deciding to wear tennis shoes instead of sandals.

The brush grew higher, the path narrower. For a moment she wavered again, thinking she might be lost. She didn't see any houses or shacks. What sort of people could live on the steep slopes of this ravine, among all these thorns and boulders? Then the path turned, climbing around a jutting shoulder in the side of the ravine. Elena stopped. A city of corrugated tin, plastic, and paper appeared before her, a jumble of square shacks attached somehow to a lush, verdant slope, patchwork structures that seemed about to slide down the hill like rickety sleds. Here and there, a wall of cinderblock. Chicken coops, laundry lines, pigs wading in the river. A rooster's cry. She started to count the shacks but lost track at fifty. The settlement rose in layers, terraces carved into the hillside. Perhaps five hundred, one thousand people lived here.

Elena took a deep breath.

*   *   *

He could not understand this sudden voyeuristic impulse that took the mother of an infant son searching for slums in the ravine.

"You're going to get hurt," Antonio said. "Think about it, a woman alone in the *barranco*. Anything could happen."

"It's not as dangerous as you think."

"You're acting very strange, going off alone like that."

Antonio was slumped in a reupholstered lounge chair, one of three pieces of furniture in what they called their living room. He frowned at her angrily, an expression that had become familiar lately: this was not the Antonio she married, the bookish man of tender smiles.

"I'm tired of being locked up," Elena said. "I'm tired of being afraid."

"You're not happy here? You're not happy with me?"

She was surprised by his infantile tone, the smallness of him suddenly.

"No, *amor*, it's not that."

"Then why do you go wandering? I have to hear about it from the people at work. People talk, Elena. It's a small town, and you're making a spectacle of yourself. The city lady who likes to walk in the ravine."

They had been going around in circles like this every day, arguing about any subject at hand. Today, her walks to La Joya. Yesterday, the maid, Carlos, the neighbors, the books she was reading. Anything she did might irritate him. Elena told herself that they were both exhausted, drained by too many sleepless nights and the ritual screams of a baby who still demanded to be fed at three in the morning after six months.

Every afternoon Antonio came home from work and sulked about his job, about San Cristóbal and the hopelessness of their situation. "We're stuck here. We're stuck in this backwater for God knows how long. I hate this. I don't deserve this."

No amount of kisses and hugs could tease back his smile. It was as if he were the one suffering from postpartum depression. "It is not uncommon," one of her pregnancy books said, "for the new mother to experience an inexplicable sadness. These feelings might make it difficult for the new mother to eat, sleep, make love, or work." A perfect description of her husband's current condition.

But she had noticed this about him before, detecting the truth even as she denied it to herself. When situations became tense, when events turned difficult, he tended to slip into this *melancolía*. It had happened when she first told him, fifteen months ago, that she was pregnant, and when they had to break the news to his mother. A fog descended over him. She had entered into this marriage imagining her husband would be a fortress of intelligence, stone walls of compassion and courage. But it turned out there were flaws in his construction; he was rigged together, like those temporary bridges on the bombed-out roads.

That night Elena lay awake beside Antonio and listened to the clock, waiting for the baby's screams to begin in the next room. Tossing and turning. Tick. Tick. Tick. Five hours of this. Time was stillness, a moonless night, the bedroom walls disappearing into infinite darkness.

"*Amor*, are you awake?" Elena asked.

Antonio moaned in assent, rolling over and setting off a chorus of creaking bed springs.

"I have an idea." It was something she had been nurturing for weeks, waiting for the appropriate moment to share it with him. "Maybe we could go to Los Angeles. I have a cousin who lives there. We could stay with her until we got settled. We could go to California."

Antonio did not answer. The ticking of the clock filled the room. It was past three and the baby hadn't started crying yet.

"With what?" he said finally. "It takes a lot of money to get that far."

"I think we've saved enough. Enough to get there, at least, and then you could get a job."

"A job doing what?"

"Anything. I could work too."

Another pause. He was mulling it over.

"I won't cross like an illegal and then go to work washing dishes," he said sourly. "And I won't have my wife clean houses. That's what our people do when they go over there. Even educated people. They wash dishes. They take care of other people's babies. It's not dignified."

Elena said nothing more. It was clear they would not be leaving San Cristóbal anytime soon. She had to resign herself to that. Her husband wasn't up to it, not now, maybe not for a while. There was no use arguing with a stone. She drifted off to sleep. For once the baby was quiet all night.

When Antonio came home the next day, he raised little Carlos in the air, his torments dissolving in the light of his son's infant smile. These first moments with Carlos were always his best, before the bitterness settled in. He smiled in imitation of the baby, whose toothless mouth opened in a happy circle while he beat the air with his fists like a tiny drummer.

Antonio was a very good father. A better father than she was a mother, Elena thought. He tickled his son and spun him around and played airplane, producing a buzzing sound with his lips that made the baby cackle. On weekends he spent hours on a blanket spread out in the courtyard, trying to interest Carlitos in blocks, balls, plastic baby books.

When Antonio put the baby down, Elena reached up to kiss her husband. A peace offering, like a hand stretched out across the table. He wrapped his arms around her, and they held each other in a long embrace, warm and forgiving. He needed her. She would not go back to La Joya. What was she looking for anyway? What could she hope to accomplish? Elena had removed herself from political concerns for more than a year now. Unopened newspapers from the capital no longer filled her living room because she no longer bothered to buy them. In the stillness of her home she could only imagine the hum and tumult of dissent, the masses on the streets, the screaming letters of their banners and signs. She was the mother of a small baby now, wedded to this house and its window and the rocking chair where she sat for hours to read and sleep.

* * *

For months it was her daily recreation, putting the baby in his stroller for the three-block walk to the Parque Central, where she sat on one of the cast-iron benches by the old kiosk and read a few pages from her current book while Carlitos slept in his blue jumpsuit pajamas, sheltered from the sun by the little awning on the stroller. Later he began to crawl on the patches of grass and then on the steps of the kiosk, a brick octagon with a high, pitched roof of red tile, built, she imagined, for brass bands and marimbas. Once Carlitos had mastered the art of walking, she stopped bringing her book along.

Elena sat on the bench and endured the unfailing lascivious stares of the shoeshine men and newspaper vendors who made the park their home. Then she walked back. Sometimes she did this twice a day, but rarely more, since each trip meant risking an encounter with Mrs. Gómez, who ran across the street to greet her whenever she passed by.

"Elena, how are you? Did you have a nice walk? Oh, let me see the baby."

The secret to dealing with Mrs. Gómez, Elena had learned, was to engage her in gossip about everyone else in town. Thus distracted,

Mrs. Gómez began to forget about Elena's mysterious presence in San Cristóbal, instead spinning sordid narratives about a variety of town personalities. Her cast of sullied and tragic characters included old maids, corrupt public officials, unfaithful husbands, and victims of vehicular accidents. Her favorite topic, however, was the town priest, a Belgian named Van der Est.

"Have you ever noticed," Mrs. Gómez asked in melodramatic tones one lazy afternoon, "how empty the church is? Even on Sunday?"

Elena had, in fact, noticed. "Why, yes. No one seems to go there," she said, mildly intrigued.

"Well, it's not by accident. After all, this is a Catholic country. We're all God-fearing people, right? It's not natural for the church to be empty. That sadistic priest, he's the reason. Because of what he did to our sacred *Virgen.*"

It seemed that Father Van der Est had tangled with the parish Ladies' Committee, of which Mrs. Gómez was a member. The Ladies' Committee wanted to make improvements to the shrine of the Virgin Mary. The statue of the Virgin was more than a hundred years old, and it was turning black from the smoke of so many votive candles. Could the priest help them raise money to clean the statue? Much to their surprise, the Belgian responded with insults. He said he was sick and tired of all this adoration for the Virgin. He said they put the Virgin before the Holy Father. He said they were a women's cult and called them pagans.

"He threw the Virgin down the front steps!" Mrs. Gómez cried. "That's where we found her, at the foot of the stairs. All scratched but nothing broken, thanks be to God. It was a miracle, of course. She was completely unharmed." Mrs. Gómez clasped her hands together piously, then crossed herself.

"He's an evil man, this priest. We've written to Guatemala City, to Rome. We've told them all about his transgressions. But nothing. What do they care in the capital about some little town? All they care is that this priest doesn't cause any trouble with politics. Not like the last priest we had, God rest his soul. He was a Communist, frankly. So the church gave us this Belgian. He's quiet. You know that saying: 'In a closed mouth, no flies enter.' Well, that's all they care about. Keeping out the flies."

Later that afternoon Elena saw the priest walking past her window, face to the cobblestones, lost in a daydream.

"*Buenos días, padre,*" she called, wishing almost immediately that she hadn't. A Sunday school reflex: you see a priest, you say hello.

He looked up at her with uncertain gray eyes, the corners of his mouth raised in something between a sneer and a smile, and walked on.

Elena brought Carlos's crib into her bedroom, as she sometimes did when she sat by the window passing the midday hours. She looked at her son, his sleep punctuated by jerky movements of his arms and feet. There was something hypnotic about watching him sleep, and she began to feel drowsy herself. Her mind drifted. Did babies dream? Were there enough clean diapers in the dresser? This would be Marisol's first task tomorrow. Suddenly a sound, faint and high-pitched, coming from outside. Elena turned an ear toward the shuttered window. She thought she heard the ringing of tiny bells. People brought instruments to the funeral processions, tambourines, a stick and a can to drum on, whatever they could find.

She opened the shutters but saw nothing.

Good. There were no coffins passing her window today. She hadn't seen one for a long time now. It was not right to think about the funerals of infants, not good for a young mother. *Purge these thoughts.*

Carlos was alive and strong, big for his age, his father's double, with Antonio's heavy Spaniard eyebrows. There were folds of skin at his wrists and ankles. Was he overweight? Was she feeding him too much? There was no one around, no one she trusted to advise her on these matters. They bought his crib in Quetzaltenango. Handmade, from pine. A whole section of the market with handmade cribs, chairs and tables too. They bought the crib for a song.

Elena took in the green scent of the wood, a freshness. There were pine forests in the hills here, at the higher elevations. Carlitos's crib filled the room with the scent of a pine forest after a rainstorm. It rained once a day in San Cristóbal, usually for an hour in the afternoon. And then the burst of sunlight that baked the cobblestones and turned the puddles into a fine vapor, water dancing skyward, returning to the clouds for the next rain.

What happened to the river in the ravine when it rained? Did it flood? Did the people of La Joya move to higher ground? Two girls filling basins by the river, drinking muddy water after the rain. The coffins were made of pine too. Life's equations.

The man in the funeral procession, the man with the straw hat, a resident of the shantytown. *My child lives, his child dies.*

* * *

There were no libraries or bookstores in San Cristóbal, so she had to go to Quetzaltenango. While Antonio pushed the stroller around the central square during one of their weekend visits, she photocopied articles from books and pamphlets on public health and sanitation. The most recent text she found was a slim ten-year-old manual from the United Nations. Marisol had said the babies were dying of diarrhea, and so had Father Van der Est when she finally succeeded in drawing him into a conversation one afternoon. But why so many in one place? She suspected the answer to the riddle was probably quite simple.

Early the next morning, before the baby was awake, she stacked all the literature on the kitchen table and began to read, taking notes on a yellow pad. It felt good to tackle an intellectual problem again, to search through the indexes and scan the footnotes.

Before Pasteur's discovery, and subsequent reforms, diarrhea was a leading cause of death among infants. . . . Both bacillary and amoebic dysentery are spread by fecal contamination of food and water. . . . A disease characterized by the frequent passage of small, watery stools, usually with blood and mucus, prevalent in unhygienic areas of the tropics . . .

Carlos woke up just before Antonio left for work. She interrupted her reading to serve them both breakfast. As soon as Antonio was out the door and Carlos finished eating, she would get back to her research. *Eat, my baby, eat. Here, another spoonful from this orange jar. Swallow, swallow. Almost done now.*

"Elena." Antonio's voice was sharp. "He hasn't even swallowed yet and you're giving him more. If you keep feeding him like that he's going to get fat. Slow down."

Carlitos was in his high chair, bib, chin, cheeks, and nose painted with ocher baby food. Of course Antonio was right, she realized this immediately. She had been distracted, she wasn't thinking. She froze with a spoonful of apricot puree poised in the air. Antonio's presence in the kitchen was making her nervous. He was reading the newspaper while she fed the baby. Always reading. He read instead of talking. He got to read while she fed the baby. There was a lingering tension between them, a smoldering resentment carried over from one day to the next. She shoveled another spoonful of food into her son's mouth.

"Well, at least I feed him," she found herself saying, the words a reflex, like a boxer raising his arms. "He wouldn't eat at all if it were up to you."

He rolled his eyes, a familiar response. Why did their arguments always fall into the same pattern? Whey did they sound like children?

"Please, not that again," he said.

"You never help. You never lift a finger. All you do is criticize and complain."

"I put food on the table. I work. I bring in money."

"Your mother's money, you mean."

A second of stunned silence. *I can't believe I said such a thing, but I've wanted to say that for a long time.*

Antonio slammed his newspaper on the table and stood up.

"We were too young to get married," he said, his face contorted. "To have children. You know it's true. This is madness."

Elena dropped the spoon, and apricot puree splattered violently on the tile floor. All right, he could raise his baby by himself for all she cared. Enough. She wanted to go home.

She pushed past Antonio, ran to the front door, and flung it open. There was San Cristóbal and its cobblestone streets, Mrs. Gómez's store facing her, rows of identical tile-roofed buildings to the right and left, the corn-covered hills beyond.

Love. If revolutionaries were always motivated by feelings of love, then what to make of her feelings for her husband and child? There seemed to be no escaping them, no escaping their demands of her, their desire to be fed, clothed, washed, humored.

Elena looked down the street at a gallery of windows, rows of closed shutters like so many wooden eyelids.

There was no place to run.

*　*　*

They walked carefully down the narrow path that went to the shanty-town of La Joya. Three-quarters of the way there, they turned left through a thicket of thorny bushes, toward the river. Elena held Antonio's hand, leading the way. They reached the riverbank and followed it upstream, climbing over smooth rocks and boulders. Elena had a theory about what was killing the babies in La Joya.

Since their last argument, since he had said those cruel words, Antonio had been on his best behavior. The last few days had been a series of acts of contrition: meals he cooked, a flurry of kisses, a bouquet of roses that appeared one afternoon on the kitchen table. They even made love again, for the first time in months. Coming along with her on this walk was part of his penance.

They continued upstream, holding hands when they could, inspecting the river. It was muddy but seemed clean enough, though Elena wasn't sure what a poisoned river would look like. Would she be able to see the germs, the source of the infection, the microscopic killers? She took off her shoes, rolled up her jeans, and waded in. The water wasn't very cold. A plastic milk container floated by, followed by a cellophane wrapper. When she was knee-deep her toes disappeared, lost in the silt caused by the rains.

Antonio helped her back onto the bank and smiled softly. He was trying very hard to be diplomatic.

"It's nice down here," he said. "There's a nice breeze. We could have a picnic one day."

"Let's just walk a little more," Elena said.

They followed the river around a long bend curving to the west at the northern edge of San Cristóbal. High above the ravine, a hundred yards or so upstream, two vultures circled, a slow, spiraling descent. Standing on a tall river boulder, Elena looked up to the edge of the ravine and saw the tops of houses, little concrete boxes, the fringes of the town. On the opposite bank the scrub-covered slope had given way to cultivated fields of corn. Nothing here suggested illness or disease.

"Let's go home," she said.

"Are you sure? We can keep walking if you want."

"No. There's nothing here. I'm sorry I made you come."

They turned back, Elena unable to hide her disappointment. Her little expedition was nothing but intellectual pride, middle-class arrogance. *I thought I could solve their problems all by myself. I thought I was a biologist, an expert in public health.*

A minute or so later Antonio tugged at her arm. "Do you smell that?"

Elena stopped, taking in the ravine air. "No, I don't smell anything."

Then the wind shifted and the odor hit her, putrid and foul. The smell of rotting milk, a smell like a finger reaching into the back of your throat. Elena coughed.

"It's awful. Like a garbage dump."

Antonio produced a handkerchief, and Elena held it to her nose. "Let's find out where it's coming from," she said.

The noxious breeze led away from the river, into the dark tangle of bushes and branches. They found themselves climbing up the slope of the ravine again, wading through the prickly underbrush, until Elena finally pulled back the last branch and they stepped into a wide clearing.

Before them was an entire hillside covered with trash, a panorama of filth. Plastic bags, toilet paper, rotting vegetables, animal bones. A fetid organic brew baking in the midday sun. A few dogs roamed the blighted landscape sniffing at the ground, snouts bouncing from spot to spot.

"Oh my God," Antonio said. "It *is* the city dump."

"Let's go to the top. I want to see how big it is."

They worked their way up the slope, struggling to keep their footing on the slippery ground. The sprawling pile of garbage oozed down the hillside like a sluggish river, boxes and wood scraps floating on the surface. At its center the pile seemed to be many feet thick. The earth was a strange, sickly gray, a color that seemed to match the smell of the air. Everything dissolved into that same lifeless gray. Yellow lemon rinds, green papaya skins, white eggshells, all pressed down by the weight of more and more garbage until they became an ashen slime.

The man who picks up my trash probably brings it here. The leftovers of a thousand meals filled this place every day. People came here to dump the buckets of excrement-soiled paper they kept next to their toilets to avoid clogging their pipes. All this rotting food and shit was becoming a permanent part of the landscape, altering the topography of the slope, killing off the vegetation.

Halfway to the top, Elena stepped on something soft and sprawled sideways, landing on her shoulder with a wet swack.

"Are you okay?" Antonio asked. "Did you hurt yourself?"

Elena looked up, her nose wrinkled in disgust, and saw that the corners of Antonio's lips were raised in a faint smile.

"Go ahead and laugh. I must look pretty funny here, huh? All covered with God knows what."

"No, love of my life. Not at all."

She took his outstretched hand and rose to her feet, blue jeans and blouse moist with gray slime.

"We found it," she said, as much to herself as to Antonio. "We found what's killing the babies. All this trash is contaminating the river. It's so obvious."

At the top of the dump they reached a lonely dirt street with a few ramshackle houses. Elena recognized this place. Marisol lived just a few blocks away. From here they could walk to their house on the other side of town.

A narrow ditch ran along the side of the road. Looking down, Elena saw a muddy liquid buzzing with flies. There was a pungent smell of urine. Feces floated in the yellowish brown creek. Sewage. She tracked the liquid's path. The ditch drained into the garbage dump and thence into the river below. This was truly unbelievable. The residents of this neighborhood ran a septic pipe right into this ditch.

"There's absolutely no sanitation here," Elena said in a daze of revulsion. "All of this sewage is draining straight into the river. This is like the nineteenth century, things I read about in books, conditions that belong to history. And I'm seeing it right here. *No lo puedo creer.* We've got to do something about this, Antonio. We have to stop it. This sewage is killing the people downstream. It's killing the babies."

Antonio bit his lip. "This isn't our home," he said after a long pause. "We're outsiders here."

"I will do what I have to do."

"Elena, please, don't do anything rash. Don't do anything without talking to me first."

As they walked home, a cloud bank passed before the sun, casting the town in gray, erasing shadows from the streets. Soon the afternoon rains began, falling in thick sheets from the sky, the hyperbole of the heavens. Elena looked up gratefully as the clouds drenched her in water and washed the stains from her clothes.

* * *

Antonio's anger arrived in the kitchen before he did, in the form of a violent bang of the front door. Standing by a pot of boiling beans, the smell of onions heavy in the air, Elena wondered what humiliation he had suffered at work, what new resentment he carried, what accusation or complaint.

She listened to his approaching footsteps and turned to face him, wearing her apron like armor. *"Buenas tardes,"* she said.

"The mayor called me into his office today. Two years I've been here and I never met the man, and today he wants to talk to me."

"*¿De veras?* About what?"

"About you, of course. What else?"

Antonio put his briefcase on the table and took off his glasses, pinching the bridge of his nose. He was angry, yes, but there was something else. Something was wrong, there was a graveness about him, a sense of fear. He put his glasses back on again, very deliberately. His hands were balled into fists. "You know, Elena," he said slowly, "I asked you to tell me before you did anything."

Momentarily surprised, Elena composed herself. They must have received her letter. Word of what she had written to the president of the departmental government in Totonicapán must have filtered down the official chain of command.

"I did what I needed to do."

"They've been following you, Elena. That's what the mayor told me. They know where you go, what you do, who you talk to."

Intimidation. They are trying to intimidate my husband. This is an old trick.

"He's lying to you," Elena said. "He's bluffing. He said that to scare you."

"They have pictures," Antonio said quickly. "Pictures of you walking to La Joya. The mayor said you've been talking to some people who live there. And he said something about other letters, correspondence to Guatemala City that has been intercepted. And then—and this was very, very strange to me—he said you're 'gathering intelligence.' About the war."

She grabbed at a chair and sat down, feeling vaguely faint.

"And do you know what else he said? Do you know, Elena?" The hostility was definitely there now, a tone of voice that was all too familiar. "He said, 'Control your wife. Control her or both of you will be in grave danger.' 'Man to man' he told me this. And then he said they know everything about us. They know where we come from and what we were mixed up in at the university. He looked at me like I was some sort of devil. As if I were a guerrilla or a terrorist or something." He fiddled with his glasses again.

"All of a sudden they know everything about our past, and now they're wondering why we're here," he continued. "Thanks to your letter, they put it all together."

The pot boiled loudly. The smell of beans and onions filled the kitchen.

"Well? Aren't you going to say anything?"

Her black beans were getting better every day.

"I'm afraid," she said.

The Wrestlers' Brigade

His new chevrons pointed skyward, gleaming yellow birds in flight against the drab camouflage forest of his uniform. He had been promoted to sergeant because he didn't flinch or hesitate when given a difficult assignment. They had swept through Huehuetenango and San Marcos and El Quiché and so many other places that he was already beginning to forget the names. He had become adept at the use of knives, guns, and grenades, and had learned new uses for his machete. And he had started to carry a cigarette lighter as a regular piece of equipment, even though he didn't smoke.

Longoria had turned many things to ash with his lighter, walls and roofs, schools and churches dissolving into the wind, taking up residence in the clouds. When there were bodies to be burned, kerosene and gasoline helped, although corpses never seemed to burn all the way. Instead they became black stones, brittle and flaky, stone people.

Although he had rarely encountered an armed enemy and his life was seldom in danger, he was proud of having survived so much war and destruction. It was exhilarating to find yourself still walking and breathing when you left a village that would soon disappear into the smoky sky. There was a sense of being fully alive, a deeper appreciation for the simpler pleasures, like drinking a beer or listening to the radio when he got back to the base.

When he put on his sergeant's uniform for the first time, Longoria lingered for a moment in front of a tall mirror in the barracks, next to the showers. His pants were tucked into his boots, the laces crisscrossing upward. The red beret on his head was emblazoned with a black jaguar patch. Longoria held up his arm and compared his tattoo with the patch. Then a glance at the chevrons again, the structure of the army in these yellow bars, hierarchies and responsibilities, layers of lieutenants, captains, majors, and colonels all stacked on top of each other. The chevrons told everyone where Longoria fit in.

No sooner had he put them on than he was forced to take them off.

A few days after his promotion, Captain Elías assigned him to G-2, military intelligence, to carry out some special "*acciones.*" For reasons that were officially unexplained but obvious nonetheless, these operations had to have a civilian veneer. The enemies of the government had to disappear in a fashion that would allow the army to say it wasn't responsible. Longoria was to wear civilian clothes. This struck him as somewhat ludicrous: with his cropped hair and muscular frame and the tattoo on his arm, he looked like a soldier no matter what he wore.

To go without his uniform made him feel tainted and dirty, like a thief. There was no pride in trying to hide what you were doing, as if it were something to be ashamed of. To make matters worse, much worse, he was ordered to work with a group of civilians, the hired guns of a certain businessman in the capital. The businessman was supposedly very rich and had financed his own private army, the Lorenzo Amaya Anti-Communist Brigade. But the businessman was not all that rich, apparently, since the men he hired for his "army" were unkempt thugs from the *reformatorio* who did not know the pleasure of shampoo or freshly laundered clothes. They were not warriors in any sense of the word.

Although no one had come out and said so directly, the reason for his assignment to this group of civilians was clear: to bring order to their actions. They were without training or any idea of tactics, stumbling through their tasks like clumsy wrestlers. He knew them by the nicknames they had picked up during their long careers as street urchins and petty thieves: Mugre, Buitre, Sapo, and Mosca. These four men constituted the entire Lorenzo Amaya Anti-Communist Brigade. They had many bad habits, like smoking and spitting on the sidewalk.

Everything had gone wrong during Longoria's first action with the brigade, the attempted abduction of a famous trade unionist in a working-class neighborhood of the capital. Longoria drove to the subversive's home in a Jeep with tinted windows, accompanied by Mugre and Sapo. Mugre, an ex-convict with wide gaps between his rotting teeth, sat in the front seat with a submachine gun across his lap. It seemed he had never held such a weapon before, because he allowed his finger to drift over the trigger and played with the safety, his hands confused by so many latches and springs. He lifted the gun, the barrel's line of fire passing across Longoria's torso.

"*¡Pendejo!*" Longoria snapped. "Don't point that at me. Keep the barrel away."

When they arrived at the subversive's address, Longoria jumped out of the Jeep with jaguar efficiency and ran toward the house under the klieg-light sun of the hot afternoon. He had not taken three steps when he heard gunfire, a patter of shots from Mugre's automatic weapon. On the sidewalk lay a septuagenarian priest and a street vendor, the two men in identical poses, hands over their bellies, bleeding profusely. Bystanders, both of them. Like the other ex-cons in the brigade, Mugre had no discipline of fire. Bang-bang at the slightest provocation.

Longoria rushed to the subversive's front door and kicked it in, his worst fears soon confirmed. The gunfire had alerted their target to the brigade's arrival, allowing him to escape out a back window.

"*¡Idiota!*" Longoria yelled when he returned to the sidewalk, where Mugre was rubbing his chin and watching his victims bleed into the pavement. "Why?"

"They were staring at me, *sargento*. They were looking at me."

Weeks later Longoria would learn that the trade unionist had reached Mexico City, where he gave regular press conferences defaming Guatemala and denouncing violations of human rights. Longoria winced every time he saw the man's name in the paper.

Mostly the brigade operated during the day and took people out of their homes. "In broad daylight," as the expression went. They stopped cars on the open highway and dragged drivers from behind the wheel. Sometimes the victims resisted, sometimes they didn't. The Lorenzo Amayas liked it when their captives fought back, grabbing onto the door of the Jeep, trying against hope to get away. Once, they abducted a couple from their wedding reception, women in fine dresses and men in tuxedos running out the doors, falling over chairs. The thing wasn't just to take the people but to make a show of it. It was street theater, a tug-of-war on the avenues and boulevards, in the parking lots and plazas. Longoria remembered his training in psychological operations and knew that the general principle of disorder and violence applied here. The point was to allow the neighbors, friends, and relatives to see, so that they would tell others. Accounts of the brigade's brazenness would grow and spread like a contagion. All Guatemala would come to know that the chaos of the Lorenzo Amaya Brigade, the cruelty of common criminals, would fall upon them like a hammer if they even thought about doing anything subversive.

Longoria would have enjoyed this work more if they permitted him to wear his uniform. He didn't see why he couldn't wear his chevrons. Politicians and generals made these decisions without thinking about the impact on morale. What sort of message was that to send to the fighting men? To say, in effect, that these tasks were so despicable you couldn't wear your uniform when you did them?

In the beginning he tried to approach the job with professionalism. He planned the actions thoroughly, staked out locations, double-checked intelligence. The work had a secret-agent quality. There were dossiers filled with photographs and classified documents, G-2 files, transcripts of wire-tapped conversations, newspaper clippings. Together the documents formed a portrait of a person and the particular problem this person presented: agitation, suspected weapons cache, guerrilla cell, defaming the army, trade union activity, and so on. You had to look over the dossier and sort out the series of minor and major obstacles the assignment entailed. There were details of daily life, habits and patterns, the routes people took to work and school, the addresses and phone numbers of relatives, mistresses, acquaintances, friends. The information in each dossier required a series of tactical decisions.

Longoria made all the decisions. He liked the sound of his voice when he gave an order. "Kick him! Get him on the ground! Look out for his teeth or he'll bite you! Pin him! His arm! Grab his arm!"

But no matter how much planning Longoria did, something always seemed to go wrong. It was hard enough to keep the four Lorenzo Amayas in one room without two or three of them breaking into a fistfight, flailing away and pulling at each other's hair. He thought about ordering them to get their heads shaved, but he wasn't sure they would obey, and headquarters might not like the idea anyway. Headquarters was a mysterious place. It did not seem right that they spent years training him to be a good soldier and then rewarded him by packing him off with thieves.

The whole situation, and his inability to escape it, frustrated him. Abductions were not easy work. The inevitable public screaming began to grate on him. After months of these disappearances he could tell which ones would be screamers just by the look on their faces when they first saw him, in that moment when the vision of him, the implication of his tennis shoes and his submachine gun and the thugs behind him, was still sinking in, that first moment when they thought Longoria might be something from a dream.

Longoria was tired of mothers pulling at his shirt, sick of wrestling with wives who just wouldn't let their husbands go. You could have a woman punch you only so many times.

*   *   *

As the Jeep rattled along, Sergeant Longoria reviewed his orders. They would spend the night in the home of the mayor of this town and then carry out the first assignment the next morning.

Longoria picked up a large earth brown file folder from the floor of the Jeep. There was the standard identity-card photograph. These tended to be at least two or three years old, and people often looked much different when you finally encountered them in real life. In this case the photograph showed a serious and stern-looking young woman, anger in the shape of her mouth, as if somebody she didn't like was on the other side of the camera. Dark features, hair pulled back in a ponytail. Very attractive, Longoria thought.

A second photograph. The woman's husband. This one a little *chele*, light-skinned and clean-shaven, in circle glasses, suit, and tie, the classic university student. Startled, as if the pop of the flashbulb had caught him by surprise. The young man in the photograph reminded Longoria of a type he had come across in the army, the petit-bourgeois graduates of the Politécnica military school who were already officers when they started out, and were promoted ahead of the real soldiers because their fathers knew men in the higher echelons of the Estado Mayor. Longoria would enjoy abducting this man.

Another picture, this one probably more recent: a fuzzy telephoto shot of the woman taken from behind as she walked along some kind of dirt path, a cluster of shacks in the background. The photograph caught her in mid-stride, and her print dress seemed to float upward slightly, suggesting a bounce in her step. Longoria was uncertain what this photograph meant to convey, why it was included in the file.

Under the photographs was a thin stack of documents. There was always more information in these dossiers than you really needed. Xerox copies of a handwritten letter from the woman, a letter from the mayor of the town, and the testimony of an informer in the municipal government. None of this he bothered to read very closely. He simply noted the address on the cover sheet and the details of his orders, which were to apprehend the two subversives, transport them to the barracks at Santa Cruz del Quiché, and hand them over to G-2.

He glanced at the subversives' names. In cases like this the names meant almost nothing to him. He stored them in short-term memory, next to what he ate for breakfast and the reading on the Jeep's gas gauge.

* * *

Elena hadn't spoken to Antonio for a week, ever since the argument about the letter. He had taken her courageous act and made her feel that it was stupid and silly. She had denied the enemy her fear, and that was worth something. She wouldn't allow herself to be humiliated by a man who let his fear paralyze him. She assaulted him with ferocious silence and barely concealed disgust until he finally broke down and apologized.

"I'm sorry, Elena. I'm sorry I yelled at you. I was angry. Forgive me, I beg you."

Antonio looked at her with weak and pleading eyes, as if to say, Help me, I don't know what to do next. Elena felt her anger slipping away. Despite everything, she felt a deep compassion for him, a sense that she had to protect him. He was a good man who could still find his way. He was the father of her son, and that was worth something too. She wondered how she had stayed so angry at him for so long. Gently taking off his round glasses, she used her blouse to wipe off the layer of dust that had gathered on the lenses, something she had been wanting to do for the past two days.

"Now I can see your beautiful eyes," she said. She stood on tiptoes and kissed him on the forehead. "We need to be strong."

"Strong," he repeated, looking very sad.

They made love that night. After a week of saying nothing, after so much coldness, all it took was one touch to trigger desires that obeyed no logic Elena could understand. It had happened many times before: an argument, followed by an apology, followed by desperate lovemaking.

He can seem so weak, but when we are next to each other, when I am next to my tall, beautiful lover, he is someone else. When he loses his sour, angry face, when his mouth relaxes into a smile, I can see the handsome man I fell in love with. The man who didn't notice how other women looked at him. Who didn't notice how people stared at us on the streets of the capital because we made such an attractive couple.

At twenty-three Elena was just beginning to enjoy making love. When she was younger, there was much about it that seemed like such a chore, like calisthenics. She had partners who led her to bed and made her believe that she was about to embark on a journey of sensual exploration, but the pleasure was all theirs. Now she had a lifelong partner, a neophyte she had educated in the subtleties of touch, the language of hands and lips and wet kisses. He had learned with time all the things she liked to do, where to kiss her, how to hold her. He didn't mind that she wanted to be on top. Antonio was not the same man who had taken her on a tryst in the back of his father's

Volkswagen. This was the best part of their marriage, Elena had discovered, its saving grace.

She woke up the next morning feeling as if she had recovered from an illness. With a long embrace and a french kiss, she sent her husband off to work.

"I'll make you a nice dinner tonight, *amor*. Something special. Something you like."

Antonio turned and walked away down the cobblestone street, his briefcase swinging from his arm in a happy arc.

A chill lingered in the morning air, but the sun was already high and strong with the promise of a warm day. Elena felt a lightness, an almost childlike buoyancy. *It's because he's trapped in this little town. That's why he gets so sad and strange. If we go back to the capital, or to Los Angeles, he will become the man I want.*

They would leave soon, in a few months, perhaps. She would wait long enough that no one could say she left because she was afraid.

Elena stood at the front door and watched Antonio disappear around the corner. A few houses down, two children were staring at her. Boys, one perhaps twelve years old, the other a little younger. Skinny children, hungry, thin-boned. *Be careful. Even a child can be an informer, even a child can work for the forces of repression.* She looked straight at them, and they stuck their tongues out at her and skipped away.

Laughing at herself, Elena went inside and began to plan what she would make for dinner.

* * *

The Lorenzo Amayas would not get up. After a night of drinking with the mayor, the four men were hung over. They had dozed off at about 3:00 a.m., leaving a table covered with glasses, lime slices, and empty bottles of Venado rum. Longoria had sipped for hours at one drink, enduring the ceaseless teasing of the mayor, who made more jokes about Indians the more intoxicated he became, until he finally put his arms around the sergeant.

"You're a beautiful man," the mayor said. "What you're doing is so beautiful. Facing bullets for our country. It's big. Bigger than just the two of us. *Es una cosa grande.*"

Now the mayor was passed out in one of the many bedrooms of this vast house. The man could sleep until noon for all Longoria cared, but he needed his squad. He needed these criminals to get out of bed and into the Jeeps, because they had to finish two assignments in this town and then be ready for the next one tomorrow. There was a lot of work to be done.

It was eight o'clock in the morning and Longoria had been awake for hours, doing push-ups and jumping jacks in the mayor's backyard. After finishing his exercises, he had gone from room to room to wake his snoring charges, but the men ignored him.

"*Levántate, cabrón,*" Longoria said as he tried once more to shake Mosca awake. But the overweight soldier of counterrevolution only threw up his arms and rolled over on his stomach.

At 10:30 they finally loaded up the Jeeps and headed out for Tercera Avenida, not far from the town square. Longoria was dressed in black jeans and a green sweatshirt that probably looked too much like an army uniform, but he didn't care. He almost felt like defying orders and putting on his uniform with the new chevrons he had barely had a chance to wear. He double-checked the laces on his tennis shoes, which always seemed to come untied. Boots were so much better, but he couldn't wear those either. Boots were a dead giveaway.

While Mosca drove, Longoria reexamined the pictures in the dossier, trying to memorize the faces of the young couple. Mistakes had been known to happen. The addresses and the faces were the only things he cared about. He was getting tired of these assignments and didn't care if this particular couple had an arsenal of weapons in their house, if it held an entire column of guerrilla soldiers.

Through the haze of pale sleeplessness that covered their faces, the men in Longoria's Jeep looked tense and anxious. Mosca seemed to be gasping for air as he drove, taking a hand off the wheel to wipe the perspiration off his forehead. It's because he's so fat, Longoria thought, not in the right condition for this kind of work. In the back seat Mugre's eyes darted around nervously, as if he wondered whether they would finally encounter a real guerrilla, someone who would shoot back for once. It was stage fright that would slip away as soon as they had the target before them.

They reached the center of town, the Jeep rattling as they rolled onto cobblestone streets.

"There it is!" Longoria yelled. "Stop!"

* * *

"There's nothing revolutionary about being a good cook," Elena thought, fighting off a faint sense of guilt as she put on the sky blue apron she had just bought at a little *tienda* two blocks away.

In the courtyard Carlitos was playing with his latest discovery, a new set of multicolored blocks. He liked to build things and then destroy them. Elena put the chicken in the marinade and went into the living room to watch through the window as he lined cylinders in neat rows, stacked squares into a little tower, and knocked everything over with a quick slap of his hand, laughing as the blocks spilled to the ground. She was relieved to hear him, because Carlitos didn't smile and laugh as much as other children she had known. She was afraid he would grow up to be a morose boy because his mother was too busy and worried to pay enough attention to him.

Returning to the kitchen, she could hear the sound of the blocks crashing harmlessly to the cement floor over and over again. She was washing vegetables in the sink, rinsing tomatoes and celery, when she was startled by the sound of screeching brakes.

* * *

The Jeep skids to a halt a good ten yards past the address they are headed for. That idiot Mosca. Sapo, who has been trailing too closely in the second Jeep, just misses hitting them from behind. Longoria makes a mental note to switch drivers for the next assignment, but he won't remember until this happens again, two days from now, in another town.

The Jeep doors open and the Lorenzo Amayas spill out onto the cobblestones. For a moment it seems like a well-coordinated drill, the men moving gracefully with machine guns and pistols at their sides, their tennis shoes landing on the street with a quiet pop. And then they run to the house and crowd around the steel door, stymied by the simplest of obstacles. They are frozen there until Longoria steps forward, pushes open the small glass portal in the steel rectangle, and reaches in to release the latch. This isn't the city, he feels like telling these *capitalinos* around him. People in the provinces rarely lock their doors, even when they should.

Now Longoria is stepping into the living room. Standing right there, in a doorway that probably leads to the kitchen, is the woman in the photograph. She looks stunned and confused, expressions that are quite familiar to Longoria and tell him there is probably nothing to fear in this house, that they've caught the subversives completely by surprise.

Longoria raises his 9-millimeter pistol and points it at the woman.

"Where's the other one? Where is your husband?" To the men behind him he shouts, "*Búsquenlo!* Check the other rooms."

The Lorenzo Amayas are fanning out through the house, knocking over lamps and furniture in the process. That's something they're good at, Longoria thinks. Knocking things over, making a mess when it isn't necessary. Turning back to the woman, he yells again, "Where is your husband?" And then, looking at the small paper folded in his hand, "Are you Elena Bernal?"

"What do you think, you bastard?"

"Where is Antonio Bernal?"

The woman says nothing, of course. She is as stoic as the rest of them, although she may be a little more spunky. Longoria wonders how long it will take to break her. The look of fear is gone, replaced by defiance. She is going to be one of the tough ones. He grabs her by the hair and yanks her violently to the ground so that she'll know he means business.

"Where is he hiding?"

"Go to hell."

The Lorenzo Amayas are turning things over, as if they're going to find the man hiding under the couch or the dresser.

"Hey, I heard something," one of the men yells from a distant room. "There's somebody in here."

Longoria orders Buitre to guard the woman, then follows the voice out of the living room and into a small courtyard covered with building blocks and toys. He enters a bedroom and discovers Mosca standing before the closet with his machine gun trembling in his hand. Suddenly the room fills with a deafening burst that splinters the wooden door from top to bottom.

Longoria opens the door and a small boy spills out, forehead hitting the tiles, tiny hands formed into fists. Scorching bullets to the neck and skull. *What's this? The dossier didn't mention any children. Or did it?* Longoria steps back to avoid getting blood on his white tennis shoes.

He yells at Mosca but can barely hear himself because the gunfire is still ringing in his ears. He slaps Mosca across the face, nearly knocking him to the ground, wanting to shoot him for being so trigger-happy, for complicating the assignment.

Leaving the bedroom, Longoria walks back across the little courtyard, stepping over the blocks, and returns to the living room, where the woman is of course screaming her head off, having lost all the composure she displayed so fiercely just a moment ago. He can see now that leaving her with Buitre wasn't a good idea. He and Sapo have already torn her dress half off and are tugging at her brassiere. They see him and stop, remembering his orders.

"My baby," the woman yells. "My baby."

"Dead," Longoria says, regretting it almost immediately, because now she really turns hysterical. She is wrestling with Buitre and Sapo, who are trying to keep her pinned to the floor.

The woman is kicking at the air. She is screaming that deep mother's scream that Longoria has heard before. And now Mugre and Mosca are in the room and Buitre is grabbing his crotch, salivating at the sight on the floor. The woman's scream pierces the numbness that has filled Longoria's ears. The situation is completely out of control.

He expected to shove the subversives quietly into the Jeep and drive them to the barracks for interrogation and clandestine execution, but now there is furniture turned upside down, a child's corpse in the next room, a half-naked woman writhing on the floor. The prisoner will be screaming in the Jeep, she will be crying all the way to the barracks, it will be useless to question or torture her.

Gunfire indoors. The sound echoes. His head is throbbing.

"Just five minutes, *sargento*," Buitre says into his ear. "Just five minutes with her."

Deeply disgusted, Longoria raises his gun, stands over the woman, and fires a bullet into her skull. He has done this so many times. It is almost a reflex.

Buitre and Sapo let go of her and move away as if her body were already beginning to rot and decay. The Lorenzo Amayas look at the corpse, then back at Longoria. There is no more screaming. All Longoria can hear is the buzzing in his ear, like the drone of a distant airplane.

The Lorenzo Amayas have been caught by surprise, and for a moment all the cruelty in their eyes is replaced by something else: *This sergeant with the tattooed arm is serious, he is even crazier than we are.* They step away from the seeping pool of blood that is now forming by the woman's head.

This woman is prettier as a corpse than when she was alive, Longoria thinks. Prettier now that she isn't screaming anymore.

*   *   *

Elena recognizes fascism coming through the door. She looks at the soldier, sees the gun in his hand and the animal on his arm, and knows that she does not have much time left on this earth. After the initial shock, a sense of sadness and regret that is almost like joy. *Vegetables in the sink and a killer in my living room.* Almost a smile on her lips. *They want Antonio, but I will not give him to them. I will not. Why am I so calm? This is unnatural. I am not a brave woman. But this man has come to kill me and I am not afraid.*

The feeling stays with her even as the tattooed man pulls her down by the roots of her hair, even as the other men tear at her dress. This is happening to someone else. She is floating above the room, defying gravity, bouncing like a balloon against the ceiling, watching this happen to a woman in a blue apron. They are turning over furniture, they are breaking vases and dishes, books are falling to the floor, but Antonio is safe, Antonio isn't here.

And then the sound of gunfire and the trance is broken. She feels the impact of the explosions on her body, sound and shock waves piercing skin. Her son, her blood, the baby from her womb. She has forgotten about the baby, and isn't that typical. Carlos. They are shooting Carlitos.

Only screams are left inside her. *My baby.* She is a living scream. She wills herself to stand, to rise to her feet and run to Carlos, but she is anchored to the ground. They are ripping something from her, links of liquid and tissue, now alive again, bleeding and raw. Now there is only regret and pain, unbearable. *I didn't protect my baby.*

Elena looks up and sees the tattooed soldier raising the barrel of his gun to her head. Surrender. No, never surrender. One more scream before the flash of light.

* * *

He would call Guatemala City and tell the major that it was impossible to work with this pack of delinquents. He would tell them that if they didn't give him a new batch of men he would request a transfer. He would transfer out of the Jaguars to a real unit where he didn't have to work with criminals.

They left the house and headed for the Jeeps. The street was deserted, although it was more than likely that many people were watching them from behind the dark slats of their shuttered windows. Longoria stared at the windows and spat onto the cobblestones. *Let them look at me. Let them get a good look.*

As they drove away, Longoria picked up the dossier and looked at the picture of the woman he had just killed, and then at the picture of the missing husband, who had saved himself merely by being absent when he was supposed to be home. There was a sheet of paper attached to the photograph, some sort of intelligence report Longoria hadn't bothered to read before. Almost immediately, to his great dismay, he noticed that the document listed the man's employment at the Department of Public Works and his hours: 8:30 to 12:00, 1:30 to 5:00. Longoria looked at his watch: 11:03 a.m. The husband was at his job just a few blocks from here; he wasn't supposed to be home at all. Longoria considered driving to the Department of Public Works and grabbing him there, but it would probably be too brash, even for the Lorenzo Amaya Brigade, to kidnap a man from a government office. It wouldn't go over well at headquarters. They could go back to the house, but by now they had lost the element of surprise. Someone would warn the man and he would flee.

If the Lorenzo Amayas hadn't been drinking with the mayor, if they had been ready to leave at 7:00 a.m., they would have arrived early enough to surprise the subversive, who, according to this document, left for work every morning at 8:15. Longoria could blame no one but himself for this screw-up, for failing to take note of the most basic piece of intelligence.

I am slipping. I am losing my professionalism. I am losing the love of my work.

After completing the afternoon's assignment—the assassination of an elementary-school teacher—and circling back to the mayor's house to use the phone, they went on to Momostenango, their route taking them through the center of San Cristóbal again. They were driving through what passed for the Parque Central when Buitre whispered into Longoria's ear from the back seat.

"*Sargento*, I have to go to the bathroom."

"What? But we just left the house. Why didn't you go there?"

"We were in a hurry. I forgot."

Mosca stopped the Jeep, and Buitre disappeared into a *tienda* to ask the proprietor for the use of her toilet. It was the only *tienda* on the square that was open, Longoria noticed, probably to serve the small group of people waiting to board a bus that was idling nearby.

Longoria got out of the Jeep for some fresh air. All around him there were women with baskets, young children at their sides. There was a stack of newspapers by the *tienda*'s entrance, and Longoria stepped across the cobblestone street to buy *La Prensa Libre*. Articles about a new leader in the Soviet Union, a man called Gorbachev. The Sandinistas fighting with a Catholic radio station. None of it was very interesting. He tucked the paper under his arm to read later and bought a chocolate ice cream from a vendor who had parked his cart next to the bus.

Across the street Mugre and Mosca were leaning on the Jeep talking. Longoria took a seat on a cast-iron bench near the *tienda*.

With a shudder and a hiss the bus door opened, and the waiting crowd began to board. Longoria looked up and watched briefly as a man tied a basket to the roof. The bus driver slipped the engine into gear with a loud clunk.

Buitre emerged from the *tienda*, adjusting his fly. "*Sargento, ya terminé.*"

"Wait for me in the car. I'll be there in a second." Longoria wanted to finish his ice cream.

As the bus rolled by just a few yards from his tennis shoes, Longoria caught the eyes of one of the passengers, a man who was staring at him from behind the window. People stared at him all the time; the tattoo and his military haircut drew their eyes. The thing to do was to stare back until you scared them, but Longoria was too bored now even for this, so he just looked away.

After the bus had rumbled down the street, Longoria noticed Mugre and Mosca wrestling by the Jeep, grabbing at each other's hair. *Little boys, I work with little boys.* As he walked across the cobblestones to tell them to knock it off, Mugre managed to get a foot behind Mosca's leg and sent the overweight killer toppling to the ground.

Part 3
Antonio and Guillermo

11
Fire Escape

Antonio squatted on the lawn by the playground, about fifteen yards from the chess tables. The tattooed soldier had finished his game and was talking to some of the men who had been watching him. He opened his arms wide, raised a palm in the air, made circles with his fingers. He pointed to the chessboard and turned to the bearded old man who had just defeated him, drawing imaginary lines like an army general or a soccer coach. He appeared to be speaking very fast.

The shaved head, the tattoo of the yellow panther. The soldier from San Cristóbal right here in MacArthur Park. To see him speak and gesture seemed fantastic, like watching a statue or a hunting trophy come to life. Just a few minutes ago he belonged only to Antonio's memory, an image that had darkened and splintered over the years, like an oil painting from a distant century. Now the soldier stood in the California daylight, his features sharp in the crystal air, the wrinkles under his eyes, the lines of the tattoo, all there for Antonio to examine and inspect.

The soldier's sudden appearance in the park was a gift, Antonio decided, something to be celebrated with loud laughter. He broke into a smile. It was a miracle, a sign from the heavens. At moments like this you could begin to believe in things like history and fate. His heart pumped fast and strong, filling his chest with wild vibrations, making his fingertips tingle. He looked around and quickly took in the layout of the park, a sunny April day with families strolling by on the grass. Just a few hundred feet away, in the park's northwest corner, there was a small amphitheater with wooden benches facing a concrete stage. A girl chased a boy through the empty rows of seats.

The soldier stepped onto the asphalt path and began walking toward Antonio, hands tucked in his pockets. Antonio turned away in a panic, looking down at the grass. The man's muted tennis-shoe foot-steps passed just a few yards behind him, a soft thump on the hard surface of the path.

As the sound of the footsteps faded, Antonio jumped up. *Don't let him get away. Attach yourself to him.* Carried forward by the vision of the soldier leaving the park, Antonio almost tripped over José Juan, who was still sprawled on his back, snoring.

The soldier walked toward the corner of Seventh and Alvarado, Antonio following a good twenty paces behind. He passed an ice cream vendor with boredom written on his Olmec features as he rang the little bell on his heavy white cart. A young couple was posing for a picture by one of the palm trees, the photographer in the baggy gray suit urging them to stand closer together. They giggled nervously and smiled, not noticing when the soldier cut behind them, ruining the picture; the photographer looked up and muttered while the intrud-er passed through his field of vision.

The soldier reached the crowded corner at Alvarado and stood waiting for a green light like any pedestrian about to cross the street. When the light changed and the people spilled off the sidewalk, Antonio lost track of him for a few moments and feverishly scanned the bodies in the crowd until he found the stiff blue rectangle of his back. *If I hold on to the navy T-shirt I won't lose him. The tattoo is start-ing to fade, it was brighter before.* Antonio could not allow the soldier to escape twice. If the soldier slipped away, how would Antonio find him again in this enormous city?

When I first saw this man, on that day so many years ago, I ran. Now I am moving with him, I am moving at him, I am not running.

The soldier stopped to look at some cassette tapes a street ven-dor was selling; squatting down, he picked one up and inspected the cover. He was a man who listened to music, and for a moment this fact was startling and strange. As Antonio watched from a few paces away, the soldier put the tape back neatly in the rows of merchandise and continued along the sidewalk toward the bus stop on Alvarado, next to a newsstand displaying Mexican tabloids with full-color pictures of mutilated corpses. Antonio's eye caught the screaming boldface head-

lines of a magazine called *¡Alarma!*: "THE JEALOUS WIFE SHOT HER HUS-
BAND! *Aquí está la cara de la degenerada.*"

The soldier joined a large cluster of people waiting for the bus.
When it arrived he was one of the first to step on, Antonio the last.
Antonio stood near the front door and looked down the aisle. The
driver did not seem to notice or care that Antonio hadn't paid his fare,
so dense was the crush of passengers. The soldier was lost somewhere
in the forest of swaying bodies.

Several blocks later the soldier exited through the rear door.
Antonio pushed past a few startled passengers and barely made it out
the front.

"Don't be so rude!"

When Antonio's feet touched the sidewalk, he looked to his right
just in time to see the soldier step into a storefront a few yards away
from the bus bench. Not daring to follow him inside, Antonio stopped
in front of two large plate-glass windows. Above them, on a sky blue
wall decorated with painted flags of the five Central American
republics, ran a series of yellow letters.

EL PULGARCITO EXPRESS
YOUR PACKAGE TO CENTROAMERICA IN TWO DAYS!
RELIABLE SERVICE WITH THAT TOUCH OF HOME
BECAUSE WE'RE CENTROAMERICANOS LIKE YOU!

* * *

Longoria wandered away from the chess tables, half wanting to chal-
lenge the old man to another game even though it would make him
late for work. To come so close and then lose because of a stupid mistake! Longoria would have won but for a single move when he allowed
his concentration to slip. At least he could revel in having kept García
on the defensive until the very end. Longoria's game was improving,
García admitted as much during their brief postmortem of the match.
"You gave me a little scare, sergeant." Sooner or later Longoria would
beat him.

He walked to the bus stop. Checking his watch, he paused to see if the street vendors had anything interesting, perhaps some music Reginalda might like. There was one singer who was her favorite, an effeminate Mexican. What was his name? Longoria couldn't remember.

The buses didn't come as often on Sunday, and he wasn't surprised to find a large crowd waiting at the stop, girls in dresses and patent leather shoes, women carrying black purses, people going to or coming from church. The ride to work would be slow, plenty of time for him to go over the game in his head again. Maybe he should start writing down his moves like the grandmasters did, so that he would have a record later of what he had done right and what had gone wrong.

There was no one waiting in line when he entered the lobby of El Pulgarcito, so he went back to what was called "the sorting room." He found Carlos Avilés there, sitting at a large table. The office manager had a stack of opened letters before him.

"Hey, Longoria, I got a real good one here, take a look," he said, holding up a photograph, a letter, and a torn envelope. "See? She's in a bathing suit. *Qué chula.*" He made a loud kissing sound. "If you see this woman come in here again, let me know. I want to talk to her. I'll tell her it's a waste for her to be saving herself for some fool who's so far away."

He returned the photograph and letter to the envelope, sealing it with tape from a dispenser he kept on his desk for this purpose. The tape was running low.

El Pulgarcito's customers were rarely suspicious when their letters arrived in El Salvador, Honduras, or Guatemala with the backs torn open and resealed with tape. They assumed army intelligence or the national police opened the letters, just like they tapped the phones and spied on the priests during sermons.

Carlos too said he opened the letters "in the interest of national security." It was common knowledge that more than a few former guerrillas lived in Los Angeles, and Carlos said it infuriated him to think that these subversives might use El Pulgarcito to transmit messages back home. There was a war going on in El Salvador, and you had to seek out the enemy wherever you might find him. Carlos sat with his lanky frame hunched over the gray steel table and peered through his reading glasses for any hint of leftist sympathies, any word or phrase that suggested belief in secularism, land reform, or raising the minimum wage. Then he copied the names of the suspected subversives on a legal pad that was always lost the next day.

Most of all Carlos was interested in doing as little work as possible. He took three-hour lunches and left Longoria in charge. Longoria, in turn, tried to leave as much work as he could to Yanira. During the morning hours, when business was slow, he liked to slip into the back and read the opened letters.

Carlos yawned, pushed back the green-skinned swivel chair, and announced that he was taking an early lunch. After he left, Longoria settled into the chair and picked up one of the dozen or so letters spread out on the table. It was addressed to a Gonzalo Venegas in the city of San Pedro Sula, Honduras.

> They disconnected my telephone because I owed $400 in long-distance calls. So now I have to write to you. There has been some bad news recently. Your cousin Williams was burned in an accident at work. He was putting on a roof and he got burned real bad all over the arms. Hot tar fell on him. I visited him at the county hospital and he is very, very depressed. They have him in a room with six other people and it smells very bad there. I was surprised to see this. The place was as bad as the hospital back home. I tried to cheer him up the best I could. But you know how he is. You can't tell him anything because he's always in a foul mood. And now this. You should write to him, or call him as soon as possible. I have never seen him so depressed.

Big deal, Longoria thought. We've all got problems. Stop whining, who cares about your friend's accident. He picked up the next letter, the address written in a hurried, barely legible script. It was headed for El Salvador.

> Well, here's the shampoo you asked me for. It says "medicated" on the bottle so I guess this is the right one. I don't see what the fuss is with this shampoo. It cost me $20 to

send this package. I hope you realize this. $20 is not a little money, not even here. We're not all rich here, you know. I can't believe you couldn't find it anywhere in San Salvador. If you had looked a little harder I might have saved these $20.

Poor man, to be persecuted by such a wife. Longoria had to deal with equally unreasonable requests from Reginalda, who thought he could get any package to El Salvador overnight, for free, because he worked at El Pulgarcito.

Longoria turned to an envelope addressed in a neat, roundish female hand to Zona 7 in Guatemala City.

I have never been so bored in my entire life. Six days a week I spend cooped up in this house, my love, looking after their little boy. His name is Jason and he is a brat, *muy malcriado*, two years old and a real terror. All I can do is read and read to pass the time. At least the couple is nice to me. She works in a museum and I haven't figured what he does yet. My English is getting better now. (If only I had taken that English class when I was still in the university. What a mistake it was to take French instead! That's what I get for being a romantic.) There is a chance I might be able to get a job at a department store downtown. Pray for me to be liberated from this boredom.

In the meantime, please, please send me a good book to read in Spanish. Any Miguel Angel Asturias you can get a hold of would be much appreciated. (Except *El Señor Presidente*, which I did manage to find here.) I am going crazy in this place. Won't you please come to rescue me?

Con Amor,
Graciela

P.S. I took my first driving lesson last Sunday. Aren't you proud of me?!

There was something Longoria liked about this Graciela. He felt sorry for her, trapped in a stranger's house, stuck in a job beneath her obvious intelligence. "Won't you please come to rescue me?" The return address on the letter was just four or five blocks from the office. He could teach Graciela to drive. He was sure he would know this woman if he saw her on the street. He was about to copy her address onto a sheet of yellow paper when he heard Yanira calling him from the front counter.

"Longoria, I need you up here. There's too many people in line. I need help."

He left Graciela's letter on the table and forgot about it as soon as he went out front and saw a half-dozen people waiting impatiently. For some reason an old woman at the back of the line caught his attention. She was at least seventy, and Longoria wondered if she knew exactly how ridiculous she looked in that yellow sweatshirt that said "So Many Men, So Little Time." Grandmothers should comport themselves with more dignity. Of course, she probably didn't know what the sweatshirt said; she probably didn't speak, much less read, a word of English.

The woman in the yellow sweatshirt moved forward in the line. She wore her salt-and-pepper hair in a long braid, and her neck was a gathering of loose cinnamon skin. An Indian, unmistakably Guatemalteca. Now she was giving Longoria a strange look, staring at him across the room. What was it about old women that they were not afraid to look you right in the eye? The baggy sweatshirt hung over a faded print skirt—hand-me-downs she might have had even before she came to Los Angeles, because of all those stores in Guatemala City that sold used American clothing by the kilo. Longoria thought she looked like a Cachiquel Indian, the ones who started causing all the trouble around Sololá. Longoria was from Huehuetenango, a good two hours from Sololá by bus, but he knew the Cachiquel people because the army had once sent him to the area for a six-month stint.

When the old woman finally made it to the counter, Longoria looked at the envelope she was mailing and saw an address in Santa Lucía Utlatlán, a little *aldea* in the department of Sololá named for the patron saint of the blind. Longoria congratulated himself. *I haven't lost my touch, I can still tell a Cachiquel from a Mam from a Quiché.* This was not an easy thing to do. It was a useful skill in the army, on patrol, to be able to tell who didn't belong, who might be the rebel infiltrator, the propagandist in the bunch. The old woman opened her mouth to ask how much it would be to send the letter, and sure enough, she spoke in that heavily accented Indian Spanish that everyone in the army always laughed at, the singsong dialect of housemaids, the voice of backwardness.

Longoria was counting the bills and coins she had stacked on the counter when she reached out and grabbed his left forearm.

"*Señora*," he said in his calmest service-sector voice. "What are you doing?"

Without answering, she began inspecting his arm like a customer inspecting a slice of beef or a melon at the market. Longoria decided that sometimes you had to humor people, especially when they were old and frail and probably senile like this woman, a grandmother in a coquettish sweatshirt.

"This mark on your skin," she said in Spanish. "I've seen this before."

"It's a jaguar, *señora*."

The expression on her face changed from curiosity to horror. "You're one of those, one of those soldiers, aren't you?" She dropped his arm and grabbed his shirt and started yelling.

"*¡Matón!* Murderer! *¡Matón!*"

Longoria was so surprised that he just stood there for a moment. Then he methodically pried the woman's bony fingers from his shirt. Undaunted, she reached across the counter again and beat at his chest with her fist, tears welling in her eyes.

"What did you do to my son? Where is he? What did you do to him? Just tell me where his body is. For the love of God, where is Demetrio's body?"

"I don't know what you're talking about. I don't know any Demetrio. You're crazy. Crazy *vieja*, get out of here."

"Where is he? I have to know." The old woman dropped to her knees, and Longoria thought she might have a heart attack right there in the offices of El Pulgarcito Express, branch number two. She began shouting to the people waiting in line. "Don't you understand? They took Demetrio and his wife. They took Demetrio and left me with his

children. I'm an old woman, and I have to take care of his children."
She looked up at Longoria. "¡*Matón!* Where is Demetrio, where is he?"

Longoria unlatched the counter door, stepped around, and tried
to lift the old woman up. She started screaming at him again as she
struggled in his powerful grip. Then she went limp. She was small but
heavy, and she smelled sour. He was dragging her toward the door
when she twisted violently and bit his forearm.

"You whore!" He dropped her to the floor. Standing over her, he
swung his arm in a broad arc and slapped her across the face, the
swack filling the room. There was an audible gasp from the people in
line, who stared as if they would spit at him if they could get away
with it. But no one moved or spoke, and for an instant Longoria felt
like he was in Guatemala and he had this control over people again,
the power to keep them frozen in place and silent as he walked
through a room. The old woman was lying on her side, coughing softly. Longoria noticed a pebble on the floor in front of her—a tooth.
Blood began to seep from her mouth. She spat a red blotch onto the
white linoleum. One of the customers, a young woman, leaned down
to help her.

The job wasn't supposed to be like this. After all, he was working
in the service sector. The service sector was supposed to be orderly
and clean. And now this old woman's blood on the white floor.

If he were still in the army, Longoria wouldn't have any qualms
about hitting someone, even an old woman in an absurd sweatshirt.
But he was trying to make another life now. His violent reactions
belonged to a distant, black past. Now he felt ridiculous for having lost
control and slapped a seventy-year-old woman. *This can only be a sign
of my own weakness, my lack of internal discipline. The rules are different here. I must learn to obey the rules, just like I did in the army.*

* * *

Antonio sat on the edge of the bus bench waiting for the soldier to
emerge from El Pulgarcito Express. He watched people go in and out,
entering with packages and leaving with receipts in their hands.
Several buses arrived at the stop and drove off, and a blur of passengers came and went around him as the day turned from nippy morn-

ing to sun-drenched noon. The soldier did not come out, but Antonio couldn't see him through the plate-glass windows. Worried that he might have slipped away somehow, Antonio stood up abruptly and went to the door.

He saw the soldier at the counter right away, talking to a stout, dark woman. The long nose and shaved head were familiar features by now, but he looked smaller than Antonio remembered him just a few hours ago. The soldier was stone-faced, an expressionless wall against the whirling gestures of the angry woman, who was waving a yellow slip of paper in his face like a soiled rag.

Antonio was afraid that if he stood there staring at the soldier for too long he would be conspicuous, so he stepped up to the counter and picked up a small flyer that listed the company's rates and special discounts. His hand trembled slightly as he reached for the slip of paper, which was in a dispenser less than an arm's length from the soldier himself.

"We only guarantee money orders if you buy them here," the soldier said in a weary voice. "Otherwise we're not responsible. That is what our *jefe* says."

Antonio was startled to hear the killer's voice so close to his ear. It was not a strong voice. Not a confident voice. He had known teenagers who had deeper, throatier voices. The killer spoke like a peasant, in a voice Antonio associated with wooden shacks and men who carried heavy loads of firewood on their backs. This was a surprise.

"I told you, the *jefe* says those are the rules."

For the briefest of moments, Antonio felt something resembling pity for the soldier. It was the most abstract of emotions, a reflex. In Guatemala's capital, where Antonio came from, you were supposed to feel superior when you heard a peasant speak with this provincial lilt; you were supposed to feel a sort of paternalistic sympathy. It was the way he said "*jefe*," something submissive in the way he said the word.

Antonio turned to leave. Almost out of the corner of his eye he saw the soldier's brown arm resting on the white counter, the tattoo facing up. Antonio was close enough to read the small black letters just underneath the animal itself, written inside a tiny scroll: "*Jaguares.*"

Antonio drifted out of the office in a daydream. The soldier, the killer of his wife and son, was a peasant. Circling aimlessly around the busy intersection, carried along like driftwood by the current of pedestrians, Antonio wandered into a grocery store, a *discoteca*, a shoe store, and then, unaccountably, into a bridal shop bursting with waves and waves of lacy fabric. Someone said something to him in a harsh voice, but none of it registered, because Antonio could only think about how the killer of Carlos and Elena was a peasant who spoke in a child's whiny voice.

This discovery had thrown Antonio off course and derailed his impulse to revenge. *I should have known from the first moment I set eyes on the man. I should have seen the campesino when I first saw him sitting at the tables in MacArthur Park.* Antonio was not sure what he expected, but not this. His rage had fled, and now there was only a vacuum in its place. He walked out of the bridal shop into the glaring sunlight of the street.

God knows what led this peasant to join the army, to become one of the army's hired killers. God knows the person he was before and who he has become since.

The easiest thing would be to forget about the man.

Antonio followed the lines on the uneven sidewalk, head down, staring at cracks that looked like rivers on a map, bumping into someone every few minutes. It did not seem fair that the situation presented him with these additional complications. He had drifted several blocks away from El Pulgarcito Express when he realized that he hadn't seen a *campesino* sitting at the table in MacArthur Park because he had been riveted by the man's tattoo and his haircut. That ugly scar on the soldier's arm, that painted animal, that was nothing natural. It was not something a *campesino* would do. His anger began to rise again. No simple peasant would paint himself in such a way. The tattoo told Antonio that there was more to this man than could be heard on the surface of his voice, something beyond his servile "*jefe.*"

Jaguares. That was what the tattoo said. Now Antonio remembered that the Jaguars were some sort of special unit of the Guatemalan army. Yes, the Jaguars were synonymous with the terror the army spread through the countryside. They burned houses and left decapitated heads at the entrances to the villages they destroyed. The Jaguars had carried out a holocaust in the mountains.

If the soldier was a Jaguar then he was the negation of what Antonio had just imagined him to be. He was a professional killer of peasants. Whatever he had been before, he now wore a jaguar tattoo. The tattoo was the key to everything. Because the soldier had that animal on his skin, he had been sent to murder Elena. Because he had that tattoo, he could kill a two-year-old boy and sit down to eat an ice cream as if nothing had happened.

Antonio circled back toward El Pulgarcito Express. That was the place to be, close to the soldier, in pursuit. Returning to the bus bench, Antonio resumed his vigil.

No sooner had he sat down than he heard a confusion of voices coming from the office, shouts of "No!" and "*¡Ay!*" and "*¡Por el amor de Dios!*" Then there was a sudden quiet. Not long afterward the front door opened and a flat-nosed old woman in a baggy sweatshirt appeared, supported by a much younger woman. The old woman was very poor, Antonio saw. She held a cloth to her mouth, and she was bleeding from her lip. "*Qué bárbaros,*" the young woman repeated as she inspected the wound. "*¡Qué bárbaros!*" Apparently someone had struck this woman inside El Pulgarcito Express. There must have been a fight over the line. What kind of office was this, where someone would strike an old woman over a place in line?

Antonio stayed on the bus bench for most of the day. One of the advantages of looking as shabby as he did was that no one paid much attention to him. A Latino man in slacks with frayed hems and a pale blue shirt that had taken on the brownish gray tinge of a smoggy sky: no one would think twice about such a man, even if he did wear an intellectual's circle glasses. There were so many strange people on the street, after all. Pico Boulevard, Vermont Avenue, Alvarado: all these places were convention centers for the homeless and mentally ill. He could melt into the landscape along with all the schizophrenic babblers, the shiftless immigrants, the paranoid wanderers and pushers of shopping carts. When he began to talk to himself softly, his lips mimicking his thoughts, it only made him more invisible.

In the late afternoon, just as Antonio began to feel the first downward pull of drowsiness, the tattooed soldier emerged from El Pulgarcito Express and made a beeline for the bus stop. As he approached, Antonio stepped away from the bench, shoulders hunched and head bowed, his best impersonation of a street person. When the bus came, he boarded two passengers after the soldier, for what turned out to be a relatively short trip to a neighborhood not far from MacArthur Park.

A few blocks after getting off the bus, the tattooed soldier turned onto a side street that rose at a slight incline and was lined with old brick buildings and vacant lots in equal numbers. He walked up a wide stone staircase and disappeared through a black security door that closed behind him with a crash Antonio heard half a block away. Antonio rushed to the door and looked up at the letters etched into the old pink portal above him: The Westlake Arms. Did the soldier live here? There was nothing to do but wait until he came out. Antonio walked across the street and leaned against a cyclone fence that sealed off a vacant lot between two apartment buildings. A man with dreadlocks was asleep on the sidewalk, lips puckered against the concrete.

Antonio decided to wait for the soldier here, next to the man who kissed the sidewalk, a spot where no one would bother him. He measured time by counting the people who went in and out of the building. At sixteen, there was still no sign of the tattooed soldier. Antonio would wait all night if necessary. A sense of purpose filled his spirit: the enemy was real and alive, right here in this building. Antonio was no longer adrift because he had attached himself to this small man who was heavy and bulky like an anchor.

I will make myself sharper. I will train my eyes to see everything, to remember everything about this street and this man.

He didn't have anything to write with, so he repeated the address in his mind until he had memorized it: 665 South Bonnie Brae Avenue. The building was tan, with terra cotta cornices and a brick fringe at the base, a structure with hints of long-faded elegance. In several spots the bricks had been painted over with black or red paint. Feeling bolder, Antonio crossed the street and climbed quickly up the front steps. In the lobby he inspected the panel of buttons where the names of the tenants should have been listed, but found that most were missing. There were only three names: Martinez, apartment 3B; Longoria, apartment 4F; Greenwood, apartment 6C. Antonio glanced through the inner door and into the hallway, a narrow corridor of arsenic green walls. An apartment door started to open, and he scurried back outside, returning to his post next to the sleeping man with the dreadlocks.

A few minutes later an old Anglo with a cane emerged and began working his way down the front steps. His bald skull was covered with angry red veins. He looked like a man setting off on a valiant expedition for food and water, muggers and addicts be damned. As he vanished around the corner, a group of thin teenagers appeared, their arms etched with fleshy frescoes of the Virgin of Guadalupe, gaudy pictures of homegirls. They camped out on the steps of the Westlake Arms, talking loudly and forcing everyone who entered or left to go around them. People tiptoed past carefully, as if walking through a minefield.

The flow of people from the building slowed, the afternoon grew old, the canyon between the lines of tenements filled with shadow. The wind grew colder, more penetrating. The man on the sidewalk woke from his long sleep and looked at Antonio with a startled expression.

"Who the fuck are you?" he said. "Where's Cindy?"

The man brushed himself off and wandered away, listing to one side, as if he might fall back asleep on the ground at any minute.

Antonio turned back to the building and examined the windows, six stories' worth, wondering whether he might be able to spot the soldier if he looked hard enough. *From a distance, the military haircut is what distinguishes him. Look for the man with the black skullcap.* Some of the windows were draped with faded curtains, others were covered with towels, blankets, cardboard. Thirty people had passed through the building now, and not one of them looked anything like the tattooed soldier.

Hours later, after the only streetlight on the block came on and began to cast a humming yellowish nimbus, the murderer stepped out of the Westlake Arms wearing a gray jogging suit and a new pair of tennis shoes. He looked like he was ready for a healthy session of exercise, perhaps at a gym or a body-building place.

If the soldier had changed clothes, he must live here. This was his home.

Antonio watched the soldier walk toward Wilshire Boulevard. There was no need to follow him any longer. Antonio could come back whenever he wished. *I've found the killer. I know where he lives.* He felt a sense of personal triumph. *I was afraid, but I didn't let him get away.*

When Antonio finally returned to Crown Hill, he found José Juan standing in the orange glow of a campfire, demolishing a wooden wine crate marked "Product of Spain" and throwing the pieces into the flames.

"Finally, he reappears," José Juan said.

Antonio crouched next to the fire with his arms around his knees, his face a portrait of stunned contemplation. Several seconds passed before José Juan asked, "Well, what happened? You left me in the park. I woke up and you were gone."

"I saw somebody I knew."

"Who?"

"Somebody I knew in Guatemala."

"A friend?"

"No," Antonio said, in a tone that let it be known he did not wish to discuss the matter further.

Antonio slipped into the snug cave of their shelter. He wanted to ponder what to do about the soldier. Instead he could only go over the events of the day like a man watching himself in his own home movies, replaying his pursuit of the soldier from MacArthur Park through the commerce-clogged streets to the apartment building. Huddled against the plastic walls of the shelter, he savored the details of the chase, the drama at the chess tables, his patient vigil at the portal of the Westlake Arms.

There was only one thing to do: he would return to the soldier's apartment building tomorrow morning. For the foreseeable future Antonio would go where the soldier went, attach himself to the man and learn everything he could about him. Surely Antonio was entitled to know everything there was to know.

* * *

They were eating at a Thai restaurant on Vermont Avenue that was very popular with the Salvadorans and Mexicans in the neighborhood, the Spanish chatter of the customers overwhelming the exchanges of the cooks and waitresses. It was a rare Tuesday night date, and this was the most expensive restaurant Longoria had ever been to with Reginalda; he was trying to forget the events of Sunday, the old woman's bony hands and her tooth, a straw-colored pebble on the floor. Reginalda liked this spicy food, hotter than the hottest jalapeño dish, strong enough to numb your entire jaw. Every few minutes the Mexicanos in the next booth slapped their thighs in pain, laughed, and asked for a new pitcher of water.

Longoria picked up his own water glass and studied the slice of lemon on the edge, wondering if he really had crossed paths with the old woman's son. He doubted it. He didn't remember any Demetrio, but then again, he didn't remember many names, period. He tried to forget the names, though it wasn't always easy. When he went on these "operations," they handed him the names, along with an address, a photograph, and a few notes from G-2 military intelligence. A dossier, they called it. He drove out to the location and carried out his orders.

"Where is my son's body?" the old woman had said. How was Longoria supposed to know? *Am I their father, am I responsible for them after they're dead? Am I supposed to bury them too? No, of course not. I am a soldier, a sergeant in the Guatemalan army, not a gravedigger.* The funerals weren't his responsibility. As far as Longoria knew, the Department of Public Sanitation handled the corpses.

Chances were he didn't know this Demetrio. There were so many actions, after all, hundreds in Sololá alone. Anybody could have killed this man, disappeared him. Longoria would just forget about it.

Reginalda was sitting across from him, waiting for her order of spicy chicken. He hadn't spoken a word for twenty minutes, but she didn't seem to mind. She was sipping her iced tea, admiring the ambiance, smiling at him because he had splurged and brought her here.

The only names he remembered were the names of the famous people, the union leaders, the writers, the lawyers, the anthropologists, the ones who were in the news for weeks and months after he killed them. He would see the graffiti on the walls just hours after his platoon dumped their bodies by the highway: "Miguel Barón lives!" "Miguel Barón, *presente!*" The names would remain on an adobe wall or the side of a grocery store for days until the officers finally rounded up some conscripts to cover them over with a bucket of paint. Sometimes you could go to the university months later and see the man from the back of your Jeep on the wall, painted to look like a saint or an angel.

"So my boss, he tells me I'm putting too much lettuce in the orders," Reginalda was saying. Longoria nodded to signal that he was listening. "More lettuce than the manual says. The sacred Taco Bell manual. And I told him I knew that. I told him I'm not a stupid woman. I told him I put in extra lettuce because it's good for the customers. They're all overweight and everything. They need more vegetables. It's for their health."

It got to the point where Longoria could almost see the newspaper headlines even before they were dead, when they were still in the back of his Jeep, quivering, sick with fear because they knew what was coming. Longoria would look at the famous detainee—a schoolteacher, a writer—and then at the identity-card snapshot G-2 gave him to find the bastard. Some of them sat in the back seat of the Jeep with defiant, almost amused expressions that matched the faces in the photographs. They had real balls, and you had to admire that. Longoria wondered if this Demetrio was one of the ballsy ones. He would look at them, tied up and bruised and bleeding, and know that he'd see the identity-card photograph in the newspaper a few days later. Or in the marches, when the Communists took the photo and made it into a giant poster and paraded it on the streets of the capital. The endless eulogies, the phrases he had come to memorize: *martyr, good father, loving mother, our leader, the bright light taken from us.*

After fifteen or so of these operations, Longoria could hear the whole country weeping even before he pulled the trigger, when he stood before the detainees in the dank interrogation room with the 9-millimeter pistol to their heads.

All this sympathy for the corpses irritated him. This old woman and all these people seemed to think they had a monopoly on grief. Longoria had survived and the corpses were corpses. Longoria could walk the earth and play chess and make love to Reginalda this very evening. That was something the old woman and the people in the marches never thought about. What about Sergeant Longoria? If he hadn't killed, he might be dead himself. So he would be thankful for being alive. There were reasons this work had to be done, even though you started to forget the reasons as time passed. When you actually had to do the deed, the reasons were what carried you forward, the speeches the officers made, what you learned about the enemy. A virus, a plague. An infection spread by ideas, a disease carried on the spoken word.

"Is something bothering you, *amor*? You look really angry," Reginalda said. "Did I say something to upset you?" When he didn't answer, she shrugged her shoulders and changed the subject. "I wonder why it is that this Thai food is so popular with the Latinos. There's nothing but Latinos in here. Did you notice that?"

Longoria nodded again. One thing was certain. This Demetrio was not one of the famous ones. His name had never been painted on a wall. If he had been one of the famous ones Longoria would have remembered his name.

* * *

Every day before dawn Antonio slipped out of the shelter into the chilly morning air and walked the eight blocks to the tattooed soldier's building, returning to his post by the chain-link fence across the street. As the sky was losing its violet hue, he would crane his neck to stare at the windows and watch the lights come on one by one. Soon the residents began to emerge from the portal, with the harried but alert faces of people about to begin a long working day: a young woman wearing a paper cap and a pale green uniform, umbrella and lunch bag in hand; a bulky Chicano in a navy blue uniform, the words "Security Officer" on his sleeves. More lights came on.

At precisely 6:15 on the first morning, Antonio heard a window slide open and saw the shaved head of the tattooed soldier underneath a raised pane of glass on the fourth floor. Antonio watched, mesmerized, as the soldier brushed a finger along the windowsill, disappeared, returned with a sponge and a rag, and wiped the sill clean. Then he scrubbed the edges of the window frame.

The light in the soldier's apartment went off, and a few minutes later he appeared on the front steps. Dark blue sweater, khaki pants, tennis shoes. Antonio followed him to El Pulgarcito and stationed himself on the bus bench. He watched people come and go on the sidewalk and at the nearby intersection, and by afternoon he knew all about the local street life. A steady stream of buses rolled past, the same five or six drivers reappearing in regular cycles, westbound, eastbound, and westbound again. The work habits of the drug dealers, who otherwise dissolved into the landscape like camouflaged animals, became clear to him. They hid drugs in the wheel wells of parked cars and used arcane hand signals to communicate with collaborators down the block and across the street.

When the day was over, he followed the soldier back to the Westlake Arms.

In this fashion Antonio kept up his surveillance for the next few days. Tracking the soldier became easy. It was important to keep a good distance away and not to stare. You did not have to look at a man directly to trace his movements. Instead you followed the outline of him, the trail of his shadow. There were always crowds on the streets and in the buses, and it was simple for Antonio to blend in. At the Westlake Arms no one seemed to think twice about the hours he spent standing, sitting, and squatting on the sidewalk. Each night, when the light went out in the fourth-floor window, Antonio went back to his camp to sleep.

It soon became clear that the tattooed soldier kept to a strict routine. The lights came on at 6:15, followed by the ritual cleaning of the window. On the bus at 7:45, *en punto*. What else would you expect from a military man?

On the third night of his surveillance the routine was finally broken. Not long after the soldier got home from work, a small woman in a shiny green mini-dress walked up the front steps. Heavy black curls flowed onto her shoulders. A few minutes later she emerged at the front door with her arm around the soldier, who looked stiff next to the swing and bounce in her walk. Perhaps she held on to him so tightly because her heels were so high she was afraid she might fall. *A frivolous person, that's why she's with the soldier. She doesn't see who he really is.* Antonio could hear her brassy voice clearly from across the street.

"*La comida tailandés es picantísima, pero me gusta,*" she said. "It's even spicier than Mexican food."

They walked arm in arm toward Alvarado Street. Antonio followed them to a bus stop. From his vantage point a block away he could see that the soldier's girlfriend was still talking and that the soldier was nodding his head from time to time. Such a curious couple. Even if he hadn't been trailing the soldier he would have noticed them. The tiny woman with the curls and the loud emerald dress, her arm around the stocky man with the shaved head. Antonio watched them board the bus.

It was a slap across the face to see the soldier with a woman, bathed in her obvious affection. The soldier's life was the negative image of his own. The soldier had a job, Antonio did not. The soldier had a girlfriend, Antonio was all alone.

This man who took my only love has all the love he wants.

As the bus pulled away, Antonio remembered that he had dated a woman here in Los Angeles several years ago. They had taken the bus too. On Saturday nights the RTD buses were filled with immigrant couples. This woman was a Mexicana he met at Dierden's department store downtown, at the appliance counter where she sold him a toaster oven. Azucena was her name. A native of Mexico City, she was smart and urbane, a lover of foreign films. They went to see a very long Italian movie called *1900*.

Azucena had lasted only a few weeks. In the end she had too much life to be with someone like Antonio. Laughter came easy to her. She told jokes with those double entendres people from Mexico City were famous for. With Azucena he could discuss art and feel something like the person he had once been, but she was just twenty-two and had quickly grown impatient with his morose moods, his bouts of meanness.

Antonio was wondering what had happened to Azucena when he

found himself standing in front of the Westlake Arms again. Something had pulled him back to the apartment building, even though he knew the soldier was gone. *Now I am gravitating to this place.* Looking up at the six stories of brick and terra cotta, he noticed that the soldier's window was open.

A strange sensation passed through him. If a man was daring enough, he could climb the fire escape, work his way to that open window, and break into the tattooed soldier's apartment. Something like that could happen while the soldier was out with his curly-headed girlfriend.

The longer Antonio stared at the open window, the louder it seemed to be calling to him. *Well, why not?*

The hardest part, it turned out, was reaching the fire escape. Whoever owned this building had some experience with break-ins and had worked to prevent just the sort of entry Antonio was planning. The windows on the first floor were sealed with bricks, and the fire escape itself stopped well above them, a little black ladder dangling over the sidewalk far from the reach of any passerby. But Antonio noticed that the sealed windows still had sills that protruded from the wall like narrow steps. If he stood on one of these sills, the bottom of the ladder would be within a leap and an arm's reach, more or less.

Soon after the street had cleared of potential witnesses, Antonio found himself dangling from the bottom of the fire-escape ladder, swinging so violently that he was afraid his glasses might fall off. He felt like a *piñata*. The old iron ladder squeaked and moaned under his weight, but the noise was drowned out by the *ranchera* music blaring from an apartment on the second floor. Using reserves of strength he did not know he possessed, he tried to hoist himself up. *I am stronger now than I was in Guatemala.* It was all the heavy work he had done in Los Angeles, lifting and digging. His muscles were coming into play again, like when he hit the old man. *Pull! Pull harder!* He was making a spectacle of himself, but who cared. It was dark, and maybe nobody would see him.

There, I made it! The rusty steps of the fire escape shook and rattled as he walked up past the second and third floors. Moments later he was standing on the fourth-floor ledge, inching his way toward the tattooed soldier's window. Grabbing the windowsill, fighting off a sudden spell of acrophobia, he threw himself headfirst into the apartment, landing with a bounce on a very small bed.

Euphoria. He *was* stronger, and here was the proof. He had conquered the ledge and the fire escape. Antonio relished this moment of private glory.

The apartment wasn't much to look at, just a single room with a door leading to a bathroom. A bare tile floor the color of algae, a dresser, and a set of barbells in the corner. How predictable. The man was a fitness fanatic.

Antonio stood in the center of the room, held captive by the silence of the walls. He did not know what he was looking for or why he had felt compelled to come here. After he decided to follow the soldier in MacArthur Park, each discovery had led him on to the next one. He had tracked the soldier to El Pulgarcito Express, then to this apartment building, and now he was in his room. He couldn't get any closer to the man than this, inside his private sanctuary.

He went into the bathroom but saw nothing remarkable, just the usual assembly of soaps and shampoos. The nose-wrinkling aroma of disinfectant reminded him that he hadn't bathed since his last unauthorized entry, when he and José Juan snuck into Bixel Gardens. He considered using the soldier's shower but thought better of it. Back in the main room, he looked under the bed and found a little plastic basket holding a roll of toilet paper and a box of condoms. Protex. Here too there was a strong odor of disinfectant, as if the floor had recently been mopped. On the bed itself the sheets and blankets were pulled taut over the mattress, even after Antonio's crash landing from the window.

The place felt like a barracks.

There was a small closet space tucked into one of the walls, and Antonio quickly riffled through the clothes that hung on a steel bar, spotting the navy T-shirt the soldier had been wearing in the park. Moving to the dresser, he opened the drawers and found underwear and socks in carefully ordered stacks. In the bottom drawer he found a blue album underneath a pile of books. Taking care not to disturb the order of the books, he pulled the album out.

On the first pages there were newspaper clippings about military engagements, and certificates showing the soldier had completed training at academies in Guatemala, Panama, and the United States. One name was repeated on all these certificates: Guillermo Longoria.

The name stunned Antonio. It had not occurred to him that the soldier even had a name, and for a moment he lingered over it, wondering what use it might be to him, if any.

Standing in the center of the room, he flipped through the album until he came to a section of photographs. The soldier seemed to attach more importance to the certificates and clippings than to the photos, which were of all different sizes and types, as if taken with a dozen different cameras: Polaroids, large black-and-whites, colored squares aged to a pink wash, passport-sized head shots. They showed the same man Antonio had seen, only younger, even younger than in San Cristóbal. One was a close-up of the tattoo. In what seemed to be the oldest picture, a small snapshot with rounded corners, the soldier was lean and small, squeezed into an impossibly tight uniform of plain forest green. Later he wore camouflage and was larger in the chest and limbs, his expression hardened into stony masculinity. The only constants were his shaved head and the way he displayed his weapons to the camera, rifles and handguns carried stiffly, as if he had held his breath until the shutter tripped.

At the end of the album, taped to the back cover, there was a white envelope. When Antonio pulled on the flap, which was tucked in but unsealed, a small stack of photographs fell to the floor. He put the album on the bed and scrambled to pick them up. He was squatting to look under the dresser when he saw the bodies, three corpses lined up on a cement floor. Scattered all over the green linoleum, everywhere, were pictures of corpses. A morgue had fallen from the album and spilled around his feet. Corpses with their eyes open. Corpses with their pants pulled down, the seahorses of their genitals exposed. Corpses with their arms folded over their chests. Corpses with hands missing. Peasants in green shirts. Living men, in camouflage, posing with the corpses, as if to say, We're alive and they're dead. And here is the tattooed soldier, the painted killer, standing over a child lying face down on a dirt path. Other soldiers, taller men, pointing at a corpse with its mouth open, a silver tooth bared. An Indian woman's hands formed into fists as if to fight off death. A man with his shoulders pulled up, frozen in his last breath. Colorless skin with machete gashes that no longer bled. Hair sticky and stiff.

His hands trembling, Antonio picked up the corpses and put them back in their envelope, where he wouldn't have to look at them. This was too much to see. Too much to know and hold inside your head. All of the corpses and all their tragedies, the lives they led, their endings captured in a killer's camera.

Antonio shoved the album back in the dresser and went to the door. The latch wouldn't open, and for a moment Antonio thought he would have to go back down the fire escape and plunge to his death. He was in no state to play spider now. This room was making him sick, this room filled with disinfectant and perversions. If he stayed here any longer the taint and smell of the soldier would stick to his clothing, a smell more disgusting than anything in a homeless camp.

At last the door gave way, and Antonio stepped into the dusty air of a long, empty corridor, much like the hallway outside his last apartment. He ran down the stairs, out of the building, into the night, and walked as fast as he could to the lot he now called home.

* * *

Frank and the Mayor sat around the campfire watching José Juan throw dead olive branches into the flames, contemplating the twists and turns in the story Antonio had just told them, about Elena and Carlos, the tattooed soldier, the chance encounter in MacArthur Park. For five days Antonio had kept the secret of the soldier to himself, not even telling José Juan, but finally he had felt the need to talk. Omitting the break-in and the photographs, he had recounted the events in a circular narrative, starting somewhere in the middle and ending back at the beginning, with the moment he discovered Carlos and Elena dead in San Cristóbal Acatapán. Now the campfire was enveloped in a sad stillness, Frank and the Mayor showing their respect for this stranger's grief by staring silently at the flames.

"I'd kill the bastard," the Mayor said finally. "Motherfucking soldier deserves to die."

"I know a guy who'll do it if you give him your welfare check," Frank said.

"We don't get welfare," José Juan said.

"Well, whatever. Give him two hundred ninety-seven dollars, then. That's how much G.R. is anyway."

"I know a guy who'll do it for *fifty* bucks," the Mayor interjected.

Antonio had thought about killing the soldier, but only in the abstract. He could not yet imagine killing another human being, even a man with so much blood on his hands. But having someone else do it, that could work.

"I don't have any money at all," Antonio said. "Not even fifty. Not even ten."

"Do it yourself, then," Frank said. "Just club the guy. With a pipe, a hammer, whatever. Push him in front of a bus." He smiled wryly. "Shit, buy me a steak dinner and I'll do it for you." At this, both Frank and the Mayor laughed heartily. "I've seen people killed for less. A lot less, as a matter of fact. I've seen people killed because they insulted some idiot's old lady."

"Me too," the Mayor added. "These days people get themselves killed just for any stupid reason."

"Antonio doesn't want to kill anyone," José Juan said in a soft, serious voice. "He just wants justice."

"Yeah, justice," the Mayor said with the faintest trace of sarcasm.

"This man should be, how do you say? *Castigado.*" José Juan frowned in concentration. "Punished."

"Who's going to punish him?"

No one could answer the Mayor's question. All four men sat listening to the tree branches crackling in the fire.

"This is true, what you are saying." Antonio looked at the Mayor. He spoke slowly, afraid his immigrant English might not be understood. "No one will punish this man. In my country there is no one to punish the army for their *barbaridades*. No court will do it. This man can go free, he can do anything he wants. He can live here, he can live in Guatemala, and no one will bother him. Like you say, no one will fuck with him."

"Yeah," Frank said. "They'd probably give the s.o.b. a medal."

The Mayor pulled his watch cap down over his ears. "Oh man, this is too much!" he yelled. "Too much! Imagine some guy killed your old lady and the cops don't do shit. They just pat the guy on the back. They say, 'Good going, little buddy.' Wouldn't you want to mutilate him or something?"

"I'd stab him," Frank said. "Like this." He rose and made a half-dozen thrusts at the air with an imaginary knife, grunting and baring his teeth. "Motherfucker deserves to die!"

The Mayor laughed at Frank and stood up to leave. Frank hung back and pulled Antonio aside, placing a hand on his shoulder.

"That's some heavy-duty shit you're dealing with," he said with great solemnity. "You need any help, partner, you let me know. Me and the Mayor are with you on this."

Antonio looked at Frank and remembered the prayers of his wife to San Martín de Porres, the black saint of Peru, when she was pregnant with Carlos. Perhaps, from the grave, Elena had asked San Martín to send this black man to help him. San Martín was the mulatto son of a slave, the patron saint of social justice, the man who swept out the poorhouses.

"*Gracias*," Antonio said as Frank walked away. "Thank you."

* * *

The next morning Antonio sat outside the shelter sifting through the black Hefty bag, looking for the picture of Elena and Carlos. He wanted to see them alive today, to remember what the tattooed soldier had taken from him. It was the picture from Quetzaltenango after Carlos Martín's second birthday. Carlitos stood next to Elena in a white shirt and red tie, his hair parted to the side, moments after his mother ran a wet comb through it, just a few weeks before they both died.

Antonio hadn't looked inside the bag for days. He opened a shoe box full of old bills and pay stubs. He found at least a dozen pictures of José Juan's family, posed shots of his wife and four children taken in front of a small cinderblock house, the dates written carefully on the back in his wife's handwriting. He couldn't have forgotten the picture, it had to be here.

After ten minutes of searching, papers and clothes scattered all around him, Antonio gave up. Most likely he had dropped it on the floor after arguing with Mr. Hwang. He drove a fist into his thigh in frustration. *I lost their picture. How could I have been so stupid!*

Antonio was tossing papers and photographs back in the Hefty bag when he came upon a stack of letters to his old Los Angeles address, written in his mother's looping script. They were the letters he had received once a month until about a year ago, when he moved to Bixel Gardens without telling anyone in Guatemala. Most of the letters he never opened because he didn't want to be reminded of home, because he didn't want to hear from his parents, because he was still angry with them for so many things. But he hadn't thrown them away either.

One of the envelopes was thicker than the rest and seemed to contain something stiff. Hoping to find a picture of Carlos and Elena, Antonio ripped it open. There was indeed a photograph, but not of people. Instead it showed what looked like a white wall. Perplexed, he began to read the letter.

February 11, 1990
Dear Son,

It's been months since I've heard from you and I am sending this letter with prayers that, somehow, you will receive it. I can only hope that you are still at the last address you gave me. Your aunt Imelda told me that in Los Angeles no one ever stays in the same place for very long. So I can only hope that you haven't moved again.

It hurts your mother not to hear from her only son. Why have you stopped writing to me? Why this silence? What have we done to deserve this? If you don't write to us we can only assume the worst has happened, that you are either sick or dead, that you've had some terrible accident. Please write to us (your father also worries about you terribly). Please give us some message to calm our fears.

I talked to your father's friend, the sub-rector at the University, who is of the opinion that the political situation has improved sufficiently for you to return. Things aren't like they were when you left. We still see bodies in the newspaper but nothing like the horrors that were happening two or three years ago. I think and hope that the time of the worst ugliness has passed. Things have calmed down. There is no reason for you not to come home.

If you stay in Guatemala City you shouldn't have any problems. It's safe here in the capital. As long as you avoid San Cristóbal, you should have no difficulties whatsoever.

In regards to San Cristóbal, I heard recently from your friend the Belgian priest, Van der Est. He remembers you fondly, of course. He telephoned a few weeks ago to say hello. I gave him what little information about you I could. Then we started talking about Carlos and Elena and he mentioned that there was still no marker on the graves. This seemed so terribly wrong to me. I persuaded him to place one for us. I hope you won't mind that I sent him 300 quetzales for this purpose. The marker is there now—a little marble plaque in the *panteón*. I have sent along a picture of it. I fear it may still be a long time before we can visit the graves in person. The war continues in places like San Cristóbal, where, sadly, it may never end.

I hope you are feeling better. Perhaps it is best, as a friend of mine suggested, that you see a psychologist. Despite my reluctance to recur to such drastic methods, it seems to me that, perhaps, you may need someone with professional skills to help you cope with the demons that have persecuted you since the horrible tragedy. Please think about it.

We were worried by the news of the recent earthquake in Los Angeles, but later relieved to hear that it was a very small one and that the damage had been minor. I looked for you in the television reports, even though I knew it was silly to expect that the camera would find you in a city of millions of people. I am content only to see a face that looks like yours, to imagine that you are safe, that you are eating well. Please write.

Love,
Your Mother

Antonio looked at the photograph, two marble squares in a large wall of similar squares. He recognized this as one of the public funeral vaults in the Cementerio General in San Cristóbal. He had been there once, to inspect the premises as part of his responsibilities at the Department of Public Works. This was where Elena and Carlos were buried, in little more than paupers' graves, surrounded by peasants killed on the highway and slum children who died of dysentery and malnutrition. The names on three of the squares next to Carlos's and Elena's were written in with crayons and pencil by families too poor to afford a permanent inscription. Thanks to his mother's generosity, his wife and son now had white marble markers etched with gold-leaf letters and swirling flowers.

ELENA SOSA DE BERNAL, MADRE Y ESPOSA
CARLOS MARTIN BERNAL, HIJO

The sight of their names filled Antonio with bitter shame. This responsibility of the father and husband had passed to someone else, to Van der Est, a stranger. Antonio had been forced to leave San Cristóbal the day of the killings, before he could make any decent arrangements for the burial. He had just discovered the bodies and was still in a trance. If Antonio had stayed for the funeral, the tattooed soldier would have killed him too, and that would have been the end of all this misery. He would never have seen Los Angeles or lived under a plastic roof. Antonio should have died in San Cristóbal.

He looked at the photograph again. He would never forgive his mother for taking upon herself a duty that should have been left to him. The hypocrisy. This woman who never cared about his wife was looking after her grave. If he were to see his mother now he would give her a real *maltratada*, one of his raging fits that made people step back in shock. He would tell her to leave the memory of Carlos and Elena alone, that she had already done enough damage with her meddling.

My mother who sent us to San Cristóbal Acatapán. My mother who said we would be safe there.

Antonio slipped the photograph into his shirt pocket and tore the letter into tiny pieces that fell around his feet. He would never make the mistake of reading one of his mother's letters again.

I didn't bury them properly. Even after they were dead I failed them.

The letter and the marble squares were proof of his impotence in the face of the tattooed soldier, his mother, and so many other things. If he had resisted his mother all those years ago, they wouldn't have ended up in San Cristóbal and Elena would still be alive instead of in a grave Antonio had never visited. "Of course you didn't remember to bury us, Antonio," Elena would have said. "You always forgot everything."

A light breeze carried the pieces of the letter across the vacant lot, white shreds of paper sticking in patches of weeds and fluttering into the mud. He could see his mother's blue handwriting on each bit of paper, snatches of her voice, giving unwanted advice, making judgments. Poor little Antonio, small man lost in an alien city, so pathetic he should see a psychologist. Pleading with him to come home so she could take care of him again. That was one thing he would not do. What was there to go back to? His mother and father? A country where the walls were covered with the names of the missing and the dead? A city of parks where Elena no longer laughed or walked or smiled?

If Antonio went back to Guatemala there would be no one to follow the tattooed soldier, no one to stand and say he was a killer. No one would know about the soldier's crimes, and he would live out his life like any other resident of Los Angeles, taking his girlfriend to restaurants and lifting weights in his room, growing old with pictures of his victims in an album in his dresser.

Antonio had seen all those pictures in the soldier's room, those anonymous cadavers. They had passed through his hands, all the peasants and students and revolutionaries and sons and daughters hacked and shot to death with no living witnesses. He knew these people only as photographs, but he could feel that they all died alone, like Elena and Carlos, in their homes and villages and fields, without anything or anyone to protect them. Now Antonio could act for them. He could act for the massacred who had been left without fathers, husbands, or brothers to avenge them.

I did not bury my wife and child, but I can stand and seek vengeance, for them and for the many, for the anonymous dead.

Now Antonio knew how Elena must have felt when she marched in the demonstrations. Now he could see why she was a revolutionary, he could understand what had been a mystery before.

This is how Elena felt, tall and strong. This is what she was trying to tell me, but I wouldn't listen. Elena knew that to march with the many was to stand tall. Elena loved me because she knew I could be a brave fighter.

Antonio felt as if he had been washed in the coldest, clearest mountain water, shocked into wakefulness. For the first time in weeks the gleam of the morning sun came into focus, the lines of the skyscrapers and bridges sharp in the distance. Antonio would stay in Los Angeles and track down the tattooed soldier and make him pay for his crimes. He would kill this man with his own hands.

It was not such a strange thing, to kill someone. Antonio could imagine himself doing it now, killing the soldier without remorse. In this city of vicious madness people did much worse things. That was what Frank and the Mayor said, and they were right. In Los Angeles people shot at the innocent, they fired randomly into weddings and funerals. If people could commit such horrible crimes for no good reason, then Antonio could bring himself to kill the soldier without feeling like an animal.

It was imperative to act immediately. It had already been seven years. Each moment the soldier lived was a crime against nature, against the laws that made planets spin and babies grow. The soldier's life, his living steps in Los Angeles, were a violation. They were a stain on the earth as indelible as the pigment etched into his skin, the jaguar on his forearm.

Antonio scoured Crown Hill for a piece of hard, heavy metal. Next to the ruins of a retaining wall he found a lead pipe, rusty at the edges, still gray and smooth in the middle, about two feet long. He tested it by striking it lightly against his open palm. *I really want to hit someone. Right now.* He started to pound on the wall, the metal clanging loudly with each blow, little bits of concrete flaking off. *Mr. Hwang, my mother, the tattooed soldier. So many people against me. I could turn this whole wall into a pile of pebbles.*

The men in the surrounding lots lifted their heads, drawn by the rhythmic clanging of the pipe, like a church bell. Soon they turned away, bored. Someone pounding on a wall wasn't that unusual here, not in the camps, where people babbled to themselves and defecated in the open air. Antonio stopped, suddenly short of breath, his arm sore.

Frank was right. Antonio would follow the advice of the black angel sent to him by his wife. One good blow to the head would probably be enough to kill. *This pipe will leave little chips of rust and metal embedded in his skull.* Being beaten to death seemed as inelegant a way to die as any. *It must be very painful to feel your skull crack open.* He would beat the soldier with the pipe, preferably with people watching. *The soldier's name is Guillermo, but the name doesn't matter. I don't need his name to kill him.* His head would be a clean target because it was covered with only the thinnest layer of hair.

In broad daylight. That's the way Carlos and Elena were killed. On a sunny morning, their bodies left on the street for everyone to see.

Antonio left Crown Hill and walked briskly back to the shelter with his pipe. He tried to stick it in his back pocket, but it was too long and slipped out. He tried again, pulling his sweater over the protruding end. He looked awkward, a large bulge attached to his back, but the pipe stayed put.

It was Saturday, nearly a week since that first encounter in the park, and the soldier would almost certainly be there playing chess tomorrow morning.

The Army of Painted Children

As soon as he talked to his friend, Longoria would forget about the old woman once and for all. What bothered him most was that she could get away with embarrassing him like that in public. In Guatemala, he would have been able to track her down and punish her. People like that were punished even if they were seventy or eighty years old, because you had to set an example. But here in Los Angeles she could just disappear into the ocean of the city, and there was no way to find her and teach her that you didn't talk to a Jaguar like that.

For almost a week now he had been carrying this lingering malaise, something resembling shame. He couldn't stop wondering whether he had actually killed this Demetrio. It bothered Longoria that the old woman had burdened him so. He hadn't felt this way when he was with the Jaguars. In Guatemala, when people looked at you with a hatred like the old woman's, or when they tried very hard not to look at you at all, it never stuck to you like this. These ugly thoughts must be lingering because he couldn't go back to the barracks and be with his brothers and forget.

In the barracks you knew you were good and honorable because you could feel the rightness of the cause in the strength of the men around you, lined up with their shimmering weapons, proud and ready for battle. Longoria couldn't be with his unit anymore because he was in California, but he could visit his friend Mauricio Lopez, the only other Jaguar he knew in Los Angeles. As soon as Longoria talked to his friend, the confusion of the past week would slip away. He would tell Lopez about the old woman and how his co-workers at El Pulgarcito had been treating him like a stranger since the day he slapped her, as if he were a different person from the man they had trusted and liked before. He would tell Lopez about the sidelong glances and the uncomfortable silences, even from Duarte, who had heard about the incident from the gossipy Carlos Avilés.

Together Lopez and Longoria had been to Fort Bragg and Panama, where they had endured the taunts of the smart-ass Salvadorans who treated them like simple backwoods cousins. Longoria hadn't been to see his friend in months, and he realized now that this was a mistake, that it was important to keep in touch with his brothers.

After work Longoria walked the four blocks from El Pulgarcito to Hoover and waited for the orange and white RTD bus that would take him on the forty-five-minute ride to Watts, where Lopez lived. One of the reasons he hadn't seen Lopez in so long was that he lived so far away, in a part of the city where, it was said, only bad things happened. Lopez's telephone had been disconnected, but it was Saturday and Longoria would just have to hope that he was there.

When the bus arrived, it was standing room only. The vehicle sagged like an overburdened draft animal, almost scraping the asphalt. Longoria squirmed through the packed bodies and found a place near the middle of the bus. An air conditioner whined overhead, unable to overcome all the human sweat and warmth. It was just like back home, like Guatemala City, the push of too many brown people heavy with exhaustion, except that on this bus no one was hanging from the back bumper or outside the front door, because that was something the gringo drivers didn't allow.

Fifteen minutes later, when half the passengers got off at Washington Boulevard, Longoria took a seat. The bus was sealed against the dry air of the streets by plastic windows shaded a smoky gray. A wild scramble of names and insults had been scratched into the panel in front of him, where the landscape of central Los Angeles was projected like a faint, fuzzy movie. Crowds of men and women massing at the intersections, nearly everyone carrying their possessions in plastic shopping bags. A revolving parade of storefronts. Imelda's Honduran Bakery. The Cheapest Flights to Mexico City! Cojutepeque Salvadoran Restaurant. The homeless, floating solo along the sidewalks, the throngs parting before them. More storefronts. El Chapín Guatemalan Grocery. Old brick buildings. Another branch of El Pulgarcito Express (number three). Here and there a shuttered window, a closed store. A huge auto parts place with tall window displays, one of the few modern buildings on this long street.

When the bus passed under the Santa Monica Freeway into South-Central Los Angeles, Longoria began counting the street numbers. He had boarded near 8th Street, now they were at 35th. His friend lived on 109th.

Longoria had been to South-Central more than once. It seemed like the rest of Los Angeles except that here the Latinos lived next door to blacks. He had never had any problems with the blacks. They kept to themselves. When you had to deal with them they were direct and unambiguous, like people he had known in the army. They didn't play games, and Longoria liked that. You could always tell what side they were on, where you stood with them.

South-Central Los Angeles looked a lot like Longoria's neighborhood, though there were fewer people on the streets. Entire blocks were empty of pedestrians. On other blocks all but a handful of the stores were shut down. Here and there he saw buildings that were only empty shells: four walls and no ceiling, painted announcements on the front almost erased by time. A few buildings seemed to have been burned out many, many years ago: scorched brick walls left standing alone, like part of a movie set, broken iron bars, twisted and rusting. Longoria looked at those buildings and thought that a war must have been fought here, though he had no idea when. A conquering army leaves this sort of mark on the landscape, the sooty signature of fire, the hand of random, celebratory destruction. The scattered ruins along Hoover Street looked familiar. Longoria wondered why this distant war had been fought.

He got off the bus at 109th Street and walked five blocks east to his friend's home. Lopez had done well for himself—he had a job as a car mechanic—and had made enough money to buy a little house for his family here in Watts. The last time Longoria talked to him, Lopez said that there were lots of Guatemaltecos living in Watts now.

Longoria went up the front steps past a lawn overgrown with dandelions and was greeted by a black steel door with an almost martial aspect. He knocked on the door and it rattled. After a minute or so of knocking and squinting through the pattern of pinholes in the steel screen, he saw a shadow moving.

The door swung open and Lopez appeared, looking so different from the man Longoria remembered that he wondered if he had come to the wrong house.

For years Lopez had kept his hair stubble-short, like Longoria, a habit carried over from their army days. Now it sprouted from his head in a tangled, asymmetrical mass of curls. Deep pillow wrinkles covered his face. Lopez had been asleep even though it was barely late afternoon. He was fully dressed, wearing a pale blue mechanic's shirt with "Mauricio" embroidered on a patch just above the left breast. Sweat soaked through the armpits, the back, the front. His green eyes had a faraway expression.

"Lopez? It's me, Longoria. Why are you looking at me like that?"

"Longoria. What are you doing here?"

"I came to visit, I wanted to talk."

*　*　*

They had first met on a basketball court, near the plaza of a little town in the mountains of Huehuetenango whose name he had long ago forgotten. It was before they both joined the Jaguars, when they were with one of the regular army units. They were lined up in haphazard rows, ready to march out on patrol, a new unit formed with conscripts from all over the country: *quetzaltecos, jutiapenses, capitalinos.* Next to Longoria stood a man with the name "Lopez" stitched crudely onto his shirt, a light-skinned *canche* with mischievous green eyes darting as they took in the scene, a big smile on his face. He was from the eastern provinces, where people were known as smart alecks and jokers. Days, weeks later, Lopez would still be smiling, though not quite as broadly as on that first morning on the basketball court. Months later, the smile would be gone completely.

Lopez seemed to find something amusing in what their new captain was saying. Longoria had no idea what could be so funny, since the captain was giving the men a pep talk about the enemy, which had been active in this area.

"Half of these subversives don't even have guns. None of them have uniforms. They carry sticks into battle, or machetes. Sometimes they try to throw little bags of lime into your eyes."

At this Lopez laughed, a brief chuckle the captain didn't seem to notice.

"They have nothing. We will crush them."

The captain was a thin man whose fair skin had turned pink in the sun. He was in his early twenties and clean-shaven, with fresh razor cuts on his cheeks and chin. "They're called the Ejército Guerrillero de los Pobres for a reason," he continued. "They're all poor, they don't have any guns. Hardly any. They're a bunch of sissies, these guerrillas. We won't have any problems."

They were to patrol the road north of town. March out ten kilometers and check for subversive activity. Come back, eat, enjoy a good meal. Extra meat this time because they were real soldiers now and they were protecting the fatherland.

Longoria had been told to keep a good five meters between himself and the men in front of him and behind him: "Protection against an ambush, so the whole company isn't wiped out. Don't stay bunched together."

The road was gravel, a meandering carpet of tiny gray pebbles. Lopez marched the requisite distance ahead, faintly whistling a song, sometimes singing the words softly. "*Mami, el negro está rabioso . . .*" This was the time of year when the *campesinos* grew bean plants around the cornstalks, the thin green strings coiling around the stiff axis. There were twirling threads of bean plants on either side of the road as the company marched up a slight grade toward the mountains. Longoria had tended to bean plants since before he could remember. It was what he would be doing right now if he weren't in this green uniform, walking gingerly on the gravel with his new boots, the first he'd ever owned in his life. He felt lucky. Marching wasn't so hard; only the city boys couldn't take it. Lopez, he guessed, had some *campesino* in him, because his step was unwavering. This soldier's work was easy compared to working on the land.

Longoria was near the middle of a serpentine line of soldiers that stretched more than one hundred yards down the highway when they came under fire, clap-clap-clap, the forest of sickly pine trees on the ridge above them breaking into a round of applause. The guerrillas were behind those trees somewhere, spitting bullets at Longoria and the men around him. He kissed the ground, becoming intimate with the pine needles and pebbles, wondering what it would feel like if a bullet hit him. Alvaro, his friend since boot camp, was lying on his stomach the regulation five meters away, his cheek pressed to the dirt as it had been pressed to Longoria's during their dance.

Longoria wondered how he would find the courage to stand up and follow the example of their captain, who was advancing up the slope toward the ridge and the bullets. After a minute or so the shooting stopped. Then the trees and branches began to speak.

"The army is a bunch of faggots! Imperialist stooges! You do it with your mothers!"

"*Your* mother!" the captain shouted back. "Communist pigs! Come out and fight!"

"The gringos give it to you up the ass!" said the voice in the woods. "Faggots!"

"Surrender. Come with us, fight for good!" said another voice, in broken, Indian-accented Spanish. "Fight for the poor!"

Several members of the company began to laugh.

"Learn to speak Spanish, you stupid Indian!"

"How much are the Russians paying you?" one of the soldiers cried out. "You *maricas*. How many Cubans are there with you?"

Longoria heard a whistling over his head, followed seconds later by a rifle report ringing across the treetops.

To his left, Lopez rose to a squat, cupping his hands around his mouth. "Hey, Turco! Is that you?" he yelled at the trees. "Turco Gómez, from Gualán! That has to be you!"

"Who's that?" the voice from the ridge called back.

"I knew it was him," Lopez said to the men next to him. "Turco! It's me! Mauricio! From the Coca-Cola factory!"

A long silence followed. Lopez cupped his hands to speak again, a wide grin on his face, like a child teasing a classmate in the schoolyard. "Hey, Turco, what are you doing over there fighting with those delinquents?"

Another long silence, and then: "I don't know any Mauricio!" Two shots rang out from the trees.

"Advance, you idiots," the captain yelled. "Advance. Into the woods."

Crouching, he began to move up the slope in a duck walk, taking cover against a tree trunk, then moving forward a little more to the next tree. The enlisted men followed in frightened imitation, a flock of ducklings in camouflage trailing behind their mother.

The sporadic shooting from the ridge grew into a steady barrage. It was Longoria's first real piss-your-pants moment. He raised his gun, fired blindly, and started running uphill. The shooting stopped again, and all Longoria could hear was the anxious rush of air through his windpipe and the pounding of his heart.

He reached the top of the slope and stood where the enemy had been. His unit searched the ridge, kicking at the ground and its bed of pine needles, but found only scattered shell casings. The guerrillas appeared to have escaped down a small valley to the west, into a thick cornfield. Or perhaps they had gone east, toward the next hill, and dissolved into another cluster of trees.

"They ran away," a soldier called out. "We won!"

"Don't be a fool," his sergeant said. "They always run away. That's how they fight."

"Hey, *capitán*, we have a casualty down here," yelled one of the men from the bottom of the slope.

Just a few yards from the embankment where Longoria had first taken cover from the sniper fire, a man lay face down, machine gun at his side. Longoria rushed down the hill, sliding on the loose dirt. The soldier who had called for help turned the wounded man over. It was Alvaro. Blood had seeped over his forehead from a wound that seemed to be behind the ear. A hand reached down to his belly.

"What bad luck," the soldier said. "No one else was even wounded, and this guy takes two hits."

"Rare Marxist metal," Lopez whispered to Longoria. "Somebody better tell the captain that the Communists have a secret weapon. Sticks that shoot bullets!"

Grabbing a tarp, Longoria, Lopez, and two other soldiers carried Alvaro hammock-style down the gravel road to a clearing, where they waited for a helicopter. In all likelihood Alvaro was already dead, though there was no medic in the company and no one felt like taking his pulse. The color had drained from his face, the blood on his forehead was a brown crust. His features looked twisted, as if he had swallowed something bitter. After they set him down, Longoria tried not to look at his friend, tried not to remember that he had been forced to dance with him in the barracks. The rest of the company stood around them, oblivious to their only casualty, talking and waving their arms, reenacting the day's brief battle in elaborate pantomimes, already spinning tall tales.

They lifted Alvaro into the metal craft and climbed inside, airborne in an instant, rising high over the treetops in a quick swoop and bank. It was Longoria's first flight of any kind. Passing over the village where the march had begun, they headed for the base in Huehuetenango. Alvaro lay motionless on the floor, his expression unchanged. Longoria felt sad that he couldn't open his eyes to enjoy the drama and rush of the helicopter ride. Alvaro was a *campesino* too, and he would have enjoyed seeing the fields from this perspective, seeing how small their little plots of land looked when you climbed hundreds of feet in the sky. This helicopter ride made all the humiliation of boot camp worthwhile. Longoria could see the pilot in the glass cocoon of the cockpit, wearing an astronaut's round helmet with wires and microphones attached. They were in a machine in the air, only the spinning wings above them holding all this equipment in the sky.

"I've never flown before," Lopez shouted over the roar of the engine, beaming as he gestured at the verdant panorama below.

"Me neither."

Longoria would forever be grateful to the army for allowing him to fly in the air, carried aloft by the pulse of the engine, like a heartbeat, hundreds and hundreds of feet above the fields. In the helicopter he could see who he had been before he joined the army and what he was now. He could see that when you worked a plot of land there were dozens, no, hundreds and thousands more like it all around you. For the first time, he could see where he fit in the world.

The helicopter ride lasted barely twenty minutes. How was it, he wondered, that such narrow spinning blades could keep so much metal afloat, lift so many people into the air? It was over too soon. Longoria and a medic lowered Alvaro onto a gurney, and he was quickly wheeled away.

Lopez asked if he and Longoria could take the helicopter to rejoin their unit, but the medic said they would have to go back in a truck. Alone on a soccer field, they watched the helicopter take off, the blades of grass around them leaning back as if in awe of the swirling machine that rose and disappeared into blue. Longoria was very disappointed.

* * *

Longoria pushed past Lopez into the living room. Musty clothes were scattered like fungi across the floor. A tall cabinet stood empty of a set of imitation china that he remembered vaguely. Bright patches of paint on the dusty walls bore witness to missing picture frames. Longoria was stunned; someone had looted Lopez's house, stolen all his property. This had been a room crowded with furniture, the requisite studio portraits of mother, father, and children on the wall. Now there was only a squat coffee table and a rumpled, blanket-covered couch.

"*Hombre*, what happened? Were you robbed."

Longoria searched his friend's face for answers. Lopez seemed a little more alert but still not fully himself. Longoria shook him by the shoulder, then grabbed his chin.

"Wake up, *cabrón*. It's four o'clock. What's wrong with you? Are you drunk? Just because they stole your things doesn't mean you should be drinking. Where's your wife, anyway? She probably left because you got drunk, right? Come on, wake up."

"Get me some water," Lopez said finally. "My throat is dry."

Stepping over the clothes in the living room, Longoria went to the kitchen, found a plastic Donald Duck cup in the sink, and filled it with tap water.

Lopez drank the water in one gulp and took a seat on the couch. He said nothing, but his jaw worked steadily, as if he were chewing gum. On the coffee table a small platoon of amber bottles stood at attention. Longoria examined the labels. Milligrams and pharmaceutical commandments. Take with food. Don't operate heavy machinery. Mellaril. Cogentin. Four times a day. Three times a day. May cause drowsiness. Lopez's name on each bottle.

"All these pills," Longoria said. "What are you taking so many pills for?"

"I've been sick." Lopez was sitting on the couch awkwardly, trying to hold himself erect, as if he were occupying his body for the first time.

"Sick?"

"The pills help me. They really help me a lot. What's the word the doctor used? I forget the word. *Estabilizar*. They stabilize me."

"What are you talking about?"

"The doctor convinced me. I didn't want to believe at first, but he showed me. I met him in the hospital. He's a really nice doctor. *Un negro*. He told me the pills would make me feel better, and they do. I just have to sleep more now."

Longoria examined the bottles again, wondering what illness his friend suffered. Maybe he'd had some accident at work; being a mechanic had its risks. The house was deserted, as far as Longoria could tell. The last time he was here, children played in this living room, the smell of home-cooked *plátanos fritos* drifted in from the kitchen.

"I didn't know you were in the hospital," Longoria said.

"It was after Dahlia left me, after she left with the baby." Lopez stopped abruptly, as if someone else had spoken and presented him with this information for the first time.

"The baby? What about the other one? What about your boy?"

"Dahlia left me and then I went to the hospital. Or maybe it was before. She took the baby."

"But where's Mauricio junior?"

"He's dead."

"What?"

"Didn't you know?"

"No! When? What happened?"

"Dahlia left me," Lopez repeated. "I don't blame her. She did the right thing. I hit her. Cuts and everything. So she left me."

"Wait. How did your son die?"

Lopez buried his face in his hands, tears escaping underneath his palms, slipping down his cheeks. Longoria had never seen his friend cry. Lopez was a Jaguar. Longoria vividly remembered marching behind him through jungles and over mountains, marching for miles and miles with his eyes trained on Lopez's boots, which never slowed because the man was either too stubborn or too stupid to admit he was exhausted. Now he was this other person, a man who cried. *I was here just a few months ago and he was fine.*

Disgusted, Longoria left him alone and wandered around the house, searching for clues that might explain what had happened. The kitchen smelled of spoiled milk and garbage. The backyard was littered with beer cans, toys, pieces of scrap wood, and an old weightlifting bench whose red plastic seat had faded and cracked in the sun. Back in the house, he discovered women's clothing and more toys scattered in the bedrooms. He went out on the porch and looked around the neighborhood.

The street was orange-yellow in the last light of the afternoon. Three girls, Latino and black, played hopscotch on the sidewalk in front of a freshly painted green stucco house with rosebushes exploding in crimson and pink in the yard. There were many nice homes on the block, an abundance of well-kept cacti, neatly trimmed bushes, and brick-lined paths cutting through lawns. A few houses had flaking paint or boarded-over windows or walls covered with a tangle of spray-painted graffiti. On one gabled roof a series of letters painted in chunky blocks faced the neighborhood like a billboard announcing the presence of "Vermont 13," a local gang.

Everything was as Longoria remembered it except Lopez's house.

The grass in front had grown waist-high, thick and unkempt, like Lopez's hair. Fed by the recent rains, the rosebushes bloomed chaotically, a carpet of petals rotting on the walkways. The chain-link fence that marked Lopez's property had become a catchment for wind-blown plastic wrappers and newspapers. What had happened to the Lopez who was a fanatic for cleanliness, the Lopez who taught him how to make his bunk so the sheets were as tight as the skin of a drum?

Returning to the living room, Longoria discovered to his great relief that Lopez had stopped crying. "What happened to Mauricio junior?" he asked bluntly. "How did he die?"

"Didn't you know?" Lopez said again, looking at his friend in irritated confusion.

"No."

"I was walking in the door from work when they told me. He was at school. That's when it happened."

"At school?"

"The gangs. They shot at the security guard. The school was for little kids, but it had a security guard." Lopez put an index finger just under his eyelid and pulled down the skin, creating a pink crescent. "*Aquí*," he said. "That's where the bullet hit my son."

"Those piece-of-shit gangs," Longoria spat.

"They didn't let me see him right away. It was the gangs that did it. The cholos. It was the guard they wanted to shoot. They didn't like the guard."

"Those gangs can't shoot for shit. They don't even aim, they just pull the trigger."

"He was standing in the middle of the playground. By the flagpole. And the bullet just came down and hit him. It happened right there in the playground."

Lopez's right hand, resting on his leg, began to tremble. "The police wouldn't let me see him." He looked up at Longoria with desperate, pleading eyes. "Why are you asking me this? Why are you making me tell it?"

"I didn't know."

"Don't make me tell it. Not again. I was doing fine, and then you come here and make me tell it." Perspiring now, he reached up to wipe his forehead with a bare hand.

"But *hombre*, I didn't know."

"They didn't let me see his body. He was just lying there in the playground for an hour."

Longoria tried to remember the boy's face. A smart little boy with his father's green eyes, about five years old the last time Longoria was here. A neat child, clothes cleaned and ironed, hair parted to the side, wavy but not curly like his father's. Mauricio junior spoke English to his father, who answered him in Spanish.

Why would a bullet fall from the sky and kiss Mauricio junior on the cheek, just under the eye? Why would a bullet find a child on an American playground in the middle of the day? Who gave the bullets their orders? The cholos? Longoria had trouble believing such a thing could happen randomly. In his experience, bullets did not find children by chance.

"Dahlia blamed me," Lopez said suddenly.

"What?"

"I didn't have anything to do with it, I was at work, but she blamed me. I know she did. That's why I hit her. Because she didn't have the right to blame me for anything."

"That doesn't make any sense. How could she blame you?"

"I've been trying to get her back," Lopez continued, pulling at his curls. "But all these things are stopping me." He got up from the couch and began pacing the room, pointing at the soiled underwear and socks. "Look at this mess. Look at me. I wasn't like this before."

"You were always neat," Longoria said, trying not to sound angry. "And clean."

"It was when I saw him. When they finally showed him to me. His body. I shouldn't have looked at him like that. But I had to. I was his father, I had to look." He paused and stared at his mechanic's hands, faint traces of oil and grease still embedded in his cuticles.

"You started drinking again, didn't you?" Longoria said. "I told you not to do that."

"No I didn't. I don't drink anymore."

"That's what the pills are for, right? To keep you from drinking."

"No. The pills are to help me forget that I saw him. Bleeding from his face, all stretched out by the flagpole."

"Stop."

"He was bleeding from his face. A bullet." At this Lopez paused, as if he were afraid to say what came next. "I saw him lying there. I saw my boy bleeding from a bullet. He was shot, Longoria. A bullet killed him."

"It was the gangs that did it. That's what you said. Not you. The gangs."

"His eyes were still open." Lopez started to cry again, tears running down familiar channels in his cheeks. "I saw him and it was like all these things I'd seen before. I started to remember all these things."

"Take a pill, *cabrón!*" Longoria shouted, reaching for one of the amber bottles. "You're losing control."

"I just started to remember." Lopez raised his hands to his temples, as if something were stuck there, to his skin. "And now I can't forget."

Longoria popped the lid off the bottle, and blue capsules tumbled into his palm. "Take one of these and shut up before I slap you. Stop acting like a woman." He flung them at Lopez, who raised his arms meekly in self-defense.

"Don't." Lopez fell to his knees and started to pick up the capsules. "They're expensive."

Longoria headed for the front door. He didn't have to listen to this. Lopez wasn't the man he remembered. The Lopez he knew was a real fighter, strong and brave.

"You're crazy!" Longoria shouted just before he slammed the steel door behind him. "Take your pills!"

* * *

Art's Gun Bonanza was in a mini-mall on Alvarado Street, about four blocks from MacArthur Park. A sign in the window cheerfully announced, "Yes, We Have AK-47s!" Longoria went straight there after his visit to Lopez even though it would make him late for his date with Reginalda.

A gringo with a shaggy mustache and a moon-crater complexion stood behind the counter. Art himself, a man with the weary expression of someone who'd been victimized by one too many robberies. He touched his hand to the holstered gun on his hip when Longoria walked through the door. A security guard in a yellow jacket was dozing off in a folding chair by the display of hunting rifles. Semi-automatic machine guns and rifles hung on a rack behind the counter, including the promised AK-47, a crescent-shaped magazine dangling from its belly. Longoria leaned over the glass case and inspected the available handguns, mostly automatic pistols, heavy chunks of gray, black, and chrome-plated steel lined up in neat rows, each with a small price tag attached by string. These were pretty weapons, practical and effective, especially the silver 9-millimeter. Longoria had one once, a gift from an American instructor at Fort Bragg.

The gang members who killed Lopez's son had probably used a 9-millimeter. The gangs were to blame for his weeping and his pills. Lopez was a warrior, but he had been broken by a single bullet fired by a cholo who couldn't shoot straight. There were so many gangs in the city, dozens of little armies, including the one that made its headquarters from time to time on the front steps of the Westlake Arms. The perpetual gunplay in Longoria's neighborhood was a danger he hadn't thought much about until now.

When he saw these cholos on his front steps, they exchanged tense glances, masculine eyes sizing each other up. Longoria saw something he recognized in the gang members, and they must have seen it in him too, because they didn't bump against him or try to intimidate him like they did other people. The cholos had eyes that looked tough and sad at the same time, the faces of boys who knew what a bullet could do to flesh, who knew the helplessness of hearing gunshots and diving for cover.

The gang members were children fighting a war, that was clear. Longoria had been in a war too, but his war was over now. For Longoria the battles had ended years ago, although he read in the papers, and had heard from friends, that they were still going on over there, in the jungle thousands of miles away. As far as he could tell, the cholos were engaged in what his instructors at Fort Bragg called "conventional warfare." Their game was to claim a position—in this case, the front steps of the Westlake Arms—and then hold it against an enemy that could be counted on to ambush them. To mark their position, their sacred ground, they had covered the black asphalt of the street with a huge graffito announcing the name of their gang, Bixel 13. It was the size of a delivery truck, so large it could be seen clearly only from the third floor of the Westlake Arms or higher. Longoria could read it from his window, but when he stood on the street it looked like a nonsensical geometry of lines, circles, and squares.

The graffito on the pavement was their flag; they rallied around it the same way Longoria and his fellow Jaguars had rallied around the sky blue and white flag of Guatemala with the quetzal bird in the center. Like Longoria, the gang members also painted themselves with their allegiances, although they took the habit to extremes, tattoos covering not only their arms but their chests, necks, and shoulders, their fingers, and sometimes even their faces. The tattoos announced a kind of devotion that Longoria understood and even sympathized with, a declaration of the blood seriousness of their loyalties.

These children on the front steps had been in combat, and you had to respect that. Still, Longoria was confused about the origin and purpose of their war. They seemed to be interested in fighting for its own sake; they fought for no cause Longoria could see, no ideology or greater historical purpose. Longoria had fought to save Guatemala from Communism, to create a country of warriors and honorable men. But the cholos held their position just to prove it could be held, making a big show of their muscles and their courage, daring someone to come and shoot at them.

And when the shooting started, they had no discipline of fire. There was probably not a marksman among them. Longoria had seen them in one engagement: a beefy, pimply teenager in a Mexican sarape, holding a 9-millimeter pistol like the ones in Art's case as he ran down the sidewalk right underneath Longoria's window, arms extended but limp, firing with his eyes closed, pursued by two skinny cholos firing just as wildly. They were like the worst unit of the Guatemalan army, like the first cannon-fodder unit Longoria had been in, a company without effective leadership, shooting at chickens and pigs, getting drunk and firing in the air.

It did not surprise him that Lopez's little boy had been caught in their crossfire. It was not uncommon to hear gunshots outside the Westlake Arms and discover a shrine of marigolds and votive candles on the sidewalk a day or so later, memorials for the dead that seemed to sprout from the spots of blood left on the pavement. They reminded Longoria of the memorials people built in Guatemala, to accident victims, to the dead of the war, to the subversives killed by the army.

Anyone could be caught in the crossfire of the war of the painted children.

After visiting Lopez, Longoria began to see that the gangs were a threat to his physical safety in the same way the old woman was a threat to his mind. Both could destroy him if he wasn't careful. The answer was to buy a gun. With a gun he could scare off the cholos and the next old woman who came to blame him for things he wasn't responsible for. With a gun he would stop feeling this confusion in his head. He would be armed again, just like he was with the Jaguars.

He asked to see the silver pistol, and Art unlocked the case reluctantly, reaching in from behind. "Nice weapon," he said. "It's got stopping power." With two quick movements of his hands, he pulled a magazine from the butt. The price tag said $275, which seemed exorbitant.

"That's the cheapest there is," Art said. "You buy it new, it's gonna cost you a hundred dollars more. Minimum."

Longoria went home, got the necessary cash out from under his mattress, and walked back to Art's Gun Bonanza to purchase the weapon and some ammunition. Art counted the money twice and then watched with a critical eye as Longoria put a full clip in the gun and stuck it in his jacket pocket.

"Hey, buddy, can I give you a little advice here? You can't carry a loaded gun around like that. In fact, you can't carry it around in public, not openly. Period. Gotta have it in a locked case in the back of your car. That's the law. If the cops catch you with it loaded, they're gonna take it away from you. And that's not all they'll do."

Longoria shot an angry glance at this know-it-all who would tell him how to handle the gun he had just bought with his own American dollars.

"Hey, I'm just warning you, that's all," Art said defensively. "I'm just trying to help."

Longoria turned to leave. These American laws were ridiculous.

"At least keep the clip out of the gun, okay?"

Longoria paused, faced the man, and made a show of letting the clip fall out. The metallic clack-clack startled the security guard awake.

"Jeez," Art said, shaking his head. "Teach me to be a Good Samaritan."

13
Basic Training

It was Sunday morning, and the park was nearly empty except for a few addicts still asleep on the lawns, their dew-covered bodies glistening in the sun. Antonio strode past a crumbling concrete statue of Prometheus with a broken torch and one hand missing. A black and white patrol car was parked on the grass next to the statue, the police officer inside sipping coffee and tugging at the bulletproof vest under his midnight blue uniform.

Antonio was planning to kill a man within two hundred feet of this patrol car, but its presence barely registered.

He wanted to see the soldier's face again, to hold the man's image in his eyes without fear. *I will look at him and I will remember Elena and Carlos and I will avenge them with one blow from this pipe in my pocket. I will do it for the peasants in his photographs, the anonymous dead. Remember Frank's advice. Strike at his head. What will it feel like? Will it be like hitting a rock? A melon? Will his skull crack and splatter?* He needed to go to the bathroom, but he would hold it until after he killed the soldier.

At the chess tables a half-dozen men were engaged in three games, to the insistent asynchronous ticking of their clocks. The air around the tables smelled of tobacco and cologne. The soldier was not here. Feeling bold, Antonio approached a gray-haired heavyset player chomping on a cigar, the man he recognized as the soldier's opponent from last Sunday. Antonio tried to speak in a casual voice as though he were looking for an acquaintance.

"Excuse me, *señor*, but do you know the younger man who comes here to play chess? A man with a tattoo on his arm? His name is Guillermo, I think." The name turned out to be of some use after all.

"You mean *el sargento*," he said without looking away from the board. "I know this man. A soldier, or so he says." He moved a black bishop forward, picking up his opponent's knight. "And a terrible chess player. He plays too defensively. Never willing to risk anything. I hate playing against him. So boring. He takes forever to move. Afraid to lose, that's the problem."

"He's afraid to win," said a man at another table. "You have to be aggressive at this game."

"Like with a woman!" a player wearing a black beret chimed in, his palm landing on the clock with a loud snap. "Aggressive!"

"We call him Longoria," the man with the cigar said. "Is he a friend of yours?"

"No. Just somebody I met once, in Guatemala."

"That's right. He's a *chapín*. He has that slow, funny way of talking, just like you. When you talk it's like you're singing, *bien cantadito*." He gave out an ancient smoker's scratchy guffaw. "So he's your *compatriota*. Well, if you wait around a while, he'll show up for sure."

"I hope he plays me," a voice called from two tables away. "I haven't won in a long time." There was scattered laughter around the chessboards.

Antonio put his hands in his pockets and began to shift back and forth as if he were trying to ward off the cold, even though it was halfway to noon and much warmer now. He would wait. The pipe was in his back pocket, sticking out several inches, like a signpost announcing his intentions. The man with the cigar seemed to notice it and gave Antonio a puzzled look. Antonio smiled at him, as though having a two-foot-long pipe in your back pocket was nothing out of the ordinary.

If only the soldier was here like I expected all this would be over now.

As time passed, Antonio began to feel absurd, lying in wait to kill the murderer with a pipe, with all his friends around him. The act had to be done today, quickly, without failure or hesitation.

Let the bastard get here soon.

All these chess players would be witnesses to the attack. They would gather around the tattooed soldier's body just as the neighbors had gathered at Antonio's front door in San Cristóbal Acatapán, to look at Elena and Carlitos. Vacant stares at the corpses, a group of people joined together by the lurid, tragic scene before them. *The chess players will be entertained, they will tell others about the soldier's death, but they will not know why it happened, the precise reasons, just like the neighbors in San Cristóbal never knew why Elena and Carlos were killed.* Only Antonio would know the truth.

The soldier ate an ice cream in the park afterward. Antonio walked over to a *paletero* standing nearby, bought a strawberry ice cream, and devoured it in less than a minute.

* * *

Sunday mornings were chess days, days to relax. After the confusion caused by the old woman, after seeing Lopez reduced to tears, it would be good to slip back into his old routines. Breakfast first. He had read somewhere that coffee helped the brain's cognitive functions, so he had a cup or two on chess days, even though he didn't normally drink the stuff. Anything to give you an edge over the competition. He walked to a restaurant on Alvarado where he liked to eat when he wanted to treat himself. Sitting at the counter, a fat American omelette before him, he read *La Opinión*. The front page was preoccupied with the trial of some police officers accused of beating a black man, a case Longoria found only moderately interesting. He skipped to the international news: the United States had recognized the independence of a country called Bosnia.

After breakfast he walked a few blocks up the gentle slope of Alvarado, past the crack addicts' motels, past the rows of pawnshops and the street vendors, until he reached the palm trees of MacArthur Park. The line of snakelike trunks climbed into the air, each leaning to the east, the sky behind them wiped clean of its customary brown tinge by the cold winds of the night before.

* * *

Antonio waited an hour by the chess tables, and still the tattooed soldier did not come. The pressure on his bladder became too much, so he walked over to an embankment of pepper tress that shaded this corner of the park and peed into the dirt. Mud splattered up onto his shoes. He returned to the chess tables and watched a game between a Cuban man in a rider's cap and a man with a long Christ-like face and a mane of wild white hair. They were at the endgame, each with a king and rook, each trying to outwit the other, until the man with the hair finally threw up his hands and said, "It's a draw." More men came to play chess, some bringing sets of plastic pieces in little leather bags, others with rolled-up checkerboard mats that they opened and spread out over the stone tables.

The day wore on, and Antonio began to think that the tattooed soldier wasn't going to show up. The park filled with families, soccer balls, balloons, baby strollers. Bored with the chess matches, he decided to sit on the lawn.

Children riding bikes, a boy throwing stones into the green lake. His violent plan stood in stark contrast to so much normality around him. *I am going to kill a man.*

He sat there for another hour or so, long enough to watch at least six people wander by to inspect the contents of the nearby trash barrels and remove an aluminum can, plastic bottle, or discarded newspaper. A waiflike little girl approached him and held a box of Chiclets in his face, asking if he wanted to buy some, two for a quarter. The girl's mother, wearing a pink blouse, came walking up behind her, pushing a baby carriage with a Styrofoam ice cooler sitting where an infant should have been, offering sodas for seventy-five cents. As she left, rolling the carriage down the asphalt path with the girl at her side, she passed a small man with pointy features who was walking in the opposite direction.

Antonio felt as if someone had punched him.

The soldier was wearing a windbreaker. It covered his tattooed arm, but there was no mistaking the narrow face and the shaved head, the thin layer of jet black hair that looked like it was painted on his scalp.

Antonio rose to his feet so quickly he nearly stumbled and fell to the lawn again.

Now is the time. Strike at his head. Shatter his skull.

* * *

Feeling liberated from the worries of the past few days, Longoria walked into MacArthur Park with a little more bounce in his step. If García was here he might beat him today. He would play black, try the Sicilian opening, then take the offensive at the earliest possible opportunity.

As he neared the chess tables, Longoria noticed a police cruiser parked on the lawn. He wondered if the outline of his new gun showed in his windbreaker pocket. But the officer was looking in the other direction, toward a group of men standing suspiciously by the lake, and Longoria went safely past him.

When he reached the chess tables, he saw García there waiting for him, the old fart, ready for the next match.

"García! I'm going to beat you today. *¡Hoy sí vas a perder!*"

García shook his hand, and they moved to one of the empty boards. They were sitting down, arranging the pieces, when someone shouted from one of the other tables. "Hey, *sargento*, there's a guy here looking for you!"

"What?" Longoria said absently. How annoying. One of the black pawns was missing.

* * *

Antonio stepped toward the stone bench, the crimson square of the tattooed soldier's windbreaker in the center of his vision. "Hey, *sargento*, there's a guy here looking for you," one of the chess players called, and that was Antonio's cue, there was no turning back. He reached for the pipe without taking his eyes off the man's head, his target. The day was exceptionally clear, the sky summer-bright. The grass was shimmering, the benches aflame with sunlight. He could hear himself telling Frank, "I did it," see the devilish smile when Frank realized it was true.

He was walking across the grass, stepping toward his target, no one was stopping him. *The old men, they don't see me.* The chess clocks sang their tick-tick, tick-tick. Antonio wanted to laugh out loud. It seemed like years since he had done something that made him feel so alive, and he wanted to cry from the happiness of it, the rush of life in his limbs. *I am walking with the multitudes now. Justice with a lead pipe, for the unknown thousands.*

Just a few feet from the soldier he raised the pipe in the air, lifting his arms and rotating his shoulders like a baseball pitcher in his windup, gathering a wave of strength in his muscles to kill the man once and for all, to rid the earth of him.

* * *

Longoria was still looking for the pawn when García yelled, "Watch out!" He turned and caught a swift movement, the whistling displacement of air by some narrow object, the sound of a man grunting. Reflexively he raised his right arm in front of his face. The object struck his forearm, sending a pulse of pain through his body. *Under attack. Someone is trying to kill me.* He dove for the grass and rolled away, a flash of memory from his military training kicking in, a maneuver he practiced at least one hundred times in a sandbox in Panama.

The two men were facing each other now, Longoria lying on his back on the grass, eyes open in a look of dazed fear, Antonio standing on the lawn, confused by the picture before him, the tattooed man breathing heavily but still alive. *Finish him. For Elena and Carlos.*

Longoria's brain was screaming, "Who is this man, what does he want?" But one good look and he could tell his attacker was Guatemalteco, and suddenly no other explanation was necessary. This was the war again, and thankfully he had a weapon in his jacket, but there was a small problem. He had lost all feeling in his right hand—the arm must be broken—and it would be awkward to take the gun from his right pocket with his left hand. But there was no other choice. He had to act quickly, because this crazed man was moving toward him with that metal club, holding it over his head like a caveman. *He looks like he really wants to kill me.*

Antonio felt only anger now. He looked at the soldier lying on the grass, and he could tell that even though the first blow hadn't killed him, he was seriously hurt. The soldier was not invulnerable, he was in pain. *I have wounded him. I have him where I want him. Now he will suffer. He will die. The head. Concentrate.* Now that they were just a few feet apart, Antonio realized for the first time that he was almost a foot taller than his enemy. The soldier was pipsqueak.

Antonio had a pounding headache. He was trying to clear his mind of a thick haze when he was distracted by voices from the crowd that was beginning to circle around them, chess players and passersby gathering to watch the spectacle, shouting and cheering and egging the combatants on. This was not the execution he had expected, calculated and quick.

"Kick his ass, Longoria! Do it."

Antonio raised the pipe for a second blow. Longoria, trying to reach into his pocket for the gun, rolled away again. Finally he pulled the gun out, but he had trouble wrapping his finger around the trigger because he wasn't left-handed. He felt clumsy and unnatural when he pointed the gun in the air, but the people around him didn't seem to notice as they dove for cover. Shock and disbelief rippled from them as they fled.

Longoria aimed for the man's torso. At this range he couldn't miss, not even shooting left-handed. The attacker was standing frozen with the pipe in the air. Longoria pulled the trigger. *Goodbye, you son of a bitch. Goodbye, whoever the fuck you are.*

The gun clicked loudly.

There was no ammunition. Longoria was feeling curiously impotent. *How stupid of me, how silly. That idiot in the gun store made me take out the clip. I haven't made that mistake since the first day of target practice in basic training, when I forgot to load the gun and the sergeant slapped me so hard on the ear I couldn't hear a thing for a week.*

The man with the pipe in his hand was moving toward him again. He could already taste the blood in his mouth. He was finished.

Antonio saw that the soldier would shoot him if he didn't finish him off fast. He was about to inflict what he was sure would be the killing blow when he heard a commotion behind him. Someone yelled, "Freeze!" and he turned to see a police officer jogging toward him across the lawn, panting under his bulletproof vest, his badge, and the rest of his equipment, his face red from the exertion. The officer saw Longoria's gun and drew his own, pointing it at him on the run.

Longoria scrambled up, let the bulletless gun fall from his hand,

and ran to the embankment and the pepper trees. In an instant he had reached the street above the park and disappeared.

The red-faced officer did not give chase. Instead he grabbed Antonio. The silver name tag on his shirt said "Johnson."

"What's with the pipe, buddy?"

The twenty or so people standing around listening to the interrogation wanted to know too. The officer cuffed Antonio's hands behind his back and made him kneel on the grass, a posture that suggested contrition, though he felt none.

"Okay, knucklehead, what's the story here? Talk to me." Johnson had called for backup. Crowds always made the police nervous, and two squad cars were rolling to a stop on the grass in front of the chess tables.

Antonio said nothing. He didn't know what to say. If he told the police that the tattooed soldier had killed innocent people in Guatemala and that Antonio had found him in MacArthur Park by coincidence, would they believe him? The police couldn't care less about international politics. He could tell they'd already made up their minds about him: he was some sort of drug dealer, because after all this was MacArthur Park, and "what else do these people have to fight about anyway?" They searched his pockets, took off his shirt, shoes, and socks, checked behind his ears, and reached between his legs. Despite the lines of dirt caked into his neck, and the sickly sweet smell of his clothes, they pronounced him "clean."

The arresting officer discussed the situation with his colleagues, whose name tags said "Griffin" and "Pierce." Since the alleged victim of the assault wasn't around to press charges, and since they really didn't feel like doing any more paperwork that afternoon, they let Antonio go. They left him sitting by the playground, barefoot and naked to the waist, his clothes piled on the grass in front of him.

14
Fort Bragg

The usual group of cholos had assembled on the front steps of the Westlake Arms blocking the way, menacing young men in oversized Pendletons and blue jeans that covered their bodies like huge curtains. Their heads were shaved nearly clean, haircuts even more severe than Longoria's, the nubby imperfections of their skulls exposed for all the world to see. Leading Reginalda by the hand, Longoria plowed right through them. He had no time for the cholos today, he didn't care if one of them reached up and stabbed him or shot him or whatever it was that these gang members did when they got angry. As he dragged Reginalda up the steps with his good arm, he felt his legs brush against the young men, but all that happened was that one of them shouted, in Spanglish, "Hey, *watchale*."

Longoria had been fighting with Reginalda, shouts and insults, for about an hour. The origin of the argument was lost, but it all revolved around his *carácter*, his being brusque and rude, *pesado*. He had gone too far, apparently, said something that hurt her feelings, and now she was making him pay for it.

"You're out of your mind, Longoria. *Chiflado*. You're sick in the head. Last night you were fine, and today you call me up all crazy and demand to see me, and then I find you with a broken arm."

They passed through the lobby and began to climb the stairs.

"The only reason I stay with you is because I'm afraid of you, Longoria. I'm afraid of what you'll do if I walk away."

She kept on talking as they walked down the hallway to his room. "Why don't you just leave me alone if you hate me? Why do you keep calling me? 'Let's go to the movies,' you say. 'We'll have fun. I want to see you.' And then when I see you all you can do is criticize. Criticize and criticize. Do you think I don't hurt? Do you think I'm a stone?"

They were alone in the room at last. He fastened the chain on the door, locked the dead bolts, and turned to face her. He was angry and frustrated and tired of arguing. Looking at her now, he wondered why he had brought her here. He wished she would leave. Why should he put up with this from her? Attacks from Reginalda, of all people. *This is a betrayal.* He felt his left hand forming into a fist. She took a step back. Her fear was tinged with disgust, as if he were a monster. And then he realized that the crazy old woman in El Pulgarcito Express had looked at him the same way. So had the tall man with the pipe, the crazy man in MacArthur Park who attacked him without explanation.

Who was the man in the park and what did he have in common with Reginalda? They both looked at him as if he were less than human, seeing something that he was sure wasn't there. He felt ugly and mean. *You try to be strong, to believe in what you are, but then the woman of your caresses looks at you that way.* This look of hers cut deeper than any insult, hurt more than a punch to the stomach or a wallop from a pipe. Complete strangers stepping out of nothingness to attack him, and now Reginalda suddenly combative, sickened by him. Longoria felt limp, as if all the wind had left him. Years of trying to be strong, of holding himself up against everything. His legs buckled, and he found himself dropping to the linoleum, kneeling before her. *Please don't look at me that way!* Wrapping his good arm around her waist, he buried his face in her belly.

For the first time in his life he wept in front of a woman.

Boys weren't supposed to cry, men even less. Tears streamed down his cheeks. He began to sob so loudly that the neighbors in the next apartment must be able to hear. Reginalda took his head in her hands, pressed him closer to her, ran her fingers through the short, stiff grass of his hair.

Yes, yes. This is what I want. For you to hold me like a baby against your stomach.

Longoria closed his eyes and held on to Reginalda, feeling helpless and weak before her scent and touch. The too tight skin of her polyester blouse, the small bulges at her waistline, the flowery mist of her perfume, the curve of her back. Everything tender about her made him want to cry.

"What's wrong, *amor*?" she asked after a long silence. "Tell me. You can tell me."

From outside, through the window, came voices, the sound of car doors slamming, engines turning off.

Reginalda's stomach rose and fell against his cheek. He wanted to stay in the trance of her heartbeat. There was so much he wanted to tell her, but the words would not come. They remained anchored to his tongue, like soldiers unwilling to break ranks, fixed in place by years of discipline. If he could find the words he would tell her about the woman in El Pulgarcito Express and the man in MacArthur Park. He would tell her what he had seen in Guatemala, what he had been forced to do in that first village on a Sunday, on market day. He would tell her about the rooms where they held the prisoners, rooms at the barracks in Huehuetenango, Totonicapán, El Quiché. He would tell her, and she would still hold him against her stomach, she would not push him away.

Outside his window, four stories down, the young men on the steps were shouting. Longoria wanted their voices to disappear, but they only became louder. He wrapped his arm tighter around Reginalda. Another voice, older, spoke now, in loud, efficient English, shouting orders. Longoria tried to block out the sounds. Why couldn't they go away? *Just go away for a minute more and leave me alone with Reginalda.*

"Hands!" the older voice yelled. "Show me hands!"

"Longoria, something is happening outside," Reginalda whispered. "I see flashing lights."

Longoria was rising to his feet, wiping the tears from his face, when he heard a loud report from below. He crouched down instinctively, pulling Reginalda with him, and looked out the window at pulses of blue and red light reflected on the building across the street. A woman's scream now, followed by the sound of feet drumming on the pavement. A brief pause and then three more shots, one right after the other. Reginalda trembled and shook with each shot.

When the shooting stopped, Longoria crept toward the window. "Be careful," Reginalda said behind him.

The gunfire had brought him back to himself. Rubbing the last tears from his eyes, he peered over the top of the windowsill and saw two patrol cars parked at odd angles. An officer was crouched behind the front end of one of them, gun drawn, peering over the hood in a pose that mirrored Longoria's own. Another officer had taken cover behind the patrol car door. They were both facing in the same direction, toward Longoria and the steps of the Westlake Arms.

Following their line of vision, Longoria looked down at the sidewalk in front of the steps and saw a young man lying face down on the pavement, arms stiffly at his sides, like a soldier at attention. His loose-fitting clothes covered him like a shroud.

"They shot Freddy," shouted a woman from the window below. "The cops shot him. *¡La chota!* He's dying, he's dying. Call 911!"

* * *

Back then, if you had told Sergeant Longoria that he would see such things in the United States, a war of painted children on his front steps, he wouldn't have believed you. He wouldn't have believed that the gringos could tolerate such disorder. Order was what he was looking for when he came to Los Angeles. Order and peace, a respite from so much fighting and confusion.

Longoria had made his first visit to the United States when he was still a soldier, many years earlier, to another corner of this vast country, completely different from Los Angeles. When life in Los Angeles seemed complicated and messy, when nothing made sense, he tried to remember that army base in a place called North Carolina, the promise and perfection of a city run by professional soldiers. On that first trip he had seen things that made him want to settle in this country, to have a room of his own and live like the gringos did.

The United States Army had met him at Pope Air Force Base and driven him in a van, along with ten other Central American soldiers, to the dormitories at Fort Bragg. The American sergeant who picked them up told them they were driving along "the All-American Highway." The road seemed impossibly wide, like nothing he had seen in Guatemala, two lanes on each side with a thick strip of grass running between. Wide enough to land an airplane, Longoria thought.

Maybe the roads were bigger here because the Americanos were bigger. Big highways for big people.

"We're gonna keep you real busy," said the sergeant, a man who spoke Spanish with a heavy accent, like a foreigner, despite his dark, unmistakably Latino features. "By the time you leave here, you will be *muy, muy cansados.*"

Longoria couldn't believe his luck, to be included in this group granted the special privilege of training on a real American base, with real gringos. It was worth the five hours he spent on the stuffy, windowless transport plane, worth the brief vomiting fit that made his Salvadoran companions laugh and slap him roughly on the back.

Now they were in the United States, and Longoria was already impressed by the size and breadth of the place, its insistent orderliness. Not a single piece of trash on the ground, not a single pothole in the road, the highway a black strip of flat perfection. The highway had traffic lights. They came to a stop in a queue of automobiles, flashy red pickup trucks with shiny chrome wheels, sleek sports cars, brand-new Toyotas. A soldier in camouflage uniform was at the wheel of each car. One of the Salvadorans asked if those men were officers.

The American sergeant looked over at the other cars and laughed. No, he said, as far as he could tell, they were all enlisted men.

"*Dios mío*, even the foot soldiers here have their own cars!"

"I want to join this army," said another Salvadoran. "An army where even a *soldado razo* can be rich!"

Later they gave Longoria his own dorm room, his own place to stay during the ten days of training at Fort Bragg. A spotless rectangle, purged of dust, with plaster walls that gleamed white. There was an air conditioner he didn't touch for fear that he would break it, the machine's whir becoming his constant companion. Not used to such cold, he slept with a wool blanket he found in one of his voluminous dresser drawers. There were extra blankets and sheets because the Americanos thought of everything.

After the hours and hours of training, after climbing over a set of square and rectangular obstacles arranged on a field like enormous children's blocks, after the bruising courses on hand-to-hand combat, after talking about "society" and "hearts and minds" and learning about the theories of Mao and Che and so much else that was just too much to remember at all once, Longoria always came back to his spotless dorm room. One day he would have a room just like this. To have a place to call your own, without a brother or a soldier or a mother crowded in with you, a place without dirt floors, without any dirt or dust at all, scrubbed clean of germs, healthy, *sano*—it seemed civilized. He was beginning to understand and appreciate the meaning of this word. *Civilization*. What the officers back in Guatemala meant when they said they didn't live in a civilized country. Being here in the United States for the first time, he could grasp the concept. This was a country where order and cleanliness reigned supreme.

They told him he could wander around during his few hours off, go to "the mall" they had right here on the base, do some shopping before he had to return home. And so he took long walks in the last hours before sunset, going off on his own.

Walking miles and miles and never leaving the base, guided by the tidy geometry of its asphalt streets, Longoria discovered many wonderful and unexpected things. There were unending black parking lots with hundreds of new tanks arranged in neat rows, turrets and guns wrapped lovingly in tarpaulin, being saved for the next war like coins in a piggy bank. He found another parking lot filled with Jeeps, hypnotizing in their identical greenness. There were separate lots for the trucks, humble but efficient, in the same forest green as the Jeeps, and yet another lot for the square bodies of the armored vehicles, proud and vain in their desert dress, beige with tinges of bluish gray.

How could anyone even think of opposing this country and what it stood for? The guerrilla snipers he had fought would lay down their arms in an instant if they came here and saw what they were up against. Longoria laughed at the thought of these Communists in the hills who had no idea of this limitless arsenal of tanks and armored personnel carriers and God knew what else. Idiots! If they came here they would see the futility of fighting the will of a country with so much strength and wealth.

Walking past the last of the parking lots, Longoria came upon a cluster of brick apartment buildings. This was where the American soldiers lived with their families. A man in a red beret emerged from one of the buildings with a martial stride, a portfolio tucked under his arm. Nearby was a sandbox where children played in swings.

Everything in this country was so well thought out. Everything was planned down to the last detail.

* * *

"Do you think that will solve everything, just because you cry? I'm happy to see you can feel things. I was beginning to worry what kind of man I got mixed up with. But crying isn't going to fix what's wrong with you."

Longoria was sitting on the edge of the bed, near the window, listening to Reginalda. Somehow the argument had renewed itself. He had been silent, mostly, since he recovered from his crying fit. From his perch he watched as the ambulance crew performed a ritual of shaking heads over the body of the fallen cholo. A paramedic unwrapped a bandage and then tossed it to the ground as if to say, Why bother?

Longoria kept his face turned to the window because he felt ashamed. He could not look at Reginalda because she had seen him crying and kneeling on the floor like a spoiled child, like a woman. A "breakdown," that's what it was. He had come across this word in Dr. Wayne García's book, without knowing what it meant. Dr. García said that if you allowed the conscious, rational mind to be overwhelmed by sensations and emotions, you were headed for a breakdown. Now he understood. He could not lose control, he could not lose hold of what he knew to be true, of his faith in himself, in what he had done and who he was.

The shots outside had shaken him out of his trance. Longoria did not believe in miracles, but it seemed to him that the gunshots on Bonnie Brae Avenue had been a message from the warrior gods in the heavens, a signal to wake up and remember. *You are a soldier who fought to defend his country. A professional soldier. A man of honor.*

"I deserve some respect," Reginalda was saying. "That's all I'm asking for."

Longoria nodded faintly in assent, a gesture that seemed to

appease her. She had been standing; now she sat down on the weightlifting bench by the dresser.

"Everyone wants respect," she said.

A movement on the street caught his eye. A crowd was forming on the sidewalk. The defeated cholos, routed from the front steps, had gathered a hundred or so feet away, behind a line of yellow tape that seemed too flimsy to keep them there. With them were some women—their mothers and sisters, Longoria surmised—and assorted residents and hangers-on, the curious.

"You shot him in cold blood! In cold blood!"

A woman in a polka dot dress stumbled toward the yellow tape, steadied by an older man, her brown features heavy with tragedy. A police officer greeted her at the tape, stretching out his arms to block her.

"Let her see the body!" someone yelled.

"It's her only son!" said a young woman.

"He didn't even have a gun."

"The body! Let her see! She's the mother!"

"He didn't have a gun and you shot him!"

They shouted at the police, some raising their fists, anger swelling and gathering in the air above them like an acid mist, a swirling cloud of bile. It infected even those who had come only for the spectacle, people who didn't know the victim or his friends. From the fourth floor, high above it all, Longoria could feel it spreading. *He didn't have a gun.* The mother disappeared into the crowd, and people reached out to touch her as if they could be sanctified by contact with her loss. *She's the mother! Let her through!* Shouted and whispered, the words passed from person to person. *The cops did it. The cops.* Like a vapor, words seemed to rise from the body of the dead cholo too. *I didn't have a gun but they shot me.*

"Pigs!" shouted a voice from somewhere below Longoria. "They shot him in the back. I saw it. Three times! I saw."

"They shot him in the back."

"*¡Asesinos!*"

Asesinos. The word startled Longoria. He stepped quickly away from the window, jarring his injured arm. When he tried to adjust the sling, he only redoubled the pain. To ease himself, he lay down on the bed gently, resting his arm on his stomach.

"Longoria, what happened to your arm?" Reginalda asked, breaking a long silence. "Is that why you're acting so funny? Yes, that's it. That's why you're so strange today, even for you. You're in some sort of trouble, aren't you? What is it? Why don't you tell me, *amor*. Tell me."

"I already told you what happened. I fell this morning. At work."

"*Mentiroso*. You think I can't tell when you're lying? After all we've been through."

Longoria closed his eyes and prayed for the pain to go away, wondering if he should give in, finally, and take the pain-killers they had given him at the hospital. He had always avoided medicines because he thought they would poison his body, deaden his mind.

"Go ahead and suffer, then," Reginalda said. "Suffer alone. Because I've had enough."

With his eyes still closed, he listened as she struggled with the locks and left, slamming the door behind her.

Over the quick march of her footsteps in the hallway, he heard a tiny explosion from outside. The sound of a window breaking.

* * *

The classes were held in a long white building with rows of windows that flooded the rooms with bright North Carolina sunshine. Longoria sat at his desk waiting for the instructor, who was uncharacteristically late: 1440 hours, ten minutes after the class should have started. Unsure of himself, Longoria shifted anxiously in his seat, his frame resisting the small space between the chair and its attached desk. The students around him looked uncomfortable too; they propped their arms clumsily on the small desks, legs overflowing, boots heavy on the floor, canteens and bullet cartridges clanking. Some stared at the black rectangle of the chalkboard, others fidgeted with the buttons of the new Casio watches they had just purchased at the base mall in imitation of the Green Berets, who said Casio was the most reliable model.

It was the first time Longoria had been in a classroom since he was ten years old. He wondered if the Special Forces instructor would be like the missionary teachers who pinched him when he came up with the wrong numbers or stuttered over the long lists of historical dates and presidents he was expected to memorize. Carrera, Barrios, Orellana, Ubico . . .

Longoria was silently rattling off the names of dead Guatemalan presidents when the instructor finally stepped in. To his great relief, this new teacher didn't look anything like those meanspirited missionaries; he was wearing the standard camouflage uniform and beret tilted smartly to one side.

The instructor was a tall, round-faced Puerto Rican who spoke excellent Caribbean Spanish. He introduced himself as Lieutenant Sanchez of the Second Special Forces Battalion. Longoria decided that Sanchez looked just like Lieutenant Colonel Villagrán, the legendary founder and leader of the Jaguars, whom he had met just two or three times. Sanchez was an older man, a bit thick around the waist, but solid. He had the frame of someone who'd enjoyed his beer over the years but hadn't neglected himself. Few Guatemaltecos were so sturdy. Longoria aspired to look like this man when he reached his forties and fifties.

Sanchez began his lecture by writing a single word on the chalkboard: PSYOPS.

Longoria stared at the word, trying to decipher its meaning. The rest of the class was equally befuddled. Lieutenant Sanchez proceeded to explain that "Psyops" meant "psychological operations" and that he was an expert in "*guerra sicológica.*" When half the students still squinted and scratched their heads in confusion, he pointed to his temple: "We use the tricks of the mind to defeat the enemy."

The soldiers nodded their shaved skulls.

"The enemy deals in deception," Sanchez said. He sounded at once serene and authoritative, like good preachers and priests Longoria had known. "The enemy deals in ideology. Ideology is one of his most effective weapons, perhaps the most effective. Disinformation, lies. To defeat him we turn his own weapons against him."

Longoria listened attentively. Sanchez said the enemy used ideas to take control of the minds of the peasants. This was easy because the peasants were so gullible, because they were poor and desperate. "They are simple people and they will believe anything. They will follow anyone."

Longoria had heard this before, from his officers in Guatemala, who believed that the peasants were to blame for everything. The country was backward because of the peasants, because of their superstitions and their bad habits, like having too many children. When the officers said these things, Longoria couldn't help looking at the ground in shame, remembering his own family. Sitting now in Carolina, he was ashamed again of the image of his former self: stooped over the soil, fingernails black with dirt, frayed sandals on his feet.

His nails were clean now. He had new boots and a new way of walking to go with them: proud and erect, the soldier's gait, the posture you learn in basic training. The lice had disappeared after that first shaving in the barracks. The army had saved him from desperate poverty, and now they were showing him the world, showing him things he never imagined, educating him, expanding his mind.

"In Psyops we fight terror with terror," Sanchez was saying. "We fight confusion by creating more confusion. We fight lies with lies." He put his hands on his hips. "And we separate the enemy from his sustenance, starve him." The guerrillas depended on the peasants for nourishment, Sanchez explained. If you cut off the source of nourishment, the guerrillas would slowly die, like a corn plant deprived of water, withering in the sun. To separate the guerrillas from the peasants you had to break the bonds of ideology, the attraction of their twisted beliefs. The guerrillas promised the peasants a paradise of free land, free seed, and easy credit. These ideas were the glue that joined the peasants to the guerrillas and held the subversive Communist movement together. To break these bonds of the mind you had to strike at the mind. And the most powerful weapon to aim at the mind was fear. Terror. The guerrillas had already mastered this: they killed suspected informers, they kidnapped the rich, they bombed cafes.

Now the forces of good had to master the art of terror as well. And the army and its allies had to use even larger doses because the war was being lost.

Some of the men in the class seemed perplexed by the instructor's arguments, but Longoria understood perfectly. This Sanchez was the most brilliant man he had ever met, a man who could shape the words so you could understand the idea, see the beauty in the logic. If Sanchez had taught him to read and write, he would have learned more, learned better. Sanchez had studied the problem of the guerrillas and their ideology, had put everything together and written it down, and now he was sharing his knowledge with this class. The peasants would only learn through brutality. Longoria understood this because he had been a *campesino* once, until the army rescued him. The peasants would be with you only if you beat them, if you forced them to take your side. You had to make them fear you before they did what you told them.

"This is what the enemy has taught us." Sanchez lowered his voice a little, as if confiding a secret. "We're speaking Spanish here, so there's certain things I can tell you that I wouldn't be able to say in English. The value of terror, the beauty of terror as a weapon." Stepping away from the chalkboard, Sanchez circled the room, the eyes of the soldiers locked on his. "You must create a sense of disorder. Disorder is your friend. Violence and randomness, that's the recipe. If the people believe death can come from anywhere, anytime, they will be paralyzed by fear. This is something anyone can understand. It's simple mass psychology. Dispense enough fear, and the people will be paralyzed into inaction. And inaction is what we're shooting for here. Inaction is equilibrium, the balance of things, the way things should be. Make them believe you are chaos personified, and they will fear you. We see this all the time. Crazy people walking on the street, everyone steps away from them, gives them room, right? You must be this way. And not just with the enemy. Because every neutral is a potential enemy unless you convince him otherwise. Do you understand what I mean when I say this? Do you understand or don't you? It's this simple: they have to believe you're capable of anything, absolutely anything. There is great power in your randomness, the chaos of you. *¿Entienden?*"

Sanchez scanned the classroom. None of the students spoke or moved. Longoria was confused by some of the terminology, but he could feel the rightness of the lieutenant's words.

What's the matter with these people, Longoria thought, why don't they say anything? Idiots! They are like cattle. Trembling with anger, he raised his arm.

"*¡Sí, mi teniente! ¡Yo entiendo!*"

* * *

The crowd below Longoria's window was growing. It occupied half the block now, spilling over from the sidewalks to the street, separated from the police only by the drooping yellow line of tape. Longoria leaned on the windowsill with his good arm and took in the scene, a welcome diversion after the fight with Reginalda. He wanted to forget about her for now, the female complications of her. She was like those unsolvable problems he found in his chess books, a riddle you couldn't puzzle out even after you'd looked at the arrangement of the pieces from every possible angle. Two attendants had just slid the cholo's cadaver into the back of a van marked "Coroner," pushing it with the nonchalance of men closing a file cabinet, for some reason shaking hands when the task was accomplished. The coroner's van was painted a muddy brown, the color of soil in a burial plot. The van door slammed, and suddenly there was silence on the street, the din of voices dissolving into the night air.

Longoria saw faces he recognized in the crowd, an assembly of troublemakers and malcontents, as far as he could tell. The middle-aged Salvadoran men who lived down the hall, the revolutionaries he had once seen carrying placards to a demonstration in MacArthur Park. The Guatemalteca who lived next door with her children— Longoria couldn't remember if she had three or four. And of course the cholos, leaning over the police tape, growing bolder as the crowd behind them grew larger, taunting the officers with lewd gestures, grabbing their crotches, pointing their middle fingers skyward.

The van drove off with the cadaver, and the street began to fill with noise again. "¡*Asesinos!*" someone shouted, with a little less vigor than before. The audience was getting restless, eager for a new diversion. Someone threw a chunk of concrete that sailed over the top of the crowd and landed beyond the police tape next to one of the officers, a woman. Incensed, she lifted the tape barrier over her head and waded into a group of cholos. Not a good move, Longoria thought. Stay in the perimeter. But no, she plowed on, elbows extended, the crowd parting before her, until she reached the cholo she was looking for. She was small but fit, with very broad shoulders and brown hair pinned up neatly under her cap. The cholo was at least a foot taller than she was, a lanky teenager with pockmarked skin and ears that protruded comically from his shaved head. Grabbing him by the arm as if she were his mother, she led him toward the police tape. The crowd whistled loudly, a collective jeer that seemed to be directed at the cholo as much as the officer. Longoria smiled; the cholo with the elephant ears was allowing himself to be humiliated by a woman.

Suddenly the cholo tried to jerk his arm away. The policewoman held tight, and people in the crowd began to pull at him and push at her. She fell to the ground, disappearing momentarily in a sea of legs, until another officer rushed to her aid with his baton raised like a saber. Longoria stood up, excited by the action, the sense that a battle was brewing for control of the street. Emboldened, the crowd surged forward and snapped the yellow tape barrier, trampling it into the asphalt.

Now more rocks were falling on the police perimeter and the officers were backing off, taking refuge behind their patrol cars, speaking into their radios, shouting words that Longoria could not hear. *Why don't they just take charge, these maricones? They draw their weapons, but they don't fire. Now they are retreating!* This was something to see. They were surrendering the field to an unarmed mob, scared off by a few rocks. Longoria was truly disgusted. The Los Angeles Police Department was not the fighting force he had imagined. In the rush to get away they had even left behind one of their squad cars, and now the cholos were climbing on top of it, pounding the hood, raising their arms in defiant celebration. One of them took a two-by-four and smashed the front windshield. What a disgrace!

Longoria scanned the crowd and tried to memorize the faces of the agitators who had ignited this disturbance. He might be able to pick them out later, turn them over to the authorities. But then he told himself that the police would never be able to catch them, that these hoodlums would melt into the city just as the guerrillas disappeared into the hills.

He was turning away from the window when he was startled by a flash of recognition. *There he is!* The man from MacArthur Park was standing in the middle of the sidewalk, four floors below. Longoria held the face for an instant, then lost it in the jostling of the crowd, the dancing shadows on the darkened street. *The son of a bitch who broke my arm. How does he know I live here?* Longoria tried desperately to find the man in the crowd again, but everyone was moving too quickly, every face was a blur.

Where is he? Where is he? Rocks, bricks, and bottles began to jump from the crowd, arching high above the street and landing at the other end of the block, where the police were ducking meekly behind the surviving patrol cars, almost out of Longoria's view. All kinds of people were running back and forth, but none of them was the man with the pipe, Longoria's enemy.

He was there, I saw him. Longoria wanted to run downstairs and confront the attacker, catch him by surprise. But no. His arm was in a sling; he couldn't fight the man with just one arm. *Was it really him?* He needed to calm down. He was losing control again, slipping into the irrational. Perhaps he hadn't seen the man at all. *I am being paranoid. I am imagining things.* Looking down at the crowd, studying the faces, he didn't see anyone who remotely resembled the tall man with the round glasses.

If the man with the pipe is out there, he could try to take advantage of the chaos on the street and kill me right now, when the police can't help me. Longoria stepped away from the window and picked up the round disks of his weights, propping them against the door one by one. And then the lifting bench itself. No, this wouldn't be enough.

Using his left shoulder, he pushed the dresser over to the barricade and sat down on the opposite side of the room, back against the wall, eyes fixed on the door.

The sounds of the crowd outside were behind him. Shouting, the patter of feet on asphalt and cement, the pop of glass bottles exploding as they hit the ground. A muffled voice on a loudspeaker, followed a minute or so later by the familiar whoosh and metal clank of tear gas canisters. Good, the police were fighting back. He rose to look out the window, and sure enough the cholos and their allies were retreating before a little plume of smoke, visible proof of what his instructors at Fort Bragg called "the outstanding effectiveness of tear gas in crowd dispersal." But it was too soon to let his guard down, so he took up his position again, across from the door, grabbing the long steel bar from his weight set to use as a weapon.

Two hours later, when order had been restored on the street and the last of the insurgents had been taken away, Longoria began to dismantle the barricade.

Of course not. He hadn't seen the tall man after all.

Department of Sanitation

Antonio walked back to Crown Hill, crushed by his failure in the park. His shoes were untied, his belt loop was unfastened, his shirt was unbuttoned. Why did something always have to go wrong? Was he doomed to constant, pathetic failure?

The tattooed soldier is still alive, walking the streets of Los Angeles, breathing the air of this day and the next and the next.

But he had injured the man, that much was certain, perhaps broken his arm with that first blow. There was an unmistakable crack when Antonio brought the pipe down. Here was a victory, something to savor and admire, like a medal. He had accomplished something. The tattooed soldier now carried this pain, a throbbing, perhaps a pain deep to the marrow, like a hundred pins piercing the bone.

The first hesitation did me in. Next time I will be ruthless. Next time I will be an arrow, a compass locked on a steady bearing.

It was late afternoon, and the shadows were lengthening in the shallow valley of liquor-groceries and stubby tenements around him, edifices of brick and terra cotta with spidery fire escapes affixed to their walls, so strange and old, anachronisms in this young city. A few more blocks and the buildings began to disappear, thinning out into the familiar series of rubble-strewn lots. Finally he reached the open plateau of Crown Hill, the blank slate in the center of the city.

He looked at the shelters grouped in clusters, plastic and cardboard clinging to the muddy earth. He saw the makeshift structure José Juan had assembled from scraps, the tarpaulin roof fluttering in the breeze. It surprised him. He had forgotten where he was living. Like a traveler who returns home after a long journey to see everything in a new light, he took in the sight of this camp and suddenly understood many things.

I have been living this way, less than human, for longer than I can remember.

I have been wearing the helmet of mourning and self-pity too long.

I am living in the streets, under the starless sky.

Antonio considered this fact for a moment. It didn't seem so daunting anymore. *I am homeless.* The phrase had definitely lost its weight and stigma. He had been following the tattooed soldier, and this new mission had cleansed him of sorrow and guilt. *I am so much taller than the soldier, stronger than him.*

He had a story to tell, and he was anxious to see his friends. He would give José Juan and Frank and the Mayor all the details: the color of the sky, the metallic taste of the air, the feel of the pipe in his hand, the sound of breaking bone. The inevitable failure and his dispassionate analysis of what went wrong. He was too rushed, he let the wave of emotion carry him forward, the surge of anger and vengeance, and didn't stop to weigh all the consequences. The parameters of the moment had escaped him, the correlation of forces on the field of battle. *I saw that police officer, and I should have known he would rescue the soldier. I should have waited, but I didn't plan.*

José Juan and the others would say he was crazy and brave to try and kill a man with his bare hands.

* * *

"You can't kill a killer just like that, without thinking."

Frank was upset with Antonio. Sitting next to the Mayor on their couch, on their mountain high above the panorama of the Harbor Freeway, he had listened as Antonio recounted his confrontation with the soldier in MacArthur Park. Now he frowned at his new friend with a sort of superior displeasure. He was annoyed because Antonio didn't consult him first.

"With a pipe?" he asked, incredulous, shaking his head. "You're crazy. Lucky you didn't get yourself killed."

"He had a gun."

"A gun? No way!"

"But it didn't fire.

"Oh man! The drama thickens."

"Maybe it wasn't loaded," Antonio said.

"Naw, it was just one of those cheap black-market guns, I bet," the Mayor interjected. "Gang bangers are dumping all kindsa shit on the streets."

"And then the police showed up."

"Police?"

"But they let me go. And the soldier, he ran away. He got away."

"Unreal. You *are* lucky," Frank said. "You're lucky the police didn't pull a Rodney King on you, beat you to a pulp like they beat that brother, a little shower of batons on your skull. You got some angel looking over you."

* * *

The sun had set by the time Antonio returned to his own campsite to sit by the fire. José Juan was quiet and cautious, as he had been since Antonio first told him about the events in the park and saw José Juan open his eyes wide in shock, as if he was afraid Antonio might hurt him. *He thinks I'm mentally unbalanced, capable of anything.*

José Juan's fear would pass. Antonio had not become a killer, nothing about him had changed. He had simply crossed paths with the tattooed soldier. The responsibility of bringing him to justice had fallen to him because there was no one else to do it. They lived in an interval of history without courts, without the passionless procedures of official justice, and so this act had fallen to him, a man living on his own in a strange city, a homeless man. *There is a balance between us. We are opposites balancing a scale, we are mathematics. I am tall, he is short. I live under the sky, he lives under a roof. He has a girlfriend, I am alone. He has a job, I do not. He is the killer, I am his victim.*

José Juan coughed, pulling Antonio out of his daydream. The light of the campfire glowed orange on his curly head. José Juan had become adept at starting a good fire and finding wood scraps for fuel. In this city of asphalt and concrete it was surprising how much wood you could find lying around. The shelter had grown from a simple lean-to built against the remains of a brick wall into a cocoon of wool and cotton blankets shielded by pine boards José Juan had found or stolen.

Shooting Antonio a look, José Juan disappeared into the shelter, which seemed more cramped every day. He had lined the inner walls with shoe boxes that served as shelves, holding razors, pencils, spoons, cups, and a satin-gloss color print of his wife and family. Alone by the fire, Antonio concentrated on his next move. He had lost the element of surprise, and the soldier would recognize him now. He could no longer sneak up on his target. But the soldier didn't know that Antonio had followed him for days and stored his life patterns in memory. The gun was Antonio's biggest problem. This man was armed, and even if he had dropped the gun at the park, he could buy a new one. He was a soldier who could easily get a weapon and who knew how to use it.

Antonio hadn't realized there was such science and strategy to the act of killing someone. The body resists its own extinction, it is a fortress with walls and armaments more formidable than you might expect. Antonio was going to need some help. He was going to need Frank.

* * *

Antonio woke the next morning to the sound of engines and the warning song of big trucks going into reverse. He turned over on his mattress and reached out to pull back the towel that served as a door to the shelter.

In the next camp, a block away, he could see disheveled men shaken from sleep, holding blankets and bedrolls in their arms, scrambling to pick up shoes, boxes, sweatshirts, hats. Their mouths were open in protest, but Antonio couldn't hear what they were saying over the din of the engines. A dust cloud grew behind them, and they seemed to be retreating from its fury, dropping papers and clothes in their rush to get away before it swallowed them up and turned them to dust men.

"What's going on?" José Juan said, rubbing sleep from his eyes.

As the dust cloud began to thin, Antonio could see a bulldozer grinding forward, lowering its shovel behind the running men. It cut into the ground and lifted something into the air: a blue tent, trailing ropes and stakes, swept up intact and dropped into a large black cube.

A trash dumpster. Then the dumpster itself rose in the air, propelled by the arms of a large garbage truck, which swallowed the contents into its roof.

"We have to go," Antonio said. "They're making us leave."

Three garbage collectors stood on the street corner, oversized lifting belts around their waists, two police officers next to them. One of the officers raised a bullhorn to his mouth.

"This is an illegal encampment. You are trespassing on private property. You are in violation of Penal Code Section Six-four-seven, a misdemeanor. This is an illegal encampment."

The two policemen began walking across the barren lot, hands on the grips of their pistols, like gunfighters walking through the center of a hostile frontier town. They carefully opened the flap of the igloo-shaped tent built two nights ago by the camp's latest arrivals, a pair of Mexicanos. Finding no one inside, the officers went on. Suddenly their heads snapped to the left, toward the shouting figure of the Mayor, who was running across the lot.

"Fucking pigs! Pigs!" The Mayor raised a brown fist in their faces, and they both took a step backward. "You can't clear this camp. Where's your fucking warrant?"

"We don't need any warrant, asshole," answered one, a white man who seemed too young to be talking to the Mayor that way, without proper respect. "All these shacks, it's a health hazard. Plus this is private property. You're trespassing."

"Bullshit! We're squatters. We got squatters' rights."

The officer looked temporarily perplexed. His partner, a middle-aged Latino with a five o'clock shadow and a thick mustache, took over.

"Listen, Mister *Mayor*," he said slowly, allowing the irony to linger on his lips. "We've been over this before. There's no such thing as squatters' rights. Not in my city. Probably not anywhere in this state or this country. So why don't you just leave like a good citizen. For once."

"Fuck you, Ramirez. This is my home. I ain't going! I ain't going!"

Ramirez sighed and threw up his arms in disgust. He mumbled something to his partner, and they walked away.

"It's the principle of the thing," the Mayor shouted at the officers' backs. "The principle! We ain't gonna take it!"

The Mayor stormed back to his camp, stopping briefly to pick up a broken bottle and fling it halfheartedly at the policemen. It bounced on the ground, unnoticed, several feet behind them.

The bulldozer advanced across the lot and crushed the igloo hut, the huge shovel descending in a cacophony of shattered wood and snapping plastic. The Mexicanos who lived there were gone, off looking for work. The bulldozer scooped up their possessions and deposited them in the garbage truck, a remarkably clean vehicle with a fresh coat of pale green paint and the word "Sanitation" stenciled on its door.

"We've got to get our things together," José Juan said, standing up in alarm.

For two furious minutes Antonio and José Juan stuffed everything they could into the Hefty bag, including the four-burner hotplate. They saved José Juan's twelve-cassette collection of BBC English tapes and the photograph of Elena and Carlos's grave, leaving little behind except some magazines recovered from the trash and the sports sections of *La Opinión*.

They emerged from their shelter with the overloaded plastic bag to find the huge shovel of the bulldozer, a scratched yellow basin, waiting for them at the towel-covered opening they called their front door. Dragging their belongings to the sidewalk on Third Street, they watched from a safe distance as the bulldozer crushed the wood and cardboard home that had protected them from the rain and wind for more than three weeks.

In a matter of moments their shelter had been reduced to a tidy patch of dirt. After the police left, after he had listened to their final warning to "stay off this property," Antonio went back to the lot and examined the ground, walking slowly in a growing spiral. There was nothing to be found but the bumpy soil beneath his feet, the crisscross of the bulldozer's long tracks, the wounds gouged by the shovel.

* * *

The refugees worked their way down the hillside in four different directions, fleeing the oily dust cloud raised by the bulldozers. They carried their possessions in shopping carts and milk crates, in blanket bundles balanced on their heads, in frayed garbage bags that trailed them like weighty corpses.

More than a hundred people joined the exodus. Antonio was startled to see a handful of women among them, walking behind male partners whose faces were familiar. It was the first time he could tell how many people lived here. The police officers had combed the entire mountain, uncovering every hiding place and niche. The bearded old man he had beaten a lifetime ago in the struggle over the hotplate stood by a cardboard shelter hidden behind a tangle of branches and took harmless swings at the air, yelling at the vanished policemen to leave him alone.

Grouped in dirty clusters, black men with black men, Latinos with Latinos, whites with whites, they assembled on Third Street, shivering in the rushing wind of morning traffic, a steady current of cars feeding into the orderly, pedestrian-free streets of the Financial District. They drew befuddled stares from the commuters accelerating and decelerating on Third, men in ties and women in suits who took in the spectacle of these refugees as if it were an image from a faded newsreel. This was something unusual, a break from the monotony of the morning drive.

Antonio saw Frank and the Mayor leading a small party of men down the steep drop of Bixel Street. He nudged José Juan and they followed. The Mayor and his friends walked like men who had been through this sort of thing before; they looked angry but not confused, and they appeared to be heading for a destination. Bringing up the rear of this procession of four blacks and two whites, Antonio and José Juan carried their Hefty bag in the fashion they had perfected after that first eviction, each man holding one end. José Juan still looked drowsy, as if he might fall back asleep at any moment. He's lucky he didn't sleep through the bulldozers, Antonio thought. He'd be in the back of a garbage truck right now.

The men descended two blocks and reached an open lot surrounded by a chain-link fence, a vast concrete floor, V-shaped, like a funnel, enclosed by two concrete walls that converged toward a tunnel entrance. Frank set down the black plastic bag he was carrying and scaled the fence, calling to the Mayor to throw the bag over. The rest of their party followed suit. The floor and the walls seemed to be vibrating, and Antonio instinctively raised his fingers to his temples to fight off an incipient headache. Narrowing his eyes, he saw that every inch of the place was covered with spray paint, a vast canvas shimmering like an acrylic rainbow sea. Color screamed from every direction, one layer of scribbles and cartoon drawings on top of another. In one corner of the lot a young man with a spray can was applying bursts of paint in broad strokes, the lone representative of the army of manic graffiti artists who had made this place their private gallery.

In single file, with Frank and the Mayor still leading the way, they marched toward the tunnel entrance across the sticky pigment on the floor. Another chain-link fence had once covered the opening from top to bottom, two stories high, but it had been systematically torn to pieces until only a few support poles and strands of fence remained. Standing under the huge gray arch, a semicircle of perfect blackness behind him, the Mayor turned to address his small band.

"This is where we make camp, at least for a couple of days," he said. "Nobody is gonna bother us here. Not in this smelly place."

"Don't go in too far," Frank added as the men began to toss their belongings on the ground. "It's scary back there."

Antonio and José Juan set their bag against one of the tunnel walls, a smooth curve of concrete covered with graffiti. The floor of the tunnel was muddy, and the air smelled green and dank. Peering into the darkness, Antonio could make out a mattress and the carcass of an automobile. The tunnel had not been used for years, at least not for its intended purpose. Like so much else in this corner of the city, it seemed to belong to another age. Just outside, baking in the orange sun, rose what looked like a concrete temple, a huge cement box with the words "Pacific Electric Rail Co." etched across the top. Antonio stepped back from the tunnel entrance and looked up. A hundred feet or so above the gray arch he could see the crumbling staircases and ancient palm trees of Crown Hill.

* * *

He was about thirty, though his long eyelashes made him seem younger. His face was light brown, with a few freckles on the upper cheeks. His name was Darryl, and he was from Michigan. He was sitting in front of the tunnel in a lawn chair, talking to Antonio. They were the only men here, left to guard the group's meager possessions while everyone else wandered in search of food, money, and work. Darryl said he was once a steelworker by trade, until an accident ruined his life.

"A whole load of sheet metal fell on top of me. Blindsided me, just like that." He snapped his fingers.

Everything in Darryl's life was fine before that fateful moment, nothing had been the same since. "I just haven't been able to get it together, you know? It just seems like nothing wants to go right. If it ain't one thing, it's another." The accident sent him on a downward spiral that ended right here, the sewer line at the bottom of the drain.

"If it wasn't for that accident, I'd be a different man."

By now Antonio knew that everyone in the vacant lots had a story like this, a quick, neat explanation for what went wrong in their lives: romantic betrayal, crippling accidents, jealous co-workers, abusive husbands, friends who turned out to be thieves, business partners who disappeared with all the money. They kept their stories uncomplicated, without nuance or ambiguity, as in a soap opera.

After talking at length about his back, Darryl revealed that he had a family in Michigan, including a teenage daughter he called collect every couple of months.

"Every time I talk to her she asks me, 'Daddy, why don't you come home?' She just doesn't understand why I stay in Los Angeles. 'Come home,' she says. Sometimes it's more than I can take. I gotta hang up the phone because I don't want her to hear me cry."

"So why don't you go back?" Antonio asked naively. "They could take care of you until your back gets better."

Up to this moment Darryl had been free with details of his plight. Now he answered curtly, "Don't want to go back. Can't. Don't see the point."

He stared at the ground, then looked up at Antonio. His glance told part of the story: brown irises swimming in a buttermilk sea, the eyes of a lifelong alcoholic. Behind this gaze Antonio could sense a truth, painful and unspoken, an old memory stored away and hidden with great care. Some act of violence, repeated and repeated. This man a child and a witness.

This was something that had happened to Antonio with great frequency since the death of his wife and son. Alcoholics, the suicidal, battered wives, the perpetually lonely, witnesses to catastrophe, survivors of war: they all came into sharper focus. Antonio could almost spot them across a crowded room. They were like brothers or long-lost friends. They were different from the other people, the unscarred, those who had never seen or lived the randomness Darryl and Antonio knew too well. These other people walked about the city like well-fed children, bathed in a glow of innocence, the happy haze of unknowing. From the grave, Carlos and Elena had given Antonio the power to see these differences, another layer of truth near the surface but invisible to so many. It was a gift to be treasured, the exile's reward, this special vision.

Sitting here staring into those milky eyes, Antonio knew Darryl was very close to killing himself.

* * *

Antonio wanted to talk to Frank about the plan to kill the soldier, but the Mayor wouldn't stop rambling. The refugees from Crown Hill were all gathered around a single fire now. Some had drifted off into sleep. Everyone was there except Darryl, who wouldn't sleep in the tunnel itself and was lying on the ground just outside.

"A friend of ours from Kansas City showed us this place," the Mayor was saying, though no one seemed to be listening. "About five years ago. Old wino, that guy was, part of a dying breed. I haven't seen him for years. Wonder what happened to him. We've been here eight times already and nobody bothers us. Except for that time with the gang bangers. That was bad. Remember, Frank? That was really bad. This tunnel belonged, I believe, to the people who ran the trolley cars. Years and years ago. The trolleys would take you all the way to San

Bernardino if that's where you wanted to go. For some reason, you might want to go to San Bernardino. I never did. That's a long way. The trolleys would go right through this hole and into downtown. Fifth and Flower. I believe it was Flower, but I may be mistaken. I'm beginning to forget things. Farley, whose shirt is that? Is that my shirt? Listen to me. Pay attention. Did you take that from my pile?"

"No, Mayor," answered Farley, a white man with a Southern accent. "It's my shirt. From the mission."

"People are taking things now. You didn't see that before. Today is different. These are the last days, and so all the evil comes out. The Ottoman Empire. It was like that at the end. Constantinople. Everyone grabbing at everybody else. Grabbing and grabbing. Take your shirt, take your coins, take your pants. Living on the row, someone tried to take my pants off in the middle of the night. The row, the motherfucking, backstabbing row. They tried to steal the pants right off my legs. Motherfuckers. This ain't the row. This is my tunnel. It used to belong to the trolleys, but the trolleys are gone."

The Mayor had been talking like this for almost an hour, drifting from point to point and circling back, his eyes fading into delusion, returning to sharpness, then fading again.

"Hey, Mayor, you taken your meds today?" Frank asked.

"I don't need 'em anymore. They cloud my mind."

"Uh-oh. Did you hear that, everybody?" Frank called out, startling half the group to attention. "The Mayor is off his meds."

"I knew it!" said Farley. "C'mon, Mayor, take the meds. You know how you get."

"I'm too smart for that. I'm too smart for pills."

"Bullshit."

"I need to be alert!" the Mayor said. "Shit's happening. I can't be asleep with pills. Don't you understand that? Alert!"

This was an argument no one could counter. It was true. Everyone needed to be alert.

"This is like Julius Caesar," the Mayor said, pulling his watch cap down over his eyebrows. "You know that, Frank? Farley, all you guys, turning on me and shit when I need to be alert. Julius Fucking Caesar."

* * *

They were huddled in a corner of the tunnel, away from the others, having a conference, as Frank called it. Antonio spoke first, in a low whisper.

"You have to help me, Frank. Until I do this thing, as long as I know he's alive, I won't be able—how do you say?—to have peace." He knew there was a better way to put this, words that would persuade Frank, but he was too nervous and his English suffered for it. "I need to have peace," was all he could say. "Have peace inside."

Frank listened to Antonio solemnly, hands clasped together, like a priest taking confession. When he finally spoke, it was not in whispers but in his normal booming voice, the words ricocheting off the round tunnel walls.

"Why should I help you? Why should I complicate my life? Complications are something I don't need."

Antonio could think of no reply.

"He killed women and children?" Frank said.

It took Antonio a second to realize this was a question. "Yes. My wife and son. And others. Many, many others."

"How many? How do you know? How can you know?"

"I've seen papers that say he was part of this unit. I saw pictures of the bodies. In his room."

"You've been in his room?"

"Yes. This unit, they have massacred people. Villages. Thousands of people, buried in graves all over my country. They are like the Nazis. He is a Nazi. He is a real-life Nazi, living in our time."

Frank's eyes lit up at this last phrase. A Nazi, living in our time. Maybe the idea of meting out justice, of fighting against the darkest evil, appealed to him. The conversation was moving to another plane. Yes. Now they were two men standing on the edge of history, like partisans camped in the hills. The crackle of the fire, the abandoned tunnel, even the layer of grime that covered their clothes bespoke heroic themes of vengeance and redemption. *Everything is against me, but right is on my side. I will prevail.* Antonio imagined himself deep in the plot of a wartime drama, Frank and the tunnel walls in flickering black-and-white.

"Okay, I'll help you. Don't ask me why, but I will." Frank picked at his teeth with his long nails, then raised a finger in the air. "But this is murder we're talking about here. Conspiracy. This is more than a friendship thing. This is a blood thing. We'd be blood after this. It wouldn't be each man for himself anymore. We'd be brothers. Do you understand? Do you understand the responsibility? We'd be brothers just like me and the Mayor are brothers. I'd expect you to stand by me when something happens. You up to it?"

"Yes. I will be a rock. I will be a rock for you."

"Deal."

They shook hands. Antonio smiled broadly and felt the strangeness of it, the mouth opening in joy like this, the sensation spreading across his face like sunlight.

Jaguar

Four stories below, someone was sweeping the sidewalk. Even on this block, with all the graffiti and the alleys clogged with the settlements of the homeless, each morning brought the impulse to clean. A Mexicana wielded a broom, stopping to pick up the larger shards of glass and the yellow police tape, which she rolled up and stuck in her apron pocket. The Asian manager of the Westlake Arms worked alongside her, hosing down the bloodstains on the concrete.

Longoria had slept fitfully. The pain in his fractured arm was intense, and the events of the previous day wouldn't stop dancing like dust before his eyes: the attack in the park, street battles and tear gas, the blackened shell of the patrol car, set on fire before the police could retake the block. Inside his apartment the dresser and weightlifting bench were not flush against the wall like they usually were, and the weights themselves were scattered on the floor.

He didn't have the energy to straighten things up. His right arm hurt too much. But his left arm, the one with the tattoo, was fine, as if the jaguar were defending the skin and bone underneath.

The jaguar protected me during the last war. Now it will protect me in this Los Angeles war. It will protect me if the man with the pipe comes looking for me again.

The jaguar was almost ten years old now, but it was still strong.

* * *

He showed off the tattoo for the first time at the barracks in Huehuetenango. Just back from Fort Bragg, flush with the sunshine and rich diet of the southern United States, he felt taller and smarter. The skin was freshly healed, and the men in his unit noticed the tattoo immediately. It was an American tattoo, expertly administered by a man called Jake, in the course of an entire afternoon, in a place called Tattoo Fayetteville: a jaguar with a sleek yellow pelt and fierce eyes, sharp and resplendent, its mouth open, exposing a pink tongue rendered with such skill that you could almost see the saliva glistening. As soon as Longoria's fellow soldiers set eyes on it they all wanted one. A crowd formed around him, holding his arm as if it were a work of art, plying him for details about Jake, lamenting that there weren't any good tattoo artists in Guatemala.

"It looks so real."

"The colors are so bright."

"You're a Jaguar for life now."

Two or three other men in the company had tattoos, none as fine as Longoria's. Next to his, theirs looked rough and amateurish, a child's effort. For several days, as they trained and prepared for a new campaign in El Quiché, Longoria found his barracks mates stealing envious glances at his tattoo. If they could figure out a way to take it from me, they would, Longoria thought. The tattoo was valuable, the prettiest and most expensive thing he'd ever owned. It cost him two months' salary, half of what he had saved since joining the army. It was his forever, it would be with him until he died. That's what Jake said back in North Carolina, that the colors might start to fade in a couple of years but the tattoo would still be recognizable when Longoria reached seventy, he should live so long. A professional soldier's life was a constant gamble, Jake said. He had tattooed hundreds of soldiers in his career, and a lot of them weren't with us any longer. Longoria had sat in Tattoo Fayetteville for hours while Jake etched his arm with that strange instrument, so he had a lot of time to listen and to absorb Jake's knowledge. Absorbing knowledge was what Longoria had done in the United States, and now he would do it in Guatemala, sharpening his perceptions, making himself a better soldier, because that was his profession now and he took pride in his work.

Jake said the skin was the largest organ in the body. Longoria did not know this. Jake said the skin was an organ and breathed, like a lung.

The tattoo announced the new species of man Longoria had become, the warrior who had been born within him. Longoria told Jake he wanted a jaguar because that was the name of his battalion. He felt good being able to explain to Jake about his unit. Jaguars were feared even way back in Guatemala's history, during the Mayan empire. The Mayans built temples to the jaguar god. Jaguars had spots that were like the camouflage uniforms the battalion wore. The jaguar stood for the new Guatemala the army wanted to build, a country of warriors and strong men, an empire like the one the Mayans had, except now they would carry submachine guns instead of spears.

Jake took out an old encyclopedia and found a color picture to use as a model. He said he knew some of the Green Berets who were training all those Latins over at the base and that they were "good guys, real he-men." In a frame on the wall, among a dizzying variety of close-up photos of tattooed snakes, crucifixes, and bare-breasted women, a man opened his shirt to the camera to reveal the Green Beret shield tattooed just above the nipple: two arrows, a sword, and the words *De Oppresso Liber*, which Jake said was Latin for "Free us from the Commies."

Even though he had been in only one battle, the tattoo of the jaguar made Longoria one with those Green Berets, a soldier who carried his loyalty in his skin. In the days after he returned to Guatemala he noticed that some of the younger soldiers seemed to take a step back when they were near him, while the civilians he encountered looked at him with a mixture of fear and carefully concealed disgust, as if the tattoo were a fungus on his arm. It was rare in Guatemala for a man to paint himself this way. He had broken some sort of taboo, crossed a boundary. Something about this snarling jaguar hinted at madness, unpredictability, bouts of rage. Even his commander looked at him strangely, this small *indio* who had grown stout at Fort Bragg and had returned with an animal on his arm, imitating the habits of the American soldiers every Guatemalan officer feared and respected.

Longoria was pleased to discover that his tattoo had these unexpected powers. From then on he always rolled up his sleeves to expose the tattoo to the Central American sky. It was born a North Carolina jaguar, but as it breathed in the tropical air it became a real Guatemalan jaguar.

* * *

A tow truck arrived in midmorning to carry away the remains of the police car. The driver was escorted by a squad of six patrolmen who formed a defensive perimeter around the hook of the truck, eyes trained on the gallery of windows above them. Using a winch and cable, he lifted the ashen chassis onto the flatbed as the officers watched solemnly, soldiers come to retrieve the body of a vanquished comrade. In thirty minutes the truck and the patrol car were gone, leaving only a rectangle of blackened pavement to mark the site of the fire.

Minutes later the cholos began gathering on the steps. Longoria could hear their chatter, the triumphant macho inflections as they celebrated their victory last night. There was no doubt the cholos had won, even though they retreated in the end. When the gangs fought each other it was conventional warfare, but last night, against the police, they were like guerrillas. The little battle was worthy of analysis. The cholos won because they employed the weapon of disorder, taking up stones against armed men, catching the officers by surprise. They understood that to win a war they had to be crazier than their opponents. Unpredictable. That was what Lieutenant Sanchez had taught Longoria back at Fort Bragg. Warriors who were prone to extremes tended to win more often than they lost.

Longoria knew that the Los Angeles Police Department could use extremes too, like what they did to that *negro* on the videotape. He had seen the tape months ago, on the television in the back room at El Pulgarcito, and had been impressed by the way the gringos handled themselves: the craziness of the baton blows, the exaggeration, so many against one kneeling man. He wondered if any of those officers had been trained at Fort Bragg, if they had studied Psyops, if they knew any of the Special Forces men. It was like the street strategies that García and the other chess players tried to teach him in MacArthur Park: attack, be reckless, forget what you read in the books. For some reason he could understand this principle when it came to real war, even though he had trouble applying it to the mind games of chess.

The burned-out patrol car was gone, but a sooty smell lingered over the street. The cholos had done a good job with their fire.

Longoria knew all about setting fires.

* * *

Their mission was to take the peasants by surprise. That's why the Jaguars had endured two days of marching instead of coming in by helicopter. But when Longoria's company reached the first houses, a tiny hamlet outside the main village, they found half the people who lived there waiting for them. A small man in a wrinkled black wool suit stood in the center of a dirt path with a Bible in his hand. Behind him a group of ten or so clapped and sang some evangelical hymn, raising their arms skyward in a gesture either of religious zealotry or of surrender, Longoria couldn't tell which. One woman seemed especially enraptured, her teeth gleaming in the sun, her head and long mane of black hair swaying to the rhythm of the tambourine in her hand.

"*¡Alabado sea Dios!*" the man with the Bible cried out.

Longoria watched as his lieutenant approached the singers. The lieutenant was a frog-eyed, mustachioed man of about thirty who usually looked composed and stoic under his red beret. Now his expression matched the snarl of the tiny jaguar on the beret's black patch.

"Hallelujah!" the pastor called.

"What are you doing?" the lieutenant demanded.

Longoria noticed for the first time that the pastor was an Indian man dressed in Western clothes. "*Gloria, gloria, es Jesús*," the group sang behind him. Their voices trailed off when the lieutenant spoke.

"We came to greet you," the pastor said timidly. "To show our support."

"How did you know we were coming? Who gave you this intelligence? What is your source?"

Longoria was waiting for the pastor's answer when a sergeant grabbed him by the arm and ordered him to search the hamlet. It was Sergeant Medina, a fair-skinned *canche* from Puerto Barrios who hated Longoria because he had been to Fort Bragg and Medina had not. Propelled by an energetic shove, Longoria stumbled toward the cluster of adobe houses, pointing his Galil machine gun at the doorways like a child in an arcade. Once inside, he pointed it at empty chairs and collections of pots and pans. He found no people, only charcoal fires that were still burning, suggesting that the families who lived here had fled in haste.

"No one," Longoria reported.

"The houses are empty, *teniente*," Medina told the lieutenant. "There isn't a soul here."

The lieutenant stepped closer to the pastor. "Where are these people, old man?"

The pastor only trembled.

"You know where they are. Don't lie to me, you animal. They ran away because they're with the guerrillas, didn't they? Tell me where they are, you bastard."

"Where are the guerrillas?" the sergeant demanded.

"Where are the guerrillas?" the lieutenant repeated.

A corporal seized one of the peasant men by the arm and took up the chant. "*¿Dónde están los guerrilleros?*"

Before Longoria realized what was happening, the soldiers were herding the singers into their church, a little wooden building with a hand-painted sign that read "*Iglesia Evangélica Pastores de Jesucristo.*" One of the boys in the group briefly resisted, standing his ground until a soldier grabbed him by his stringy hair and dragged him inside.

"But I'm with the party," the pastor pleaded. "I have my papers right here." He pulled a laminated card and a folded document from his pocket and held them in the air.

The lieutenant took the card and examined its plastic skin with his frog eyes, seemingly impressed by the authority of the party seal. Then, without explanation, he threw the card to the ground and pushed the old man violently toward the door.

"The MLN gave them to me," the pastor insisted, trying to retrieve his card. "The papers say I'm with the party."

"We've seen all the papers we need to see," the lieutenant said. "Anyone can get papers."

Longoria was confused. The MLN was one of the right-wing parties that supported Guatemala's president. In the complex set of political classifications and acronyms he had just begun to master, the letters M, L, and N, when put together, should have made the old man a sympathizer, a friendly. The Movimiento de Liberación Nacional was on the side of the army, they were not even neutrals. What the lieutenant was doing didn't make any sense. But then again, Longoria had discovered that many things in the army didn't seem to make sense at first, until you thought about them for a long time and found a way to fit all the elements together. Maybe the lieutenant, who after all was a more experienced soldier, had access to some other information that exposed the old man as a fraud.

Suddenly the boy who had resisted bolted from the church, heading for the jungle in a panicked sprint.

"Stop him," Sergeant Medina shouted. "Longoria, you!"

Longoria gave chase, dropping his pack because it weighed him down. When he saw he wasn't gaining any ground on the boy, he fell to one knee and calmly aimed his machine gun at the rapidly shrinking target. He missed high, three times in a row.

"*¡Cese el fuego!*" he heard the lieutenant order from fifty yards away. "Cease fire!"

Longoria lowered his weapon, and the boy galloped into the safety of the jungle. Bewildered, Longoria walked back to the main group.

"No shooting! No shooting!" Sergeant Medina yelled. "Everybody in the next village will know we're here. Knives only."

Knives only. Longoria was still registering the words when he saw five soldiers entering the church, machetes drawn.

They better know what they're doing, he thought. Machetes were very sharp. He had cut himself more than once as a child, before he learned how to handle the long blade. You found out how sharp a machete was when you cut yourself.

Seconds later a woman stumbled out the church door, her arms and face covered with deep gashes. Sergeant Medina blocked her with his shoulder, like a wrestler, and sent her sprawling to the ground. She tried to scramble to her feet, but the sergeant put his boot on her back and pushed her into the dirt. Straddling her, he unsheathed a hunting knife from his hip, grabbed her by the hair, and slit her throat.

Such a strange thing, the silent rush of blood, turning black when it seeped into the earth. Legs trembling, arms flapping. And now the rest of them were doing it too, stumbling out of the church, boys with stains on their crotches, girls holding up ripped dresses. They raised their arms in the air and fell, making noises that came from the lungs and stomach, not the mouth or tongue, a secret language of grunts and moans. What were they saying? What was the meaning of the noises and the blood spilling from their throats, the roll and spin of their eyes? They tossed and shook on the ground. What were these signals the body gave off before it finally surrendered to stiff silence? What were the children saying?

Now Jaguars were spilling from the church too, and for a moment it was like a game on a playground. Children running in circles around the huts, soldiers chasing after them with clumsy strides because they were so big and the boys and girls were so little. The children were crying, but it sounded like laughter to Longoria, the excited laughter of the schoolyard. *You can't get me, you can't get me.*

And then the soldiers looked like *campesinos* again. Because this was hard work, raising the machete to cut and hack. They chopped and grunted like men trying to clear a sugarcane field, strings of perspiration running down their necks. Steel against bone. Hack, hack. This was work you couldn't do without spattering pink and red and brown all over you. The Jaguars looked like camouflage *campesinos*, dirty and sweaty, muscles working in *machetazos*.

* * *

Setting fire to the church was Longoria's responsibility, the first important one they had given him since he joined the Jaguars. He could feel Sergeant Medina's eyes on his back as he snapped nervously at the little silver box he had just been given, trying to put a flame to the adobe bricks. He turned the small wheel with his thumb but produced only a few sparks.

"What are you waiting for?" the sergeant yelled behind him. "Do it! Burn it now!"

If Longoria didn't set the fire, if he didn't get the box to work, the sergeant would laugh at him, he would think that the jaguar on Longoria's arm was a fraud. Already this sergeant had made sarcastic remarks about Longoria's trip to Fort Bragg, asking who this peasant was to receive such an honor. Sergeant Medina said Longoria went to Carolina only because he was the *preferido* of Captain Elías, and he said it in a way that suggested something truly disgusting. Finally the box did its job. First a wisp of smoke snaking skyward, then a little cone of fire, the dance of saffron tongues, and the whoosh of a hot wind.

All the bodies had been dragged inside the church. If the people in the church miraculously came to life again, they wouldn't hear the sound of the flames. They wouldn't hear anything, not even their own screams, because one of the Jaguars had cut off their ears to fill a little burlap bag with souvenirs.

Screams were the last sounds the people in the church made when they still had ears and could hear themselves. The pastor and the children screamed before they died because they were afraid of passing over to the other side. Who could blame them? No one wanted to pass over, because on the other side there wasn't anything, just darkness and silence. Longoria might be on the brink of passing over to the other side himself. He could easily wind up like one of those corpses in the church, and that would be the end of him, of all his thoughts and desires. He wouldn't be able to march anymore, to clean his gun or admire his tattoo. Even the jaguar on his arm would wither and die. That's how it was in a war. One moment you could be clapping and singing, full of life and the Lord, your arms reaching for the sky, and the next you could be a corpse, no more alive than a chair or a spoon or a wall.

Longoria made the walls of the church come alive with his cigarette lighter.

* * *

There were those who hadn't unsheathed their machetes, those who stood by and watched while their comrades-in-arms exhausted themselves in the labor of cutting and chopping. The other soldiers did not look at them with disdain, they simply ignored them. There seemed to be some kind of understanding among the men. Not everyone was strong enough to carry out such orders.

As he marched from the hamlet of the singing children to the village of Nueva Concepción, Longoria began to see how the Jaguars could be divided. He could sense that each man felt repelled by the others. It did not seem right that they could all be marching together with such different expressions on their faces. Some still wore their warrior masks, jaws locked and ready for more combat, as if they expected the rest of the unit to turn on them like a column of guerrillas. Others had surrendered to a stunned contemplation, and one man wept, a Kanjobal Indian who kept repeating words in his language that no one else in the company understood.

The only thing they seemed to have in common was the jaguar on their berets and on their sleeves. That jaguar was always snarling an identical snarl. The faces of the men in the uniforms might change, but the animal on the patch was always fierce. The jaguar was a hunter; that was why the Mayans worshiped him for generations, that was why the Jaguar Battalion wore his image.

Like Longoria, the lieutenant must have sensed the disunion. He ordered the men to halt and looked down at the muddy soil at his feet, his frog eyes shifting as he searched for words.

"All the people in this area support the enemy. That's how they know we're coming, and that's why they run away. That's why they lie to us when we ask them where the guerrillas are. They all know where the guerrillas are, but they lie. I lost six men right here, right at this village, because the guerrillas surprised us. They surprised us even though these snakes knew they were coming."

"That's right, *teniente*," Sergeant Medina shouted. "They're all snakes. They betrayed us."

"When all these people are gone we won't have any more problems," the lieutenant continued, "because there won't be anyone left to give the guerrillas anything to eat. We're going to go through this place and level it, do you understand? The guerrillas will go away and we won't have to fight them anymore."

Longoria recognized in the lieutenant's speech what the instructors at Fort Bragg called "leadership." The men were beginning to fall apart, so the lieutenant gathered them together with words. Longoria was glad that the lieutenant had done this, because he was afraid of what might happen if the guerrillas found the Jaguars divided.

* * *

When the Jaguars had taken Nueva Concepción, they sat down to eat. Two women tended to beef sizzling on a grill and slapped masa between their palms to make tortillas, weeping and working, wiping tears from their faces with their sleeves. They were the last living representatives of the hundred or so people who had filled the town market until a few hours ago. Clap, clap, they took yellow balls of masa and squeezed them into flat discs. Three dozen so far. They worked over the fire, surrounded by the contents of the market stalls: baskets of tomatoes upended, mangoes squashed into a slippery pulp, new tin buckets dented, candles broken, handmade brooms splintered. The lieutenant wanted enough tortillas for the company's two-day march back to headquarters. The older of the two, a stooped woman with knots of muscle in her back and a few strands of gray in a black mane, seemed to understand what would happen when she finished. Sergeant Medina pointed his Galil at her, and she clapped the masa faster.

The Jaguars had entered the market firing a steady barrage from their Galils, peasants sprinting and falling across the square in a futile attempt to outrun the racing bullets. When we finish this work, Longoria thought, the guerrillas will go away. He aimed at the moving targets, and this time he got a few, hitting a man in the small of the back and a woman in the neck. He watched, fascinated, as they fell like canvas tents collapsing when you took away the frame, the life of their bodies instantly transformed into dead weight, their muscles no longer able to keep them upright.

Now there were only these two women left, vendors of tamales, spared the executions that followed the taking of the market, sweeping bursts of machine-gun fire in a ditch by the road. They were making tortillas because the Jaguars had eaten all the tamales. The women must have known some of the bodies in the ditch, because they had not stopped crying. Overwhelmed by grief and fear, they worked clumsily, slowing down or falling to their knees until the sergeant stuck the barrel of his gun in their ribs.

When the men had devoured all the steak, chicken, and vegetables they could stomach, when the last of the tortillas was made, Sergeant Medina pulled Longoria and the Kanjobal soldier aside and gave them the order to execute the cooks.

"Take them over there," he said in a whisper, pointing to a corner of the market strewn with smashed chicken coops. "And be quick."

Longoria grabbed the older woman by the collar of her blouse and led her away. She flung her arms at him without much conviction. To look at her was to remember the market women he had known as a boy, the outstretched arms that gave him sweet tamales, mouths opening to a silver-toothed grin. Market days were special days then, the happiest he could remember, filled with the wonder of so many new sights and different people.

She slipped from his grip and tried to run away but lost her footing in the slush of trampled vegetables on the market's cement floor. Longoria heard a chorus of derisive whistles from the other soldiers. Sergeant Medina was looking at him as if to say, This Indian is not worthy of the beautiful jaguar tattoo on his arm. His tattoo is a joke. Longoria caught up with her in two long strides and slammed her against the cement. *This woman has humiliated me.* If he didn't kill her now, he would be a laughingstock like the Kanjobal, who was crying like a baby over the kneeling figure of his prisoner, unable to carry out a simple order.

"Just shoot her, you stupid *indio!*"

Standing over his own prisoner, Longoria pulled the trigger. The first bullet pierced her stomach, and she looked straight at him in disbelief, wheezing as she gasped for air. Her arms floated up and she reached for him like the market women of his boyhood. "*Por favor,*" she said meekly. "*Por favor.*" She was passing over to the other side, and the quicker she passed, the sooner she would close her eyes and stop looking at him. He fired another round into her, but still her eyes did not close. Another round and another, his muscles tense against the weapon's recoil as the eyes rolled in circles, brown balls spinning in a creamy soup. Longoria kept shooting until his machine gun wouldn't fire anymore.

"Hey, look at Rat-Face!" Sergeant Medina called out. "He's a real killer, that one. Fierce! A killer rat!"

* * *

Longoria was racing down the stairwell of the Westlake Arms, uncharacteristically late for work after another night of fitful sleep, when he bumped into a cholo who was loping up the steps. They both fell in the crash of limbs.

"Hey, what the fuck!"

"*¡Hijueputa!*" Longoria spat back.

"You fucking with me or what?"

It was the elephant-eared one. They stared at each other, facing off with identically clenched jaws and flexed muscles. Longoria could see "María" tattooed on the cholo's neck in a pretty swirl. Perhaps that was the name of the girl whose image adorned his biceps, the bounce of her curls reaching almost to his elbow.

Longoria had encountered this young man on the steps dozens of times but had never noticed the word on his neck because they had never stood this close before. The cholo had never stopped to look him in the eye this long, he had always looked away. The battle with the police had emboldened him. If I can fight a cop, his eyes seemed to say, I can fight you too, soldier.

Finally, with more bumping and jostling, they allowed each other to pass, Longoria's jaguar brushing against the homegirl on the cholo's arm.

Adventure in Beverly Hills

Not long after the bulldozers came to Crown Hill, José Juan Grijalva disappeared.

He got up one morning before everyone else, as usual, and bundled himself against the pre-dawn chill in a thrift store coat he wore over the sweater he had been sleeping in for the past three weeks.

"*Me voy a la Main y la Washington,*" he told Antonio, who was groggy but awake, lying on three layers of cardboard that were just enough to keep the wetness of the muddy tunnel from seeping through. "I'm going to look for work. Want to come?"

Antonio shook his head. He didn't feel like going to Main and Washington. He never did. He was surprised José Juan asked since he had told him many times that he considered it pathetic and undignified. You stood on the sidewalk, scanning the traffic like a prostitute in search of a john, pushing and shoving with a hundred other men so that you could be first in line when a pickup truck with building materials in the back finally slowed down and stopped. Then you held up the three or four fingers that indicated how little pay you would accept for an hour's work.

"*Como quieras,*" said José Juan, shrugging his shoulders as he walked away. Eight days later he had not returned.

Now Antonio missed his friend and wondered why he had left. Maybe it was the tunnel and its fetid air, even more dismal than the plastic and cardboard shacks on Crown Hill. Maybe he was scared off by all the talk of killing and vengeance that had begun to fill the conversations by the campfire. Maybe he thought Antonio would make him an accomplice to the murder of the tattooed soldier and they would end up in prison together, co-conspirators in a political assassination. José Juan had always been the cautious type. Breaking the law, resorting to violence, that was something he'd never do. He wanted a place in Montebello or East L.A., one of the nice Chicano suburbs, a house with a van parked in the driveway. If he played by the rules, maybe those things would come to him.

"Hey, what happened to your buddy, the curly-headed guy?" Frank asked one afternoon.

"*El moro?* I don't know. He's gone."

"He was quiet, but he seemed like a nice guy."

Maybe José Juan had simply decided to return to Mexico, defeated at last by the separation from his family. Maybe he was worried that his wife would take up with another man, someone who could provide for her—an understandable reaction for a woman left alone with four children. But at least he could have said goodbye. José Juan was always gracious and polite, and it seemed strange that he would leave like that, without a word to the friend who had suffered with him through so much.

Of course, it was also possible that he had been mugged or run over by a car or arrested by the immigration police. So many different tragedies could swallow a poor man in Los Angeles. Antonio was always reading in *La Opinión* about immigrants who died on the freeway or in factory accidents so far from home and family that there was no one to pay for their funerals.

Antonio could only hope and pray that nothing like that had happened to José Juan. He missed the companionship, missed talking to someone from his own culture, more or less, someone who at least spoke the same language. He remembered their last trip to the Los Angeles Memorial Coliseum, to see Guatemala play Mexico, the game they ended up listening to on a radio just outside the stadium because the tickets cost more than they expected. It was a few weeks before the eviction, and they were broke. The radio announcer launched into a long "*Gooool!*" and the cheer of the crowd arrived a second or two later, forty thousand people taking in breath all at once and shouting, the extended roar peppered with horn blasts and firecrackers. José Juan shouted his own "*Gol!*" and jumped two feet in the air because Manolo Negrete had just put the Mexicans ahead of the hapless

Guatemaltecos. Even though they couldn't see the action, Antonio knew his team would be shorter, frailer, and less skilled than the Mexicans. They always were.

When the game ended with the score 4-0, José Juan put a brotherly arm around Antonio's shoulder. "They'll do better the next time, *hombre*. They've got all those good new players, Paniagua, Castillo. They're young and fast. In a few years they'll be a lot better."

"No they won't," Antonio had said with a frown. "Guatemala always loses."

A friend like that shouldn't just leave. He should tell you when he decides to go back to his country.

But the worst thing about José Juan's absence was that it made it impossible, for the time being, to move forward with the plan to kill the soldier. Everything hinged on being able to buy a gun. Frank said that was the only way to finish off a trained killer. You had to surprise him, plug him from behind, or you ran the risk of getting killed yourself. That was how Frank explained it. For this reason Antonio needed at least a small gun, something Frank called a .22, or preferably a bigger one, like a .38. Frank said there was a difference between a .38 and a .22—"a huge difference"—and he sounded like he knew what he was talking about. But even a .22 cost money, and Antonio was down to his last dime. He had planned to ask José Juan to lend him the forty or fifty dollars Frank said he would need.

Without José Juan, Antonio's plan to kill the tattooed soldier was in strategic limbo, but he could still work out the rest of the details, deciding when and where to stage his ambush. Frank suggested a "reconnaissance mission."

"We have to know everything about the guy," Frank said. "Where he sleeps, where he eats. Every detail."

Antonio said he already knew these things. "I can take you to all the places. I can show you everywhere he goes, everything he does."

The tour took a day. Antonio led the way, Frank following along with good humor and moderate curiosity, like a student on a field trip to the museum. It occurred to Antonio that he had never known a black man this intimately. There were only a few blacks in Guatemala

City, and it was the nature of Los Angeles that the many races stayed separate, everyone on their own turf, Latinos with Latinos, blacks with blacks, whites with whites. It was only in the little camp in the tunnel that Antonio had seen the races mixing, all thrown together because they had no place else to go.

The only other black man Antonio knew as well as Frank was San Martín de Porres, the sixteenth-century Peruvian saint whose face adorned a palm-sized devotional card he carried in his pants pocket. He had bought the card for a quarter at one of the *botánicas* on Broadway, a few days after deciding to kill the tattooed soldier, in hopes that the image of the saint would remind him of Elena and inspire his quest for justice. But next to Frank, San Martín seemed mild and meek. He was saintly by definition, and not the fighter that Frank was, not the powerful and funny black man who was now helping him plan the murder of the soldier.

Walking toward the tattooed soldier's apartment on Bonnie Brae, they made slow progress because every half block or so Frank saw somebody he knew and stopped to talk. These acquaintances were an odd assortment, but they shared the same gray pallor, general emaciation, and slumped posture. "They're all hypes and hubba heads," Frank said. "I used to be in that life, but not anymore." They met a skinny white woman named Nancy who started to flirt with Frank, saying he had beautiful eyelashes. Antonio looked at Frank's eyes and saw that this was true. The lashes were long and curled at the ends, giving him a slightly feminine appearance that was offset by the stubble on his chin and the thickness of his neck. Nancy started to rub up against Frank but stopped abruptly when he said, "Hey, babe, I'm flat broke."

A block later they reached the Westlake Arms. Antonio pointed out the window of the tattooed soldier's room.

"He lives up there on the fourth floor, right next to the little ladder. He's at work right now, so he won't see us."

Frank craned his neck to examine the window. It was closed today, precluding any acrobatic break-ins from the fire escape. Antonio took off his glasses and cleaned them to get a better view.

There was a white curtain that hadn't been there before. Maybe after their confrontation in the park the soldier had started to take precautions.

They walked around to the alley and the dumpster in back.

"He takes out his trash in the morning," Antonio said. "Every day, I think."

Frank seemed especially intrigued by the narrow corridor of the alley, his eyes lingering on the rear fire escapes that climbed up the building, the crisscrossing wires, the shacks of the homeless tucked against one wall.

"You say he comes here every day?"

"Yes. With a little red trash can."

Frank chuckled. "You really got this guy down. You know everything about him. You know where he shits, you know where he sleeps. You really got him."

Next they went to the bus stop where Antonio had seen the soldier standing with his girlfriend, the pretty Latina in the shiny shoes. Antonio began to describe her in detail, but Frank interrupted him.

"No, no, that's no good," he said. "We have to leave the girlfriend out of it. She's got nothing to do with it."

They walked two blocks to the park and the chess tables where Antonio had attempted to bludgeon his enemy, then another mile to Pico Boulevard and the storefront office of El Pulgarcito Express, branch number two. From across the street, keeping a safe distance, Antonio pointed at the plate-glass windows.

"He works at the front counter. See?"

Frank squinted and shook his head. The counter and a few bodies were visible through the glare of the glass, but little else. "Wait a minute," he said. "I'll be right back." He crossed the street and returned a few seconds later, barely aware of the traffic, grinning broadly.

"Holy shit! I saw him! He was right there. Tiny little motherfucker, just like you said! Ha! With the tattoo and everything."

"Let's go, Frank. I don't want him to see me."

"That sick s.o.b." Frank clenched his fist as they walked away. "He looks like a killer. Looks like a Nazi with his buzz-cut hairdo. I seen him once, and I already wanna kill him. I wanna do him bad. I could see it in his face. I could see those kids you said he killed."

* * *

"I think the alley is your best bet," Frank said. They were sitting near the tunnel entrance in the afternoon sunshine, watching a group of graffiti artists add yet another layer of paint to the concrete walls. Pulling spray cans from canvas backpacks that hung languidly from their shoulders, they worked in elegant bursts, accompanied by the click-clack of little metal balls as they shook the cans to keep the paint flowing.

"No one'll see you there. You can hide in one of those boxes. Behind the dumpster. Whatever. Then, when he comes down, you take him out. Like this, pow!" He pantomimed firing a gun. "And then you make a run for it down the alley, blend into the crowd. Get on the first bus you see."

It all made sense. The thing was not to get caught. To accomplish the act and go unpunished, to live afterward like a normal person, that itself was the real act of defiance against the crimes of the tattooed soldier. Antonio would kill him, and then walk and breathe in the open city as a free man. He would go back to work, find a woman to love, start a family again and grow into old age with them. While the soldier rotted underground, Antonio would stand in the sunlight and welcome the coming decades, the new generations. He would watch his children stand tall and prosper: they would go to school, do all the things Carlitos never could.

Antonio was lost in his thoughts, half listening to Frank, when he spotted a lone figure jumping the chain-link fence at the entrance to the lot, a swarthy Latin in a bleached white shirt and leather shoes ill suited to climbing. The man landed about fifty yards away, nearly slipping on the concrete, and the graffiti artists looked up from their work, wondering if he was a cop or maybe the owner of the property. The man ignored them and walked toward the tunnel. "Antonio!" he called out, waving his arms. "It's me!"

Antonio and Frank stared at him and then at each other with identical expressions of astonishment. It was José Juan.

"He's clean," Frank said, echoing Antonio's thoughts precisely. José Juan had the freshly showered look of a man who slept in a real bed.

"I got a job!" José Juan exclaimed in English, raising his arms in a triumphant V. He embraced Antonio, who felt an unexpected rush of nostalgia. *I didn't realize how much I missed him.*

"*Moro,* look at you," Antonio said, laughing and wiping at the corner of his eye. "You're a new man. What happened?"

"Look at those shoes," Frank said with a low whistle. "Sharp."

Antonio looked down at the tassels of José Juan's tapered cordovan shoes, now stained with the mud of the tunnel floor. His friend looked slimmer because he was no longer wrapped in the bundle of clothes they had to wear to stay warm, and he had gone to the barber for the first time in months. He could have been one of those smooth playboy types Antonio usually found so annoying.

"I'm living in Beverly Hills!" José Juan blurted.

"What?"

"Beverly Hills," he repeated.

"No way," Frank said. "How?"

He pulled out a milk crate and José Juan sat down to explain. Too excited to concentrate on English, he spoke in Spanish, with Antonio translating for Frank.

"*No me lo van a creer.*"

"You're not going to believe this," Antonio said.

"Start from the very beginning," Frank suggested.

"Okay. *Todo comenzó en la esquina. En la Main.*"

"It all started on the corner," Antonio translated. "On Main Street."

"Where the dayworkers are," Frank interjected. "All the Mexicans looking for jobs."

"*Sí.*"

In this fashion José Juan proceeded to tell his story. He had gone to Main Street to look for work, but when he got there he quickly lost hope. The place was more crowded than he had ever seen it, maybe three hundred men standing at the intersection, pushing and shoving toward the cars and trucks that stopped there, a dense pack of bodies forming around each prospective employer. José Juan wasn't strong enough to get to the front, and after a while he gave up and went off to sulk on a nearby side street.

Sitting on the curb with his head buried in his hands, he began to contemplate, for the first time, going back to his pueblo in Mexico and facing the ridicule that would surely be heaped upon him for his failure in Los Angeles. Just then a green Hyundai stopped inches from his feet, and the Korean driver called out, "You want work?" José Juan jumped into the car, not bothering with the matter of pay, and slammed the door just as a horde of men came running from Main Street and began to pound on the hood, holding up four and some-times just three fingers. Miraculously the driver managed to escape that crush of humanity without running anyone over. A few minutes later they were in Koreatown.

The man owned a huge pink apartment building and wanted José Juan to hang up some signs. They were all in Korean, but José Juan assumed they said something like "For Rent: Koreans Welcome." He had to use a ladder for the signs the boss wanted on the second floor and on various lampposts in the neighborhood, but no matter how slowly he worked, José Juan couldn't stretch the job out past three hours. He finished at about one o'clock, and the Korean man paid him nine dollars.

"*Nueve dólares cabales, ni un centavo más,*" José Juan said, shift-ing on the milk crate and leaning down to scrape mud flakes off his shoes.

"Nine dollars exactly," Antonio translated. "Not a penny more."

The pay was bad enough, but then the *coreano* didn't even give him a ride back to Main Street and he had to take the bus. That cost him $1.35.

"Those Koreans are jerks," Frank commented. "But what about the Beverly Hills part?"

"*A eso voy.*"

"He's getting to that," Antonio said.

José Juan made it back to Main Street about two o'clock. All the action on Main was in the morning, and if you were there after noon you knew you wouldn't get any work. Most of the men at the corner had gone home and the few who remained were already starting to get drunk, so when a big Ford truck pulled up, José Juan and a black Honduran guy named Roberto were the only ones to offer their services.

"I told myself, I can't believe I am so lucky," José Juan said, switching momentarily to English. "Twice in one day I am lucky."

The next thing he knew he was in Beverly Hills, of all places, in a house that looked like one of those haciendas in the Mexican soap operas, a big, beautiful white house with the prettiest red tile roof. The man who had hired him was the head gardener, a polite and friendly Asian who wanted José Juan to do some simple yard work. The pay was better this time, six dollars an hour instead of just three. He started out in back, cutting a huge lawn that surrounded the swimming pool. That's where he was an hour later when he spotted the maid.

"*Una Mexicana guapísima.*"

"A very pretty Mexican woman," Antonio translated.

"Uh-oh," Frank said mischievously. "I think I know where this is headed!"

When the Mexicana saw him looking at her, she disappeared into a cute little house in the back. José Juan thought he'd scared her off, but then she came out with a glass of cold water and said, in the sweetest voice, "You've been working so hard. Look at you, your clothes are so dirty from work. You should take a drink." They talked for only a few minutes, but that was all it took for José Juan to find out that she was just like him: all alone and separated from her family. She had two little boys back home in Guanajuato, living with their grandmother.

"And the father?" Frank asked. "The father of her kids?"

José Juan shrugged his shoulders and smiled. "*¿Quién sabe?*"

It was a long time since José Juan had talked to such a nice woman. When he finished work at about six o'clock and the polite gardener offered to drive him and Roberto back downtown, he lied and said he had a cousin in Santa Monica and that he'd take the bus. He walked two blocks down the street, saw the gardener driving away with Roberto, waved to them, and then circled back to the hacienda to talk to that very pretty, very lonely Mexicana.

Well, to make a long story short, he had been sleeping with Cristina in the little house behind the hacienda ever since.

"You dog!" Frank shouted with glee.

"But you're married," Antonio said.

José Juan ignored this last remark and explained that Cristina's employers were away on a long trip and so nobody bothered them. This rich family worked in the movies, and they were in Europe at something called a "film festival." And so it was just José Juan and Cristina alone in the little guest house, which was just like the main house only much smaller, with an identical red tile roof. Living with Cristina had been like paradise, but the best part was that she had a friend who got him a job at a garment factory on Washington Boulevard, just a few blocks, as a matter of fact, from the street corner where the whole adventure started. He had been working there for a week, making five dollars an hour. And even though he hadn't been paid yet, Cristina had loaned him some money so he could buy some new clothes, which was what he had done just before coming to the tunnel to see how his friend Antonio was doing.

"What a story!" Frank said.

"But there's more," José Juan said in English.

"More?"

It turned out that Cristina had a brother in South-Central who was doing real well, with a good job in a factory that made water heaters. He had just bought a house out there in the black neighborhoods, by Fifty-third and Normandie. And even though this brother was going to share the house with his in-laws, they were still going to have trouble making the payments to the bank. To bring in a few extra centavos, they needed to rent out a small room in the back. The room had space for two people, and its own private bathroom.

"They say they'll rent us this room for just one fifty a month," José Juan told Antonio. "And we don't need any deposit. When I get my first paycheck, next Friday, we can move in. You and me, Antonio. There's room for both of us."

Antonio, who had been translating every word, stopped suddenly. "What did he say?" Frank demanded.

There was a brief silence as Antonio wondered if it could be true. *I must not be such a bad person if this friend has come back to rescue me. José Juan knows I don't deserve to live in this tunnel.*

"We're not going to be homeless anymore," Antonio said finally. "He found a room for the two of us. Very cheap."

He looked around at the mattresses and sleeping bags tossed on the floor near the tunnel entrance, at the pots and pans blackened by fire and the plastic bag that held all his belongings. He looked at his hands and saw the dirt under his fingernails, reached for his neck and felt the layer of grime.

"You're not going to be homeless," Frank said.

* * *

José Juan gave him the money right away, two crisp twenties, just enough to buy a cheap gun on the black market. "You can pay me later," he said. After a final embrace he left the camp to rejoin Cristina in Beverly Hills.

"She's going to make me dinner. Just two more days before the family gets back, so we have to enjoy it."

The next morning Antonio and Frank rose early for the long walk to the Eastside, where Frank knew someone who would sell them a gun cheap. How did he know such people? Without Frank, Antonio would be completely lost, unable to solve this most basic of problems.

An hour later they arrived at their destination, a series of bluish gray apartment buildings just on the other side of the concrete ravine of the Los Angeles River. A large sign announced "Pico-Aliso Housing Project." Frank led Antonio into a maze of buildings and grassy plazas, looking for an address.

They reached a doorway where a tough-looking teenager in baggy pants was cradling a baby boy in his arms, cooing at the infant as he kissed him on the stomach. As they headed for the next apartment over, the teen glanced up at them with mild suspicion, revealing a teardrop tattooed under his eye.

Frank knocked on the door. "Hey," he said when a large Latina woman in a nightshirt appeared, hair shower-wet, the room behind her smelling of staleness, of closed windows, old carpets, and cigarettes. "I'm looking for my buddy John De la Torre. He around?"

At the mention of this name, the woman looked at Frank as if he had insulted her or spit at her feet. "John De la Torre! You know John De la Torre?"

"Uh, yeah," Frank said tentatively. "I'm looking for him. He's my friend."

"Your friend!" she yelled, and then laughed. "That's a good one. I didn't know he had any friends left!"

"Isn't this where John De la Torre lives?" Frank asked.

"Used to live," the woman said. "Now we don't even let him in the fucking house, and when we hear he's in the neighborhood we double-lock the doors. Three times he's cleaned us out. A junkie is what he is. And a thief." She paused, eyebrows raised in alarm. "Is he out now? Is that what you're telling me? They finally let my brother out of jail and didn't tell us? Son of a bitch!" She turned and shouted, "Hey, they let Johnny out of the big house and didn't tell us."

"What?" came a voice from the apartment.

The woman turned back to Frank and pointed a menacing finger at his chest. "If you see that s.o.b., you tell him and tell him good. Tell him not to even think about showing his sorry-ass face round here till he gives me back my TV."

"And my jewelry too!" the unseen voice added.

With that, the door slammed in Frank's face. "Looks like John ain't here," he said to Antonio with a sardonic smile.

They were walking away from the door when they were approached by a boy on the brink of adolescence, a sheen of oil covering his pimply face. He was dressed in the T-shirt and stiff, oversized jeans that seemed to be a neighborhood uniform.

"You looking for John?" he asked.

"Yeah."

"What for?"

"To buy a gun," Frank said without hesitation.

"Oh." The boy looked at the ground, as if he were thinking about what to say next. "I know someone who's got a gun."

Antonio's sense of surprise and horror quickly passed. Of course this acned cherub knew where to get a gun. It made perfect sense.

Frank contemplated the boy with a mixture of distrust and curiosity. "How much?" he said after a brief pause.

"Don't know. You gotta ask her."

"Her?"

"Yeah. Monica, she's my cousin. It's only a twenty-two, but she wants to dump it."

Frank and Antonio found themselves following the boy around the corner of the building. He walked with an easygoing shuffle, his pants legs rubbing together in a muted song. Antonio wished he were taking them to a playground or a sandbox, instead of to a woman selling a gun. Maybe it was all a game. The boy led them deeper into the labyrinth of apartment buildings, each the same bluish gray as the others. They walked for ten minutes, to a building that seemed no different from all the rest. The boy knocked on a door, and a thin girl appeared, perhaps sixteen years old, with cinnamon skin and hair dyed a brownish orange.

"Can you talk?" the boy asked.

"Yeah, what's up?" the girl said.

"These guys, they're friends of John De la Torre. They wanna buy the gun."

Monica looked at Frank and Antonio with a frown, offended by their grungy appearance, perhaps, or by their association with the sullied name of John De la Torre.

"It's just a twenty-two," she said.

Frank looked embarrassed now. They both felt like fools or worse, engaged in this repugnant commerce with children.

"We'll take it," Frank said finally. "How much you want for it?"

"Twenty bucks."

"Sold."

Monica disappeared into the apartment and returned with the gun wrapped in a musty dishrag. She handed it to Frank.

"Don't want it no more," she offered as he inspected the contents. "I got a nephew, he's real little, just two. I'm afraid he's gonna find this thing."

Antonio gave her one of José Juan's twenty-dollar bills.

"Here, take these too," she said, reaching into her pocket.

Antonio stretched out his hand, and the girl dropped a dozen or so bullets into his palm. They looked like pieces of brass candy. Glancing up, he saw her smiling broadly, as if she had unburdened herself of an awful weight.

Back on the bridge over the Los Angeles River, Antonio soon forgot about the girl. He was mesmerized by the little packages of explosive fire that were rattling in his pocket. One of these bullets would do the job. He would make the soldier swallow this brass candy. Frank had the gun tucked under his sweater and would soon teach him how to use it properly.

Antonio was one step closer to killing the soldier from San Cristóbal. The man in the park who ate ice cream after murdering Carlos and Elena.

Antonio asked Frank if he could hold the gun.

"Be my guest," Frank said. "Better you than me."

Metal tucked inside his jacket now. *I was a bus boy once, but today I am an armed man. Antonio of the dirty plates is a warrior today.*

Bullets seemed to be the only instrument capable of transmitting Antonio's will. They were projectiles of rage. He thought he might be scared once he actually had a gun, but instead the .22 was fueling waking visions of spinning blades and blunt instruments, flamethrowers and avalanches of falling boulders. Obstacles would be crushed, smashed and destroyed, in the same way the buildings on Crown Hill had been flattened. There would be an evenness to the world again, land empty for a new beginning. Bulldozers converging on the chess player with the shaved head, the man who carried corpses in an envelope.

18
Halloween

The flashlight gave off a weak yellow crescent. Antonio was afraid the batteries would run down and they would be stuck in pitch darkness. They had set out from the tunnel opening twenty minutes ago, slogging along the muddy floor, stepping around puddles of brownish water. Frank stopped once and pointed the flashlight beam at the tunnel ceiling, a broad arch of crumbling concrete the texture of sandstone. Moving the light across the brown-gray surface, he found what he was looking for, a three-foot-long stalactite glistening ice white. A drop of water fell from its tip.

"Ain't that pretty," Frank said. "It's all that rainwater from Bunker Hill. All that rain that falls on the stockbrokers. That water has minerals and it leaves this shit right here."

Antonio had only a vague idea what Frank was talking about. He just knew they were somewhere under downtown and that the plan was to walk deep into the tunnel and take target practice so that no one would hear the shots. Frank carried the gun and a plastic milk crate, Antonio the bullets and some bottles and cans. They walked a little farther and set up their firing range, stacking the bottles and cans on the milk crate. Frank took the gun from his jacket and handed it to Antonio.

"How do I load it?" Antonio asked.

"What do I look like, a thief? I ain't never fired a gun in my life."

"But I thought . . ."

"I guess you just open up the round thing there and put the bullets in the little holes."

Antonio fumbled with the weapon and finally opened the cylinder, taking six bullets from his pocket and slipping them in. He had spent the morning counting his fifteen bullets over and over again, and now the plan was to take nine practice shots. That would leave him with enough ammunition to keep the gun fully loaded. Frank said it was important to practice, even if it was just nine shots, so that he would have a steady hand when he confronted the soldier. Plus they had to test the gun to make sure the girl in the projects hadn't sold them a dud that wouldn't fire at the crucial moment, when he was toe to toe with his prey.

With Frank standing safely behind him and pointing the flashlight beam at the target, Antonio raised the gun. He closed one eye and looked at the sight, a tiny bead at the end of the stubby barrel. Then, holding the gun with two hands, he shut both eyes and pulled the trigger. It was a little harder than he expected, the metal stabbing into his finger.

The gun went off with a flash he could still see behind his eyelids, the explosion echoing with a thunderous clap against the curved tunnel walls. Antonio was temporarily deafened, and blinded too, because Frank dropped the flashlight in a belated attempt to cover his eardrums. He picked it up again and pointed it in Antonio's face.

"You okay?" he yelled.

"Yes."

Frank turned the beam of light toward the milk crate. The bottles and cans were still in place. "I think you need to get closer," he said.

Antonio moved forward until he was about twenty feet from the target. At this range he could easily hit the bottles with a rock. Frank covered an ear with one hand and held the flashlight with the other. Antonio fired again and struck the crate, knocking the bottles over without breaking them.

"Hey, not bad," Frank said. "Get even closer."

After rearranging the target, Antonio stood just five paces away and fired two shots in quick succession, shattering a bottle with the second one. He took two more steps forward, until he was within easy spitting distance of the milk crate, and fired two more shots, knocking off a can.

"I guess that's the trick," Frank said. "Get as close as you can."

Antonio understood immediately. The secret of the gun was to think of it as a knife. Press it close to the soldier's torso and then fire. Think of it as stabbing, the bullet cutting fire into his flesh, tearing at muscle and capillaries. Antonio liked the directness of the act, the idea that he would have to be close enough to the man to feel him breathe.

What a beautiful thing this gun was. It fit neatly in the palm of his hand, a small chunk of metal and oiled mechanisms, and yet it equalized everything. When the orange-haired girl in the projects sold him the gun, she gave Antonio the power to take the tattooed soldier's life. The advantages of his military training and muscular physique would be erased by this palm-sized chunk of metal. Antonio felt tall again. He remembered that the soldier was a small man, a pipsqueak. Killing him would be child's play.

With a gun anyone could be a killer. Guns were very democratic instruments, Antonio decided. They did not discriminate. With guns the weak became strong, the frightened brave. Anyone who held one became invincible. A tattooed soldier, a teenage girl. Even a poor, timid bus boy who slept in a cave.

*   *   *

The television droned in the rear office of El Pulgarcito Express, a small black-and-white affair with a butterfly antenna. Duarte crouched over the set and adjusted the antenna's metallic arms to make the image on the screen stop jumping. He was trying to get Channel 52, a Spanish-language station with a notoriously weak and unpredictable signal.

"*Cabrones*," he said, twisting one of the knobs. "They're too cheap to get a stronger transmitter. Just a few thousand more, but they won't invest it. Typical Latinos. Skinflints."

Frustrated, he turned to the other Spanish station, Channel 34, but quickly changed it after encountering a commercial for "*Jabón Palmolive.*"

"News," he shouted at the screen. "*Queremos noticias.*" Finally he settled for one of the English-speaking stations.

Longoria stood next to Carlos Avilés, watching Duarte play with the TV. The boss had told them to come back here and see what was happening

"It's those police officers," Duarte said, "the ones that beat up that *negro*. The verdict is in." Seeing that Carlos looked perplexed, he added, "They put them on trial for beating up that big black guy, remember? On the videotape."

Longoria remembered the case well, although he had not been following the recent developments. Duarte finally got a clear signal and stood back, eyes fixed on the image of a room filled with Americanos in suits. They all seemed to be holding their breath.

At the announcement "Not guilty" Duarte punched his fist into the air, repeating the gesture as the television called out "Not guilty" again and again.

"*¡Eso!* This is really going to hurt the blacks," he gloated. "They're really eating shit now."

"Congratulations, *jefe*," said the office manager, ever the sycophant, patting Duarte on the back. "It's good news, no?"

"Of course it is, Carlos. Those blacks have been getting away with murder. *Maleantes*. This will teach them a lesson."

Duarte looked like a man who had won a great revenge, his expression at once happy and meanspirited. Longoria left him at the television with the office manager, returning to the front counter to help Yanira. She always slowed down when she was working alone; the lobby, which had been nearly empty just a few minutes ago, was now half filled. Tired people with boxes and envelopes stood impatiently between rope barriers, the line almost to the door.

Two hours later, at 6:00 p.m., Longoria went into the back room with a stack of packages and saw that Carlos and Duarte were gone. The room was dark, but the television was still on, flickering white and gray. In a hurry because the lobby was still full, he dropped the packages on the table and was about to return to the front when something on the screen made him stop. A shot from a camera high in the air showed a group of young men and women, teenagers and children, running in and out of a building, objects in hand, as if engaged in a relay race. For a moment it seemed like a contest of some kind, a sport he had never seen before. A cluster of people stood around the front of the building, waiting to loop in and out of the doors. The gringos were always inventing new sports, and he wondered what this one was called. He wondered if the rules were as complicated as American football, a game he could never understand.

"Longoria!" Yanira pleaded from the front counter, and he went to help her.

An hour later the lobby was empty, as were the streets outside. Standing at the plate-glass windows, Longoria pondered the strange stillness on the sidewalk. The shoppers and commuters who crowded around the bus benches on most evenings were nowhere to be seen.

"It's quiet all of a sudden," Longoria observed.

"Thank God," Yanira said. "I'm tired."

Vaguely troubled by the missing people, Longoria drifted around the office and soon found himself back in front of the television set. The station was switching from one image to the next, rapid fire, so fast that it was hard for Longoria to make sense of what he was seeing.

A large rectangle, four walls and a roof of flames, the picture so bright it seemed it might burn a hole in the screen. Cars with spiderweb windows speeding away from an intersection in twilight, adolescent arms hurling projectiles at the metal cocoons, all of this seen from an eye in the air. A circle dance of young men around a kneeling woman, forearms and biceps spitting rocks at her back. An ancient ritual, a public stoning. "SOUTH-CENTRAL," say the letters at the bottom of the screen. And then more flames, more burning rectangles, a whole row of them, a family of burning buildings. And now the eye returns to the ground, the eye is someplace completely different, seeking out the face of a black woman in a smart blue dress, microphone in hand. There she is, now she's gone. The camera pans. Where is she? the camera asks. The woman is lost in a jumble of faces and arms. People are stepping up to the eye. Why they are doing that? Why they are showing off their missing teeth and braces and silver caps to the camera? And there is the woman again, a reporter. Her mouth is open and moving, but Longoria can't hear what she's saying because there is no sound, just pictures. He is afraid to step close to the television to turn up the volume. The television is doing crazy things, and he might get an electric shock if he touches it. Young men and women in T-shirts mill around the reporter. They are Latino and white and black, all colors. "CIVIC CENTER," say the letters at the bottom of the screen. The camera loses the woman again, looks for her, finds a police car instead. Black and brown and white arms emerging from the T-shirts rock the police car like a seesaw. The car flips over very slowly. When it crashes upside down Longoria can almost feel how heavy it is. And now people are standing on its exposed belly. They punch at the air and open their mouths to scream. Tiny flames begin to creep from the smashed windows. Déjà vu. The police car is on fire and people are laughing, showing their teeth to the camera again. Happy teeth. Burn and smile.

Another shot. A line of white helmets and shields, black batons held at the chest. Police officers, the LAPD.

What was happening on the screen was a battle bigger than anything Longoria had ever seen. It was being fought all over the city, by huge crowds, masses of people. Memories rushed forward, taking hold of him by the chest. Fire and laughter. Violence welling in the eyes of the crowd, the march of police forming battle lines. He could feel it now, this resurfacing of animal instincts. So much like the taste of blood that passed through the Jaguars when they entered a village, when not even the doe-eyed children and the farm animals were safe from their machetes and machine guns. Longoria, agent of disorder, carrying a lighter and a little can of fluid with a smell he really liked. To see this here in Los Angeles, fire dancing from house to house, singeing everything in its path, was to remember the names of villages turned to ash: San Miguel, Nueva Concepción, Santa Ana.

He should have seen it coming. If he had been living like a true soldier, the new war wouldn't have caught him by surprise. When he was with the Jaguars in Guatemala, he read and studied the newspapers, understood the political currents. If his mind was still battle-sharp, he would have sensed the explosiveness of the city, the correlation of forces on the street.

Longoria realized that he was caught in the middle of a war without a weapon to protect himself.

Reginalda. For reasons he couldn't explain, her name began to resonate, drowning out the rest of his thoughts. Reginalda. Something might happen to Reginalda. He had to find her.

* * *

A black man in a watch cap jumped over the fence surrounding the graffiti-covered lot and headed toward the tunnel entrance, where Frank and Antonio were breaking up pieces of scrap plywood for the fire. The man looked like a monk in his long, hooded jacket, hands in his pockets.

"Hey, look who's back," Frank called out. "Our leader!"

"Never mind that shit," the Mayor said. He looked angry but rational, his recent madness gone. "You heard what happened with Rodney. The trial."

"What trial?"

"Rodney King, fool."

"Oh. What happened?"

"Motherfucking cops got off, that's what."

"What?"

"They got off. Every one of those white boys that beat my man Rodney. Scot-free. They're walking the streets now. With smiles on their faces. Not guilty. Every last one of them, not guilty."

Frank looked stunned. Antonio had heard about this case but had not followed it in his obsession with killing the tattooed soldier. He wished he knew more about it so that he could understand the rage and hurt that seemed to overtake his two black friends. They looked like people who had pinned great hopes on something and suddenly had those hopes shattered.

"What are we gonna do about this, Mayor?" Frank said finally.

"I don't know, but the shit's gonna hit somewhere, I know that. People are going to Parker Center right now. They're gonna have a little demo. I heard it on the radio."

"Right here in downtown? Shit, let's go."

In a flash Frank and the Mayor were climbing over the fence and running toward the Civic Center. Left behind to guard the camp, Antonio started the fire and sat alone next to the flames. The afternoon light turned deep orange, the shadows lengthening around the tunnel entrance. Soon it would be dark. Antonio held the unloaded gun in his hand and pulled the trigger, watching the cylinder turn and the hammer fall over and over again.

* * *

It was about ten blocks from El Pulgarcito Express to the apartment building on Normandie where Reginalda lived with two roommates. Longoria walked briskly, passing through neighborhoods where everyone except the homeless and the junkies was locked inside, huddled around a television set. Occasionally he caught a glimpse of the spreading conflagration through an open window, the screen flickering from one incendiary image to the next, a pyromaniac's slide show. When no cars passed by and quiet briefly settled in, he could hear the distant sound of sirens. Otherwise there was no sign that the battles gripping the rest of the city would spread here. There were no crowds on the street corners, nothing like what he had seen on the television. He was relieved, because the injury to his arm would make it hard for him to defend himself if he was attacked. In the sky a helicopter headed south, toward what people were already calling the *"quemazones,"* the great burning.

Longoria had been to Reginalda's apartment only twice before in the whole time he had known her. Almost always they talked by phone, meeting elsewhere and spending the night in his room. She would be surprised to find him on her doorstep. He wanted to see her, he wanted to wrap his good arm around her waist. Perhaps his impulse to protect her would inspire her to forgive him his mean silences, his crude remarks.

Reaching her building, he walked through an unlocked steel door into a small alcove, then out a glass door into a courtyard where an empty swimming pool was surrounded by two floors of apartments. Reginalda lived on the second floor.

Her door opened to the ubiquitous sound of the television set and the face of an unknown teenager with smart, penetrating eyes.

"I'm here to see Reginalda," Longoria said.

"*No se encuentra*," said the girl, whose voice was familiar; she sometimes answered the phone when he called here.

"Where is she?"

"Who wants to know?"

"My name is Longoria."

The girl's eyebrows rose in recognition: so this was the famous Longoria. She nodded and took a good look at him, leaving him with the vague sense that she had sized him up and the assessment was less than favorable. For a moment he felt like an evil character in a soap opera, making his entrance to jeers and whistles from the audience.

"Reginalda went out," she said curtly. "I don't know when she'll be back."

"Tell her Longoria came to see her," he said, turning to leave.

"Is that all?" she called out behind him. "Is that all you wanted to say?"

Longoria walked away.

* * *

One by one they began to filter back to the camp, long after nightfall. They were returning from four hours of running street battles with the police, a night of broken glass and baton charges. First Farley, the Texan, with blood dripping from a cut to his forearm, an injury suffered when he stepped through the smashed windows of a matrimonial supply store on Broadway. Then Darryl, who silently plopped down on his sleeping bag with a drunken smile. And finally, halfway to dawn, Frank and the Mayor, announcing their return to the tunnel with boisterous laughter.

"Hey, my little Spanish friend, we're back from the war," Frank said. "Back from the revolution."

"Victorious days," the Mayor said. "These are victorious days."

Both men were grinning, their faces more alive than Antonio had ever seen them.

"The battle of Parker Center," the Mayor said bombastically. "That's what they'll call it. The historic battle of Parker Center. When the people got theirs."

"Fucking cholo," Frank said with a laugh. "Remember that? He nailed that cop. A rock right in the fucking helmet. Wham! Fucking cop was all dizzy and shit." He imitated a man about to fall over like a slowly spinning top.

"I never thought I'd live to see the day when we'd attack the *L.A. Times*," the Mayor said. "We besieged the place, that's the word. Besieged. For me that was the highlight. Breaking those motherfucking windows."

"I hit that window on the third floor," Frank interjected. "Where the lights were on. Still got that old baseball arm."

"God, I feel good right now. So good!"

"But we didn't get anything. I saw people taking stuff."

"Man, this is more than *that*," the Mayor said, sounding slightly offended. "You know what I'm saying. This is more than just getting things, fool."

"I know that and you know that. But people are getting things anyway, stereos and shit. I just want my share."

"Stop with that."

"We coulda got something if we'd gone down to South-Central like I said. That's where the serious action is."

"Don't be crazy. That's the last place I'm gonna go on a night like this. Get my sorry self shot at, have the cops beat me. I don't need that shit. I'm too old. That's for the youngsters to do, the new generations."

They were still talking when Antonio set his head down on his pillow of old shirts and pulled a blanket over himself. He was happy for them, for the unexpected excitement, for their jubilant laughter, so different from their mood earlier, when the anger of the injustice still gripped them. He drifted off to sleep to the rise and fall of their voices, visions of running people and flying rocks slipping into his dreams.

* * *

By the time he made it back to his room, Longoria had forgotten about the *quemazones*. Reginalda hadn't been home when he went to see her, long after dark. Her absence was an anomaly, a shock, a slap in the face. In the middle of the evening. There might be a good explanation, but Longoria couldn't think of one. She didn't work at night, churches were not open at night, there was no decent place for an unaccompanied Salvadoran woman to go after dark. Not in this neighborhood. He began to imagine her out with another man, dancing with him at a club, going to his apartment. What else could she be doing? Only a few days since their last argument, and already she was going out at night on her own.

If she was not at work and if she was not with him, she should be at home. This woman had no loyalty.

Sometime after midnight, agitated and unable to sleep, Longoria got up and walked down to the pay phone in the lobby.

On the seventh ring, a sleepy, scratchy voice answered. It was the nosy roommate.

"Is Reginalda there?"

"What?"

"Reginalda."

"She's not here."

"She's not there?"

"No."

Before Longoria could demand to know where she was, the phone clicked dead.

He slammed down the receiver. Now he was certain that she was with someone else. This had turned out to be an evening of surprises, punches to the stomach. The city was burning, and Reginalda had betrayed him. Reginalda whom he met at Taco Bell, the only woman who'd ever kissed him with real passion, the only woman he'd ever danced with. Reginalda could make him dance. She wrapped her arms around him when they danced. He could feel her touch slipping away, passing to another man.

If he saw her, he would want to kill her. At the very least, slap her.

She better have a good explanation for not being home after midnight.

* * *

Antonio felt hands on his shoulders and opened his eyes wide to see a freshly shaved face, dried specks of blood on the cheeks. It was José Juan, smelling of soap and shoe polish, the scent tickling Antonio's nose.

"It's nine-thirty in the morning and everyone is asleep." José Juan sounded amused. "What's wrong? Did you have some kind of party last night?"

Antonio rubbed his eyes and tried to shake himself awake.

"*Vámonos, compadre*," José Juan said. "I want to show you the house. Our new house. Our new room."

"You mean in South-Central?"

"Yes, the one I told you about."

"But what about the riot, *moro*? I heard things are going on down there."

"No. I was watching the TV this morning at Cristina's house. That was last night. It's calm now. There was a lot of burning, but everything is fine again. Daylight calms people down. The fires stopped this morning. Anyway, that's why I want to go, to see if the house is okay. If Cristina's family is okay. They closed down the factory, so I have the day off. And I already have the money for the rent." He tapped at his front pocket. "I got paid early. We can move in today if you want. No more sleeping in the cave."

"Today?"

"I think so. Why not?"

"Maybe I should pack first."

"We can come back later."

"I just need one thing."

"The hotplate?" José Juan joked.

Antonio reached into his pillow of shirts and retrieved his gun and bullets from inside a dirty sock. José Juan watched him load the gun and frowned.

"*¿Para qué es eso?*"

"You know what it's for."

From the tunnel they walked uphill to Third Street, leaving the men in the camp fast asleep. As they went by the bulldozed lots, they

noticed a new cyclone fence and freshly painted warnings against trespassing. Soon, maybe in a week or so, people would begin to tear
down the fence and reinhabit the place.

At the corner of Third and Bixel they caught the bus, which was
three-quarters full. Antonio could see no sign of the street battles
Frank and the Mayor had described last night. Here on Third Street,
at least, there were no burned buildings or broken windows, just the
usual crowds of Latinos gathered at the bus benches, glaring at the
traffic with impatient eyes. Maybe Frank and the Mayor had been
exaggerating, making up stories. He wouldn't put it past them. José
Juan tugged at his sleeve to indicate that their stop was coming up.

"You want the Vermont Avenue bus?" the driver asked as they
were descending the rubber-coated steps. "South?"

José Juan nodded, holding up his transfer.

"I'm not sure it's running. Because of the riot last night. It might
only take you as far as Washington. That was the last I heard on the
radio."

Then the driver turned to make the announcement to the rest of
his passengers. "For anybody going to South-Central, I cannot guarantee that you will get there!"

Duly warned, Antonio and José Juan stepped off the bus and
crossed the street to the Vermont Avenue stop. There were two giant
parking lots at this intersection, asphalt fields serving the customers
of two supermarkets, a Vons and a Ralphs. Here again was a picture of
ten-in-the-morning weekday normality, shopping carts squeaking
across the tarmac, street vendors crowding the adjacent sidewalks.

When the Vermont bus arrived five minutes later, Antonio and
José Juan boarded and stood in the center aisle, gripping the steel
overhead bar. Jostled against the bodies of strangers, Antonio put his
arm over the gun in his pocket so that no one would feel it. *What a
stupid thing for me to do, carrying a loaded gun on a bus.* What if it
went off and wounded an unsuspecting rider or started a panicked
scramble for the doors? He was imagining various ballistic mishaps
when the bus screeched to a halt and a commotion spread at the front,
passengers expressing outrage in Spanish, Cantonese, English.

"This is bullshit!"

"*¿Cómo puede ser?*"

"I got my orders," the driver yelled back. "This is as far as I go. Washington is the last stop. I'll be goddamned if I'm gonna take this bus into a riot zone. Take it up with the RTD if you don't like it."

Antonio and José Juan stepped off the bus and stood on the sidewalk, trying to get their bearings. They were pedestrian castaways on the corner of Washington and Vermont, about thirty blocks from their point of departure and another thirty or so from their destination. Too much traffic at this intersection, a dozen cars in the blink of an eye. They decided to walk east to Hoover, to see if the buses were running there, but found only groups of stranded passengers cursing the signs that promised "Bus Stop."

"We might as well walk. From here it's an hour, maybe more," José Juan said. "Should we do it?"

"Why not? What else do we have to do?"

They headed south, toward the hazy silhouette of the University of Southern California, a brick tower jutting from the skyline not too far away. It was a sunny spring day, already pleasantly warm, the last traces of winter finally gone. Antonio didn't mind walking, especially with a good chance that he would be able to take a warm shower once they reached the new house.

They had been walking for twenty minutes when three fire trucks and two patrol cars zoomed past them, barreling south down Hoover toward the university. As the siren cry of the caravan faded, Antonio heard even more sirens in the distance. He stopped, fascinated by the sound. Unseen ambulances and fire trucks wailed into the city sky, calling out to their brethren, who answered back from all sides. A vast herd of emergency vehicles was assembling in the streets around them and migrating en masse to South-Central Los Angeles, where Antonio and José Juan hoped to live.

"Look," José Juan called out. "I see a fire. Two fires! Three!"

Past the brick buildings of the university, black columns of smoke billowed into the air.

"I think we better go back," Antonio said.

"Why?"

Antonio stared at his friend, incredulous. "There's a riot going on down there!"

They turned away from the pillars of smoke and walked north toward Washington Boulevard, at a brisker pace. Approaching the intersection, Antonio heard an alarm and saw a crowd of people descending upon two white buildings, a large structure and a smaller cube atttached to the side: an auto parts store and its garage.

"Something's going on here."

A few people were bolting from the white buildings now, running in funny waddles, deftly avoiding collisions with the people still trying to get in. A man in a hairnet came trotting down the middle of the street, oblivious to the cars around him, rolling a brand-new tire between the lanes of traffic. Other men followed, carrying car batteries, repair manuals, windshield wipers, cans of STP oil treatment, rearview mirrors, paper air filters.

"It's because of that *negro* who got beat up," Antonio said, thinking out loud. "Because the police beat him up."

"What *negro*? They're Latinos," José Juan said. "They don't know any *negro*. They don't care about any *negro*."

The waddling looters laughed and ran, eyes darting as they escaped the scene. They were scared and excited all at once, with a breathlessness in their expressions, a happy disbelief. *No one will catch us. No one will catch us because we are hundreds.* Antonio had never seen anything like it. It was the same impulse that made people push to get on the bus first or grab for the items on the sale table, a latent impulse set loose and multiplied, now a collective spirit. Another alarm sounded, and Antonio saw that a fire had started in the garage behind the main store. Employees in blue uniforms stumbled outside, soldiers of a vanquished army, some with torn shirts and scratch marks on their arms. Men and women, cashiers and clerks, they wept and comforted each other. *We tried to hold them off, but we couldn't. We've been attacked by the mob, but we survived.*

"Maybe we should take something," José Juan said. *"Aprovechar."*

"It's an auto parts store," Antonio said sarcastically. "We don't have a car."

"I guess you're right."

A crowd had formed around Antonio and José Juan, taking in the spectacle from across the street. The number of onlookers seemed roughly equal to the number of looters. A tall Mexicano in a chef's uniform, white cylinder on his head, folded his arms across his chest and spat at the ground in disgust. On this side of the street, he seemed to be saying, we still respect the law. We are not people who loot, we respect the laws of this country even if we are not citizens. Antonio focused on a Filipino man who was running away with a red toolbox in his hand and the ecstatic smile of a lottery winner on his face. He stopped for a moment to look up at the sky, as if he half expected the great claw of law enforcement to descend upon him. Next to Antonio on the sidewalk, a young Latina woman in red heels and a black dress began to weep.

"Why are they doing this?" she said, stamping at the ground. "Why?"

Antonio did not share her sense of outrage. The whole thing was too much like a street fair, with alarm bells and shattering glass and crashing metal substituting for carnival music. People were breaking windows, cars were driving up to the intersection and smashing into each other. The flow of traffic, so thick and fast just an hour ago, had slowed to a crawl. Apparently word of the festival at Pep Boys had spread, because cars were stopping on the sidewalks or in the middle of the street to discharge their passengers into the store.

"I have to go," José Juan said abruptly.

"What? Go where?"

"It's not far from here."

"Now? Where? You have to go now?"

"It's just three blocks."

José Juan turned away, but Antonio grabbed him by the arm. "Tell me where you're going." He was afraid his friend was about to place himself in some sort of danger.

"I'm going to get my money from *el Armenio*. Or get even, at least. He owes me five hundred and sixty dollars."

"You're crazy."

"Or maybe I'll just set the office on fire. That seems to be popular today." José Juan gave a wicked smile and touched his pockets. "Do you have any matches?"

"No!"

José Juan jerked his arm away and disappeared into the crowd of pedestrians who had taken over the northbound roadway on Hoover Street.

What does he think he's doing? Getting even. Someone had declared this the municipal day of settling accounts, a day for all vendettas, private and public.

Now young men with rocks were roaming the streets. Where did the rocks come from? How did they get rocks in the middle of the city? Antonio looked closer and saw they were just chunks of concrete and brick, pieces of crumbling walls. There were plenty of crumbling walls in this neighborhood and thus no shortage of ammunition.

Antonio wandered around the intersection and watched as several smaller stores on the block began to surrender their merchandise. Hoover Hock and Pawn returned its goods to anyone with a rock or crowbar. The Washmont Mini-Grocery donated its inventory to the crowd. Women in tattered dresses pushed shopping carts filled with disposable diapers: diapers now, but maybe dresses later. Antonio was almost knocked down by a man with a huge samurai sword, pawn tag still attached. The samurai man fell to the sidewalk but quickly rose to his feet, sprinting away, cutting at the air with his sword to open a path through the crowd.

Housekeepers, garment workers, bus boys. Mexican, Honduran, Costa Rican, Nicaraguan. And of course his countrymen, the Guatemaltecos. It was a day without submissiveness, a day without coffee to pour or strangers' babies to feed or the whir of sewing machines in a factory. It was a day to liberate toolboxes and diapers from their glass cages. A day when all the pretty objects in the store windows would mock them no longer.

Antonio saw a boy of eleven running from a grocery store with a bag.

"Hey," he called. "What did you get?"

The boy stopped, his face brightening with a catlike grin. He opened the bag for Antonio to see: lollipops and chocolate bars, jelly beans in clear packages. Red-hots. It reminded Antonio of that American holiday, the one where the kids dressed up in costumes and went from house to house. What was it called? He could not remember.

The boy disappeared into the smoky air on Washington Boulevard. There were many fires burning on this street now. The sunlight retreated, erasing the shadows of running people from the sidewalks. Flames from a burning warehouse ignited a palm tree and leapt up the trunk to the crown. Antonio wandered back to the auto parts store in time to see two more cars filled with looters collide in a metallic crunch.

A shoving match ensued. Two men began to wrestle, punches were thrown, a baseball bat was produced. And then, inevitably, a gun. A shot rang out and one of the combatants doubled over in pain as the people on the street scattered, instinctively ducking for cover. The shooter, a bulky middle-aged man, stood over his victim, a gaunt teenager, and then he got back in his car and drove away, a dangling rear fender scraping the asphalt. The teenager gripped his side and bled into the street.

"Where's the police?" a woman yelled.

Antonio touched his hand to the chunk of metal in his pocket.

There were no police. There was no authority or order of any kind. It was the municipal day of vendettas, and the police were staying home. There was nothing to stop José Juan from breaking into the office of his tightwad employer and setting the place on fire. He'd probably found some matches by now. There was nothing to stop a man from settling a dispute with a gunshot to the belly.

Antonio began to walk north along Hoover Street, toward Pico Boulevard and branch number two of El Pulgarcito Express.

Below 19 Crown Hill

The insistent ringing of an alarm bell half a block away from El Pulgarcito Express announced the arrival of the mob. Sticking his head out the door, Longoria could see the twisted steel gate of the Payless shoe store, black bars bent so the looters could squirm in underneath. First they broke the windows with a pipe, then they used the pipe to jimmy the bars. Two men of about twenty-five, both looking vaguely Salvadoran, coordinated the action, displaying the desperate ingenuity that was characteristic of Centroamericanos everywhere. Two, three, four men followed. Collective action, another Central American trait. Longoria wanted to run over and bend the bars shut again, sealing the store and trapping the looters inside, but he realized this would be a foolhardy act. Trying to stop the looters now would be like running across the thick stream of traffic on the freeway: you were sure to be hit.

The fatal mistake of the Payless crew, Longoria decided, had been to close their doors in the first place, to pin their faith on locks and metal barriers. Running away and leaving the store unattended invited the crowd to attack. If every store owner on this block had held his ground, like the Cuban proprietor of the *discoteca* on the next block who stood on the roof with a shotgun, his mouth twisted in a canine snarl, they could have turned the mob back. But all it took was one weak link to break the chain.

For much of the morning Longoria had been monitoring the television, following the geographic progression of the riot, now in its second day. It spread northward from its cradle on faraway Florence Avenue, past the university, finally spilling over the bridges and through the underpasses of the Santa Monica Freeway. What surprised Longoria most was how quickly it had happened. Was some guerrilla cell masterminding the operation deep within the fabric of the city? Perhaps not. The real problem was the complete surrender of the Los Angeles Police Department, which lacked the resolve to take charge of a messy situation. They were unwilling even to fire their weapons, to do anything that might spill blood. Two good battalions of Jaguars, he calculated, could easily retake the city.

But no. He wasn't with his unit anymore. He was on his own, for all intents and purposes, inside El Pulgarcito Express. Yanira paced back and forth across the lobby, which had been deserted since ten, begging to be allowed to leave. Duarte and Carlos Avilés had left two hours ago for branch number three, six blocks south of the freeway on Normandie, hoping to defend what seemed at the time the most vulnerable outpost in El Pulgarcito's eight-branch empire. Longoria tried to call them, but all the lines were busy or dead. Duarte had taken the only gun in the office. The police were nowhere, unreachable by phone, radio, or scream.

As he looked out the plate-glass windows, which he noted were especially vulnerable, Longoria tried his best to summon his army stare, to fend off the looters with his rapacious eyes, the exotic scar of his jaguar tattoo. The stare and the tattoo had served him well in Los Angeles. They had helped Longoria establish himself as a man who couldn't be fucked with, as the gringos would say. But today, when he desperately needed their power, they were failing him. Something was wrong, and it wasn't just the fact that his arm still ached and throbbed from the attack in the park.

The old woman and the man with the pipe were to blame. Reginalda was to blame for leaving him when he needed her most. She had planted all this doubt in him. She had made him cry.

Across the street a lanky young man sat on the curb and stared at Longoria through El Pulgarcito's windows. He was in his teens or early twenties, Longoria's age when he was first promoted to sergeant. Skinny brown arms dangled at his sides, reaching now and then for two chunks of concrete at his feet in the gutter, next to the storm drain. He wore white shorts with blue stripes, and his knees knocked together nervously. He looked at once eager and apprehensive, like a girl waiting to be invited onto the dance floor.

When the first wave of looters arrived, the young man grabbed one of the chunks and stood up. When more and more people began to stream onto the street, when the baying of the alarm at the Payless had been joined by a hoot-hoot from the appliance store next door, the young man looked up and down the block. Longoria gave him a long stare, his meanest, but the young man just smiled at him. Taking a running start, he hurled the heavy chunk of concrete toward El Pulgarcito with athletic skill, throwing it sidearm, like a discus. Longoria barely had time to duck behind the counter next to Yanira before his ears filled with the sound of glass crashing around him. Yanira screamed. Another rock came sailing through what was left of the windows.

"Go out the back!" Longoria ordered. He was frantically looking for something to throw back when he saw the young man climbing into the lobby, his shoes crunching on the carpet of broken glass. Three other invaders of similar ages and builds followed, and for an instant it seemed that the young man had magically transformed himself into a platoon of looters.

Outnumbered, Longoria abandoned any notion of putting up a fight. Moments later he followed Yanira out the back door, surrendering El Pulgarcito Express, branch number two, to the mob.

* * *

Antonio saw the shattered windows and knew instantly he would not find the tattooed soldier here. The soldier was no longer at El Pulgarcito Express, because its windows and walls had been violated and he was not a man to tolerate such a thing. The soldier shot first and asked questions later. Antonio knew the man now. If a crowd was ransacking the place, then it followed that the tattooed soldier must be elsewhere.

He had walked fifteen blocks through Los Angeles ablaze, oblivious to the disorder around him because he was imagining what it would be like to confront the soldier again, this time with a gun. It seemed that there was nothing to stop him. Only once during his hour-long march to El Pulgarcito Express did he see the police, four officers in white helmets, three men and a woman, trying to keep a crowd from looting a bank on Venice Boulevard. Antonio stopped: he would be in serious trouble if the police searched him and found the gun in his pocket. He stood in the middle of the street as the officers chased a group of people from the bank's shattered front doors, inflicting truncheon blows on those they could catch up with. Seconds later many of these same people were across the street, invading a furniture store. The officers hesitated, then ran in a V formation toward the looters, only to watch them circle back to an electronics store. It seemed this bizarre dance might continue all afternoon. Realizing that the officers were fully occupied, Antonio had walked quickly past.

Two blocks from El Pulgarcito, his heart began to pound wildly. He stopped to compose himself, knowing that he would have to be clearheaded to do this act. *The gun is like a knife. Get close and stay calm.*

And then he had reached the office and felt the adrenaline draining from his veins. The soldier was gone. There were only men and women and children carrying off typewriters and chairs and adding machines. A skinny young man in shorts with blue stripes was transforming the surviving panes of glass into crystal debris. The crowd had inflicted some revenge on the tattooed soldier's place of work, but the man himself had escaped.

Antonio joined a group of people gathered on the street as if for a block party or *quinceañera*. A thin grandmotherly woman watched a man step out of the office with another typewriter. She looked tough, like she might want to take something herself, and laughed as she shook her bony fist at the building.

"*¡Qué bueno!* Take everything. Take it all. *Gusanos sinvergüenzas.* They deserve it. Burn the place down."

"They won't cheat us anymore," said the man next to her, an old Mexicano with a puffy gray pompadour. "They can't cheat us now."

"The packages never got there," the grandmother said. "Or when they did half of what we sent was missing."

A dark young man emerged with several posters in hand, portraits of El Salvador's right-wing presidential candidate, slogans declaring "ORDER, PEACE, WORK." He'd ripped them off the walls, and now he made a show of tearing them in half, throwing the pieces to the ground, and stepping on them in a little jig. Another man joined him. The grandmother clapped.

"¡*Así!*" she shouted. "Get him, *muchachos!* Stomp him!"

Antonio moved on, searching his memory of the soldier's habits for clues as to where he might be. Above all it was important to act quickly. The chaos on the streets might soon evaporate, like the spring storm fronts that swept over the city and left a few drops of rain before dissolving into blue skies and sunshine. And then the tattooed soldier might live forever.

*　*　*

Longoria stood at the entrance to Reginalda's apartment building, unable to get inside because a man and his wife were trying to force their looted sofa through the narrow steel door. He had come here because he couldn't think of anyplace else to go, anyone else he wanted to see besides Reginalda. Perhaps she would have an explanation for her absence the night before. He wanted her to have an explanation.

All along this residential block people were shuffling back to their homes with shoe boxes, cassette players, and microwave ovens tucked under their arms. Everything was in its original packaging, nothing secondhand today. Two women drove up, left a stack of dresses and blouses on the porch of a neighboring building, got back in their car, and sped off.

The couple in front of him were especially ambitious looters. To run off with an entire sofa took a lot of nerve. The plastic cover and factory label were still attached. Just an hour ago he would have been outraged, but by now the couple's behavior seemed almost normal. Longoria could see part of the woman's dress riding up as she struggled with the far end of the sofa; she must be strong to hold it for up so long. It was a pretty sofa, yellow with a floral print, but probably much too big for their apartment.

Finally they made it inside and Longoria followed, taking the stairs two at a time. The door to Reginalda's apartment was open. He stepped in and froze. The living room floor was littered with boxes, a toaster and a curling iron peeking from plastic nests, two pairs of leather pumps spilling forth, clothes piled on the couch, the room thick with the cellophane aroma of new merchandise.

Reginalda was one of the looters. Longoria flushed, the disgust he felt for this day and this city gathering sourly on his tongue. Reginalda had betrayed him, she had joined the other side, she was with the enemy. He walked through the living room, down the hallway to her bedroom, and found her sitting on her bed talking into the telephone, her back to the doorway. The slender shoulders, the curly black hair Longoria had run his fingers through, everything about her so familiar. He was hovering over her, but she had not felt his presence and was laughing into the receiver. The sound enraged him even more, as if she were laughing at him, laughing with all the looters who mocked order and mocked Longoria.

He grabbed the telephone, and she turned and screamed. He threw the phone to the floor, closed his left fist, and punched her square in the mouth. *You spent the night somewhere else, and now I find you stealing.* Falling back on the bed, Reginalda raised her arms to shield herself, like a boxer pinned against the ropes. Then she held a hand to her mouth and laughed when she found no blood.

"Is that the best you can do? Is it? Get out of here, *maricón!*"

"Thief!" he yelled. "You were stealing."

"What are you talking about? I didn't take anything. Those aren't . . ."

Longoria left without listening, venting his fury on the merchandise in the living room. He shattered a window with the brandnew toaster and threw the pumps at the wall, knocking down a framed poster of Luis Miguel. As he ran down the steps, he nearly collided with a girl hugging four pairs of jeans to her chest, a girl he vaguely recognized. Reginalda's roommate.

He stepped into the sunny madness of the streets. All around him people were running, but he walked at a deliberate pace, feeling the anger drain away. He shouldn't have hit Reginalda, even with his left arm. Would she ever speak to him again? Of course she wouldn't speak to him again.

He walked for almost thirty minutes, headed in no particular direction. His last contact with the world of women, and of people in general, had been broken. He had cut himself adrift in a city of flames. There was nothing to do but go back to the Westlake Arms, to his room with its scrubbed floors and the waste basket he emptied every day, a sanctuary of cleanliness. There were no fires, no crowds in his room.

He looked at a street sign to get his bearings: it was two miles to his apartment. On Vermont Avenue he saw black smoke spewing from the windows of a Thrifty drugstore. Firefighters perched on tall ladders poured braids of white water into the roof. They were trying to save the supermarket next door but did not seem to notice or care that a hundred looters had rushed in through the unguarded entrance, women mostly, Latino and white and black, running up and down the aisles, filling their arms with milk cartons and luncheon meats and cans of tomato sauce even as smoke and water cascaded through the ceiling.

The place was about to collapse on these people. They were going to kill themselves. And for what? For steak and chicken, oranges and fabric softener? He watched them through tall glass panes that had miraculously survived the assault, reaching for jars and cardboard packages, violating the neatly stacked shelves, knocking things over as they raced for the front doors. Hamburger Helper, cornflakes. On any other day Longoria would have yelled at them. *You call yourselves mothers? What would your children say?* On any other day he would have told them to obey the law, to respect the order of the shelves and aisles. *Wait your turn and pay!*

Covering his face against the heat and the pungent smell of ash, Longoria followed the double yellow lines that ran down the center of Vermont, usually a pedestrian no-man's-land. A fire truck zoomed down a cross street, bumping over the uneven pavement, a police car in its screaming wake.

And then, at a distance, emerging on the smoky horizon as if from a dream, he saw what was instantly recognizable to him as an armored vehicle of the United States Army, a desert brown Humvee. At last! Longoria began to laugh. The U.S. Army had come to save him, one of their own, a soldier trapped behind enemy lines. With the police in retreat it would be left to the army to restore order. The army would not fail.

A minute or so later the Humvee rolled past him, a caravan of green trucks behind it, just like those armored boxes he had seen so many years ago at Fort Bragg in those parking lots of steel and rubber. Longoria raised his arm to wave but stopped when he heard jeers from the people on the sidewalk. He looked into the back of the first truck and saw two rows of seated soldiers tucked under oversized helmets, like big green mushrooms, staring out at the burning city and the crowds with teenage eyes of fear.

Longoria looked at their faces and saw himself in the moments after his forays in the villages, smoke and flame and chaos all around him. Soldiers rolling into battle, men setting fires. Longoria playing with his cigarette lighter, the Jaguars marching through the dance of ash in the hot wind. It seemed that the demons of his memory had taken flight and were loose on the streets of L.A. A trick of the mind, a hallucination. Everything spilling from his head onto the streets. Burning walls sagged and fell to the ground with a creak and a sigh. The Olympic Mini-Mall took a final bow. Tattooed cholos kicked at the glowing embers and ran from the orange rush of flames.

Longoria had expected Los Angeles to be like that beautiful military base at Fort Bragg, a city of tidy houses and well-behaved people. He had carried his cigarette lighter into the mountain villages so that Guatemala could start all over again, from scratch. The new Guatemala would be a place like Fort Bragg, like the United States. Instead the infection had followed him to Los Angeles. Even when you killed the children, the infection still spread. What would Lieutenant Colonel Villagrán and Lieutenant Sanchez of the Green Berets say if they saw this? Children were all around him now, their bodies painted like his, a guerrilla army of tattooed cholos assaulting the pawnshops and malls. How many more children would have to die before the infection went away? A sense of futility overwhelmed him, and then an inchoate feeling that he had been tricked in some way he didn't understand.

He was too tired to think anymore. *Just make it home.* The Westlake Arms was about a mile away. He would go to his room and sleep.

* * *

Antonio had been at the Westlake Arms for an hour, moving from hiding place to hiding place. He started off in the alley behind the building, then slipped into the lobby and sat in the stairwell on the second flight of steps. This seemed the ideal place to catch the soldier by surprise, until some tenants on their way upstairs glared at him as if they were trying to memorize his features for a future police lineup. He decided to wait outside.

The gun was in his pocket, loaded and ready to go.

Flakes of ash floated in the air like snow. Antonio had never seen snow, but he imagined it resembled ash, that it wobbled slowly to the ground, riding invisible currents. The burning smell was overpowering, a carbon taste on his tongue. In the weeks since the eviction, after all those scrap-wood campfires, smoke had seeped into Antonio's clothes, his hair, his skin. Today the smell was everywhere, carried aloft by hundreds of fires, a city of mini-malls and palm trees ablaze.

Hiding in the shadows behind the front steps, Antonio peered over the concrete staircase. He expected the tattooed soldier to come from the south. Everyone seemed to be running from south to north today. Waves of people drifted over the sidewalks and the street, so he didn't have to worry about looking too conspicuous. In a blue windbreaker and dirty jeans, hands in his pockets, feet shuffling nervously on the concrete, he looked a lot like a man waiting to meet a drug dealer, which on this block meant he blended in just fine.

Not that anyone would be paying much attention to him anyway. Everyone was caught up in the looting, too busy liberating merchandise or defending homes and businesses. A certain segment of the population was behind locked doors, waiting it out. Antonio could see them in the six-story grid of windows on the building across the street, worried eyes peeping from drawn curtains, immigrant mothers and fathers calculating the relative dangers and wondering at what point they would have to grab the children and make a run for it.

When the tattooed soldier finally showed up and Antonio shot him, he would draw the attention of these people, dozens of witnesses who would register his face and height and weight as they watched him run from the scene. They would see the body of the tattooed soldier bleeding into the black tar of the street. It would be something like a public execution.

Antonio began to draw energy from the thought, just as he had when he attacked the soldier with the pipe in MacArthur Park. The difference now was that he had a gun. With a gun it would be quick and clean.

There was a shot in the distance, the unmistakable pop and echo. Another pop, and then two more in quick succession. Somewhere a man was pointing and firing, his anger palpable in the sound of the bullet cutting through air.

My madness is everyone's madness. The day of vendettas and bravado. A Zacapaneco took it seriously when you doubted his manhood. When he was a boy, Antonio's father told him stories about men who settled their differences with *machetazos*. Antonio didn't have a machete, but he had a gun.

The tattooed soldier turned the corner.

Ashen face, rodent features, shaved head, right arm hanging limply at his side. The man looked defeated already, he had no fight left in him. Antonio could sense this from behind the concrete steps. Something in the universe had shifted and rearranged everything in Antonio's favor. For a moment he felt like the neighborhood bully: this was like the time he picked on the weakest kid in his school and gave him a bloody nose in a fight over a bicycle. Not a fair fight. But the thought quickly passed as the soldier walked toward him. A man who is almost home, a tired man, imagining the feel of his bed, the creaking of the mattress as he lies down, a man who wants to rest. Walking home like any normal citizen. Antonio's fingers felt numb, and he squeezed them into a fist to bring the muscles to life.

He glanced at the building across the street and saw a woman draw back a curtain. *Seven years of Los Angeles and now this moment.* A skinny girl sold him the gun. Antonio closed his hand tighter around the grip, placed his finger on the trigger. The soldier had his eyes fixed on the sidewalk, and there was no one on the block but him. The street was empty, another miracle. Everything just right.

Antonio stepped out of the shadows with a light and silent stride. Four feet from the soldier he drew the gun and called out, "Hey, you!"

The soldier looked up, and at that instant Antonio fired. The bullet like a knife. Brass candy.

For Elena and Carlos and the blood on the tiled floor.

The soldier grunted and stumbled backward, clutching his stomach as he fell to the sidewalk.

Antonio heard the rattle of a window opening in the Westlake Arms. He turned and saw a white wino with grimy skin and a stubbly beard standing twenty paces away, looking him straight in the eye. Where had he come from? The wino turned and began to run, dropping his paper bag, the bottle inside popping when it hit the sidewalk.

"He shot my wife and son!" Antonio shouted at the wino's heels. He turned back to his prone victim and straddled him, pointing the gun at his head.

"*¿Quién?*" the soldier moaned. "Who are you?"

I am the avenger of a martyred wife and son.

The soldier was in pain, frightened and surprised, wheezing as he breathed through his mouth. He touched his wound, a red stain that was just beginning to show on his light blue sweatshirt. Antonio raised his eyes to the windows, where a dozen or so people were staring at him. On the third floor a woman held a hand over her mouth.

"*Mató a mi hijo y mi esposa!*" Antonio shouted up at the building, but the words seemed unreal and hollow as soon as he said them. What were words next to the image of a man standing over his bleeding victim? No one would believe him. *They can't see what the soldier is.*

Now the soldier was pushing himself up off the sidewalk with his one good arm. It seemed he was barely hurt. Antonio lowered the gun on the struggling body and aimed at the shaved skull. *This one is for the pictures in the envelope.*

Antonio squeezed the trigger, and the soldier slumped back to the ground. A fresh bloodstain appeared on the upper chest, just below the curve where the shoulder meets the neck.

The city is burning all around us. The sirens are singing goodbye to the soldier.

"Hey, you! Get away from him!"

A big Latino man in a sleeveless T-shirt was standing at the top of the front steps, a gun in his hand, dark tattoos smudged on his forearm and neck. His gun was bigger than Antonio's.

"Leave him the fuck alone or I'll shoot your ass."

He doesn't understand what I'm doing here. He thinks I'm just some psychopath, vomit spit up by the riot.

The Good Samaritan on the steps was raising his gun now and halfheartedly pointing it at Antonio. The bloodstain had spread across the blue field of the tattooed soldier's sweatshirt, a ruby dampness on his stomach and chest.

He is dying now. The wound in the stomach will kill him. My work is done.

Sneering at the man on the steps, Antonio turned on his heels and walked away.

* * *

His first thought: *I am bleeding.* And then: *I don't deserve this.* In years of battle he had never been wounded. First touching his stomach and seeing the blood on his fingers, and then the lingering gut pain. A chance to look at the man's gun as he yelled at the windows. It was a small gun, a .22, the smallest there was. *For this I am lucky.* Then the shot to the shoulder, just missing the neck and the jugular. *Twice lucky.* The soul of a Jaguar felt no pain. The animal stare of the jaguar.

I can still move my legs, so there is no damage to the spine.

The man from the park had come to attack him again: persistent, this man was, like a horror film monster, showing up at the most obvious yet least expected place, right here on his front steps.

The sound of the footsteps. Turning on his side, Longoria

watched the killer calmly walking toward Wilshire. Who was he? Who were the wife and son?

He couldn't let this man get away. He would be persecuted by men with pipes and guns and old women with sharp teeth until he caught up with the shooter and found out who he was. Longoria rose to his feet slowly.

"Lie down," his rescuer said protectively, descending the steps. Longoria had lived in this building for years, but he did not recognize the man in the T-shirt. "You're wounded. Don't get up."

"Get away from me."

"Call 911," the man shouted at the upper floors.

"We're trying, but there's no answer," a woman said from the sky.

Longoria felt as if the street were the floor of a helicopter or the deck of a ship at sea. Still, he took one step and then another, and soon he was walking uphill to Wilshire.

"Crazy-ass motherfucker," the man said behind him. "Lie down. You'll bleed to death."

Now Longoria remembered seeing the Good Samaritan in a blue security guard's uniform. *He thinks he's a policeman, and that's why he came to help me. Birds of a feather. Does he know I'm a soldier?*

He was amazed to find himself bleeding and walking. The fingers over the wound in his stomach were glistening with blood. *My blood.* And yet he was walking. He could see the shooter's blue windbreaker two blocks away, headed toward Third Street. *He will not expect me to be following him. He will not expect such strength and resolve, such resilience.* To rise, as if from the dead, and catch up with the man who has left you to die on the sidewalk.

This is nothing. I am strong because I have been working since I was five years old. His earliest childhood memory, stooped over the soil, his mother at his side, showing him how to drop seeds into little holes in the ground, making a game of it. Later, taking the hoe, too big for his soft child's hands, and hacking at the hard earth until his arms and back were so tired he wanted to cry. People had no idea what he had been through, and they were always underestimating him. They did not know who Longoria really was.

Before his arm was injured, he had bench-pressed two hundred pounds.

He stumbled on a square of concrete jutting from the sidewalk and fell to the ground. Lying there with his head resting on the sandpaper surface, he touched the wetness on his belly, a wound in his side, right over the kidneys. *I should be fainting just about now.* He hadn't fainted because he had been shot with a .22, a pinprick as far as the Jaguars were concerned. His vision was becoming hazy. If he lost any more blood, maybe he would soon be light enough to fly, maybe the wind would pick him up and carry him like a feather on the soot-laden breeze.

I have to get up. Back on his feet, he looked around and saw the shooter turning onto Third Street. He was getting away. If Longoria could find this man, he could plot his revenge, exterminate the danger, live free of fear.

Crossing Union Avenue, two blocks from his apartment, another vision, dreamlike. Columns of soldiers standing in rows in front of the Vons supermarket, where he had come once with Reginalda to buy something feminine. Soldiers standing in rows, waiting for orders, waiting to fall out. What are soldiers doing in a supermarket parking lot? He must be imagining them. But no, they are as real as the dimming sunshine of late afternoon and the crowds of people gathered on the street as if it were a holiday and not just another Thursday in April. He can still remember today is Thursday, so his mind must still be sharp. It occurs to Longoria that if he simply wanders into the little army camp here in the parking lot, the soldiers will take care of him. The United States Army has the best military hospitals in the world. They will dress his wounds and fill him with plasma, and he will be just like new.

But the pull of the shooter is stronger than anything, and so Longoria follows along, ignoring the sanctuary of the troops bivouacked at Vons. Soon he finds himself stumbling into a barren area of the city, a place with fewer and fewer buildings, fenced-off fields of green. Longoria has the strange feeling that the missing buildings have floated up into the air like balloons, in the same way his head is floating now, bobbing somewhere above his body and leading him deep into this empty land. He cannot feel his feet touching the ground. The soles have no sensation left. Now, mercifully, he is walking downhill, and isn't this easier, to allow gravity to do the hard work. Longoria is coasting down the steep incline when his legs collapse underneath him. He cries out and he falls to the pavement, rolling down the hill and landing with a plop in the gutter.

The shooter turns around. Their eyes meet for an instant, just as Longoria's close and he slips into the quietest, sweetest darkness.

He dreams that he is being carried aloft by a breeze so strong it seems to have grown arms. He is floating, but still heavy somehow, like a zeppelin.

Opening his eyes, he finds himself slung over a man's shoulder. Good, Longoria thinks. I am saved again, rescued from my folly, from so much walking and bleeding. He is being carried down a hill and then over a fence that has been stepped on, flattened. So many walls and fences have fallen today. He would like to thank this man, but suddenly it has become nearly impossible to form any sound but a groan. Blood is trickling from his mouth. If he could speak, he would say that this is not the best way to be carried, because his stomach is pressed against the man's shoulder and each step brings the sharpest pain, the pain of metal in your gut.

And then it's as if the man has heard his thoughts, because he is lowering Longoria to the ground, taking him by the arms, dragging him along a cement floor. Longoria can see the sky again. He can see the face of the man who is dragging him, a brown face with round glasses.

Longoria feels warm wetness spreading over his legs. He has peed himself, his bowels have exploded in a sickening mess. Blood is dripping from his mouth, from the wound in his gut, from the wound in his shoulder. Liquid is seeping from him at every opening, he is being drained.

He can see the face of his killer against the sky. Perspiration drips down the killer's cheeks, his eyes dart back and forth, he is short of breath. They are at the foot of a green mountain, wild plants and shrubs all around them, forlorn palm trees and tall milkweed. Are they still in the city? Surely Longoria is hallucinating now. The sky disappears, replaced by a gray arch, and the concrete floor beneath him yields to mud.

It is getting darker, as if someone were shutting a coffin. Longoria is very scared. He opens his mouth to scream but can only make the weakest of sounds, a faint groan. *Don't do this. Don't take me here. I am afraid.* It is getting darker and darker, and Longoria can't tell if it's because he is getting weaker or because he's being taken from the sunlight. The roof is closing over him. The only escape is to pull his arms from the killer's grasp, but there is no muscle, no will left in them. Longoria slides deeper and deeper into the tunnel. The last light fades, the killer's features dissolve into black and disappear.

He is in total darkness.

Now there are only sounds. The labored breathing of the killer, the plop-plop of his footsteps. Without warning, Longoria's arms fall to the mud. Every sound is amplified now. He hears a rush of wind through the man's mouth, a grunt of exertion, then an object whistling through the air and landing in a pool of water.

"Guillermo," the man says.

Longoria is startled by the sound of his given name, a relic from his childhood, lost long ago.

"That's your name, isn't it?"

How does the killer know?

"Do you remember Elena and Carlos? San Cristóbal?"

Longoria tries to speak, but the sounds that come from his throat make no sense. If he could speak he would say no, he doesn't remember. There were so many villages, so many people. They have slipped into the farthest reaches of his memory, years and months blurred into a single image: fire and ash. He cannot remember.

Footsteps on the muddy floor, fainter and fainter.

Ask me something else, talk to me. Don't leave me here.

Longoria tries to get up, but he is anchored to the ground. He is being swallowed by the muddy floor. The last liquid is seeping from his body, into the earth. He would like to cry, but he cannot. He can no longer feel his feet or his hands.

There is a burst of light. Glowing golden in the darkness of the tunnel is a cornfield. Stalks rise from the black mud and push against the cement walls, fleshy leaves shining, tiny husks bursting like green embryos. A dark woman stooped between the rows of plants. She cuts into the earth with a hoe, grunting in a quiet and familiar way, then turns to look at him. Stretching out her hand, she gestures for him to rise. Stand up, quickly, there is work to be done.

Guillermo forgot to bring back the soap because he went to the theater instead, but his mother is not angry at him. She wants him to stand and work, because the plants need human hands to help them grow.

With invisible strings she pulls him up, and now he is walking toward her through rows of corn. Leaves brush his face, cool and moist. Rainbow-colored trousers hang loosely from his waist, fabric she wove at the loom. On his feet are sandals, strips of old leather held together with wire and twine. He smiles at his dirty toes, mud caked in the nails. So strange and happy, after all these years, to be wearing his peasant clothes again.

And now words from his mother in a language he has nearly forgotten.

"*Balam*," she says.

* * *

Antonio stepped into the sunlight and saw a note held down by a rock on one of the old chairs by the campfire. José Juan had come looking for him; they must have missed each other by minutes. "Meet me at the new place," the note said. There were directions to an address on Fifty-third Street in South-Central. "The buses might not be running yet," José Juan had written. "Walk if you have to. It's not that far."

He slowly took in the surroundings and rubbed his shoulder, which was sore from the effort of dragging the soldier into the tunnel. The body was about three hundred yards inside, past the first curve. For a few frightening moments he had become disoriented, circling in the darkness, panicked by the sensation that he would be trapped in the tunnel forever, punished by God for taking a man's life.

Everyone in the camp was gone, as they always were during the day. There were no witnesses to the final act, no one who could step forward and enter the tunnel to save the soldier's life.

Antonio felt a sticky dampness. He looked down and saw that a blackish stain covered almost half of his brown sweater, the wool already turning stiff. *The soldier has soaked into my clothes. This wetness is him, his lifeblood.* He quickly took the sweater off, and the shirt underneath, gagging as he choked back the juices rising from his stomach. *Look at me, I am the clumsiest, sloppiest killer.*

He took the tainted clothes and buried them in the mud of the tunnel floor, checking one last time to see if the soldier's blood had passed through the fabric to touch his skin. Diseases were transmitted through blood. Antonio inspected his shoulder but found nothing, though he thought he felt a drop under his chin, a spot he couldn't see without a mirror. He picked up some mud from the tunnel floor and wiped it on his neck, just to be sure.

Now he saw things that had escaped his attention when he dragged the soldier through the camp to the tunnel entrance: a brand-new clock radio next to the sooty coffee pot that had endured so many fires, a bleach white sweatshirt announcing "Sunset Strip" next to piles of dingy hand-me-downs.

His plan was to wait here until morning to make sure the soldier was dead. There was only one way out of the tunnel, through the arch under which Antonio was sitting. The Mayor said the other end of the tunnel was closed off when someone built an underground parking garage. If the soldier came back to life, he wouldn't be able to escape without going past Antonio.

Resurrection did not seem beyond the tattooed soldier.

With an injured arm and two of Antonio's brass candies in him, he had still managed to chase Antonio for almost a mile. What a shock, to turn around and see the man stumbling to the ground twenty minutes after shooting him. After making sure that no one was watching and that the soldier was quite helpless, Antonio had picked up the bleeding man and hidden him in the muddy crypt of the tunnel so that he would finally die.

Exhaustion had whittled Antonio's passion for revenge down to the simplest of desires: to be rid of the man.

That was just like him, to follow me. A picture had formed in his mind of the soldier as proud and obstinate. Follow the man who shot you, show him he has not hurt you. Foolish, self-destructive pride. A man who would never change his ways, never repent his sins. Antonio went over in his mind what he knew about the soldier's life. There were no redeeming qualities. He collected pictures of his victims and kept them in his dresser, a set of barbells his only other furniture. The insignia of a murderous regime was imbedded in his skin. He played chess, which was not a bad thing, Antonio supposed, but his only sympathy was for the curly-haired girlfriend, who seemed like a nice enough person. She smiled at the soldier as if there were something to like, something she saw that no one else could. What would she think when the soldier stopped calling her? What would she think when she found out he had disappeared?

Enough. Forget him.

Frank and the Mayor arrived just as darkness began to fall, relieving him of the loneliness of his thoughts. "Oh man," Frank said. "Oh man, oh man, oh man. What a day!"

"We seen some ugly shit out there. The ugliest."

"The fun was gone after the fourth hour. Right, Mayor? The hoodlums took over. No spirit out there. Just me, me, me."

Frank had a transistor radio he had taken from a Thrifty drugstore. The Mayor carried some white packages under his arm.

"You got something," Antonio said, surprised.

"Underwear." The Mayor looked slightly embarrassed. "What can I say? I got the bare essentials. The bare necessities."

"We saw somebody get shot," Frank said. "At the Thrifty, right after the Mayor got his shorts. Security guard opened up on the crowd. Asshole! Crowd scattered, then one of the gang bangers answered back. Probably the only gang banger in town who can shoot straight. Nailed the guard. The guy just fell, like this." Frank placed his arms stiffly at his side, imitating a falling tree.

"There was blood everywhere," the Mayor added. "And not a cop in sight. It was anarchy, fucking anarchy."

Frank opened a package of batteries and loaded them into his radio. "The silence is broken," he said. Switching from station to station, he found only news broadcasts.

"I'm tired of the fucking news. News is all there is."

Finally he found a classical station that was playing what sounded like a funeral dirge. To the wailing of oboes and bassoons, Frank and the Mayor went to sleep, pulling their dirty blankets over their chins like children taking a nap, exhausted and satisfied by the excitement and wonder of the day.

Antonio spent the night awake, watching the light of the campfire flicker on the tunnel walls, half expecting the tattooed soldier to emerge from the black arch. Shortly after dawn he took Frank's flashlight and went back inside, stopping when the beam of light touched the outline of the body. The soldier's feet pointed toward the tunnel entrance, and the black well of his mouth opened to the ceiling, as if to gather the water that fell around him in steady drops. The eyes were locked in an empty stare.

Would he ever forget the horror of the eyes, the face of a man at the moment he reached for his last breath? The soldier with the peasant's voice. He would carry this memory next to the image of Carlos and Elena on the steps of their home in San Cristóbal. Twin images, emblazoned on the front and back of a book filled with his wanderings. The blood of Los Angeles was colorless in the black-and-white light of the tunnel. The blood of Guatemala was crimson under a tropical sun. The blood of Los Angeles might soon begin to fade. The blood of Guatemala was indelible.

A park in Guatemala and a park in Los Angeles.

If I hadn't seen him at the park, the soldier would still be alive now, playing chess, walking to the bus with his girlfriend, lifting weights in that barracks of a room.

* * *

Frank and the Mayor were still sleeping. Antonio gathered a few belongings from the Hefty bag, just one shirt and some underwear and socks. He left everything else behind except José Juan's hotplate. He was going to a new home now, and he wanted to start with new things. Everything clean. It would be easier to look for work when he was living under a real roof again.

He wanted to say goodbye to his friends, but with the tattooed soldier's corpse in the tunnel it was better to leave no connection to this place, no way to trace him from here. It would be safer that way. One day, perhaps, he would come back to thank the man who had helped him in his mission. "We'd be blood after this," Frank had said. Antonio would not forget, he would find a way to return the favor. That would be the right thing to do.

Soon he was on Third Street, walking toward Vermont Avenue. He had decided to walk all the way to South-Central, fifty long city blocks, a trip that would take him all morning and part of the afternoon. Right away he noticed that the multitudes of running people were gone and no more columns of smoke blackened the sky. After two days the *quemazones* were over. A few people gathered around the hulks of mini-groceries and gas stations, like passersby drawn to a car wreck, fascinated by the twisted metal and the charcoal scent of burnt fuel. A syrupy smell assailed him as he passed a liquor store, all those bottles of cheap wine now a sugary ash.

He was halfway to South-Central when an army of people with brooms materialized. Where did they get so many brooms? They pushed at the streets with straw, harvesting mounds of pale green glass, teasing them into dust pans and shovels, lifting them into boxes and trash bins.

A woman on the sidewalk glared at him. Antonio was puzzled until he realized it was because of the hotplate. He was carrying this appliance under his arm, the cord dangling halfway to his feet. She thought he was a looter. All the Mexicanos and the Centroamericanos stared at him with contempt because he looked like a brazen thief and brazenness was something that belonged to yesterday. Today, their eyes said, we are a different people. We are the people we were before all this ugliness led us astray. We do not take things that don't belong to us.

Antonio laughed to himself. He was the last looter.

The incendiary mood of the night before had definitely passed.

It had evaporated just like Antonio knew it would, a fleeting storm gone out to sea. Already he missed it. He was nostalgic for the running crowds, for the sense of power, for the world turned upside down and the supermarkets where everything was free. An insurrection had taken place on these streets, a beautiful disorder. It was the window he stepped through to kill the tattooed soldier. And now it was shut. The rebellious waitresses and nannies and bus boys had gone back to their overcrowded apartments. For the foreseeable future the revolutionaries had retired to the glow of their television sets and the variety shows beamed in from Mexico City.

Elena would have loved to see the throngs of nannies taking over the streets of an American city, like the garbage workers they had joined in Guatemala all those years ago. She had led him to the demonstration by the hand when they were lovers, to teach him something. In the same way she had shown him the slogan painted on the wall of the philosophy building at the Universidad de San Carlos, underneath the mural of a dashing Che Guevara.

The revolutionary is guided in all his actions by great feelings of love.

All the brooms on the streets now—they were definitely an act of love. The sweeping and the sweeping, strangers meeting to collect a treasure of shimmering shards. We are cleaning now. Here is the true brotherhood of the city. But the brooms could not do their work without the fields of broken glass, without the soggy ashes that covered the sidewalks. Antonio wondered if throwing a rock was an act of revolution and thus also an act of love. José Juan running off to set a fire, Antonio pulling the trigger. Ten thousand people taking things and breaking windows because they were angry. Smash, smash, smash. We are free.

Carlitos, my baby, he liked to destroy things too. He built little houses with his baby blocks and knocked them over with a slap of his hand. He laughed when the blocks came crashing down.

No, it was absurd to mistake rock throwing and looting for an act of love, but Antonio was willing to allow for the possibility. If only Elena were here, in Los Angeles. Elena would know, she would be able to give him a definite yes or no. After all, she had studied and thought about these questions of love and revolution and had given her life in search of the answers. If she were alive, Elena would put her arms around Antonio and kiss him on the cheek and say, "Of course you're confused, my love, you always were."

If she were alive, Elena would put her arms around him and whisper all the answers in his ear.